LOST IN
TRANSMISSION

WIL McCARTHY

BANTAM BOOKS

LOST IN TRANSMISSION
A Bantam Spectra Book / March 2004

Published by
Bantam Dell
A Division of Random House, Inc.
New York, New York

ISBN 0-553-58447-2

Manufactured in the United States of America
Published simultaneously in Canada

OPM   10   9   8   7   6   5   4   3

aspect rings changes on J.M. Barrie's *Peter Pan* (1904). And certainly the theme of 'lighting out for the territories' harks back to Mark Twain's *Huckleberry Finn* (1884)... All these potent riffs are fleshed out in a comprehensive portrait of humanity transformed by advanced technologies. What more could any SF reader ask for? Next year will see the publication of the third volume in this fascinating series, *Lost in Transmission*. I, for one, wish it were to hand right now." —Paul di Filippo, scifi.com

"If Robert Heinlein had written *Lord of the Flies,* he probably would have come up with something like *The Wellstone*." —*Rocky Mountain News*

"Wil McCarthy considers post-scarcity economics, leadership politics and immortality—all in an adventure that would have made Robert A. Heinlein proud." —BookPage

"McCarthy's satirical humor and mastery of the hardest of hard science—he actually is a rocket scientist—are just as much in evidence here as in his earlier novels. It's lots of fun." —Netsurfer Digest

THE COLLAPSIUM

"Wil McCarthy is a certified science fiction treasure, a real-life rocket scientist with a gorgeous writing style and rapier wit to boot. [While his] high-concept physics ideas... are deft and fascinating, it's his characters and story that make *The Collapsium* a book to savor, a complex and layered story in the grand tradition of science fiction's masters." —Therese Littleton, Amazon.com

"Ingenious and witty... as if Terry Pratchett at his zaniest and Larry Niven at his best had collaborated." —Roland Green, *Booklist*

"[A] comedy of manners about High Physics, immortality, mad scientists, and murder. Great fun [with a] Wodehouse-meets-Doc-Smith aesthetic. As ingenious as the physics and special effects are, it is their juxtaposition to the wit and comedy that gives the novel its particular flavor. [A] playful, thoughtful book." —Russell Letson, *Locus*

"Top notch. Terribly good fun. This very funny book has something for everyone."
—Niko Silvester, *Entertainment Tomorrow*

"McCarthy knows his physics, and makes it extremely easy to suspend disbelief. He creates a world that is both foreign and amazing . . . but in McCarthy's hands it appears all but inevitable." —J.M. Frank, *Mindjack Magazine*

"Quite entertaining. The science is larger-than-life, and so are the characters." —Rich Horton, *SF Site*

"I don't recall the last time a book made me laugh out loud. I did so here on page 146, and at the book's end I did so again . . . though my eyes were moist as well. McCarthy has created a story here that is distinctly Asimovian in flavor, though his voice is very much his own."
—Ernest Lilley, *SFRevu*

"Prepare to use your grey matter. [McCarthy] fills his pages with lovingly rendered descriptions . . . but it is the strength of his scientific imagination that really shines through."
—Rob Williams, *SFX Magazine (UK)*

"A most dazzling future. What follows is a mind-spinning struggle that recalls a Henry Fielding novel of manners, Michael Moorcock's epic sagas and the cosmic free-for-alls of Doc Smith. There's fascinating science aplenty, mad scientists, robots running amok . . . What more could you want?" —Terry Dowling, *The Weekly Australian*

"A decidedly odd but enjoyable mix of mannered, decadent comedy and far-out physics. I liked and was even prepared to believe in [it]." —David Langford, *Ansible (UK)*

"A wonderfully off-kilter space operetta, best described as a sophisticated version of those golden-age serials of the '30s populated with slightly mad scientists who happen to have total mastery of nanotechnology and black hole physics." —Netsurfer Digest

BLOOM

"*Bloom* is tense, dynamic, intelligent, offering a terrifyingly vivid view of how technology can rocket out of our control." —David Brin

"What clever and compelling science fiction! The *Bloom* future is all too believable." —James Gleick, author of *Chaos: Making a New Science*

"Wil McCarthy makes ideas jump. *Bloom* grabs you from the very first scene and doesn't let go till the last page. It's irresistible." —Walter Jon Williams

"An ingenious yarn with challenging ideas, well-handled technical details and plenty of twists and turns." —*Kirkus Reviews*

"Succeeds on many different levels, combining a unique literary style with complex scientific speculation and political intrigue. Wil McCarthy's most entertaining and thought-provoking novel yet." —Preston Grassman, *Locus*

"McCarthy is an entertaining, intelligent, amusing writer, with Clarke's thoughtfulness [and] Heinlein's knack for breakneck plotting." —John Mort, *Booklist*

"An intense narrative of survival. *Bloom* works on several levels even while beckoning the reader into deeper mysteries. McCarthy proves once again that he has the wit and narrative power to take us to the outer reaches of space and down into the vast unknown of human, and inhuman, consciousness." —*Barnes and Noble*

"Complex and inventive. Hundreds of pages of smart, suspenseful science fiction. 'Our Pick.'"
—Curt Wohleber, *Science Fiction Weekly*

"The writing is vivid. Readers who can plug into the prose and navigate its dense circuitry will find themselves rewarded with a wallop of a finale that satisfies high expectations for high-concept SF." —*Publishers Weekly*

"The science is consistent and integral to the story, and the characters are much more plausibly drawn than are so many folks in [other speculative] fiction. In nearly every passage, we get another slice of the science of McCarthy's construction, and a deeper sense of danger and foreboding."
—Jim Hopper, *San Diego Union-Tribune*

"An astonishingly original concept, one of the most chilling versions of nanotechnology yet envisioned. McCarthy is able to make the idea . . . seem quite believable. The pacing of the book is also excellent. McCarthy has a real talent for hard-SF concepts and thriller plotting."
—D. Douglas Fratz, *SF Age*

"A feast of exposition [that is] tasty as well as nutritious. His sworn agenda to balance hard science, adventure and characterization is vindicated by the completed product. *Bloom* is a fine synthesis between Hard and Literary SF, a trick many have tried, but few have managed."
—Ernest Lilley, *SFRevu*

"Technology gone wrong provides hard-SF terror in this fast-paced thriller of nanotech-as-mold. Recommended."
—Russell Letson, *Locus*

By Wil McCarthy

Aggressor Six

Flies from the Amber

The Fall of Sirius

Murder in the Solid State

Bloom

The Collapsium

The Wellstone

Lost in Transmission

acknowledgments

With thanks to Kathee Jones and Laurel Bollinger, who insisted this part of the story could not be skipped over, and to Anne Groell and Rich Powers and Gary Snyder, who helped give it shape, and to Cathy, whose influence is more pivotal than she sometimes suspects. Thanks also to Paul F. Dietz and Malcom Longair for help with the astrophysics of condensed matter, to John H. Mauldin for his authoritative book on starships, and to Chris McCarthy for his data on Barnard's Star.

This story rests on a foundation of ideas built up over many years, with the help of dozens of people who've been copiously cited for it elsewhere. Nevertheless, special thanks are owed to Shawna McCarthy, Mike McCarthy, Vernor Vinge, Scott Edelman, Chris Schluep, Anne Groell, Bernard Haisch, Richard Turton, and Sir Arthur C. Clarke.

Any errors in this book are, I assure you, the printer's fault.

no quiet today

"Hold on tight," Radmer says, too late to do any good. The first air pocket comes and goes like a kick on the guts. *Whump!*

Radmer is old enough—more than old enough—to remember the fiery slam and tumble of entering a planetary atmosphere from orbit. The howl of plasma, the glow of radiators . . . Piercing the atmosphere of Lune is nothing like that. For one thing, he's coming in under four kps, so there is heat but not fire. For another thing his vehicle is not some graceful, gull-winged shuttle, but a crude sphere of brass, navigated by eyeball and sextant and steered with charges of dinite explosive. Inertial stability comes, in theory, from a gyroscope made of a potter's wheel, but Radmer has been too busy steering to kick the thing and wind it up. Beyond the bootside porthole, he can see the world of Lune spinning crazily.

The Squozen Moon: a world crushed and greened and left to its own devices, still in orbit around the pinpoint collapsar of Murdered Earth. Lune is so much smaller than a real planet. More delicate, more precious, and yet the largest—by far the largest—of the habitable worlds still bathing in the light of Sol.

No longer whispering, the air is dense enough now to sing and screech against the hull of the sphere. But even from this altitude, deep into the atmosphere now, this world looks small and very round. Because it *is*: barely 1400 kilometers across. The size of a province, an inland sea, a large hurricane. Not quite to human scale, but nearly. Nearly.

In the two-hundred and first decade of the death of the Queendom of Sol, in a space capsule made by armorers and watchmakers and artillerymen, General Emeritus Radmer— once the architect Conrad Ethel Mursk—is preparing to land in the province of Apenine, in the nation of Imbria, on this tiny world of Lune. Or hoping to, anyway. Where exactly he comes down will make the difference between a warm meal and a ghastly—

With a bump and a screech, the brass sphere hits another air pocket, an eddy in the storms of the upper atmosphere, and Radmer's payload—his most precious of cargoes—is thrown hard against its restraints. The capsule whirls. Then there's another bump, and another, even harder one, and the screech of air is louder than ever, and Radmer realizes they're not in the upper atmosphere at all. They've just punched through into the troposphere. Where the weather lives.

The clouds are sparse today in this particular location, but they form a definite deck, a stratum of atmosphere rushing upward with visible speed. As the brass sphere spins down toward it, Radmer cannot help worrying that the rough ride will damage the payload. That would be bad—very bad—for the course of the war, because this particular payload has cost lives and fortunes to retrieve from the empty tropical paradise of the planette Varna.

"Isn't there a parachute?" the payload asks.

"Not yet, I'm afraid," Radmer answers.

The payload is a human being, yes—a man with ancient and critical knowledge about the way things used to work. He is older than Radmer by several hundred years, and looks it. It seems incredible—criminal!—to subject his wizened frame to this jerking, hammering fall through the sky, but the world of Lune will not save itself. It is up to these ancient men, these Olders, to do what they can.

Radmer cannot pop the parachute because they are still too high, and the air too thin. Even if the chute opened fully, which he's not at all sure it would, the capsule could drift on the trade winds for hundreds of miles. And if they come down outside the borders of Imbria, then Radmer and the payload are in deep shit indeed. But Radmer has got to do something about this tumbling, or when he does open the chute it will foul, and kill them both with even greater certainty. He has landed on streamers before, but in the sheltered environment of a small planette. Lune is a much realer world, unforgiving of error.

"Rip another oxygen candle," he tells the payload, just to keep him busy. Then he leans his own seat forward and begins, finally, kicking the potter's wheel. The thing has wound down completely. It will take fifty kicks just to get the springs engaged. And after that, several minutes of steady kicking, steady spinning, to store the energy of his muscles in the flywheel made by Highrock potters and inserted into the capsule by master clockmaker Orange Mayhew.

Hopefully, by the time Radmer does pop the chute, the inertia of the spinning disc will have stabilized the capsule somewhat. If not, there are other tricks he can try: spinning the hull against the sphere's fixed inner platform, or even— God help them—popping open the hatch to serve as a kind of fin or rudder.

Dutifully, the payload loosens his harness, leans back his seat, opens the cabinet behind him with hands stretched out behind his head. He finds the steel canister of an oxygen candle, clutches it between his legs, then closes the cabinet and readjusts his seat and straps.

"This is the last of them," the payload says.

"That's fine," Radmer answers distractedly. It doesn't matter. At this point they will either land safely or die, and the freshness of the air will make no difference at all. But the payload pulls the canister's ripcord just the same, then holds on for a minute, feeling for the heat of the iron/chlorate reaction. Then, satisfied, he pulls the old canister out of its niche and places the new one where it sat, pulling down the bracket to hold it in place. Then he leans back, opens the cabinet again, and places the spent canister where the fresh one had sat.

This task requires no great genius to accomplish, but Radmer is relieved by the sight of it nonetheless. The payload can still learn, still reason, still take on and master a new task he has previously only seen. This is good news indeed: he is not one of the indeceased, the Olders whose neural pathways have simply worn out. Over the fifty-seven hours of their voyage and the weeks of preparation that preceded it, Radmer has felt some doubt on this point. The two of them had quickly run out of conversation, and without it the old man retreated into a kind of stupor, simply waiting for something to happen.

But perhaps this was merely patience. One does not live long—not *this* long—without patience.

"I may throw up," the payload warns. "I'm not accustomed to this spinning. To any movement, I suppose."

"Go ahead if you must," Radmer says. "But I would rather you watched the ground for glints."

"Glints?"

"Of light. The sunlight reflecting from our enemies as they move across the landscape. If it's all the same to you, sir, to the extent that we can steer this tub, I would rather not drop in their midst."

"Hmm. I see."

And perhaps he does. The details of the war seem to slide off him without effect, but the gist of it cannot be too hard to grasp. He leans forward to peer through the porthole.

While the payload is absorbed in this task, Radmer winds the wheel and winds it, and winds it some more. And indeed, the tumbling of the craft has begun to slow, its momentum soaked up by the wheel. He would of course need three wheels, arranged at right angles, to really stabilize the capsule. Or if he had the time, he could reorient the entire ship and soak up angular momentum on each axis singly. But even without any of that, this humble mechanism works surprisingly well. Perhaps the chute will not foul.

"There is a mountain," the payload says.

Radmer looks down, follows the old man's gaze. Indeed,

he can make out of the green sprawl of the Aden Plateau in the twirling landscape beneath them as, in a brief flicker of whiteness, the cloud layer comes and goes. The capsule has fallen a long way, tens of thousands of kilometers. Now it is barely a kilometer from the high ground of the plateau, and it truly is time to deploy the parachute. Radmer gathers up the chains that control it, stares out the window for a moment, then yanks hard.

The parachute doors clang open, and the drogue snaps in the breeze for a moment before hauling the orange-and-white silk of the main chute out behind it. Radmer can feel but not see the canopy as it inflates, and the capsule jerks as if caught by something springy. The lines of twisted, vacuum-weakened hemp creak with sudden strain, but decide to hold.

So. Aden Plateau, an uninhabited area, is not where Radmer had intended to land. But things could be worse; the city of Timoch is only twenty-two kilometers beyond the bluff's easternmost edge, so perhaps his navigational abilities—or his luck—are not as hopeless as he'd feared. Unfortunately, the easterly winds are carrying the capsule to that edge. It appears, in fact, that the capsule will land on the *slopes* of the plateau, rather than on its flat summit. This is extremely dangerous, because there will be nothing to prevent the capsule from rolling down a sixty-degree slope two kilometers long. Aye, and a battering tumble like that could easily kill the payload, not to mention—strange thought—Radmer himself.

His steering authority is virtually nil, but with no better prospects at hand, he tugs the chains to pull in one side of the chute, to encourage both a slow curl to the west and a more rapid descent. To race, in effect, against this unlucky wind. The effect is subtle but definite. Using the plateau's eastern watchtower as a reference, he can gauge his change of course and see—with considerable relief—that it is enough. The capsule will stay clear of the edge, and alight on the plateau's flat upper surface.

Unfortunately, Aden is grassy on top, with no trees or other serious vegetation to cushion their fall. They come down just thirty meters to the west of the tower, and they hit the ground hard with a clang of metal and a whump of dirt and begin rolling at once. The view through the portholes is more confusing than informative as the whirling edge of the precipice looms, as the brass sphere wraps itself up in silk and parachute cords. But again luck seems to favor them: the inner platform remains stable, and with it the men themselves, who don't even get dizzy while the capsule rolls right up against the old watchtower's metal fence. And though the fence groans and falls back in protest, the capsule stops dead, fully ten meters from the drop-off.

They have arrived. Radmer has completed an interplanetary mission. An interplanette mission anyway—using little more than a bridge and some pulleys, he and the artisans of Highrock have hurled this capsule at the sky, and then with dinite he's blasted it back off the surface of Varna, the tiny world where the payload lay marooned. And somehow, it all worked. Not quite according to plan, but well enough.

"Sorry," Radmer says, fighting a sudden wash of fatigue. "Welcome to Lune, sir."

"Hmm," the payload answers, peering around him uncertainly. Feeling the crush of gravity again, the insistent tug on limbs and jowls and eyelashes. He flexes an arm experimentally. "It feels . . . different."

"What does?" Radmer asks. "The gradient?"

Lune, like Varna, was squozen to the point of Earthlike gravity and no farther. But the radius of Varna is three thousand times smaller; its gravity drops off much more rapidly with altitude. Still, Radmer had never *felt* that difference, or imagined that it could be felt.

The payload nods, though. "Yes, the gradient. This world is . . . large." And since his name—Bruno de Towaji—is virtually synonymous with the study of gravity, and the interrelationships of gravity with electricity and information, biology and even politics, Radmer is inclined to believe him.

"It's a long time," the payload says, "since I felt the tug of a flat surface. But there's something right and proper about it, isn't there? Now, I don't mean to sound ungrateful, but you must get me outside. I need to stand; I need to *breathe*."

"As do I," Radmer assures him. Throwing off his harness, he drops to the curved hull beside the payload's chair, grabs the slick brass handle of the hatch, and turns it. There is a sound, not unlike a gasp of surprise, as the inner and outer airs mingle. And then gravity is pulling the hatch inward and down, and daylight floods the sphere's interior with jagged pools of light and shadow.

The capsule is cold inside, and the winter air of Apenine is colder still, though blissfully fresh as it oozes inside, pressed and tugged by a wind which sings against the hull.

"I will precede you," Radmer says to de Towaji. "A standard precaution in time of war; your life is vastly more important than my own."

Amused, the old man snorts. "That remains to be seen, lad. But out with you; I'm right behind."

Stepping out into the cold wind, Radmer stretches and yawns, then groans. Looking up, he sees right away that the watchtower has been ransacked. The enemy's forces do not burn, do not pillage per se, but in their quest for anything made of metal they have torn the tower apart, sundering its floors, scattering and pulverizing its contents. Little remains except the base of the outer shell itself, all cut stone and poured concrete.

"They have been here," he says. "Recently."

"Your enemies?" the payload asks, stepping up beside him to survey the damage.

"Yours now as well," Radmer corrects. "I'm sorry, sir, but they will likely kill you on sight."

"Perhaps," the payload says thoughtfully. "Or perhaps not."

To the east, the city of Timoch is visible in all its glory, a cluster of towers surrounding the Central Lake, with smaller buildings sprawling around it for many kilometers in a starburst of arrow-straight roads. In time, the sprawling, spreading city might have reached the slopes of Aden Plateau itself, had this bitter war not intervened.

Almost ten million people live here. And on Lune, that makes it a big city indeed. "That's the city of Timoch," Radmer says.

But de Towaji isn't even looking. His eyes are to the south. "There are glints of light," he says.

Radmer looks. Damn. The reflections are plainly visible in

the midday sun, probably a squad of twenty. Radmer's luck—
which has held remarkably well up to now—has finally run
out. But a glance back in de Towaji's direction reveals the old
man now studying the sky with that same slack interest.

"Did you lose something up there?" Radmer asks impatiently.

The payload says nothing for a moment and then mur-
murs, "Such a beautiful day. One forgets what a real sky is
supposed to look like, so pale. Why, the horizon is nearly as
white as the clouds! And to think, the sky of Earth was paler
and brighter still. Terrible about the Earth, isn't it? How I
miss that place, that enormous collection of places. Forged
by God himself."

"Lune's atmosphere is almost eighty kilometers thick,"
Radmer says, "and dynamically stable. Thermal motion is
well below escape velocity. These clouds, this weather—it's
not fake."

"I recall that, yes. I did help design this place."

"Ah. So you did. My apologies, sir."

"It was a long time ago. It hardly matters. We've come
down in a bad spot, here, haven't we?"

Shielding his eyes against the sun, Radmer counts the
glints. Twenty of them, yes. For whatever reason, though the
enemy have no discernible officers or other command hierarchy, they travel in platoons, which are quickly combined and
re-formed on the rare occasions when they suffer significant
casualties. They're only five kilometers away, perhaps six.
Radmer watches them for several minutes.

"They shouldn't be this far north already. Imbrian forces
should have held them at the border. And as you say, it is an
unusually clear day. That's bad, for they'll have seen us come
down. Seen the parachute, seen the sphere. This is probably
the same force that raided the tower, now on its way back to
home territory with a load of nails and wheel hubs and such.
But two tons of brass will interest them greatly. They're
headed this way again."

"Why do they shine so?" the payload asks. "What are they
wearing?"

"They're not human," Radmer reminds him, again impatiently. The word "Sire" hangs unspoken on his lips.

Radmer hands the binoculars over, and the payload, examining the glints more closely, gasps. Then laughs. "This is your enemy? Your army of doom? Tiptoeing around on those dainty feet?"

Angrily, Radmer snatches back the binoculars. "Try facing one up close, then. Try facing twenty of them, or a hundred, or a thousand. This may seem unreal to you, Bruno—an awakening from your own dreams into the nightmares of someone else—but that is a tiny piece, yes, of the army which has devastated this world. Don't make light of it in my hearing."

"But those are household robots!" the old man protests. "They should be mopping your floors, shining your shoes. Those aren't soldiers. They aren't even in good condition; what are those boxes sticking out of their heads?"

"They have been fashioned into soldiers," Radmer says. "They've been modified, multiplied beyond number. The last I heard, there were four million of them. They will kill anyone who opposes them, and quite efficiently, thank you. In Nubia, the Senatoria Plurum commanded a full surrender by all forces and citizens—no resistance of any kind—but discovered to their woe that if unopposed, the enemy will also dismantle any signs of authority or government or the rule of law.

"What happens after that is anyone's guess; in the final reports from Nubia, these 'household robots' were trampling cities into the dust, carrying away every scrap of metal they could find. To make more of themselves? To make something else? Some siege engine to lay waste to our final strongholds? You laugh, Sire, but my children are dead. A great many children are dead, and the fates of those behind enemy lines are unknown. The handful of reports we've received are, shall we say, not encouraging."

Hearing this, the payload visibly reconsiders his stance, his position in the world of Lune. Radmer feels a burst of sympathy for the man; in truth, very little has been explained to him, and Radmer's own voice may have lost some urgency through the ages, ground away to deadpan by the wars and peaces and startings-over. Perhaps he has understated the dangers.

"I apologize for offending you," the payload says officiously, echoing that thought, "but I could not have known these things, since you haven't told them to me. We've barely spoken. There was a time, Architect, when you addressed me with trust and respect."

"Aye, that hasn't changed," Radmer says. "But we are not peacefully marooned on your little planette, and this world does not know me as a builder. Here I'm a sort of . . . pastured warhorse, I suppose you'd say. I'm separated from my army, and my job—my absurd mission—is to get you into that city. You are a commodity, Sire, an armament. You may or may not be able to help us, but for now my job is to deliver you safely."

Even farther away, past the city itself, he can see the enormous white tents and globes which line the seashore, although the ocean itself is beyond the horizon, invisible. That's the camp of Lune's largest remaining human army, the last hope of a world.

Now the payload is angry. "Perhaps your mission would go more smoothly if I were aware of the pertinent details. You say this place is unreal to me. I'll admit, that's so. Could it be otherwise? I've never seen this world inhabited. I don't know its people, and something tells me I don't know you either. You have become something . . . quite different. But recall, please, that until twelve days ago I thought my time on history's stage was ended."

While de Towaji holds forth, Radmer turns and rummages through lockers in the hull of the sphere. "I've brought only the lightest of weapons," he says, fishing out a pistol and a stubby little blitterstick. "And very little ammunition. Stay very close, Sire, and do exactly as I say. Your life depends on this, and the fate of this world depends on you. You understand? Is that clear enough?"

"Very clear. Thank you."

"Good. I'm sorry to be so brusque, but things are about to get very hot around here. If there's time later, I promise we'll talk." Radmer locates a metal hook about the size of a dinner fork or particularly large gate key. He finds a good-sized rock and plops his ass down on it. Then, with the hook, he begins tugging at the laces of his boots. "Watch what I do. You're going to repeat these actions. You will want your boots very tight."

"Er, I believe they're tight enough already."

"So you say. But if you survive the first contact you'll be running and jumping and dodging for your life, and the ground may be slick with mud or blood or lubricants. Believe me, I've seen men step right out of their boots, dying for want of a proper knot. There is *no limit* to how tightly you should lace them. You can tug on this lace puller until your toes turn purple, until you lose all feeling in your feet, and still, when the moment comes, you will find these boots sliding and flopping around you, barely attached."

And Radmer can see right away that the payload thinks he's crazy, thinks that years of strife have tipped his mind over some precipice. People in the grip of a panic will latch onto small details in exactly this way, it's true, but Radmer has not panicked in more years than he cares to think about.

The view, now that he bothers to notice, really is gorgeous. From these heights, in this clear winter air, he can see not just Timoch but fully a third of the nation of Imbria—its lakes and forests and prairies, its smaller cities to the north and south, and to the west the jagged mountains of the Sawtooth Range, towering kilometers higher than even the Aden Plateau itself.

But it is a nightmare come true: the enemy right here within Imbria's borders, within a day's march of the capital itself. He scans the beautiful scenery for other glints and sees a few, although they don't have that too-bright look of super-reflective robot hulls. These are the ordinary glimmers of glass and metal, of water and perhaps even ice, down there in the daily hustle and bustle of the wintering city and its suburbs. But the fact remains: a tendril of the invasion has reached the heart of Imbria. Radmer will not get the payload into Timoch, not before the enemy soldiers can reach him. Alas.

There will be no quiet today, no peace, no crackling fire at journey's end, unless the city itself begins to burn. Radmer does not fear death—not much, anyway—but the stench of futility hangs nearby, and this is a thing he has dreaded since the Barnard Exile. Since his first taste of responsibility, of oversight, of problems so insolvably large he hadn't even known he was failing at them.

So Radmer pulls on that lace hook for all he's worth, taking firm command of the one variable he can control. And knowing it will never be enough.

book one

the pioneeriad

chapter one

unto a nameless world

Radmer vividly remembered his last sight of the old moon, before King Bruno's terraforming operations had begun to squeeze it....

He was called Conrad Mursk in those days, and he was standing on the bridge of the QSS *Newhope*, falling past the Earth and moon on a sunward trajectory. They had started their fall at Mars, and would keep on falling until they were within a million kilometers of the sun. At that point, scorching even through their superreflectors, they would swing around and rise again.

Their path was like the orbit of a comet: long and narrow and lonely, descending briefly to kiss Mother Sol and then racing back up into the dark again for another long orbit. Except that they'd be firing their fusion motors down there at the bottom, unfurling their sails, catching the light of the sun and the laser boost of a dozen pocket stars to hurl them into deepest space. Past Mars and Neptune, past even the Kuiper Belt and the Oort Cloud where the true comets lived. To the stars themselves.

The windows on the bridge weren't made of glass, weren't made of anything really. They were just video images on the wellstone walls. Holographic—though with nothing close by to look at, this was difficult to discern. The images could of course be tuned and magnified and filtered to the heart's content, but looking out the portside window at that moment, what Conrad saw was probably an unadulterated view: a blue-white Earth no larger than a grape, with a fist-sized moon lurking in the foreground.

There was no man in it. With Luna tidally locked to its parent planet, Conrad was looking at the Farside, the side faced permanently away from Earth, where there were no familiar landmarks at all. Funny: he'd been living in space for most of the past eight years, but he wasn't sure he'd ever seen Farside before. It looked flat and gray, mostly featureless, and the half that was lit by sun revealed no superreflective gleam of dome towns. The dark half of it, washed out by brightness, revealed no city lights, no sign of human presence at all.

This strange, precivilized moon drifted down the window, from fore to aft, with quite visible speed, like a soap bubble blown from a plastic wand and settling to Earth. But a bubble was small and close, whereas Luna was a quarter-million kilometers away, and huge. The QSS *Newhope* was falling *fast*, at twenty-seven kps—almost thirty kilometers per second. As fast as a comet. They were still a hundred and fifty million kilometers from the sun, but perihelion—their closest encounter with the furnace of Sol—would occur in just thirty days.

Practically speaking, there were human beings who had traveled faster than this. Several hundred of them, in fact. But *Newhope* was the largest object ever to break the ten kps barrier. Not the most massive, though, for it was capped fore and aft with shields of collapsium, a foam or crystal of tiny black holes, and the mass between these "ertial" shields kind of . . . dropped out of the universe or something. The ship and crew had mass, had inertia, but not enough. Not as much as the universe wanted them to. Such vessels could be flicked around effortlessly, with even the tiniest of forces generating enormous accelerations, barely felt by the crew inside.

But not many ertially shielded craft had ever traveled this fast, either. Generally speaking, it wasn't considered safe—any more than a hail of bullets could be considered safe. Interplanetary vacuum or no, there was a lot of debris to run into out here.

Conrad Mursk was sitting behind the captain and to her right, in the first mate's chair. Around them were the three other bridge officers: Astrogation and Helm; Sensors, Communications, and Information; and System Awareness. And as it happened, the captain was turning to look at Conrad at that very moment, her face framed beautifully against the window, a part of the planetary tableau. Conrad looked from her face to the moon to her face again, thinking that perhaps she had something to say, some fair words to mark the occasion. The little blue planet down there was her home, after all. But she eyed him instead without speaking, without acknowledging the view at all.

"You okay, Cap'n?"

His use of the title was partly in jest. Her name was Xiomara Li Weng, or Xmary to her friends, and she had no closer friend than Conrad Mursk. Technically speaking, this was a violation of all sorts of Naval protocols and traditions, but then again the two of them weren't really in any sort of navy, weren't even Merchant Spacers in a commercial fleet. Never had been, unless penny-ante space piracy counted as a branch of service these days. In fact, like everyone else on this ship, they were prisoners. Convicts, exiles, *fakahe'i*. This long adventure, this hundred-year voyage to Barnard's Star, was their punishment for years of antisocial behavior in general, and for the Children's Revolt in particular.

"Would you take a walk with me?" the captain asked, ignoring his ribbing along with the stunning view.

"Um, certainly," Conrad answered. "Walk" was a euphemism indeed, since every deck on the ship was a circle exactly thirty meters wide. There wasn't a whole lot of walking you could do. But there was an observation lounge, and that was what Xmary meant.

"Robert," she said to the astrogation officer, "you have bridge."

"Aye, miss," Robert said. He had long ago faxed his skin a bright shade of blue, with hair and eyes to match, and it had the effect of making everything he said and did seem sassy, though his tone was innocent enough.

She paused. "You want to keep it all night? Ninety-three days on this tub and you've never had the bridge for more than half a shift. You'd be all right with that, I assume?"

"Absolutely, miss. I've conned bigger tubs than this one, if you'll recall."

"I'm aware of your record," she said, wearily displeased. Indeed, she'd been along for part of it, dodging navy ships in the wilderness of the outer solar system. "And will you please call me Xmary?"

But Robert just smiled. They'd had this conversation before, and he seemed determined, for whatever reason, to stand on ceremony. Robert was a sort of pirate himself, having led a group of squatters onboard a Mass Industries neutronium barge for almost five years. Hell, he'd practically run the place—a vigilante handyman and amateur mass wrangler. He was also an avowed anarchist who'd railed for years—uselessly, Conrad thought—against the natural human tendency to form hierarchies and elect leaders. But for all of that, he still seemed to have an anomalous bit of Navy in him.

"Carry on, Number Three," Conrad said to him crisply, just to carry the theme a little farther.

"Aye, sir. Carrying on, per your instruction."

Conrad narrowed his gaze with what he imagined to be a Naval sort of ire. "Are you getting smart with me, Astrogation?"

"Doubtful, sir," Robert replied bluely, "although if I feel any symptoms of smartness coming on I'll be sure to report them."

"Do that, yes," Conrad said, then couldn't keep from laughing.

For a variety of logistical, historical, and presumably sentimental reasons, the bridge was actually at the center of the ship's next-to-forwardmost deck, just five meters behind the ertial shielding. It was the only crew-accessible space on this particular deck. All around it, above and below and ringed around the sides, were storage tanks—the eight tons of water the ship's plumbing required as buffer and ballast. It also served as shielding, against radiation and particle impacts and God knew what else.

Conrad hadn't designed the ship, and truthfully, he wasn't all that familiar with the reasoning behind its design. He was only twenty-five years old—still a juvenile by Queendom of Sol standards—and had never held a job of any sort until *Newhope*'s passengers had elected him first mate of the expedition three months ago. He was still learning his way around. Xmary, for her part, had just turned twenty-seven and had even less sailing experience than Conrad did. Systems was a twenty-year-old boy, Zavery Biko, and Information was manned (womaned?) by Agnes Moloi, who was twenty-nine. Blue Robert M'chunu, the old man of Astrogation, was thirty.

It wasn't by coincidence that Conrad knew all their ages. This was his area of specialty: the crew. If he knew nothing else about them—nothing else about anything—he knew their birthdays, their hobbies, their interests and skills. He wasn't sure what to do with the knowledge, but he did his best to keep it fresh in his mind. The launch ops crew were getting on each other's nerves even before the passengers were tucked away, feeling the first twinges of cabin fever even before the Diemos Catapult had drawn back its arms and slung them sunward. Conrad's own personal passion was for architecture, for the subtle interplay of shapes and materials, but he knew a little—a very little!—about holding a crew together through difficult circumstances. It was a responsibility he took as seriously as he'd ever taken anything. Which wasn't saying much, but there you had it.

"Have a nice walk, right?" Robert called after them, in an innocent tone which managed, nevertheless, to convey a sense of lewdness.

Leaving the bridge involved climbing ass-first down an inclined ladder—or sliding sideways down the handrail if you felt like it, which Conrad usually did. The lounge was three decks down, and took up nearly half the level all by itself—one of the few indulgences the ship's designers had permitted her crew and passengers. At the moment, the ship's complement was twenty live people: the launch ops crew. The other forty-eight hundred were in storage, as data patterns in

Newhope's wellstone memory cores. And eighteen of those twenty were currently either sleeping, working, or messing around on the galley level. For the moment at least, he and Xmary had the lounge to themselves. Alas, the Earth and moon were no longer visible through the windows, though he supposed he could remedy that by pulling back on their magnification a little.

Instead, he engaged a voice lock on the hatch, then turned and yanked down his captain's pants. This was his other main joy and passion, and the only other responsibility he took at all seriously. Within the minute they were fuffing on the cool wellsteel plating of the deck, kissing and hugging and working out the kinks. That they should do this as soon as the opportunity arose was not terribly shocking; they'd been intimate partners for years. And since everyone in this thirtieth decade of the Queendom of Sol had the eternally, immorbidly youthful body of a twenty-year-old, it was considered right and proper to squeeze in a vigorous fuff or two in the course of every day. Well, the men considered it so at any rate, and the women did not protest it overmuch.

When Conrad and Xmary were done, they lay tangled in each other's arms, resting. Still on the floor, not even bothering with the couches or trampolines because they were young in their minds as well as their bodies and liked the sense of immediacy that a nice, cold floor could provide.

"Now that's what I call a walk," Conrad said.

"Hmm," Xmary grunted noncommittally. She liked a good fuff as well as anyone, but that wasn't why she'd asked him down here.

"You want to talk?" he asked, taking the hint.

"Oh, now you want to."

"My head is clear," he agreed. "My full attention can be brought to bear. You have some problem? Some little worry itching at the corners of your mind?"

"The usual." She sighed. "I hate my job. I hate it for me, anyway. Captain of a fuffing *starship*? What do I know about that? Robert is spacewise; it should be him. *I* should be in storage with the passengers."

Conrad shrugged. "People like a woman in charge; they've

had a queen ruling over them for three hundred years now. Well, I guess the oldest person in storage has only had a queen for forty-five years, but even so, we're all products of society, aren't we? You think we want *Blue Robert M'Chunu* for our captain, who doesn't believe in leaders or followers? Who went five years without wearing clothes, just on general principle? I don't think so, dear. I really don't."

"There are other women available," she sulked. "I was always a party girl. I'm tempted to say *just* a party girl. The rest of my life has been . . . a fluke of circumstance."

"Aye," he said, kissing her hair. "There are other women. And some of them were in the August Riots, and some were space pirates, and some were confidantes of the Prince of Sol. You alone were all three of these things. You fooled the queen to her own face, and talked a Palace Guard into doing your illegal bidding. You turned your back on the chance to be a princess, and sowed confusion in the streets of Denver. Shall I go on?"

"Don't bother," she grumped. "*You've* at least been a first mate before. Well, sort of."

"Sort of," he agreed, laughing. In fact, he'd never held the actual title, and had clung to the de facto position only through threats and blackmail, onboard a rickety homemade *fetu'ula* commanded by a suicidally depressed prince. And— this part wasn't funny—eight people had died along the way. Horribly, for the most part. They'd later been restored from backups, but the whole experience had left a bad taste in Conrad's mouth that was still with him these eight years later.

"Sorry," she said, catching his shift of mood. "You probably don't like your job, either."

"Not particularly. It's a hundred-year voyage, and even if we're in storage for a lot of that time, we'll still be living a lot of years in . . . this." He spread his arms to indicate the narrow confines of the lounge. "And I'm supposed to hold things together? Me? The Paver's Boy of County Cork?"

"This is our punishment," she reminded herself.

"Aye." Now he was the one sounding bitter. "We're punished for wanting a future. Well, we've surely got our fill of one now."

"A pretty good one," she said, rising to the bait. "A whole star to ourselves. A new king, a new society. That's not so bad."

"No, it isn't. Am I squishing you, by the way?"

"A little. I wish we could turn the gravity off in here."

He snorted. "Now *that* would be rude."

Once you'd lived in space for a while, you got used to the idea that *all* the stars were out there for you to look at, all the time. After that, you always felt sort of cheated when you were standing on a planet, which blocked half the sky all by itself, and had an atmosphere that washed out the remaining starlight except at nighttime. Fuffing in zero gee was like that: always a good time, and you got used to the total freedom of it. In gravity, you always had some surface pressing against you, and you found yourself wanting to reach right through it to get in the proper position. Actually there were special beds designed to accommodate spacers and former spacers in this way, and Conrad had toyed more than once with the idea of installing one in his quarters.

But turning the gravity off was a no-no. It was generated in the aftmost compartment of the ship's crew segment, about halfway down the long needle that was QSS *Newhope*. Conrad even knew the buzzwords to explain it: *a zettahertz laser— that's a trillion gigahertz, you know—operating at four watts and refracted through a pair of Fresnel condensates to form an isotropic beam exactly thirty meters wide, terminating at the collapsium barrier of the forward ertial shield. The photon becomes a spin-positive graviton at high enough energies, and will penetrate a light-year of lead.* You couldn't deflect it, or control it on a room-to-room basis. It was gravity, pure and simple, and you either had it inside the ship or you didn't. So while Xmary had the authority to turn it off for an afternoon fuff, the inconvenience to the rest of the crew would be substantial. Along with their sniggers and smirks.

Anyway, it wasn't really zero gee without the grav laser; thanks to the ertial shields there were all kinds of screwy momentum and inertia effects in here. People got the spins, got the upchucks, got the willies and the shakes when the gravity was off. You'd have to fuff quickly to avoid serious trouble.

"Floor hologram, please," Xmary said. Beside them, a few meters away, a murky cube appeared. Well, kind of a cube—holographic displays emanating from the floor tended to look really good when you were standing up, and really bad when you were actually lying on the floor itself. Her calling for one was, in its own way, an announcement that they should get up. And indeed, she was disentangling herself, reaching for her clothes, letting them shimmy onto her like living things.

Conrad reached for his own uniform's pants, inserted his feet, and let them slide up. There were all kinds of clothes in the Queendom, including spray-on, wrap-on, and clothes that looked like a ball of putty until you stepped on them or smacked them with your fist, at which point they came alive and sort of straitjacketed themselves around you, taking on some stylish cut and color. In this regard, Conrad and Xmary were a little old-fashioned for their generation. They liked to see the shape of their clothes before they put them on. They liked to pull them from the fax, look them over, request modifications, and then dress.

And indeed, this "classique" style remained by far the Queendom's most popular, though in actual composition it only vaguely resembled the leathers and textiles of ancient times, or even the synthetic fabrics of the Old Modern era. Queendom fabrics were spun largely of silicon for one thing, and their fibers were a thousand times finer than a human hair. But like the wellstone of the hull, these wellcloth fibers moved electrons around in creative ways, forming structures that mimicked the properties of atoms and modules, radically altering the cloth's apparent composition.

And they adjusted themselves independently, aye. Shouldn't they? Conrad had worn natural cloth from time to time—even been forced to in his days at Camp Friendly—but the stuff didn't keep you warm and dry, or cool and airy, or whatever. It didn't stop projectiles, or harden to sponge-backed diamond in a fall. It didn't even look good, not really.

So he and Xmary weren't Luddites or Flatspacers or anything, and anyway these *Newhope* uniforms were pretty raw—green and black, flecked with hints of subliminal starlight. Xmary's had two impervium bars on the collar, where Conrad's had only one. And hers shaped itself differently around her rather different form, but otherwise they looked about the same. Which is to say: gorgeous. Anyone could be young and beautiful, but to be *stylish* was a thing the Queendom admired greatly. It was perhaps the one area where the opinion of youngsters was still considered important.

Once the two of them were on their feet, the hologram looked a lot better, except for a stripe running down the length of it, just left of center. This defect remained stationary as the holographic cube rotated through it. Weird. Beneath it on the floor, Conrad could see a narrow, matching streak of discolored material. Frowning, he got down on his knees and scratched at it with his fingernail, feeling the difference between that and the faux metal plating around it.

"Huh. Something wrong with the wellstone," he muttered.

"Broken threads?" Xmary asked.

"It looks more like contamination." Here was another thing he knew a bit about: matter programming, and the perils and pitfalls of wellstone. He was going to be an architect someday. "The composition of these threads has been altered. They're still working, still shuffling electrons and forming pseudoatoms, but not the right ones."

"It's in a perfectly straight line," the captain said, "but it's not aligned with the ship. It just slices through. I'll bet it's a cosmic ray track."

"Hmm. Yeah, probably. There's a spot here on the bulkhead as well. Some kind of heavy particle firing through here at the speed of light." He traced a path in the air with his finger, matching it with a sort of projectile noise. "I'll note it in the maintenance log, and if the nanobes haven't fixed it in a few days, we'll wake up damage control."

"Sounds good," she said, then shuddered. "We're taking the same kind of damage ourselves. Our bodies."

"We did on Earth, too. Maybe not as much, and maybe not as high energy as that." He nodded at the streak. "But there are charged particles flying through us all the time. Poking holes in our cells, flipping bits in our DNA...It's one reason people used to grow old, isn't it? Before there were fax machines to reprint us from scratch?"

"Yuck, Conrad. I don't need a biology lesson, especially from someone who failed it in school. Anyway, let's see a graphic of Planet Two, please."

The floor thought about that, pausing for a moment before deciding she was talking to it. Then the translucent, holographic cube was replaced by a translucent, holographic sphere. But not a featureless one; it was paler around the middle, darker and bluer at the top and bottom, and clinging to it all around was a thin haze of refractance, a suggestion of atmosphere.

The captain cleared her throat. "Planet Two, my dear."

"Best guess, anyway," Conrad answered. "A five-year-old could draw this."

"Well, they *have* detected oceans, and some suggestion of a small polar cap."

"Who has? I don't know how they get that," Conrad protested. He'd done a little amateur astronomy himself—in space, where it was a matter of life and death—and he knew how difficult it was to resolve a dim, distant object as anything other than a pinpoint. "All they've got is an analysis of the light reflecting off the planet's atmosphere, right?"

"Well, the air is breathable."

"Maybe," Conrad said. "Barely. I heard you'd die from the carbon dioxide."

"Breathable to something, I mean. There is life there."

"Hmm. Yeah." That much at least was undeniable. There wouldn't be free oxygen in the atmosphere—probably not even free nitrogen—without biochemistry to replenish it.

"Fix this image in your mind," Xmary said. "Don't ever forget. We won't always have these silly jobs. Before you know it, we'll be building a world of our own."

Conrad's smirk was somewhat bitter. "If you believe these clowns, which I'm not convinced you should, then Planet Two is four times the mass of Earth. Its day is, what, nineteen times too long? Fix *this* in your mind, dear: unprotected on the surface, you'd die in a couple of hours. The planet merely soothes the Queendom's conscience; Barnard is no friendlier than Venus, or the wastes of the Kuiper Belt."

"People live on Venus. And in the Kuiper."

"Sure they do. *We* did. But we could fax ourselves to Earth anytime we needed to. Fresh air, sunshine . . . We won't have those things at Barnard. Not for a long time."

There was a sound at the door, a scratching and thumping as if someone were nudging it with an elbow. And then, ever so faintly, the sound of voices. There was an unsealing noise, like someone hawking to spit, and then the hatch was swinging inward.

"Hello?"

"Hello?" Xmary called back.

"Are we decent in there?" The voice belonged to Bascal Edward de Towaji Lutui, the former *Pilinisi Sola* and *Pilinisi Tonga*, the Prince of Tonga and of the Queendom of Sol. Now, newly elected as King of Barnard.

That hatch had been verbally sealed, but of course locks meant very little in a programmable world, where Royal Overrides could compel the obedience not only of machines but of the very substances from which they were made. At least the king had had the courtesy to knock.

"Hi, Bascal," Xmary said. "Come on in."

The hatch swung inward, and Bascal stepped into the room. He was wearing the same sort of uniform that Conrad and Xmary were, but his was purple and bore no insignia. He wore no crown or other signs of office, unlike his mother the Queen of Sol, who wore a ring for every civilized planet in her domain and carried, at least on formal occasions, the Scepter of Earth. But Barnard's civilization—all twenty people of it—hadn't had the time to develop such trimmings. Perhaps they never would.

Bascal's skin was the tan color of mixed ancestry, or "hybrid strength" as he liked to say: a dark Tongan mother and an olive—if brown-haired—Catalan father. Bascal was a son of the Islands, now exiled to hard vacuum, hard time, hard life among the stars.

"Hi," he said, a bit sheepishly. "Are we interrupting?"

"Not now," Xmary replied. "A few minutes ago, you would have been."

"Well, that's all right then." Bascal stepped inside, away from the hatch, and a woman trailed in behind him. Her uniform—green and black like everyone else's, though it didn't go with her bright blue skin—bore the markings of an engineer.

"You know Brenda Bohobe," Bascal said.

Xmary looked annoyed. "She is my Chief of Stores, third engineer, and fax machine specialist, Your Majesty."

And more. Brenda had been one of the Blue Squatters, along with Robert and Agnes and the others. Conrad and Xmary had met her at the same time Bascal did, in the midst of the Children's Revolt. The king was just being pedantic, a failing he seemed to have fallen into in the wake of his election.

"Hi, Brenda," Conrad said.

Brenda looked back at him with an expression that was both irritated and smug. "You didn't mess the place up, did you?"

"Not that I know of, Engineer Three." Conrad tried to say this in a way that dressed her down but didn't make him sound overly concerned about it. He was technically her superior, after all. But it was grinding, her always sniping at him like that.

"Ah," Bascal said, his eyes lighting on the hologram. "Planet Two. Now there's a site for naive eyes, who've never yet caught glimpse of a thing undoable. Plotting its takeover, are we? Scheming its subjugation to the fist of Man? Or are we making friends, filling out a shopping list to surprise it with the gift of ourselves? That's the fist of Woman, I reckon: to love a thing into submission. Either way, my friends, I'm encouraged to see you fuffing by its light. I was going to name the place—such is my privilege, I'm told—but I figure we should wait for the formal introductions. Find out what she's like, how she treats us."

"You need a shave," Conrad observed. It was just an expression; what Bascal really needed was to reprogram the cells in his face to stop producing unsightly hair. Either that, or simply step through a fax machine, commanding it to give him a real beard.

"Do I? Who says?"

"What, are you growing a beard? *Growing* one?"

"The old-fashioned way," Bascal agreed. "It seems more proper than just printing one, or printing myself attached to one. I'm not dressing up here, Conrad—I'm growing into a role."

"It's a lucky thing everybody's in storage," Conrad prodded. "You look like you're growing into a pirate again. Or a hobo."

"Ha, ha. You slay me, sir. A king does need a beard, though, don't you think? It provides a certain sense of gravitas."

Conrad smirked. "Even a king in exile?"

"Especially a king in exile, boyo. I have no real duties here. I command the expedition, but your darling Xmary here commands the ship. My citizens are in a state of quantum slumber, and even when they awaken, they'll be much too busy to look to me for anything more than emotional support. Unlike my parents, I really am a figurehead. I rule myself and nothing more."

Xmary smiled, without much warmth. "It takes more than a beard, Your Majesty."

Bascal's answering smile was equally polite. "I never said otherwise, Captain. It's a grave responsibility, to look good doing nothing. Eternally, no less, for we shall never die! But give me time and I'll do nothing better than anyone has ever done it. I'll be the King of Nothing, and Nothing will bow down before me in admiration."

Xmary laughed at that, though she clearly tried not to. She and Bascal had had a fling once which had ended bitterly, and as far as Conrad could tell, that sort of thing never really healed over.

"Don't you have a ship to steer?" the king asked gently. "I saw the Earth outside my window. These are treacherous shores, awash in paint chips and spalled flecks of wellstone. The detritus of civilization: bullets, every one."

"Robert has the con, Sire, and my complete confidence."

"Ah, good for him. Though this ramrod of a ship may be thin for his tastes, as well as freakishly light."

"Still," Brenda said, "it's a safe feeling, knowing he's up there."

Instead of Xmary, yeah. Conrad opened his mouth to dress Brenda down more firmly—

But if there was one thing the King of Barnard knew, it was how to head off an unpleasant conversation before it got too far along. He turned to the window and spread his arms. "Where is it? The Earth? The moon? We came up here to see them, to revel in their glow."

"You're a few minutes late," Conrad said. "If you like, I can rewind it for you. Or change the magnification or something."

But Bascal just waved the suggestion away with a frown that was partly genuine. "No, no. It wouldn't be the same. I can see the Earth in playback anytime I want, right?"

"But not the real thing, maybe never again," Brenda said sourly. Or maybe that was just her normal voice; it was hard to tell the difference.

"Well," Conrad said, in his best official, first-mate tone, "perhaps we'd best surrender the room." He turned to Xmary. "Shall we finish our walk?"

"Sure."

When they were outside, sealing the hatch behind them, Conrad muttered to her, "Those two are spending a lot of time together. I never see him anymore without her attached at the hip. Are they an item? Have they been?"

"For a while now," Xmary said. "You know, for a first officer in charge of crew issues, you're not very observant. You might want to work on that."

"Well, I'm slow, but I get there eventually." He thought for a moment before adding, "Do we need a title for her? Something like Philander or Sackmate, but for women? You know, to denote her formal status as consort to the king?"

"How about Shrew?" Xmary suggested sweetly, plopping herself on the handrail and sliding down out of sight.

#### chapter two

perihelion tides

Four weeks later, the bridge was crowded with nonessential personnel. Xmary and Conrad of course, and Robert in the Astrogation seat, and Agnes Moloi at Information, and Zavery at the somewhat redundant position of Systems. Bascal and Brenda were here too, in special chairs that had been installed for the occasion, and beside them was Ho Ng, the Chief of Security. Thankfully, Money Izolo and Peter Kolb, the first and second engineers, were down in the engine room itself, monitoring the reactors. But Bertram Wang, the second astrogation officer, was here, standing because there were no extra chairs, nor space to install one.

The occasion: perihelion. *Newhope*'s closest approach to the sun. "When we fire the motor," Robert was saying, "a ten kps nudge here at the sun becomes one hundred kps excess at escape. It sounds like a free ride, but that's how the orbit numbers work out. Of course, ten kps is nothing in the grand scheme of things. We need almost thirty *thousand* kps—a tenth of lightspeed—to get where we're going in a hundred years. The fusion burn is mainly to correct our course, to change the plane of our orbit so that we're actually aimed at Barnard's Star. We'll get most of our actual impulse from the sail. Once we unfurl it, the sun is going to push the loving shit out of us, and laser stations are going to push even harder. If we weren't ertially shielded, the acceleration would squish us all to paste in a fraction of a second."

"Who are you talking to?" Conrad asked. There wasn't a soul on the bridge—on the whole of the ship—who didn't know these facts backward and forward.

"Posterity," Robert said with a shrug, and then, thinking about it, added a theatrical flourish. "This is all being recorded, sir. This is a major event in human society. The dawn of a civilization."

"True and true. Shall I say some grand words?" Bascal asked of no one in particular. "We leave behind us the troubles of the old . . . ahem. Hmm. We leave behind us the troubles of the old, to find and create a set of new troubles which are entirely our own. We do this . . . because a civilization which cannot die, and cannot grow old, also cannot grow young. All it can do is give birth to fresh civilizations."

"Very nice," Conrad said, clapping politely in the air.

"Oh, dry up. Captain, what's your status?"

Xmary frowned at a display on the arm of her chair, then turned to Robert. "Astrogation: status report."

"Position is only 9.16 kilometers off nominal, ma'am," Robert answered grandly. "Velocity is off by 1.34 meters per second. Position uncertainty is less than two centimeters, and velocity uncertainty is 18.4 nanometers per second. Orientation uncertainties are well below the vibrational tolerances of the vehicle. In a quantum universe, you don't get much more accurate than this."

"How's our dust count?"

"Zero impingements, ma'am. Agnes has got the nav laser firing once every five seconds, clearing the path ahead, so what hits us is a gas of single atoms, highly ionized."

"I'm familiar with the principle."

"Anything else, ma'am?"

"Thank you, Astrogation. That will be all. Engineering?" She turned to look at the bulkhead behind her. The word and gesture together formed a command which opened a holographic window to the engine room. This was actually twenty-eight decks below, or *aft* if you wanted to be technical about it, but the resolution on the holograms was orders of magnitude finer than the human eye could discern. The illusion was perfect: that the engine room, with its reactor controls and status displays, was located immediately capward of the bridge itself, when in fact there was nothing but empty space there, rushing by at six hundred kilometers per second.

Conrad could see Peter in the background, leaning intently over something and frowning. Money Izolo, another Blue Squatter who'd long ago reverted to his natural shade of deep purple-brown, looked up at the sound of the captain's voice and found himself staring into the bridge.

"First Engineer, what's your status?"

"Well hi, Xmary. Captain, I mean. Our status is good, yah. The fusion motor is generating fifty kilowatts, mainly for lighting and environmental controls. The deutrelium stream is focused and crystallized, with no detectable density anomalies. We are prepared to go propulsive at any time. Antimatter reactors are idle, with full hermetic sealing on the storage cells. Failsafes three layers deep. Would you like me to read you the temperatures?"

"Thank you, no," Xmary said. She looked away, and the engine room winked out of existence. Like many an object in the quantum universe, it did not exist when there was no attention being paid to it.

Xmary glanced pointedly at Agnes. "Information?"

"I have nothing to report, ma'am."

Xmary turned a serious expression on Bascal. "Your Majesty, my status is good. I mean nominal. We are 'go' for fusion burn, after which we will unfurl the sail and begin accumulating our departure velocity. Would you like to give the orders?"

The king frowned, thinking about it. Conrad understood, or thought he did: if Bascal gave the orders, he was micromanaging, and undermining the authority of the ship's duly elected captain. But declining the invitation was a consequential act as well, which could make him look indecisive or something. Overly delegatory. But he had to say *something*, so he leaned forward, fingering the black curls of his new beard, and said, "As you were, Captain. This moment belongs to you."

"Well," Xmary said, glancing at her armrest panel, "the moment is still a few minutes away."

Conrad didn't know what to think about all this formality. He really didn't. The last time they'd done anything like this, they had been criminals, or at least delinquents. Squabbling among themselves, making it all up as they went along. It was recklessly, foolishly dangerous—commandeering a pocket star to launch them across the wastes of the Kuiper Belt!— and everybody knew that and was okay with it. Well, mostly okay. There had, after all, been a mutiny, and there'd've probably been another if the Navy hadn't caught them when it did.

Hell, as recently as eighteen weeks ago they'd all still been criminal wards of the state. Even Bascal had had no official rank; he was the Prince of Sol, but that meant very little given that he'd been banished from Sol for a period of not less than one thousand years. In training, the exiles had all taken turns at different jobs, under strict orders to figure out who was good at what. There had been no fixed chain of command, no hierarchy. All for one and one for all. But here they were: a king, a captain, a crew.

In his Poet Prince days, Bascal had written frequently about the "verdant fires of youth," but where were those fires now? Co-opted in some way. The Queendom authorities had grabbed them, molded them, forced them unwilling into these roles. The queen had in fact given the child rebels exactly what they'd always asked for: a chance to grow up. To take on responsibilities of genuine consequence. Well, they had that now. All that and more.

And somehow it all felt very premature, very forced. Except on pirate ships, Conrad had never met a captain who was any younger than fifty, and most of them were much older than that. In fact, the oldest person in *Newhope*'s memory cores was just forty-five, and Conrad had never met anyone that young who was in any position of responsibility. They were children, these *Newhope* exiles. Like all the revolutionaries, Conrad had railed against that label, which seemed destined to cling to them forever like a bad smell. Children with no room to grow up, no space to grow into. But now, at age twenty-five, he felt nearly as resentful at being made responsible for himself. For a whole ship and crew.

Damn it, adulthood came too suddenly, and at too steep a cost. There was a lot to worry about; it wasn't fun. And he supposed that was the whole point. There was no use complaining about it, but it did feel eerie, watching his friends behave this way. Himself, too.

"You look troubled all of a sudden," Bascal said to him.

Conrad looked around the bridge, then back at his king. "I just feel that something is slipping away. Our precious youth. Look at us: we aren't playacting, here. We are actually doing this thing. We'll never be young again."

"No," Bascal said with a wistful, half-pleased look. "We won't."

"How does this happen?" Conrad mused. "When does it steal upon you? The green-hot fires fade into cool wellstone light. Five years ago we would have screamed and jumped at a moment like this; now we just look at each other. I wonder why that is."

Bascal's face broke out in a smile, and he got up from his seat. The bridge's little fax machine was not far from his elbow, and he whispered something to it. A number of objects spilled out into his waiting hands, and he took one of these and threw it hard against the floor. It made a popping sound, and burst with a spray of ribbons and confetti which covered a radius of nearly two meters. Ho Ng and Brenda had it all over their shoes. The king turned his smirk on Conrad. "Feel better?"

"Actually, yes." Conrad could feel some tension going out of him. Whether this was a moment of triumph or gloom was entirely up to them, right? And really, if all this was being recorded for posterity, then the tone they set here today would speak directly to the future society they hoped to build. "Give me one of those things."

Bascal tossed one to him, and it exploded with a snap in Conrad's own hands. "Ha!" he cried, and would have said more if not for Xmary's hard glare, directed first at him, and then at Bascal.

"Majesty, can I ask you to cut that out? This may be the time, but it certainly isn't the place."

The tone in her voice set off a cascade of memories in Conrad. Years ago, onboard the pirate ship *Viridity, he* had been the voice of reason. Not because he'd wanted to, or was particularly good at it, but because there'd been no one else. People were too afraid, too angry, too wrapped up in their own affairs to think about any bigger picture. But here, now, the opposite seemed to be true.

Okay, messing around with confetti was fun, but it didn't fundamentally change the fact that they were doing as they were told: meekly exiting the Queendom of Sol. It seemed a strange answer to their years of rebellion. They had lost their revolution—they'd always known they would—but the fact that they'd fought at all, taken on such hopeless odds, was a kind of victory all by itself. It had won them a star of their own, and a starship to carry them there. But did they have to be so obedient about it?

"Information," he asked, "are there any isolated sensor platforms within one hundred kilometers of our current position?"

"There are three holding steady in our forward arc," Agnes answered crisply, "with matched velocity. They're leading the way, essentially." Then added: "Um, sir."

"Hmm. How about the aft arc?"

She frowned. "May I send out a wideband ping? I get forward readings from Navigation, but the aft data is much sparser."

Conrad looked to Xmary, who nodded uncertainly.

"Wideband ping, please, Information," Conrad said to Agnes.

"Aye, sir. Pinging now, all frequencies."

Conrad was impatient. After only about five seconds, he asked, "Well?"

"Eleven targets in our aft hemisphere, sir. Seven of them running silent, in addition to the three pingers. They all look like news cameras to me, but it's hard to be sure. They're the right size anyway, half a meter or less, with a wellstone reflection signature. Most of the targets are clustered just aft of our equator, probably hoping for a cinematic angle on the motors and sail."

"Posterity wants a good view," Robert said.

"Let's give them one," Conrad suggested, feeling suddenly, wickedly playful. "Robert, how difficult would it be to fry one of those bastards?"

"Beg your pardon, sir?"

"Fry it. With the fusion exhaust. It's a stream of monochromatic helium, right?"

"And protons, I think. Ask Engineering. Let me see if I understand you correctly, sir: you want to orient the main motor not at our navigational optimum, but at a piece of private property? A reportant device, a news camera? For the purpose of destroying it?"

Conrad cleared his throat. "Too many damn voices of reason onboard this ship. Yes, Astrogation, that is exactly what I'm asking you. It might be nice to leave this system in style. Give them something to remember us by. And the question stands: how difficult would it be? We needn't use the main motor; we have the four nav exhaust ports as well, right? I just want to point something hot at the nearest target of opportunity. I am asking you—correction, I am *ordering* you—to plot a solution."

"All right," Robert said unhappily. "Solution plotted. It's, uh, not difficult. About 12.6 degrees off optimal, if we use the portside nav motor. A three-second toot ought to do it. Sir."

King Bascal burst out laughing. The old gleam was back in his eyes, and he said, "It was wanton vandalism that got us in this fix in the first place. I like it. What are they going to do, punish us? Fine us? Add an extra year to our sentence? Make no mistake: my parents have spy devices all over this ship. Our wellstone's programming must be lousy with them—microscopic sensors that move and shift and disappear when examined—so as long as we remain in comm range, maybe five AU for low-gain transmissions, they'll be watching our every move. And that by itself is a good enough reason for me:

because they'll see us do it. But I can't give the order myself. Captain?"

Xmary frowned at the king, and then even harder at Conrad. It was they, more than anyone, who'd led her to a life of crime. Well, Yinebeb Fecre as well. Feck the Facilitator. But that whole August Riot thing was small-time mischief against the larger backdrop of piracy and plunder. Bascal's crew had been gearing up to destroy a neutronium barge, cargo and all, when the Navy finally caught them.

The captain's gaze wandered over to the astrogation niche. "Robert, confirm your solution, please, and forward it to the steering program. We'll give that camera six seconds in the fusion stream, and then reorient to our departure vector. There's no sense telling a joke and then leaving out the punchline."

"Now, ma'am?"

"Yes, please."

The motor had been fired at low power when they departed from Mars orbit, and its reactors had operated continuously since then in a nonpropulsive mode, generating power for the ship and crew. And yes, it had been fired propulsively during drydock testing, for small fractions of a second. But this was the first time they'd opened her up, jamming the throttle to full power. The sound of it was incredible: low and shrill and visceral, like a continuous punch in the gut. Like the end of a world, or the beginning of one.

"Bloodfuck," cursed the Chief of Security. "We're really gone now."

And so they were.

#### chapter three

in which a wake is keenly felt

Queen Tamra-Tamatra Lutui and her king, Bruno de Towaji, stood on the balcony of their Summer Palace on the island of Tongatapu. Above them, the stars of the night sky were washed out by a single pinpoint of indigo, painfully bright. That was *Newhope*'s sail, illuminated by the launching lasers, racing past the Earth's orbit at one-twentieth of the speed of light and still accelerating madly. The ship was actually quite far from the Earth itself: nearly as far from it as the sun. But even so, the laser light reflected from its sails—bright as a hundred full moons—was painful to behold against the blackness.

It made Bruno's heart stir with pride, because even by Queendom standards, the energies at play here were enormous. *Newhope*'s ertial shields—among the largest hypercollapsites ever constructed—had consumed the entire output of Mass Industries Corporation for eleven whole months, single-handedly tripling the price of collapsium on the futures markets. The launching lasers were sacrificial—trillion-dollar platforms that were melting themselves down and pushing themselves up out of the Queendom as they fired. Like slow-motion bombs, exploding in a highly directional way over a period of ten days.

Fortunately, that was the most complex piece of hardware involved, and while its construction was exacting, it took no great genius or mathematical insight to operate. The starship's internal technology was generally quite crude—open faxes and enclosed reactors, with tanks and plumbing to shuttle material around, and wellstone plating and cabling to control the flow of information and the semblance of matter. And crude was good, for it was safer that way, and cheaper, and gave the wayward children of Sol their best chance of success. The boys and girls were on their own now, separating themselves from the Queendom across the widening chasm of lightspeed communications.

The king and queen had thought to send a historic transmission, a final message. And here the moment was at hand, the microphone waiting expectantly in the balcony's railing, grown a few minutes ago for expressly this purpose. But tears had begun to spill from Tamra's eyes, trailing down her walnut cheeks, and she seemed at a loss to make any sound at all. Choked up, as it were. Mute with grief. For who had conceived and imposed this sentence, if not Tamra herself?

In the end, it was Bruno who leaned down to the microphone and murmured, "Godspeed, children. May every chance be in your favor, and if love makes any difference, be assured you have ours in abundance."

Now Tamra was sobbing aloud, and the king felt his own eyes grow misty. He put an arm around her shoulder and hugged her, offering what comfort he could. Their only child, perhaps the only child they would ever have, was gone now to seek his own way.

"His heart's desire has been granted," Bruno said. "He is a king, duly elected by people who love and admire him."

"Barely."

"Ah, so you've found your voice."

"Barely," she repeated, with a laugh and a cry.

It was true, though: Bascal's election had been somewhat less than a landslide. Only thirty-nine percent of the transportees had actually voted for him, while a shocking twenty-four percent had voted for alternative political systems: republics and democracies and communist utopias long discredited. Bascal's camp friend, Conrad Mursk, had gleaned fifteen percent of the vote himself, as had Xiomara Li Weng. Xmary.

Bruno wondered if Bascal regretted letting that girl escape into the arms of his friend. Perhaps not; perhaps they hadn't been suited for each other and were wise enough to recognize the fact. But she would make a formidable woman. She *was* a formidable woman, the captain of mankind's greatest adventure.

"He's got good friends at his side."

"And bad ones," the queen said matter-of-factly. "More than enough bad ones. I wish we could separate them out somehow."

"True. True enough. But none are in positions of significance."

The queen declined to respond to that. Instead, she tossed her hair back and said, "You like little Xmary. In her little captain's uniform."

"I do, yes. She's a formidable young woman. And her young man, this Conrad Mursk, has been a better friend than Bascal deserves. I say that as a pained and disappointed father."

"Mursk is a coaster, though a likeable one. Or his peers seem to think so, at any rate; he took second and third place in a lot of the voting. He could almost have been the captain, or the engineer. He might even have been king. Gods, what a thought."

"I don't know," Bruno mused, running a hand along the balcony rail. The damned thing had a sense of drama; his fingers left a wake of pseudogold in its wellstone surface, fading to trails of some gray-black material like coal ash, which finally faded again to whitewashed iron. "There's something of substance about that lad. Not intelligence, not charm; his talents are modest in both regards. But he gets his way nonetheless, eh? We could send our boy packing in far worse company. And we've backed these children up, every one, with copies in deep, safe storage. If they all died tomorrow, it would be as though they never left."

"And if they die in nine hundred years?" she asked, mist-ing up again. "What will their childhood backups mean then? Their adult selves will die and be reincarnated here, minus the wisdom their adventures should have taught them. They'll have to take our word for it, or else live the same mistakes all over again."

"So gloomy," Bruno said, moving his hand up to stroke her chin. "Our first decade together seemed to last forever. That first century was long, and often beautiful. But the time blurs, doesn't it? The racing by of years has nothing to do with mortality. It's something in the wiring, part of our essential definition as human beings. These ten centuries, my dear, will hustle by like a spring morning. And if our son chooses not to return at the end of it, why, we'll go and visit his new family. Granny and Grandpa, driving out for the holidays."

The queen smiled at that, and for a moment Bruno caught sight of his reflection in her eyes. Here was a man who had invented collapsium, had invented ertial shielding, had laid out the telecom networks that were the Queendom's very backbone. He was the richest man who'd ever lived, and by most accounts the smartest (although he personally would never believe it). He had fought great battles, even rescued the sun from destruction, this former Declarant-Philander of Spanish Girona. But there was nothing complicated about him.

"Never change," she instructed. "Bruno, Bruno, you are my anchor. By which I mean, you drag me to the bottom and hold me there until my struggles cease, while the waves break overhead."

"Ah. And are you drowned yet? Have I filled your lungs with the bright saline of hope?"

She didn't answer for a while. On the railing, her own fingers left trails of glittering diamond, hard and clear, which refracted the light of *Newhope*'s sail, and of its rippled twin in the ocean's broad mirror. And when she finally spoke, all that came out was, "You must fill me with more than that." For she had the body of a twenty-year-old and the grieving heart of a mother, and neither could be soothed by words alone.

#### chapter four

# of creation and power, and the finding of oneself

Conrad was minding his own business, sliding down the ladder railing and whistling some half-remembered tune, when everything around him lurched violently to starboard. The railing was yanked out from under him, and he flailed backward, and would have hit the floor if the wall hadn't come along and hit him first.

"Ow!" he cried, just as the floor really did come up and smack him in the butt. "Little gods!"

"Collision avoidance. Sorry, people," said the voice of Robert M'chunu over the intercom.

"Get processed," Conrad muttered under his breath, picking himself up and probing gingerly for bruises.

This kind of crap was just a fact of life onboard a starship. Given their speed of travel and the range of their sensors, if there was any debris in their path which was too large to be disintegrated by the nav lasers and too small to be spotted telescopically and plotted around, they had about ten seconds to get out of its way. With lateral thrusters belching fusion exhaust at one full gee, you could juke laterally by about half a kilometer in this length of time. And that was usually enough; it was the safety margins that really killed you, made you juke five or eight or ten kilometers instead.

If the thing you were avoiding was the size of a thumbnail or a particularly large grain of sand, and it was bearing right down the ship's centerline, then you really only had to dodge fifteen meters to let it skate past the edge of the hull with nary a scratch. But that did nothing to protect the sail, which was needed to slow down again at Barnard, and which was actually still giving them some fairly substantial push, even out here in the Oort Cloud, ten times as far from the sun as the orbit of Neptune.

And fuck if it was empty space. The last-minute dodges—"jukes" they were called—were happening ten or fifteen times a day. This was down substantially from the third-day peak of a hundred and four, but damned annoying nonetheless. Human bodies simply weren't meant to withstand this sort of sustained battering. Even null-gee hockey players would fax themselves a fresh body after every game, but here onboard ship, in the middle of operations, there generally wasn't time. For this reason, all nonessential personnel were being cycled—very willingly—into fax storage. The ship had been quiet before, but now it was *deathly* quiet. As the thrum of the nav engines faded away, the air resumed its stillness.

The skeleton crew—now a partial skeleton crew—actually had no particular use for Conrad Mursk. He didn't keep the engines or the fax machines running; he didn't navigate; didn't maintain or forecast or repair. Thus he was tempted—more tempted every day—to jump in the fax and let this part of the mission be over. Stored as data, he'd experience no time or sensation of any kind. He would simply step out of the fax in a hundred years, and everything would be great. But somebody did have to look after the crew as a whole, and anyway Conrad felt it was bad form for a first officer to go to sleep while there was still work being done.

So he dusted himself off, climbed gingerly back onto the railing, and slid four decks down to Engineering.

There, Money Izolo's crew of five was down to just himself and Peter Kolb. And Peter didn't look too happy. He was holding his eye and glaring balefully at a waldo hanging down from the ceiling. This was one of those things you could stick your arms into, to operate robotic arms inside one of the re-actor cores. But it necessarily had some solid and angular parts, whose indentations were clearly visible in the flesh around Peter's eye.

"Hi, Petes," Conrad said, pulling out the sketchplate which held his to-do list. (He was a big believer in lists; they had saved his life more than once during the Revolt, and were anyway vital in holding entropy at bay.) "You okay?"

"I think I popped my eyeball," Peter complained.

"*Popped* it? No way." Conrad immediately felt better about his own bruises, and guilty for whining about them, even to himself.

"He's fine," Money said from across the room. He was staring intently into a holie display on one of the wall panels and waving a wellstone sketchplate at it to absorb the image, and presumably perform some calculation on it. "Quit clown-ing around, you. I need those cooling parameters updated."

"No, seriously," Peter insisted. "I'm hurt."

"Let me see," Conrad told Peter. And then, when Peter didn't pull his hand away, more firmly: "Let me *see*. That's an order."

Reluctantly, Peter uncovered the wounded eye, and Con-rad couldn't suppress a groan of disgust. "Eeew. Yuck."

"Did I pop it?" Peter asked worriedly.

"You did *something* to it." Truthfully, Conrad couldn't really tell what he was looking at. There wasn't a lot of blood, and as far as he could tell there was no eyeball jelly leaking out or anything, but something unpleasant had happened to the eyelid, and to the eye underneath. There were vertical gashes of pink and white where nothing like that was supposed to be, so that it barely looked like an eye at all.

"All right," Money relented. "Go visit Stores and have yourself reprinted. But hurry back—I need those numbers or we're going to vent some irreplaceable coolant mass. Under-stand? Mass we'll have to do without for a hundred years, or maybe forever."

"Yes, sir," grumbled Peter, brushing past Conrad and hur-rying out the door.

"You could be more sympathetic," Conrad said.

It was an understatement, but Money just shrugged. "It's always something with that kid. Maybe he'll be more careful next time. Meanwhile, power demands on this fusion reactor are jumping around like spit on a heat sink, and the cooling system is not keeping up."

"I'm surprised that isn't automated," Conrad said. "You've got hypercomputers, right?"

"Well, yes and no. *Newhope* was designed with people in mind. There are built-in tasks for us, and of course there are always issues the designers didn't foresee. For example, this predictive cooling algorithm looks as though it was based on some kind of weather program, like for a domestic climate controller. It never has worked very well, and until we get it replaced, I'm using Peter."

"I see."

Money turned back to his panel for a moment, then looked up at Conrad again. "Was there something you needed?"

Conrad nodded, glancing once at his sketchplate for confirmation. "Yeah, but it's pretty much just a status report. I'm trying to stop by all the stations today that still have crew, and see how everyone's doing. Looks like I've got your answer, or part of it anyway."

"Things could be easier here," Money admitted.

"You have a lot of issues like this?"

He pursed his lips for a moment. "Oh, a few. Five or six. Keeps us busy enough."

"Okay," Conrad said, nodding and frowning with the false wisdom he had learned at leadership school. As probably the smartest of the former Blue Nudists, Money was not the sort to be ordered around. He needed a gentler touch, a bit of praise and persuasion. "So you're fully burdened. You don't anticipate freeing up anyone else for storage?"

"Not until the engines stop firing, no."[1]

"Hmm."

"Even after that Peter and I, and one or two of the others, will have to stop by occasionally, to check on efficiencies and

1. See Appendix A-1: Engineering Issues

such. Maybe tweak a parameter here and there, or spec out a new monitoring routine.

"The comm antenna is another issue. We're already using the whole sail for this, so there's no room left to expand communications. As our distance from Earth increases, we'll have to increase transmitter power to maintain our data rate. Or just live with a lower data rate, I guess. We *are* supposed to be on our own. But to answer your question, I think we need another ten days here at half-crew, and probably five or ten more with a single person on part-time watch. Then we can talk about storage. But truthfully, we need to go last. Or nearly."

"Why so?"

Money shrugged. "Fax machines take a lot of energy. Of course they recover a lot of energy, too, forming chemical bonds and such. But the demand is asymmetric. With no crew, you don't have to worry about it, and with a thousand people sharing one machine, you can project your energy needs with statistics. But right now we've got almost as many fax machines as people, and it's getting to be a grind."

"And here I've been taking them for granted," Conrad said thoughtfully. "Do we need some kind of rationing or scheduling system? Would that make your life easier?"

"Yah," Money said vaguely, "I don't know about that. Talk to your Chief of Stores. She's my main energy customer after propulsion."

Just then, Peter Kolb came back, stepping through the hatch like a new man, no longer holding his eye.

"Better?" Money asked him.

"Much," Peter answered testily. "And don't ask me again for those cooling numbers. I'm on it."

Conrad found his Chief of Stores in the aft inventory, cursing and glaring. She was sitting on the floor beside the fax machine—the largest one in the ship's habitable compartments—with a bunch of tools and sensors and sketchplates spread out around her.

"Is this a bad time?" Conrad asked, wincing inwardly because there was no good time to talk to Brenda Bohobe. Not for him, at any rate.

Brenda looked up sharply, as if surprised to find anyone penetrating her little bubble of a world. "Oh. It's you. Hi."

"Some trouble here?" he asked.

"The start of some trouble, I think." She chewed her lip for a moment. "This is the fax most of our passengers stored themselves through, and in the last hundred or so, the system logged an increase in energy consumption. I've run the plots, and it looks shallow but exponential."

"So the machine is slightly broken, and it'll only get worse over time?"

"Right."

"Wonderful. Have you identified a cause?"

The look she gave him was hard. "I have, yes, thank you. These kind of surges are always related to error correction. Now before you get too excited, let me say that a print plate doesn't last forever, and the large ones tend to die more quickly than the small ones. And this one here has probably got a million tons of throughput left before it gives up the ghost. With proper maintenance, it'll last for hundreds of years."

"And that's what you're doing now? Routine maintenance?"

"I didn't say it was routine. There are burned-out faxels which my nanobes can't replace. To avoid molecular defects in the items being printed and stored, error correction has to judder back and forth around these. Like a snake's head swaying to improve the view."

"So then," Conrad said with some relief, "there's no danger of pulling the passengers out of storage as cancer-riddled morons?"

To his surprise, Brenda actually laughed at that. She had kind of a sadistic laugh, but good-humored just the same. "Unless they went in that way, no. What I'm doing right now is scrubbing behind the print plate's surface, bringing all marginal faxels up to full capacity. I don't know where this damage is coming from."

"Probably cosmic rays," Conrad told her. "We're seeing

traces of it all over the ship. It's going to be a fact of life until we slow down and get back inside a large magnetic field of some sort. But you get cosmic rays on Earth, too. Is this sort of damage unusual? Have you seen it before?"

"Not unusual, no. Just more than I'm used to seeing."

"Well," Conrad said with a smirk, "you could always print another fax machine."

He was joking with her. The print plate of a fax machine had, like, extradimensional quantum attributes that couldn't be stored or described atomically. People and oranges and even whole spaceships could be produced by fax machine, and most of the parts for another fax machine could be as well, but the print plate itself had to come from a special factory, and every square centimeter of it represented—according to rumor—a year's labor from a thousand patient elves. The amazing thing, when you thought about it, was how dirt-common these things had become even before the rise of the Queendom. By some accounts, as much as ten percent of the economy—both human and monetary—was involved in the production of fax machine print plates. Alas, that was pretty much everything Conrad knew on the subject.

What he said to Brenda was, "Are there programs to monitor this damage while we're all in storage?"

"Of course," she said impatiently. "My crew and I will be pulled out if any of these machines degrade beyond a threshold value. But like I said, they've got a long life ahead of them. We take good care here."

"So, do you anticipate going into storage yourself soon? Or releasing some of your people?"

In response, Brenda scowled and threw up her hands. "I don't know. Ask me when I'm finished with this! I'm going to look at all the other machines, too. Louis McGee is worthless, how about you store *him*?"

"He is on my roster," Conrad confirmed.

"Good. Now leave me alone. Please. Sir."

Conrad looked for Robert on the bridge, but found two of him in a service-core crawl space just forward of Engineering.

Though the space was crowded and close, Conrad stuck his head in.

"Some trouble here, Astrogation?"

There was a thump.

"Oh, hell," said one of the Roberts, rubbing his head. "Don't startle me like that. Yeah, it's the sweep radar. I've reconfigured the antenna, but now it needs more power. I'm trying to boost the range."

"Can't you do that from the bridge?"

"There's a safety interlock," said the other Robert. "Bertram's on the bridge right now, issuing commands, but there's got to be a human thumb on the control point here as well. All critical systems need at least two nonidentical operators to modify. Some of them require five."

"Even the ship can't override it?"

"Especially, the ship can't override it. Isn't that right, Ship?"

A speaker appeared in the wall of the crawl space. "Absolutely, sir." The voice was vaguely feminine, almost childlike. "I am completely at your command, and nothing could please me more. Of course I'm programmed that way, but *feeling* it is, I should think, a higher level of obedience."

"So," Robert prodded, "you enjoy your work, even when it consists of letting me tinker with your guts?"

"Immensely, sir, although I do hope you'll be careful."

"Right, right. Warn me if I'm doing something stupid."

"My programming demands it," the ship confirmed. And then, as quickly as it had appeared, the speaker was gone again, vanishing with the faint crackle of programmable matter operating at needlessly high speed.

Conrad personally didn't talk to the ship very much. The idea didn't bother him, exactly, but his first ship had been the pirate *fetu'ula Viridity*, whose only intelligent hardware had been a snotty fax machine. Not much of a conversationalist, and not much point in even trying. Over the years he'd trained on half a dozen other ships, some of them quite charming, but Conrad really didn't see the point in getting chummy. He didn't talk to houses, either. To its credit, *Newhope* seemed to sense this about him, and kept mostly silent in his presence. But it was just like Robert to have a personal relationship with the equipment.

"So, when you were on that neutronium barge, did you talk to it as well?"

Both Roberts smiled, and one said, "Not so much, no. Barges are funny that way; they're not really intended for crew, and I don't think *Refuge* ever really got used to having us there. It didn't matter how we talked to it or what we did, we were always kind of anomalous, a constant source of surprise and confusion. Of course, we weren't exactly authorized, which may have had something to do with it. But *Newhope*, why, she and I are friends."

"You make friends with robots as well?" Generally speaking, robots had a kind of collective intelligence thing going; whatever thoughts they had in their wellmetal brains, they were shared and spread across the brains of nearby robots, or household hypercomputers, or anything else that might be handy. They could be shockingly intelligent, but with a sort of mindless, mechanistic quality just the same. Idiots savant. And when they appeared together in the same sentence, the terms "friendly" and "robot" had certain other connotations— sordid ones which a lesser man might take amiss.

But what Robert said was, "Ah, sir, you just don't know the right robots. Think of that one that follows King Bruno around. What is it, Hector? Hugo?"

"Oh, yeah. Hugo. I've met him. It."

"Eerie, isn't it? There's nothing human about it, but it's definitely . . . there with you. More so than this ship, or any hypercomputer I've spoken with. I could be friends with a machine like that."

"Bruno spent a hundred years training that one. And it's still not finished."

Robert laughed. "Who among us is finished?"

"Hmm," Conrad said. "So, this activity here . . . Will it take you long?"

Robert glanced briefly at his thumb, making sure it was still on the interlock switch, then looked back at Conrad. "You trying to hustle me into storage?"

"Something like that. Have you got a timeline?"

In the confines of the crawl space, Robert shrugged. "Two days for fine-tuning? A week? I'm just guessing. We don't really have to do this at all, but I thought it might smooth out the ride. We've got predictive algorithms trying to steer us at low thrust into minimum-density zones, so we don't have to spend all our time juking around dust grains, but unfortunately this is where astrogation starts to become a challenge."

"How so?" Conrad had studied astrogation, along with a lot of other subjects, but it was one of the many things that had gone in one side of his head and straight out the other, leaving no impression at all. Conrad wasn't sure if he was a stupid man or not, but he knew, at least, when somebody else knew a subject better than he did. Which was most of the time, alas, but that realization itself was maybe not so stupid.

The nearer Robert wriggled in the crawl space, adjusting his position while keeping his thumb on the interlock. He gestured with his free hand.[2] "There isn't any kind of fixed reference for where we are. Near a known object, yes, you can take some range measurements, but not out here in the middle of nowhere. So even where we have echo-ephemeris dust maps—which are extremely spotty out here, by the way—we can't say with any certainty where we are on the map. So we're still flying blind."

And suddenly Conrad understood. "Ah, it's like driving a motorcar at night."

"Hmm? A motorcar?"

"My father paves roads for a living. Well, maintains the paving, anyway. I used to do a lot of testing with him."

"So," Robert said, "you're in some sort of wheeled contraption then? Rolling along in the dark? With, like, searchlights shining out in front of you?"

Conrad nodded. "Right. And there's wildlife out in the country, and if you hit a deer or something it can bounce you right off the road. But you never know where the deer are going to be, and your headlights only shine so far, so the faster you drive, the less reaction time you have."

2. See Appendix A-2: Astrogation Issues

"And the more violent your maneuvers have to be, when you suddenly see that deer in front of you. Okay, it's exactly like that. So I'm turning up the brightness on our search-lights."

Just then, an alarm sounded, and Bertram Wang's voice echoed throughout the ship, calling out, "Collision avoid-ance! Brace for—"

The lurch was not terribly violent when it came. Maybe a hundred-meter juke, one-fifty, tops. But the sound of crash-ing equipment echoed down the ladder, from one or two decks up, and the sound of human cursing followed close be-hind it. Then, while Conrad and Robert looked at each other, came the slam slam bang of angry footsteps coming down the wellsteel rungs. Seconds later, Louis McGee appeared, throwing himself down in front of them and stomping up to the entrance of the crawl space.

"Goddamn it, Astrogation." Louis seemed, for a moment, to be preparing to ask a question: Why can't you be more careful? Why can't you watch where we're going? Why don't you give us a little warning next time? But instead, he grabbed Robert by the foot, hauled him bodily out of the crawl space, and punched him hard in the stomach before Conrad could intervene.

"Security!" Conrad shouted at the walls, and the walls re-sponded in the voice of *Newhope*: "Security alert, deck four service core." And then Conrad was prying Louis off of Robert, with a head- and armlock he wasn't really sure would hold. But as Robert struggled to his feet, and as the other Robert wriggled free of the crawl space, their own efforts aided Conrad, and the three of them were able to restrain Louis effectively.

"You all right?" Conrad asked.

"No," Louis said angrily. "I banged my fuffing head for the third time today."

"I wasn't talking to you, numbskull," Conrad barked. Louis was the third inventory officer, and had no business being out of storage this late, anyway.

"I'll be all right," Robert said, a little breathlessly. "He mostly just surprised me. Well—uh!—maybe I'll step through a fax just to be safe."

"You stupid ass," Conrad said, smacking Louis across the top of the head. "Now I'm going to have to figure out a punishment. High space naval discipline, oh my little gods. You're probably going to have to be *flogged*, my friend. What would make you do something like this? Right in fuffing front of me?"

And with that, Louis started crying. "I want to go home. Oh, I want to go home."

"Oh, brother," Robert said wearily. "Here we go."

Conrad was inclined to agree. They'd had their share of freakups onboard *Viridity*, and even occasionally onboard more civilized craft. It was only a matter of time before they had some here. A lot of people didn't take well to space—the distances, the dangers, the isolation. And no one had asked to be here, not really.

"I've got a big brother," Louis whimpered. "He's forty-nine years older than me, and he always knows what to do. But it's taking three weeks to get his replies now, and it's only going to get longer. Three months, three years, *twelve years* when we finally get to Barnard. What good is a big brother if it takes him twelve years to give advice?"

"Just calm down," Conrad told him. "Take deep breaths."

Just then Security, in the person of an unescorted Ho Ng, came clanging down the ladder. He surveyed the scene, glancing dispassionately from face to face before meeting Conrad's gaze. "What happened?"

"Freakup," Conrad said. "Escort him to storage, please. We'll worry about treatment options sometime in the future. Meanwhile, just get him out of here."

Ho pursed his lips, studying Louis for a long moment. "What did he do, sir?"

"It doesn't matter."

"It does if we want valid security and psych statistics. Did he damage equipment?"

"No," Conrad said. "He threw a punch."

Ho considered that. His eyes settled on Robert, noting the

gut-pained kink in his stance. "Assaulting an officer. Out here that's a flogging offense."

"Only if I say so," Conrad corrected. "Or Xmary does. There are extenuating circumstances, and in my opinion Mr. McGee here is not fully responsible for his actions. Do you want him flogged, Astrogation?"

"No, I forgive him," Robert said.

Conrad nodded. "Right. Louis? Do you have anything to say for yourself?"

"I want to go home. I didn't want to be here, I was never part of the revolt. I was just, you know, there at the time. Can you fax me home, sir? Please?"

"Oh, for crying . . . Louis, you work in the inventory. You know as well as I do that we haven't got the data rate to transmit a person. Take some mental notes, if you like, and we'll mail them back for appendment to your archive. Do you want to be locally erased?"

"No!"

"Then you're pretty much stuck here, right? Ho, just take him."

"With pleasure, sir." Ho grabbed Louis' arm and roughly hauled him toward the ladder.

"Gently, Security," Conrad warned. He knew Ho from their pirate days, and trusted him about as well as he trusted a starving dog. Security was a real interesting job choice for him, the result not of a vote but of a writ issued by King Bascal shortly after his coronation. "Ho likes responsibility," Bascal had said at the time. "It's good for him, and that's good for us. You want him idle instead? You want him tuning the engines?"

But as Ho and Louis ascended the ladder together—not stopping at the nearest fax machine but continuing all the way to the top—Conrad heard the echoes of Louis' yelping and squawking for a long time, and knew that Ho would gladly break an arm or two if the opportunity arose.

"Jesus Christ and all the little gods," he said to Robert. "I need to get my ass into storage pretty quick here. Maybe I should punch you myself."

chapter five

through every waking moment

Time? Any physicist will tell you it's just another dimen-
sion, not so different from space, and its relentless forward
movement is an illusion imposed by conscious minds rather
than an inherent property of the universe itself. Remove consciousness and time does not pass, does not have any dynamic properties at all. It simply *is*.

The first thing Conrad saw when he stepped out of the fax
machine was Bascal's face. Or something like it, anyway. The
king looked different: at once chubbier and more gaunt, his
skin looser. There were even strands of gray in his hair, and in
his beard. But his eyes were the thing that really stood out.
They had a milky, unfocused look to them.

"Bascal?"

The careworn face lit up with a smile. "Ah, Conrad. So
glad to hear your voice again. It has been . . . too long."

Conrad felt a cold shiver. "What year is it?"

"Well, let's see." Bascal's smile collapsed into a frown of
concentration. "We did the first correction burn at one year,
and the second burn at ten years, and that was thirty years
ago. So we're forty years into the journey. Yeah, forty."

"And nobody thought to wake me before now?" Conrad
didn't know whether to feel relieved or insulted.

"Yes, well, we would have," Bascal said. "You're due next in the rotation, I believe. Xmary will sit out the next burn, but that's not for a while yet. That's not why I brought you out."

Well, that sounded encouraging. Conrad cast a look around him, scanning for signs of trouble. They were at the forward inventory, on deck fourteen, twelve levels aft of the bridge. It was all done up in projective holograms: a tropical theme of sand and palm trees, elephant grass and vanilla. And right away, Conrad noticed flaws in the imagery, indicating streaks of dead material in the wellstone of the walls and ceiling. But not too much—the damage was no worse than he'd expect after forty years of cosmic wear and tear—and other than that, there was nothing obviously amiss.

"What's going on?" he asked.

Bascal stepped away from the fax's print plate, gesturing for Conrad to follow. "Our colonization plans need . . . revising. Some surprises have trickled along in the news from Earth, and . . . Well, the truth of it is that I was lonely. You're my best friend, and I don't feel like doing this without you. All right?"

Conrad felt his brow furrowing. "How long have you been out here, Bas? You're supposed to be in storage."

Bascal smiled sheepishly, his face showing off deep creases. "There is a lot to do, you know. A lot to study. I'm to be the king of an entire planet, an entire solar system. The first truly new civilization since the conquest of the Americas. I thought I'd, you know, pack in some wisdom along the way. I've got six master's degrees now, do you know that? I was going to try for a Ph.D., but, well, it seemed wrong to specialize in any one field. That's not really my place, I think."

Conrad was both awestruck and horrified. "You mean you've been bumping around the ship all by yourself, for forty years? Some kind of hermit? So when we get to Barnard, we'll all still be kids, but you'll be a pleasantly seasoned man. A grown-up, here to lead us in the ways of the world. Is that it?"

"Yeah, basically." The king did not seem particularly embarrassed by this admission. "But I realized I can't do it alone. I need help; I need friends. It's a powerful insight! So you see, in spite of the doubts written all over your face, there is a bit of wisdom accumulating."

Conrad studied his friend's face and body. "How long has it been since you faxed a fresh body? You look terrible. Your eyes, especially. Can you even see me?"

Bascal frowned, looking him up and down. "You know, I thought you looked a little...dim. I put it down to all the reading I've been doing. But I think you're right—there's something rather wrong with me."

"It's the cosmic rays," Conrad said. "They're eroding your retinas and your corneas, and God knows what else. Stop here. Don't leave this room. I'm not going anywhere with you until you step through that print plate."

The king paused, then nodded. "Very well. It's your advice I seek, and this sounds like strong counsel. One gets...neglectful. My father lived alone for decades, on a planette out in the Oort Cloud, but it occurs to me, talking to you now, that I've been a hermit for longer than he. The people finally dragged him back and made him their king. That was more than Mother could ever do. But there is no one to drag me anywhere, and nowhere to be dragged to, so a hermit I remain."

Though he hated to bring it up, Conrad asked, "No one? Not even Brenda?"

"Oh, I've seen her," Bascal said distractedly. "We have our little flings every now and then. Although I suppose it has been a while. Funny, that I brought you out instead of her. But we get different things from different people, don't we?"

"Aye, Your Highness," Conrad said with some amusement, although there was something creepy about this situation.

Bascal stepped up to the print plate and murmured, "Repair and reprint, please." Then stepped through. It was like watching someone brush through a slightly sparkly gray-black curtain, or sink into a pool of liquid paint. The print plate didn't move, didn't part, didn't resist. It simply accepted Bascal's body, whisking it apart into component atoms. And then, a moment after Bascal's back had vanished into it, his front reemerged, stepping clear and bringing the rest of his body along behind it. He blinked, suddenly young and fit again, sharp of mind and fleet of foot.

"Oh. Wow. That feels better."

"I'll bet," Conrad said. "You should consider, you know, making it part of your regular schedule."

Bascal's youthful face broke into a smirk. "Ah, you kids, you think you know everything."

Conrad sneered at the joke and then said, more seriously, "So what is this bad news from Earth?"

"Ah. Yes. Trouble with the atmosphere, I'm afraid. More than a hint of chlorine in it. Not nearly as much as the oxygen, thank God, but more than enough to be toxic. There is also sulfur dioxide, which gives us some clue about the biological processes that must be involved. I have a master's degree in the subject, by the way."

Conrad shrugged. He'd never expected the atmosphere to be breathable, anyway. He'd never expected the planet to be habitable at all. "I wouldn't worry, Bascal. Most of the settlement designs are already provisioned for doming over. Chlorine is pretty corrosive, I seem to recall, but if we use chlorinated plastics in the dome material, or even probably just standard semiconductors—basically wellstone in the off state—I doubt that will matter. It's more an inconvenience than anything else—some extra filtration when we pump in fresh air. It's really not that big a deal."

"Oh." Bascal looked as though the light had gone out of his sails. "Well. That's all right then."

The two of them looked at each other for a long moment. "You want to have lunch?" Bascal asked finally.

As it happened, Conrad had eaten dinner only thirty subjective minutes ago—his last waking act. He wasn't hungry, and he wasn't bored or lonely. In point of fact, he was very eager to get to the next mission milestone, and from there to Barnard itself. He'd spent enough time on this ship already! But *forty years*? That was a long, long time to be alone, without ever once having lunch with your best friend. Bascal had inflicted the fate on himself, of course, and it was crazy—it was *crazy*—to go and do a thing like that. But the king had his reasons, weird as they were, and the desperation in his eyes was unmistakable now.

"Sure," Conrad said, and watched Bascal's face relax.

The next time Conrad stepped out of the fax, he saw ex-actly the same thing. Well, not exactly the same; Bascal looked fresh, for one thing. And the holograms were different: an underwater theme of translucent reefs and fish, with the illusion of depth and a hint of surface light somewhere up around the bridge.

"You've got a fresh body this time," Conrad said encouragingly.

"Newly printed," Bascal agreed.

"And how long did you let yourself go before that?" Conrad accused. "Were you blind? Arthritic? Was your mind playing tricks on you?"

"Maybe a little," Bascal said with a dismissive wave of his hand. He looked impatient.

"You know, we really should modify those fax filters. There's no reason you should become decrepit like that, just because you haven't faxed in a while. Why should our bodies age? Why should the radiation damage accumulate instead of being repaired? Or bouncing off?"

"I don't know," Bascal said, pausing to think about it. "That's a good question. I'll add it to my list of things to do." And he reached into his pants pocket and pulled out a little wellstone sketchplate, and said to it, "Item: modify fax filters for aggressive immorbidity and repair." Then he looked at Conrad and nodded smugly.

On a hunch, Conrad asked, "Bas, how many items are on your list?"

Bascal glanced down at the sketchplate. "38,450. Or rather, 38,451, thanks to you."

Wow. Conrad's own lists rarely exceeded ten items, and the longest of his life had been under thirty. "That's a lot of items."

"I suppose so. I suppose it is. How are you, Conrad?"

Quietly annoyed, Conrad answered, "I'm exactly the same

as the last time you saw me. It was, like, five seconds ago. But you're older and wiser and weirder, right? You've got another master's degree."

"Four, actually. Atmospheric dynamics, planetology, stellar plasma dynamics, and biochemistry. Truthfully I'm running out of things to major in. Soon I may have to start accumulating doctorates."

Little gods. Knowing he didn't really want to know, he asked, "What year is it?"

Bascal counted on his fingers, in that weirdly fast way his father had taught him. "Let's see. Four, eight, twelve, sixteen... We're sixty years into the voyage, so it's Q353, 3.5 centuries since my dear mother's coronation. Perhaps we Barnardeans should mark our dates from my own ascension, though, or from our departure, which conveniently occurred on the same date. By that calendar, it's year 61. Sadly, our voyage has been quite uneventful, except that our positional uncertainty has grown outrageously. Four hundred AU and climbing. Astrogation is having fits about it.

"The good news is that Barnard, tiny speck that it is, is finally visible to the naked eye. You have to squint, but you really can make it out. A little red dot, just off the shoulder of Ophiuchus, the Serpent Bearer. As we draw closer to it, those errors should start to come down again. That metal-poor piece-of-shit star, also known as Gliese 699 from the Dim Star Catalog, has only four ten-thousandths the luminosity of Sol, and seventeen percent of its mass. It's practically a *sila'a*, like the pocket stars we used to have in the Kuiper Belt. Remember those, Conrad? Remember hacking that one by voice to get a launch beam out of it? That was fun. Anyway, Barnard is an old man—already twenty percent older than Sol—but he'll outlive her by forty billion years, maybe more."

"Okay, thanks for the lesson. So why did you wake me up this time?"

"It's good news, actually," Bascal said quickly. "It's the surface gravity. We were worried about the planet's high mass, right? Four times the mass of Earth. But the Queendom astronomers have been studying its infrared profile, and they figure it's got about two and one-quarter times the diameter of Earth, as well. That means the gravity is around .8-gee, not bad at all. And being so close to the star, it's got some greenhouse heating which makes the atmosphere a lot thicker than you would suspect. About three bars of pressure—that's three times what you'd experience at sea level on Earth. That's not so bad, eh? Low gravity, thick air—you could practically fly. Hammer spikes into the air and climb it. What do you think about that? How does that affect your habitat designs?"

Conrad struggled not to sigh. That *was* good news—much better than he would have expected—and on some level he should be happy about it. But Planet Two was still very unreal to him, very hypothetical, and he resented being nagged in this way. If you could call it nagging, when it happened at twenty-year intervals and longer.

"That *is* good news," he admitted. "We won't have to crawl around like slugs. It hardly seems like a punishment at all."

The king grinned. "So? Shall we do some redesigning?"

"Well, I hate to tell you Bascal, but although I did some of the initial sketches, those habitat designs have been vetted by real architects. The structures are gravity-insensitive, or nearly so. All we do is build them and move in. Sorry."

This news seemed to grind Bascal. "I thought we were on our own here, liberated from the long and overprotective arm of parental love. We should be so lucky, eh? They'll be looking over our shoulders till the day we die. Which is never."

Conrad felt a smirk coming on. "Well, you never know. We might get lucky and meet death somewhere along the way."

Bascal glared at him. "Yeah? Be careful what you wish for."

And for no reason he could think of, Conrad felt a shiver run down his spine. Did Bascal know something, suspect something? Or was it just a general gloom that had settled over him in his time alone? He said, "There will be plenty of other work, Your Highness, without redesigning things that have already been carefully designed. There's a whole world to be built. Why don't you just pop yourself into storage, and we'll see when we get there?"

The king's smile returned, if wearily. "You make it sound so reasonable."

"Isn't it?"

Bas waved a hand, looking conflicted. "I just don't know, Conrad. This plan seemed so sensible when I started. Now, well . . . If it was the wrong thing to do, I should just commit suicide, and refresh an older copy of myself who maybe hasn't gotten so crotchety and demented. But I can always do that later, right? Meanwhile, it makes sense for me to stay my course. Because if this *is* the right thing to do, and I blow my only chance to finish it properly, then that opportunity will never come again. A hundred years of wisdom is nothing to sneeze at. That's a big thing, well worth a bit of sacrifice."

"But it's so hard," Conrad protested.

Bascal grimaced. "My friend, it is much harder than you can possibly imagine. As bad as you think it is, multiply that by ten. Multiply it by a hundred, and you still have no idea. Maybe I'm just going bananas here, but I'll let a doctor make that determination once we've arrived. Well, we don't have any doctors, but I can let a psych program or medical officer interview me and transmit the results back to Earth for confirmation. Then I can pick any archive copy of myself along the way. I can choose my optimal self, from a library of stored snapshots. The Catalog of Bascal Edward. How many people have that privilege, without also excising decades of critical memory? Not many, my friend. Not many at all. But in the meantime, yes, it's difficult."

He paused for a minute and then added, with pathetic hopefulness, "I'd be honored if you'd join me for lunch."

Now Conrad did sigh, because he'd eaten two meals in the past two hours, and did not feel like eating a third. Did not feel like even watching someone eat another meal. He said, "I'm not really sleeping in here, you know. No time is passing at all. I almost wish it were."

Bascal blinked. "You've already eaten?"

"Twice."

"Oh. I didn't realize. Seriously, though. Would it kill you to spend the day with me? Spend a *couple* of days. Maybe you can help Robert with the navigation."

"Robert is awake?"

Bascal nodded. "Brenda, too. We had Xmary last month as

well, but that was just for a couple of hours. Command decisions; I'm sure you know how that goes."

And Conrad felt a stab of anxiety at that remark, not liking the implications. "How long has Xmary spent out of storage? Altogether, I mean."

"Oh, I don't know. Six months more than you? Maybe a year. I'm not sure, Conrad. Why, are you worried?" It was the king's turn to smirk. He singsonged, "Everybody's getting older but you, Conrad! *You're* the impatient one, hustling along to journey's end without stopping to smell the rosewater. You'll be a boy when we get there, and the rest of us will have some seasoning on us. Unless, you understand, you spend some time outside the memory core."

And this at least was a relief, because Bascal really hadn't changed all that much. Not in his interaction with Conrad, anyway, which had always been light and humorous, yet vaguely conspiratorial, vaguely coercive.

"That's quite a sophisticated twisting of my arm, Your Highness. This 'seasoning' has done wonders for you, I can see."

"So you'll stay, then?" The plaintive tone had left Bascal's voice. "I'll make it a request rather than a decree, since you and I are not really friends at the moment. My boy, I've seen you for two hours out of the last sixty years. Don't presume too much, all right? I am your king, and you're some snot-nosed kid I used to know." Then he paused, touching his chin. "Well, that's not quite fair. You're with me in spirit a lot of the time, even if you're not aware of it yourself. But anyway, yes, I'd enjoy the chance to synch up with you again. I'll bet even Brenda would enjoy your company."

Sourly: "Doubtful. How long has *she* been out?"

Bascal laughed. "Not as long as myself; don't worry. Altogether she's had about six years of subjective time, spread out over the voyage. One year for every ten of mine? That sounds about right."

"Thaw her out when you need her, eh? Is it three days a month? Five weeks a year?"

"Whoa, be careful," the king said seriously. "Don't talk like that around her. She's older and wiser, too, but she's still sensitive, and you always had a habit of tweaking her. Just don't, okay? Or the next time you step out of that fax, you might have fifty-seven arms and no mouth. I'm only half joking. A fuffing Hindu god is what you'll look like."

After a moment's silence, Conrad suggested, "Why don't we go to the observation deck? I'd like to see Barnard."

"Well, we'll need to put a realtime window on the ceiling for that. Obviously, Barnard is dead ahead, so you can't just look out through the side of the hull and see it, or up through eleven decks. Even if we turn the sail and bulkheads transparent—which would bleed all our heat into space, by the way—the ertial shield's lensing effects are highly nonlinear. Might as well be looking up through the surface of a lake. There is a nose compartment just above the water tanks, I guess, where you can get a blurry sort of view with your own two eyes. I haven't been there in years, and I wouldn't advise going up without a radiation suit. Every particle in free space hits that nose like a cosmic ray. Kinetic energy rises with the square of velocity, so at .1 C even a helium atom can rip up your genome a bit."

"Yeah, I know all that," Conrad said. He knew some of it, anyway. "Can we just print some radiation suits and go? I *would* like to see it with my own two eyes. How's the sail holding up, by the way? We had talked about maybe furling it for the journey."

"I know, but that didn't work out. It was never a good idea, because what were we supposed to use for forward shielding? Nobody likes eroding the sail on interstellar grit, but it sure beats eroding the forward hull of the ship. We just bleed some power off the reactor to bathe the fabric in infrared, keeping the nanobes warm, and they can repair a typical hit within a few days. Which is about how long we've got between punctures these days, so they mostly stay ahead of the damage. It still adds up, decade by decade, but the thing's not going to fall apart anytime soon. Not in the time frame we're concerned about." He touched the wall. "Brenda, hi, it's Bascal. I've got Conrad Mursk here with me. Remember him? Our first mate? How'd you like to meet us in the forward blister? He wants to see the stars with his own two eyes."

"Hmm," came the sleepy reply, after a few seconds' delay. "Hi there, sweetie. I'll go get a suit."

"Get three, would you?"

"Sure."

The view was interesting, if a little disappointing. Ophiuchus was not one of the clearer constellations. Although the sun passed through it once per year as seen from the surface of Earth, the Babylonians had left it out of their zodiac, relegating it to a sort of eternal cultural limbo. It might've been their tenth month, between November's Scorpio and December's Sagittarius, but it just wasn't that dramatic a picture. The "Snake Holder" didn't correspond to any of the great myths, and the stars which formed the image were not much brighter than the other ones around them. This was especially true when you got outside the Earth's atmosphere.

Still, Conrad had become well familiar with the image during training, and could pick it out now against the background stars. And Barnard, as advertised, was visible: an orange dot just off the hero's right shoulder. It was not the brightest star in the heavens—not yet, not by a long shot—but it was the brightest star in the constellation: a definite interloper, changing the picture to a more humanlike from by appearing in a patch where the Queendom's more distant view showed only empty space.

"There it is," Bascal said, attempting a shrug in his space suit.

Brenda had gone all-out with these: Fall-era battle armor with a centimeter wellcloth all the way around, extra rigidizable padding at the shoulders and knees, boots like shipping containers, and a high, clear dome above the head, halfway between a Roman arch and a gothic one in shape. It was without a doubt the bulkiest space suit Conrad had ever worn, and while there was room for the three of them up here, it was a tight fit. Conrad usually felt claustrophobic in a space suit anyway, even tumbling free in the empty vacuum, and having three other space suits jammed up against him, head-to-head in a kind of flower or teepee shape, did not improve things.

Worse, even the open space above the ceiling dome felt distant and contained. The view through the ertial shield really did look like he was peering through a lake: the stars were clearly visible, but they rippled, they shimmered, they broke apart into tiny rings of rainbow light. And there was a faint glow as well, a bluish haze, which Bascal said was Cerenkov radiation: the scream of particles exiting the hypercollapsite and slowing to the classical speed of light.

"It doesn't look as red as I expected," Conrad said.

"'Red dwarf' is a bit of a misnomer," Bascal agreed. "I mean, the surface is still white-hot. Hotter than that, really. Main sequence stars are really ultraviolet-hot, and blue giants radiate a lot of X-rays. But the eye can be funny, can't it? Put Barnard right next to Sol and the difference would be more apparent. Anyway, that speck is where we're headed. That is where we will live out the term of our exile, or more probably, our lives, and since that term is infinite, we'd best make an effort to be happy about it. Personally, I think it's quite a pretty star."

"You write much poetry anymore, Bas?" Conrad asked.

"Not much, no. Sadly, my artistic engine was fueled by injustices of the status quo. Now that I *am* the status quo and the injustices are my own, I find I have less to say, and less artfulness in the saying of it. But I do get your point: this is a sight which should inspire. I'll give it some thought."

"King Hermit here can barely be bothered to write log entries," Brenda said. "He is the colony's chief historian, but you'd never know it to look at his books."

"There's not much happening," Bascal protested. "What am I supposed to say? 'Reactor output reduced by seventy-five watts, to account for Captain Li Weng's return to fax storage. There is one less mouth to feed.'"

Brenda laughed again, and didn't answer. In the silence, in a moment of particular strength or particular weakness—Conrad wasn't sure which—he blurted, "Brenda, Bascal tells me I antagonize you. He would know, I guess, but the truth is, I've always felt the reverse: you going out of your way to antagonize *me*. But either way, it's kind of stupid. I'd like it if we could get along."

"That's interesting," she answered seriously, and without too much of the rancor Conrad had come to expect from her. "I think you and I definitely got off on the wrong foot, back onboard *Refuge* all those years ago. But I was right to be suspicious of you. You *did* get us caught. If not for you, we'd've lived out the entire twenty-year run in secret."

Conrad couldn't deny that. In those days, he and Bascal had ripped their way through more lives than just hers. On the other hand, it was a goddamn revolution. And a successful one, sort of. He was through feeling guilty and defensive over what they had accomplished. But had he been too hard on Brenda since that first ugly meeting? Too critical, too ready to see fault?

"We did get off on the wrong foot," he agreed.

Bascal, perhaps sensing the conversation's potential now to veer off in a less productive direction, changed the subject. "Conrad has some suggested updates to the fax filters. I think it's a good idea, and actually I sort of wonder why we didn't do it a long time ago."

"Is it the immorbidity extensions?" Brenda asked. "It is a good idea, yah, and everyone seems to come up with it sooner or later. But it's incredibly difficult. In the Queendom there's no need for it, because everybody faxes daily anyway. I'm sure their finest minds could come up with a fine solution, but who's going to pay them? And here on *Newhope* we don't have a billion geniuses to draw on. Instead, my team is five people who never finished traditional school. But I have some ideas on the subject, and the next time I have a few months free, I may press ahead with some models and calculations."

It was interesting, Conrad thought, to hear her talking this way. She *had* changed since those early days, or at least let some hidden aspect of herself rise to the fore. This made him wonder, with a gut-gnawing anxiety, whether Xmary might have changed as well. For better? For worse? Any difference was unwelcome, if he hadn't been there to witness it, to share it and change along with her. Should he try to catch up? Spend six months, spend a year, spend five years out of storage, adding season to his soup? Or would that just send him off in still a different direction, increasing the distance between them? Damn it, this would be much simpler if people would stick to the plan, and simply stay in storage where they belonged. On a hundred-year coast between the stars, there was very little work that actually needed doing. Was he the only one who saw that?

"Brenda," he asked tentatively, "can you set up some sort of trigger, to bring me out with Xmary the next time she comes out of storage? And vice versa? I think it would be good if she and I spent some time together."

Brenda smiled, and there was a knowing, womanly quality to it. "I think something like that can be arranged, yes. That's another point which you're not the first to raise."

Inside the helmet dome, Conrad nodded his thanks. "This all seemed simpler back in the Queendom, didn't it?"

She wiggled a little beside him, in a way that made Conrad think she was trying to shrug. "Different time, different place. Did you think we would leave all our problems behind? We left some, but you pick up new ones wherever you go."

Conrad snorted. "Maybe we need a filter so people come out of the fax feeling happy. Adjusted, you know, feeling like they enjoy their lives."

Brenda's laugh was polite but humorless. "If I could do that, sir, I'd be a declarant in Her Majesty's service. Well, all right. To be fair, the Queendom has toyed with that approach from time to time, but there are dozens of ethical questions wrapped up in it. Where does free will enter in? What are the limits in changing someone else's mind? Without knowing that, we'd be on dangerous ground indeed."

"We're on dangerous ground already," Conrad pointed out. "Though I see your point."

She snorted. "Hell, I'd settle for just having people come out feeling rested."

as a stone is skipped
across the water

Suitably chastened, Conrad did indeed spend more time out of storage over the next couple of decades. A lot of that time he spent with Xmary, and it was nice, but he learned— as Bascal and Brenda had—that they didn't want to spend *too* much time together in the small confines of the ship. A few weeks together, a few weeks apart, a few months in storage, and then start all over.

Their alternating supervision was kind of needed anyway, because there *was* a certain background level of activity required to maintain the ship—more so as the hardware aged—and a lot of that had been going on without benefit of senior officers. Which might or might not be a good thing, depending on your point of view, but it had side effects like excessive unauthorized energy allocations, raiding of the mass buffers for spur-of-the-moment projects, and peculiar forms of vandalism, such as the word EXHALE! inscribed twenty thousand times in the floor and walls and ceiling of the observation lounge.

The lettering was elegant: inlaid impervium on a brushed-platinum background. Very tasteful, even beautiful. And reprogramming the wellstone to wipe away the display was no great exercise for Conrad, who'd been programming since the age of sixteen. But it struck him as a bad sign for morale, somehow—both a symptom of poor discipline and an encouragement for worse. Only the tiny size of the crew and the brief, staccato nature of their assignments prevented it from being widely seen.

Meanwhile, news continued to trickle in from Earth. It was nothing like the Nescog feeds they'd grown used to as children, but the Queendom had thoughtfully erected an array of hundred-megawatt transmitters, so the bandwidth of their transmissions was not tiny by any means. *Newhope* was receiving eight hundred separate channels of full sensorium, including news, entertainments, continuous library feeds, and of course personal message traffic, which had taken on a wistful tone as the speed-of-light turnaround time edged past the decade mark.

When Conrad got a message from his parents, it was as though he'd found it in an attic somewhere, dusty and long forgotten.

> *Hello, lad. Dad here. Hope you've not forgotten us in your travels. I thought you'd like to know we repaved the Kerry bypass this year, with genuine cobblestone on top of a gravel and asphalt base. She's a beautiful road, Conrad, and I wish you could drive her with me. Mother sends her love. You know, it occurs to me that you've been gone from us now for nearly three times as long as you were with us to begin with. Funny, that we should miss you so much, when the time we spent raising you— badly I might add—is such a tiny fraction of our lives. That's immorbidity for you. We were born expecting to die—you know that—and we never did really adjust to the change. It's easier for you, I think. At any rate, you've many exciting adventures ahead of you, lad, and I wish you all the best.*

Unfortunately, *Newhope*'s own transmitters were nowhere near as powerful, their return bandwidth nowhere near as broad. Conrad's reply, which took seven hundred watt-hours out of his personal energy budget, was, "Hi, Mom. Hi, Dad. Not much going on here yet. All my love, Conrad."

Of course, he was in storage for most of the time anyway, so he got five or six long letters for every terse reply he sent back. It seemed to him that Donald and Maybel Mursk, with lives of their own in a community far older than the Queendom of Sol, must surely be forgetting about him by now. His face growing dim in their memories, his voice and mannerisms increasingly remote, historical, irrelevant. The thought was at once sad and liberating.

Meanwhile, the Queendom astronomers continued to refine their predictions about the nature of Planet Two, and of the other, less habitable planets in Barnard system. For good measure they sent along information about other systems as well, the planets of nearby stars, toward which ten other colony ships had already been launched. *Newhope* was no longer the sole hope of humanity, the sole cradle of its wayward children. This thought, too, had good and bad sides for him to contemplate.

From what Conrad could see, there had been a lot of experimentation in starship technology, and most of the later ships were of wildly different design than *Newhope*. Higher thrust, greater terminal velocity, more spacious interiors. *Newhope* had even received a couple of personal messages from the crew of this or that ship, to one or another of her own sleeping passengers. Their content of course was private, and also many years out of date, having necessarily been relayed through stations in the distant Queendom. But Conrad was curious about them nevertheless. What were they saying, these other colonists?

The transit distances these other ships had to cover were all longer than six light-years, so while they were faster, they had departed decades later and had farther to travel. Some of them quite a bit farther. Except of course for the Alpha Centauri ship, The QSS *Tuscany*, which had been among the last to be launched, owing to the lack of suitable planets and moons in the chaotic resonances of that triple-star system. But asteroids and Kuiper belts made a decent home too, for the right sort of people, and eventually the Queendom had accumulated ten thousand volunteers willing to make a go of it. If all went as planned, they would be the Queendom's second colony.

Strangely, unlike the *Newhope* crew and passengers, the other ships carried mostly volunteers. The Children's Revolt was long over and never repeated, and the Queendom did not seem much inclined to exile its rank-and-file criminals. Instead, it reserved that dubious honor for children under forty, whose crimes were clearly social or political in nature, so that the population of prison transportees on the other ships held fairly reliably at fifteen to twenty percent.

The rest of the passengers were just people—children and adults alike—who admired the failed rebels, or envied their exile, or wanted either a fresh start of their own or a long, long adventure among the stars. And being volunteers, they presumably had the luxury of turning back if things didn't work out, leaving their exiled comrades behind or else dragging them back in storage, to be shipped out again to some even chancier and more distant locale.

Anyway, fortunately for Conrad's ego and the morale of *Newhope*'s crew, their own personal colony ship had enough of a lead that it would still arrive first. Whatever else might happen, they—the Barnardeans, the architects of the Children's Revolt—would be the true pioneers, the first to win and settle another star. *Tuscany* would make starfall two years behind them, followed by a whole string of arrivals stretched out over the next couple of decades.

Conrad wondered about the costs involved. King Bruno had complained, more than once, that *Newhope*'s construction alone was a strain on the Queendom's resources. How had they managed to build ten more ships, all larger and more sophisticated, in the seventy years following her departure? Maybe they couldn't afford it, but had felt nonetheless that it was one of those things that simply needed doing. Since their parents would never die and the planets weren't getting any bigger, the children of Sol did, in the end, need a place to live and a means to get there.

In this manner did Conrad while away the decades of *Newhope*'s transit. And then, in year 89 of the Barnardean calendar, the level of shipboard activity took a sharp upward spike as Robert's position errors dropped off their high plateau and began, finally, to shrink. The star was close enough now to provide very exacting Doppler and proper motion readings, to be triangulated against the starry backdrop shifting behind it.

Postponing the third correction burn turned out to have been a wise decision on Xmary's part, because the erroneous position and velocity estimates would have pointed the ship in the wrong direction. The resulting waste would have come to several megawatt hours, or dozens of kilograms of their precious deutrelium fuel supply. Xmary had been hoarding against uncertainty, and the strategy had paid off; with more fuel now for accurate correction, and of course for the deceleration burn itself, their arrival date had moved up by six and a half weeks—welcome news to all.

Of course, Conrad had largely stopped keeping track of subjective time by then. It hardly seemed to matter. But even unaccounted for, the months and years added up. Like an office tower in a downtown district somewhere, *Newhope* was spacious for a quick visit and comfortable for a day's work, but much too fuffing small to be your whole world. To occupy for years on end, without ever going outside.

In his pirate days he'd spent eight weeks on a tiny *fetu'ula*— a sailship patched together from pieces of a ruined planette— and it had driven him to the edge of breakdown. He was older now, better able to handle it, but the situation was a *lot* worse. There were quiet corners to retreat to, holie displays and programmable surfaces to change the decor and the sense of scale, and even neural sensoria to provide the illusion of space and company. But illusion could only go so far when there was no relief, no hope of rescue or capture or early release. No one was waiting for them at journey's end, except their own sleeping passengers, and they *could not go outside*.

First mate or no, he was sick of this ship, and the sooner he could get off it and into some fresh (if perilous) environment, the better.

Preparations for the third and final correction burn were extensive—almost in line with the grand perihelion burn itself. And Conrad found himself spending a quarter of his time, and then a third, and then half, outside the fax. Xmary did the same, and with their work to distract them, the time they spent together was pleasanter than it had been in the doldrums. Less strained, less formal. More fun. Still, there was an uneasy edge to it. One time when he greeted her stepping out of the fax, she looked at him and said, "You again."

She'd meant it as a joke—or so he told himself—but like most jokes it had a sting of truth to it, and that particular shift he had stayed out of her way as much as possible, not caring to test his luck any farther. On the subject of women most men were fools in any era, but Conrad Mursk at least had the wisdom to fold his hand when he saw no hope of winning. As a result, things were better the next time.

And then one day, quite suddenly, they were juking again. Not once or twice a month, but four times in a single day, and three the next, and seven in the day after that as they entered the debris fields of Barnard's upper Oort cloud. This was a genuine milestone—a huge milestone—because Barnard's Oort cloud was only a tenth the size of Sol's. To run into it, to juke around and through it, you had to be pretty damn close to the star.

It was inconvenient, the constant fear of battering from floors and railings and bulkheads suddenly jerking this way or that at full gravity, but even so the crew—Conrad included—cheered every time it happened. They were getting close. It was really happening.

It was in the middle of this, on a bridge running at three-quarters staff—a bridge full of eyes and ears and gossiping mouths—that Brenda and Bascal had their final argument.

Xmary didn't know what to think when Bascal and Brenda started fighting. She had done her share of fighting with both of them: Bascal because she used to go out with him, and Brenda because she was a generally unpleasant person with a habitual disrespect for authority. And certainly, those two had fought before, usually over minor things that an outside observer would have a hard time understanding, much less agreeing with. But the king's fights with Brenda were normally short and hot and superficial, and when Xmary saw it happen—which wasn't often—she figured the two of them pretty well deserved each other.

But right from the start there was something different about this particular fight. It was quieter, tighter, tenser.

"Don't touch me," Brenda said, snatching her hand away. They were sitting side by side, in the special guest chairs that had become a more or less permanent fixture of the bridge.

"What have you got, a bee up your dress?" Bascal said, though Brenda, like everyone else on the bridge, wore a standard uniform. Xmary was ambivalent about this; the uniforms looked spiffy and gave everyone a sense of importance, and of the solemn nature of their duties. That was good. But the kids had all been wearing them forever, with no civilian population to compare themselves against. As symbols the uniforms had become virtually invisible, and when the colors and insignia faded into the background, losing all cultural significance, what further purpose did they serve? She had thought, more than once, of changing them all to a bright lime green or screaming pink—something the optic nerve simply couldn't ignore. But she guessed that would simply grind people without solving the underlying problem. Bascal wore his own uniform, too: his purple one. The insignia and cut were a little bit different, but this, too, was hard to notice anymore. Unless you really stopped to look at it, as she was doing now.

"I just don't want to be touched," Brenda said.

The king chuckled mirthlessly at that. "Well there's a surprise. You never want to be touched. Touching grinds you, throws sand in the gears of your otherwise charming nature. I *should* know better than to try, but hope, as they say, springs eternal."

"Write a poem about it," Brenda shot back. And here was a low blow, because everyone knew Bascal had been trying for years to come up with a decent poem—about Brenda, about anything—but had found himself utterly blocked. This was not surprising, considering he'd spent almost a hundred years cooped up in the same fifty-four levels, without a walk in the sun or a cool, shady rest beneath a coconut tree. Oh sure, the wellstone could be made to produce sunlight, even a fair simulacrum of sky, and the texture of a palm tree or a summer breeze could be imitated. But in practice, these things were annoyingly difficult to do, and surprisingly unworth the effort when you bothered. You couldn't spend *all* your time sulking in the dark, obviously, but you did wind up spending a good deal of it that way.

"Ms. Bohobe," Bascal said wearily, "you are a treasure. Shall we bury you? Design a clever map which leads to you if the clues are properly understood? Then we burn the map, you see. That'd be a nice diversion."

Brenda sat very still, and said, "You burned the maps to me a long time ago, Your Highness."

"Did I? Or was it you?"

"You, Sire. All you."

"*All* me? I'm to assume the entire blame for your unhappiness, here on the happiest place in the universe?"

Brenda just looked at him. "Does it matter, Sire? I'll take the blame myself, then, just so long as you keep your damned hands off me. As far as you're concerned, I *am* buried."

And there was a sort of patient finality in her tone that Xmary had last heard coming out of her own mouth a century ago, when she herself had broken it off with Bascal. She hadn't even been angry with him at that point—not very angry, anyway—and to a certain extent she'd felt sorry for him. But sometimes the splinter had to come out, and you couldn't worry too much how the splinter felt in the process.

Under the circumstances, she ought to have sympathized with Brenda, who had stayed with Bascal for longer than Xmary could ever have hoped to. And though Bascal had mellowed, become nicer and funnier, more rounded as a human, he was still pretty much the same guy he'd always been—the guy Xmary had broken off with all those years ago.

But whether it was a mark of judgment or simply a flaw in her own character, Xmary found she could not side with Brenda in any argument. She found herself feeling angry on the king's behalf. He was trying to be nice to Brenda, to soothe her with a mix of logic and humor, and she was having none of it. Having none of *him*. He'd probably done something to deserve this—not one thing but a hundred, a thousand small things. But still he did, in some greater sense, deserve better.

Oh, boy. With a shock, Xmary realized that even after all this time, she still had some intimate feelings for Bascal Edward de Towaji Lutui. She shuddered at the thought—what a mess *that* would be! And she felt immediately bad for Conrad, sitting beside her in his first mate's chair, looking uncomfortable. She and Conrad had done their share of fighting, too, and she had been her share of mean to him. He was no angel, either, or he'd never have been on this ship at all. But he was a good man, and did his best to treat her well, and she knew that on some level he feared and resented her past loves, and most especially Bascal, who after all was Conrad's own best friend.

And that was a sorry thought all by itself, because most of the time the two of them seemed to tolerate rather than actually like each other. In practice, Conrad and Bascal were always stewing about something, getting over something, looking forward with trepidation to something that was about to happen between them. But aside from Conrad, she had no close friends herself these days, unless you counted Blue Robert, so she was hardly in a position to criticize.

When Bascal next spoke, his voice was resignedly unhappy, and cold. Xmary could hear him giving up, letting go. "Not deep enough, my dear. Not nearly deep enough."

This was Brenda's one chance to make it better, to apologize and smooth things over. Bascal paused long enough to make the chance unambiguous, but she didn't take him up on it. Sighing, he stood, straightened his collar, and headed for the stairs.

Xmary and Conrad shared a look, and then Conrad and Robert, and then Robert and Xmary. Everyone was looking at everyone, except Brenda, who looked down at the ray-streaked wellstone of the deck until a seemly interval had gone by and she could, with dignity, slip away herself.

That night, and for days afterward, Xmary hardly spoke to

Conrad at all—hardly dared to—but touched and hugged him every chance she got. She met his gaze; she smiled warmly. She clung. If he was not her flotation device, her air supply, her anchor against the winds of fortune, he was something not far removed from that. Something vital.

And so she asked herself: Will I stay with him when we've unpacked and debarked? For a thousand years? Ten thousand, a million? I could live without him. I *have lived* without him, and the odds are virtually certain, in an infinite universe, that I will again. But God help me, I can't imagine it.

To the best of her knowledge, Bascal and Brenda were never intimate again, and when Xmary asked him about it, years later, all he said was, "Dear girl, human beings weren't meant to love forever. Indeed, I fear sometimes that we weren't meant to love at all."

starfall

Technically speaking, the pressure of Barnard's light on the photosail had begun to slow *Newhope* in the year 92, when its light finally became brighter than Sol's. In practice, though, this effect was negligible until year 98, when *Newhope* was well inside the Oort cloud; and it was quite minor until the very end of year 100, when they were finally inside the orbit of Gatewood, the outermost gas giant, some thirty-six light-minutes from the star itself.

Of course, there were no launching lasers—or rather, braking lasers—here at Barnard, and while a number of complex schemes had been floated before their departure, involving lasers shining away from Sol, bouncing off the sail in funny ways to brake it here at Barnard, the mission planners had finally decided on the simplest of solutions: carrying lots and lots of deutrelium for a really hard deceleration burn.

So *Newhope* screamed into the system at .06C—eighteen thousand kps—running tail-first with the fusion motors burning at medium power, supplementing the nav lasers in their effort to vaporize any debris in their path. Flitting—in a single crew shift!—past the orbits of giants Gatewood and Van de Kamp, the nearly hospitable Planet Two and the barren rock of Planet One. Disappointingly, only the latter was in a position to be seen clearly, and that for only a fraction of a second. By this time the braking effect of the light sail was not negligible, not even minor, but then, neither was the gravitational attraction of Barnard. The two balanced each other that first shift, and then on the second shift the braking effects began to dominate, began to slow *Newhope*'s travel measurably, though still not nearly enough. The fusion motors still provided twenty times more braking than the sail, and then as the ship approached perihelion—or peribarnardion, as Robert insisted on calling it—the deutrelium valves were opened all the way, the throttle set at maximum, and in the safe cocoon of the ertial shields, *Newhope* decelerated at almost two hundred gravities.

The view through filtered portholes and simulated windows was staggering. Barnard was smaller than Sol, with a weaker surface gravity, and though its temperature was lower, and its energy output a *lot* lower, its surface was markedly more active: a riot of flares and sunspots and coronal anomalies. The space around it was lively with proton storms, prompting Robert to remark, "Eighty percent of our hull mass is given over to radiation shielding right now, and we're still getting an unhealthy dose. Even our clippers and frigates, when we build them, will need battleship plating in this system, or the crews will be down with cancer in no time."

"Even our orbital colonies will need to be shielded," Bascal added. "P2's trifling magnetic field isn't much of a defense. You have to remember how *close* it is to the star, snuggled right up against its meager warmth, only forty-five light-seconds away. We're lucky the atmosphere is so thick, or we'd die of radiation sickness right out on the surface."

After that, some more dramatic words were spoken and recorded for posterity, but Conrad never did remember what they were, and never heard them played back or spoken of again.

And then, with alarming swiftness, Barnard was shrinking behind them. Or ahead of them, if you wanted to think in *Newhope*-centric terms, for the bow of the ship would remain pointed at Barnard for the foreseeable future, until orbital capture was complete.

"Information, can we have a graph of deutrelium consumption over time?" Conrad asked.

"Deutrelium consumption is constant," Agnes protested.

Indeed, as Money Izolo had told Conrad many times, the flow rates were very tightly controlled for a given throttle setting, to minimize damaging thermal anomalies in the reactor. "Snaps," he called them.

Conrad sighed. "Deutrelium *stores*, I mean. Give me a graph of the deutrelium level in the tanks. And talk to engineering: find out how much of our supply has decayed over the course of the journey. The stuff has a half-life, right?"

"It has two half-lives," Robert said. "One for the deuterium and one for the helium-three."

Conrad rolled his eyes. "My, isn't everyone a stickler today. Your precision is commendable, Robert, and my own lack of it an embarrassment to us all."

"Just give him what he wants," Xmary cut in with an authoritative voice. By now, everyone knew you didn't quibble with Xmary. You could disagree with her, bring her serious issues, even take the initiative to accomplish necessary things without asking her first. But any sort of nitpicking, any splitting of hairs or academic nose tweaking, and you would bring out the old party girl in her: judgmental, hypercritical, and impatient of needless posturing. "Don't be such a leak," she had said to Agnes more than once, right here on the bridge. And to Robert: "Don't speak to me again until you've ingested a drug, mister. I don't care which one." And to Conrad: "Plan on just shutting up for a while, all right? There's a plan for you."

Bad enough if she said these things in command tones, but she generally managed to make them funny, which was worse. For the most serious cases she reserved the Ugly Hat, a punishment so lame and undignified that no one had risked it in decades. The Ugly Hat was a full meter tall, and composed of equal parts feather and sequin and madly flickering wellstone, like a blitterstaff that had spent the weekend in Gamboll City.

So without further comment, Conrad's requested graph appeared on the ceiling half a minute later.

"Engineering," Conrad called down after that, "time to deutrelium depletion?"

"At current rates of consumption, sir?" Money returned.

"Obviously at current rates of consumption."

"Because we want to leave some reserve in the tanks. Safety margins, yah? And inevitably there's ullage as well, the fraction we can't easily extract from the tanks and plumbing."

"Money, not now," Xmary warned. "Just tell us what we need to know." He accepted the warning, and conferred for a few minutes with Robert in hushed intercom voices, and then went off by himself for a few minutes before coming back to the comm window and relating to Conrad that the burn was expected to last another eighteen hours, and that four tons of deutrelium—less than one percent of the original supply—would remain in usable form when they were done. They would need that fuel for in-system maneuvering, for transit to P2, for all the things that *Newhope* would be called upon to do once they had finally come to a halt. And since *Newhope* was the only transportation they had, at least for now, it would be called upon to do a great deal.

So the burn thundered on, barely felt in the ertially shielded and gravity-lasered confines of the crew quarters, terminating just as they passed the orbit of Gatewood on their way back out again. *Newhope* continued upward, not back toward Sol but in a direction only slightly bent from their original approach vector. Barnard's gravity was on their side, now, and though its light pressure was behind them, pressing on the sail and technically speeding them up, the *tack* on the sail (actually a dancing chorus of clear and silver patches, as the sail itself was immobile) allowed them to absorb the force in a lateral direction. This amounted to a minor deceleration, on the order of ten microgee.

"Now comes the frustrating part," Xmary said to her bridge crew. "We go where we must, and not where we really want to."

Strictly speaking, they *had arrived*. They had captured into Barnard orbit. But their orbit was cometary; they wouldn't reach aphelion—apoapsis, apobarnardian, whatever you wanted to call it: the high point of their orbit—for another ten years. They could, of course, burn up their remaining fuel and stop more or less dead, but this would be dangerous in the extreme, and wouldn't really help in the long run, because they'd need the sails to maneuver their way back to Planet Two anyway. And that would actually take longer. Instead, they would make a complete circuit around the star—a tight cometary ellipse, shedding speed all the while through the slow, steady push of the sail—and brake once more at the bottom. Twenty-two years from now.

"Back into storage?" Robert asked with a groan.

"You especially," Xmary agreed. "I don't need two more decades of boredom and frustration building up in my astrogation team just when we're finally doing something tricky."

Robert would have looked about as thrilled if she'd asked him to put on the Ugly Hat. But he nodded, and later that shift, Conrad personally escorted him to the fax machine at the forward inventory. "I just want to be *there* already," Robert said to him as he stood by the print plate. "I want to run a position check and find that we've been there all along, that all this was a bad dream."

Conrad could only shrug. "People used to say life was a journey, not a destination. My mother still says that, or anyway she did a hundred years ago. I'm not sure it's true anymore; people live forever and never seem to go much of anywhere. But *we're* different, Robert, or we ought to be. Once we're finished decelerating, we still have to unpack and make our way to the planet itself. And then we've got orbital colonies to set up, and then the first ground colonies, and then industry, and then agriculture and maybe even terraforming if we have the stomach for it. And the whole thing is going to take us hundreds of years even if we hustle, which I'm not sure we particularly need to. And even when we're finished with all of that, this place will never be like the Queendom. That's the whole point, isn't it? So why are you impatient? What, exactly, are you waiting for?"

Robert stared at him for a long moment, and finally said, "Paver's Boy, in subjective time I'm almost thirty years older than you."

"Your choice," Conrad said, shrugging. "I'd've spent even more time in storage if I thought I could get away with it."

Robert waved a hand, impatient with that reply. "No, you're right. You're the one with the proper attitude, the *immorbid* attitude. And knowing you as I do, I can't for the life of me think where this wisdom of yours has come from. I've always believed in anarchy, in ad-hocracy and collectively half-assed solutions to the problems of life, but suddenly you make me wonder. Could it be that simply holding a position of authority—even petty authority—wakes up a little piece of us that knows how to lead? That knows what's right and proper. I've got my eye on you, young man. I'll be studying this."

Then he turned and stepped and vanished through the fax's print plate.

The irony of it, of course, was that Conrad himself was burning with impatience. "Pretends," he told the empty air. "The part that *pretends* to know what's right. Blue Robert, you nudist pirate chieftain, you know as well as I do: leadership is the art of lying."

And yet . . .

It should be said that immorbid people gripe about time in much the same manner that Old Moderns once did about the distance of a telephone call or the altitude of an aircraft: with great conviction and very little practical consequence. Consider it a form of boasting, perhaps, or a vestige of the hunter-gatherer wiring which remained, in spite of everything, permanently baffled by the marvels of technology. In any case, for the vast majority of *Newhope*'s crew, the time passed in no time at all.

Barnard's meager supply of asteroids—mostly the cosmic equivalent of coal—were nothing to write home about. *Newhope did* write home, of course, because the Queendom astronomers were squirming with curiosity, and were owed a favor or two for all the information they'd transmitted ahead to *Newhope*. But there were no minor terrestrial planets in these belts, nothing big enough that its own gravity would pull it into a spherical shape, as with Ceres in Sol system. In fact, only four asteroids were larger than two hundred kilometers across—all residents of the more populous inner belt, between the orbits of Van de Kamp and P2. These worldlets were egg-shaped and very dark, and Bascal, struggling for a name worthy of the journey that had brought him here, dubbed them the Four Horsemen: Bellum, Fames, Obitus, and Morbus.

The outer belt consisted mainly of rubble: irregular, sharp-edged chunks of carbonaceous chondrite and low-yield iron ore no more than a few kilometers wide. The total mass of the two belts together came to less than a tenth of Sol's own Asteroid Belt. Fortunately, in an energy sense, the outer belt was the easier one for them to get to, requiring less than half the fuel they'd need to reach the inner one.

So that was where Robert and Bertram steered them: to the outer belt, which they insisted on calling the Lutui Belt. Whether this was meant as a compliment to King Bascal or some sort of subtle dig in the ribs was neither clear nor specified. Nor asked, for that matter.

Newhope's first orbit carried her high up into the Oort cloud, but Barnard provided some fairly significant braking on the second pass, which dipped down into the upper reaches of the star's chromosphere, or middle atmosphere. How the ship—120 years old by now—rattled and groaned between her ertial shields! How she whined at the inconvenience, and sweated through the scorching heat! But she saw them through, riding the particle flux and magnetic disturbances as though she were born for them. Which of course, she was.

The density of the chromosphere was not all that much—about equivalent to the "vacuum" in low orbit above the Earth. But plowing through a quarter-million kilometers of it raised a substantial cumulative drag, shaving hundreds of kps off their speed. And then, of course, there were the photo-braking effects from the pressure of Barnard's light on the sail. This was also significant, shaving off another fifty kps, which was enough—just barely—to lower their apogee down into the upper reaches of the Lutui Belt.

This process took a lot of attention and a few more years of their precious youth. This time, more people were needed outside of storage, although the shifts and duty periods were by no means evenly distributed. The old grew older while the young remained as they were. At the start of the journey the crew's oldest member was just seventeen and a half years older than the youngest, but now—even discounting Bascal himself, and the stored passengers whose subjective experience of the journey was zero—that gap had widened by decades. Conrad learned an astrogation term to describe this: dispersion.

"Throw a handful of rocks on the floor," Second Astrogation Officer Bertram Wang explained one day over beer and blintzes in the observation lounge, "and they'll skid to a halt at various distances: some at your feet, some coming to rest against a far obstacle. Most of them are just scattered in between, in a pattern we call 'Gaussian distribution.' If we draw a graph of crew subjective ages—a histogram, it's called—I'll bet it follows this pattern. A bell curve, you know, with Bascal at one extreme, the median peak around twenty-seven years or so and, I dunno, Martin Liss at the tail end. Remember Martin?"

Indeed, Conrad remembered him well. Had even gotten him killed once, when Martin suffocated in a makeshift space suit during one of the more hazardous operations of the Children's Revolt. He was technically the ship's medical officer, but the job was so redundant that he'd been pulled out of storage only twice over the entire course of the journey. "Yeah. All right, let's try your graph."

They did, and it came out much as Bert had predicted it would.

"But these aren't random events," Conrad objected. "These are people with free will, making conscious choices. Pebbles that get up and walk around."

"Yeah, well," Bert replied with a shrug. "Choices are a stochastic phenomenon. Meaning you can apply statistics to them, which I'd call a fortunate thing, or else there would be no science of politics at all. Everyone would just—I dunno—guess what to do and hope it all worked out."

Conrad laughed at that. "You're saying they don't?"

"Not always, no. If our dear king is clever as well as cracked, he'll keep some people around to check the math on his various plots and schemes."

And here a prejudice showed through: implicit in any discussion of aging on *Newhope* was the observation that along with the alleged "seasoning," it fostered a particular kind of craziness, which Xmary dubbed "decade fever." At the far, peculiar end of the spectrum was King Bascal, yes, now 145 years old, with more than half that time spent in the company of two persons or fewer.

"I wouldn't talk like that too openly," Conrad warned Bertram. "But you're not the only one worrying about it."

Bascal, speaking to Conrad on an occasion some nine months later, was upbeat and expansive on the subject. "Ah, my old friend, or rather my *young* friend, my childhood chum who still has baby fat around the cheeks! There is so much more to life than you've yet guessed. It is such a rich and intricate process, of which you've tasted so little!"

"And how would you know that, exactly?" Conrad answered with rising irritation. "What have you tasted lately?"

"A fair question," the king conceded. "To the untrained eye, I've been doddering around in a cellar for a century and a score now, probably—if not obviously—deranged. But in fact, my dear boyo, there's not just one of me bumbling around the ship. When I'm alone, I print dozens of copies of myself, each with a different work assignment. There has been, at times, a whole society of me, with its own social structure, differentiation of labor, and even a sort of service economy—necessary because I don't always agree with myself about who should do what. Especially when the work is unpleasant. One gets to know oneself very well indeed under these circumstances, and knowing oneself is the first step along the path to understanding others, and therefore what life is all about.

"In addition, laddie-oh, I've absorbed one thousand classics of written literature, in ten different languages. I've also watched at least half a million hours of television—all the classics of the Queendom, and of the societies which preceded it—and I have seen and read the major analyses of them as well, and even added my own voice to the body of criticism. You tease me for abandoning poetry—" In fact, Conrad had done no such thing. "—but there was a hubris to my early works which I now find inexcusable. Chief among the presumptions of youth is the spouting of platitudes, which are understood intellectually but which exist without experiential context, and are therefore not *felt*. Thus, in an information sense, they're meaningless: a repetition rather than a reformulation. As a poet I was an utter fraud, and have been atoning at length for that sin. When I know enough, when I've learned enough, the muse will visit again, and this time her gifts will not be abused."

And if the words themselves made a certain amount of sense, albeit one of fatalism, they were delivered with a strange, plodding sort of mania, like the downhill slide of some immense glacier, cracking and grinding its way over any possible objection. One might as well argue with a storm, with the orbit of a planet or the slow rotation of the galaxy itself. That was decade fever. That was Bascal Edward. The two had become indistinguishable.

"I also converse with the ship, of course. By now, its outer personality is shaped primarily through its interactions with me. Not that you would know this, robophobe that you are. And if that social scene begins to feel barren, why, I simply create other personalities as needed. I once spent a decade raising a family of robots. They're in storage now, but I'll bring them out—I will!—when I have a palace to move them into. And of course there is neural sensorium, which is real enough when you've nothing better to compare it to. I have seen London and France, my boy, and more than my fair share of underpants as well."

Conrad had no idea what that was supposed to mean, but it had an elderly sort of sound to it: wistful and boastful and vaguely, smugly superior. Not for the first time in his life, he wondered whether he and Bascal were still friends, whether they really knew each other at all. But Bascal certainly seemed to feel a bond, and since they couldn't avoid each other anyway, that pretty well decided the matter.

Robert and Agnes were not as bad, as insufferable, as

fevered by the passage of time. But they had logged their share of solo hours, too, and of years in various too-small societies with bizarre, insular customs of their own. They still wore their uniforms—everyone did—but their own had mutated in strange, subtle ways: the shoulders too broad, the waist too narrow, the braids and insignia so bright that they actually glowed a little. And there was a hint of transparency to the fabric—perhaps an echo of their old nudist ways, though it looked more funerary than sultry. Sometimes Conrad would find them wandering around the ship like ghosts, together or separately, lost in thought and mumbling to themselves. Agnes had brightened the blue of her skin as well, and Robert had added a subtle pattern of tiger stripes to his that through some trick of the light was plainly visible through the corner of your eye, but could scarcely be seen at all when you looked right at it.

"I've spent my life steering this ship," Robert would say sometimes, in an angry, almost accusatory sort of way. "Don't you tell me how to count beans, sonny. Your rank at this point is an absurd formality."

Of course he said nice things, too, like, "You're a fine young man, Conrad. I always thought so. Follow your passions, and this long, long life of yours will ease by like a pleasant dream."

Farther down on the decade fever scale, Brenda and Peter and Bertram and Money had racked up a couple of decades each, and didn't often let you forget it. Even Xmary was puffing herself up a bit, and Conrad, who lagged her by a good eight years, supposed that he himself was not immune. When the ordinary colonists came out of storage, what would they make of *Newhope*'s crew? And of their child-king, yeah, who in their subjective time frame had only just been elected a few weeks before?

Well, maybe the move to larger environments—orbital colonies and finally domes on the planet herself—would do them all some good. After all, no one here was an expert in colonizing a new star. In this most crucial of senses, they would all be on equal footing. Not solid, but definitely equal.

But the problems were already starting as Conrad pulled

out a few teams of people who, in their studies, had specialized in astronomy and geology, or matter programming and
zero-gee construction. Where possible, he introduced them
to the ship no more than five at a time, and for no more than
seven days at a stretch. But still it amazed him how quickly
they grew bored and frustrated, claustrophobic at the confines of *Newhope*, and cranky—very cranky—at being told
what to do. On more than one occasion bitter arguments
erupted, and Conrad had to remind himself that these children, many of them, were only a few years removed from
their days of revolution, and weeks at best from the Queendom's training and reeducation camps.

So he gave them every possible benefit of the doubt. Until,
inevitably, the first of the Barnard freakups occurred.

What happened was that a fight sprang up between two of
the newcomers. One girl was from the uprising in Calcutta,
and the other from the sole revolutionary action on the surface of Mars, popularly known as the Chryse Feint. They
started arguing about who knows what, and it came not only
to blows, but to the Indian girl dragging the taller, thinner
Martian to a maintenance airlock leading down to the un-
pressurized storage levels where the mass buffers and other
equipment lived. There were security alerts all up and down
the ship as the one girl—or woman, Conrad supposed—
dragged the other down fourteen levels, past a dozen onlook-
ers, most of whom tried to intercede in one way or another.

There wasn't much to the Indian woman, who weighed no
more than Conrad had at age fifteen, nor was there any real
power behind her jabs and thrusts. But she knew exactly
where to hit—the inner curve of an elbow or knee, the base
of the nose, the soft tissue of the ear.

When Conrad got there she was actually working the controls of the airlock, speaking voice commands and thumbing
authentication circles, even rotating the locking wheel on the
inner hatch itself. If she did not intend to murder the taller
girl, she certainly made every effort to appear as if she did.

Fortunately, it was no trivial matter to open the lock, especially with the white heat of rage slowing her down.

Conrad arrived at the same time as Ho and two of his heavies: Steve Grush and Andres Murillo.

"What's going on here?" Conrad and Ho asked at the same time.

"Help!" cried the Martian girl, whose name Conrad could not for the life of him remember. She was not technically a member of the crew, so her uniform bore no insignia, and looked like what it was: a prison coverall. The Indian girl—Geetha something—wore a shorter, broader version of the same garment, and looked no better in it.

"This shitnick Earther is trying to kill me!"

"It certainly looks that way," Conrad agreed, though Geetha had stopped with the controls and was simply restraining the other girl.

"I was just scaring her," she said flatly.

"Sure you were," Ho chortled.

"Let go of her," Conrad said, "and tell me what happened. Why are you doing this?"

"She was careless. She nearly burned my hand. She nearly burned it right off, and somebody has to show this Martian bitch some damn manners. You understand? Some damn, some goddamn manners."

"I was nowhere near you! We weren't working together, and there is no way that telescope mirror would have burned you. The sunlight is too weak, you stupid twat! I could focus it right in your fucking retina for twenty fucking minutes, and you'd still be fine."

Geetha let the other girl go, but promptly brandished a fist at Conrad. "You think you control me? You think you tell me what to do?"

"The chain of command thinks so, yes," Conrad said. "And our lives depend on it. We can't have this kind of behavior going on. If you have a grievance, bring it to me. That's my job. If you feel you're in immediate danger, talk to Ho here, or just shout 'Security!' at the nearest bulkhead. They'll break up your disputes, one way or another."

"I fought people like you," Geetha said through clenched

teeth. "I fought to get people like you off my back. Out of my face, out of my fucking life. But here you are, like a big fat bag of pus. Chain of command my bleeding twat, fucker."

There was a time, Conrad realized, when he and his brothers and sisters in arms had used such language, and worse. But perhaps he had matured, or the youthful fires within him had cooled, because he found it shocking now, and offensive, and flatly unnecessary. He resisted the urge to tell Geetha to watch her mouth. At this point, that would be counterproductive. What he did say was, "Compared to some of the ships we trained on, this one is fairly spacious. Maybe not as big as the habitats you grew up in, but not tiny, either. Still, there is nowhere to escape to.

"You can't even throw on a suit and go outside, because even though the radiation has finally died down, we're under maneuvering thrust half the time as we nudge, frugally, toward our target asteroid. You'd get lost, or slung to the end of your tether, or knocked in the head and burned. And there's no reason to go out anyway, if we use the fax machines wisely and judiciously, and treat each other with some minimum level of respect. I don't see a minimum level of respect here. Do you?"

"She started it," both girls said.

And the Martian girl, finally free to do so, launched a punch at Geetha's stomach. Geetha launched a blow at the Martian girl's face and for good measure, a wild kick in Conrad's direction as well.

"Oh, I don't think so," Ho said. And with that, he drew a gas pistol from a holster hidden in his uniform somewhere, aimed it at the two girls, and pulled the trigger twice. It went *Pop! Pop!*—a vaguely comical sound, except that a round, red hole appeared in the side of each girl's head, and the two of them collapsed to the deck in a tangle of limbs. There was an immediate pooling and spreading of blood.

"What did you do?" Conrad said, dumbfounded. "You shot them. You bastard."

Ho was matter-of-fact. "Judgment call, sir. One of these girls was clearly irrational, and both were violent and presented a danger not only to themselves and each other but very clearly to you as well. I felt it would be better if they were both dead for a while. The ship has instructions to record all such incidents of violence, so we can show them the whole scene when they wake up, and maybe they'll think twice next time they feel the urge."

Conrad looked from Ho to Steve to Andres, blinking. Something wet and warm ran down his forehead, and he wiped it away, then glanced down at himself and realized he was covered in tiny, bright spatters of blood. "Who . . . who authorized this? Who gave you permission to kill people?"

"It's implicit in my job description, sir. It has to be. If you feel this particular action was in error, take it up with the captain. She may see your side, in which case I'll receive a punishment, and I don't think the captain much likes me so that's probably what will happen. But I would do it again, sir. And I have backing from the King of Barnard himself, so if shove comes to push, I have some ability to push back. I'm not stupid, Mr. Mursk, and don't appreciate your treating me like I am."

Conrad continued to gape in disbelief at these men from security. "Who said anything about your being stupid?"

"You've always thought so," Ho replied. "It's no great secret. You can think what you like, sir, but don't come down here and try to do my job for me. You haven't got the stomach for it."

At that, Steve Grush spoke up. "He *is* right, sir. He did the right thing under the circumstances."

Conrad shook his head. "He could've used a tazzer. He could have put them both to sleep, or separated them and dragged them to the fax."

"See, that's where *you're* stupid," Ho said. "What's the difference, if I tazz them or if I brainshoot them? Either way they lose a period of consciousness. Either way, they wake up with a hole in the memory, and none in the skull. And the fact is, I don't have a tazzer with me right now, so I made a judgment call."

Conrad straightened, and glared at the other man. "Don't enjoy your job too much, Ho—not under my command. I'll talk to the captain, but unless you hear differently, you are to stop carrying projectile weapons, or any other form of lethal force, onboard this ship. That applies to the people under your command as well. You will proceed to the aft inventory and request a tazzer, and you will keep said tazzer with you, fully charged, at all times. When you need to immobilize a person, that is the instrument of first choice, with your own body being the instrument of second choice if for some reason the tazzer fails to operate. Do I make myself clear?"

It was an effort to keep his voice from quavering. This was not a reaction of fear, although he and Ho had certainly had their run-ins in the past. But Conrad had just watched two people murdered right in front of him, the blood splattering in his face, and although the two could be revived by any fax machine, and probably would be within a couple of days, the sight of their murder wasn't something he could shake off so easily. His body was screaming, Fight or flee! Barf or faint, do *something*!

Ho seemed to sense this and was about to say something, probably along the lines of Conrad being soft, or a pussy, or needing to leave the hard decisions in the hands of someone capable. And once a thing like that was out in the open, on the record as it were, it would hang over them all for the rest of eternity. And that just wasn't acceptable, so Conrad held up a hand and jumped right in with, "I don't want to hear any argument about it, Ho. You're already in violation of any reasonable code of conduct. Throw insubordination on top of that, and it could be a long, long time before you come out of storage. *Do I make myself clear?*"

Ho just rolled his eyes. "Very clear, sir. Full of mystery you are not."

Conrad straightened farther, staring down the three security officers. "That will be all, Mr. Ng. The three of you are dismissed. Send someone else to clean up this mess."

The three did as they were told, shuffling out of the chamber and up the stairs, but they seemed more amused than upset by Conrad's reaction, and he guessed, wearily, that the matter was far from settled.

chapter eight

the unpacking

The target asteroid was nameless and would remain so, both because it was a minor body—smaller than *Newhope*—and because it was about to be destroyed. Or rather, reshaped and reborn. They pulled up alongside it on August 1 of the year Barnard 123, or Queendom 416, or—according to Robert, in a particularly pedantic mood—2680 by the old Christian calendar.

"Well," Conrad said, cracking his knuckles, "it's finally time to unpack."

But when he turned to Xmary, sitting beside him on the bridge, her face was misty rather than exultant.

"What's the matter? Cap'n?"

The corners of her lips twitched up for a moment, and then sank once more. "My ship," she said sadly. "My beautiful ship. In a few minutes, we'll split open her belly, pull out her entrails, and feast upon her corpse."

Robert looked back at them, clearly about to say something, but Conrad headed him off. On matters of crew morale, Conrad had clear jurisdiction, and concerning the emotional well-being of Xiomara Li Weng in particular, it was as close to absolute as these things ever got.

"It's not as bad as all that, ma'am. We're not pulling out

Newhope's entrails, just, maybe, pumping her stomach. And, you know, going through her pockets. She'll never be the same, it's true: the clean, needle lines of her shape will be broken up a bit. To my mind, she's spreading her wings. Or perhaps she's a stork with four thousand babies to deliver, plus whole communities for them to live in, and infrastructure to support them. But *Newhope,* my dear, will live on. For a long time, I think."

But Xmary was shaking her head. "She won't be aerodynamic, Conrad. She won't be *properly equipped.* She won't ply the starways ever again—not without a major overhaul, or unless we strip her down even farther. From starship to tugboat, in one vicious cut." She dropped her voice to a murmur, so that only Conrad could hear her—although technically, the wellstone around them was more than capable of picking up her voice, amplifying and recording it, and since the fundamental programming had been laid down by Queendom engineers, one had to assume it was doing exactly that. But barring the unlikely return of said starship into the hands of said Queendom engineers, this mattered little.

It should also be noted that in the Queendom, belief in far-future "quantum archaeologists" was widespread and unshakable. People generally agreed, for whatever reason, that their actions, their imprints, their electromagnetic *ghosts* would be open to future scrutiny, even where the events themselves took place in the absence of witnesses. *Information persists,* people were fond of saying. This was a reasonable supposition, and in many ways provably true, for such archaeologists already existed in small numbers. But for the most part the belief sprang from the same irrational roots as the urban and rural and faery myths of earlier ages. And the queen's subjects could not know of the terrible changes in store for Sol and her planets—changes that would crush a great deal of this information completely out of the observable universe.

Be that as it may, the conversation was as private as it could reasonably be in a programmable environment, in a quantum universe, with live human beings all around. And so the two of them spoke and thought and emoted without artifice, without any thought of audience or posterity. Such exchanges are, when preserved, the rare treasures of quantum archaeology.

Xmary went on, in her quiet voice. "I hate this. I never wanted to be the captain of a tugboat. What kind of job is that, for a spoiled girl from Denver?"

For a moment, Conrad was surprised to hear her say this. Unpacking was good, right? Getting the hell out of this prison! But then, thinking about it, he supposed he too might feel some ambivalence about it if his role were about to shrink and shift so dramatically.

In point of fact, he was personally very excited, because once the initial colony structures were printed and assembled, there would be need—enormous need!—for the design of new buildings and support systems. The Kingdom would require an architect or two, and while Conrad had only ever designed and built one major structure, and that a mere school exercise which was torn down afterward to make room for another project, Conrad knew he had it in him to do the job. He was a decent matter programmer in the aesthetic sense, as the bridge's current motif of white gold and pearl could attest, and really a pretty good one on the materials science side as well.

Why, at age seventeen he'd pulled the lining out of a mid-sized planette and fashioned it into a rigid one-way super-reflector—the photosail of the good ship *Viridity*. He'd handled that ship's climate controls and waste disposal systems as well, and had even taught Xmary enough about programming to support two abortive mutinies. During his later studies, he'd even discovered a new material, which was named after him in the *Encyclopedia of Elements and Compounds*: Mursk Metal. It wasn't the strongest or the brightest or the most conductive of materials, but it had the interesting property of "intermittent optical superconductance as function of temperature." From 84 to 104 Kelvin, and again from 200 to 231 Kelvin, the stuff was a pure insulator with an optical band gap of almost 10 eV. Opaque, yes, but at every other temperature it transmitted photons with zero energy loss, making it a new and unique member of the optical superconductor family. Conrad, all fired up to design his building, had intended the stuff to be used as window glass. To the best of his knowledge no one had ever used it that way except himself, but somebody at World University had later found an application for it in hypercomputer designs.

Conrad supposed he was still technically accruing royalties on that in his Queendom bank accounts. Twenty dollars a year? A hundred? The price of a good massage, anyway, or a couple of fax trips around the solar system. None of this meant much of anything by itself—probably half the adults in the Queendom earned occasional royalties on something or other—but it was a visible sign, something that Conrad could point to in an argument to defend his supposed architectural abilities. In fact, no such argument had ever come up, nor was it likely to. The point was simply that Conrad was going to do some designing, both in orbit around P2 and on its surface, and no force in the Kingdom could prevent him, or was likely even to try.

What he said to Xmary was, "I think it will be exciting. You never wanted to be a starship captain either, but you've been doing it for nearly half your subjective life now, and have grown nicely into the role. Right? And it seems to me there's a lot more to do on an interplanetary vessel than an interstellar one. For a hundred years you traveled in a straight line, and for twenty-three in a big spiral. Now you'll have a new destination every couple of months. A new cargo, a new mission. Maybe not as many lives will depend on you at any particular moment, but no civilization could possibly rise here without your efforts."

That didn't seem to mollify her. She said, "Conrad, I want to live on a world. I want to stay with *you*. But then someone else would be *Newhope*'s captain, and what would I be? A party girl? I *will* drive the tugboat. I'll stay here with *Newhope*, bumping around Barnard system, but you won't. I know you won't. You're going to Planet Two."

And here was a thought which had honestly never occurred to Conrad, though surely it should have. In his mind, somehow, Barnard system was conceived as a single place. But in fact, of course, it was hundreds of light-minutes across, and consisted of many thousands of individual places, not even counting the surface of the planet, which was an infinity of places unto itself. None of which would contain Xmary.

Suddenly, he felt his own eyes grow misty, though he kept his voice brave. "Oh. Well. Not to worry, dear; you'll be stopping frequently at P2. I mean, I have to assume you will. As the main population center, it stands to reason it will also be the center of industry, and therefore the main destination for cargo. Right? So you'll pop down to the planet, or I'll come up, and we'll see each other nearly as often as we have on *Newhope*."

"Not as often. Not nearly as often."

Conrad sighed, because she was right. There was no sense kidding themselves about it. They had loved and fought, grown bored with each other in the perpetual sameness of *Newhope* and then rekindled their passions as Barnard approached. And every step—even the negative ones—seemed to make them stronger in the end. But here was a new challenge of an altogether different sort: time and space, unfettered.

"Well," he said carefully, "maybe so, but it's only for a while. When we get the collapsiter grid installed, we'll be able to fax back and forth at leisure, and this whole ship will be just one more room in my big, beautiful house. We'll have the speed of light between us, and nothing more."

"And when is that?" she asked sadly. "Twenty years from now? Forty? A collapsiter grid doesn't just grow, like a houseplant. It's built up from pieces of pieces of pieces."

"Maybe," he acknowledged. "Maybe that long. We'll see, I guess."

But the time had come for personal conversations to cease; the target rock was in position, snared with electromagnetic grapples and pressors, and a team of gleaming humanoid robots was out there wrapping physical lanyards around it, to keep it from sliding around during passfax operations. The bridge was plastered with views from various points on the ship and a few—lurching sickeningly—from the robots themselves.

Xmary raised her voice to normal command levels. "Brenda, what is your status?"

A well-window appeared in the bulkhead, showing Brenda Bohobe in the aft inventory. She looked up and said with all seriousness, "Ma'am, the passfax clears every diagnostic I can push it through. It has been edge-on to the particle flux for most of our journey, and has suffered some cosmic ray streaking, which I've repaired, but no other serious damage or degradation. As far as I'm concerned, you can throw open the doors and begin operation."

Xmary nodded, her demeanor once again professional and leaderly. "Information?"

"Nothing to report," Agnes said.

"Systems?"

"Everything is nominal," said Zavery.

"Engineering?"

When Money Izolo appeared, he said, "The door has three latches, ma'am, and I've opened them all singly, while leaving the others closed. They all function, no problem. I can't test the force on the hinge motors, but I can verify that the coils are working, so there is virtually nothing that can go wrong."

"I've heard that before, mister. Are you prepared for unknown emergencies?"

There was a twinkling in Money's eye, and he said, "Tell me what the unknowns are, ma'am, and I'll tell you if I'm prepared for them. We're as ready as we can be, yah? Let's quit dawdling already, and unpack our bags."

Robert, for once, was not queried. He'd done his job already, guiding the ship alongside this nameless rock, and as far as the unpacking operations were concerned he was nothing more than a spectator. He fidgeted under the strain of this, but did not offer any opinions. Nor did Bascal, who sat a good deal more regally in his "temporary" chair behind the captain's.

Xmary paused for a few moments, sucking her teeth and frowning, before saying, "Open the doors, please, and activate the passfax."

Newhope's mass buffers were already full, stocked with the assortment of elements a fledgling colony was expected to need, although the more reactive atoms had been compounded with carbon or hydrogen and stored as small, inert molecules. But the colony structures were all stored as data, in the same shielded memory cores which held the colonists themselves, and to instantiate them all would take nearly ten megatons of raw material. Hauling that mass all the way from Sol—even within the confines of an ertial shield—would be wasteful madness. Might as well haul the artifacts themselves! Instead, *Newhope* was designed to live off the land, making use of the materials native to Barnard system.

In a sense, *Newhope* was a fax transaction unto herself: both the transmitter and receiver, and also the carrier of the signal. In fact she *was* the signal, packaged as small and as light as the Queendom engineers could cram her. All she carried were emergency supplies: the organics and alkalai metals and electrolytes of human bodies and foodstuffs, and the heavier metals and semiconductors of wellstone and other programmable materials. There was also a supply of basic industrial metals, heavy on titanium and gold, plus a contingency periodic table with at least a ton of every stable element, just in case. And some of this would no doubt prove handy—perhaps even priceless—in the metal-poor environs of Barnard.

"He's an elder star, our Barnard," the king said to no one in particular. "Not one of the original Titans—the hydrogen supergiants that blew themselves to plasma in the first gigayear of creation—nor even one of their helium-swollen children the Olympians. He's safely removed from that bitter past, that stellar ice age when even lithium was still a dream. He tastes of metal, and it's a good thing or we'd've never come to see him in the first place! But he is not of Sol's young, fat lineage. He's a grandchild, this runt star of ours, not some great-great spoiled in a carbon-rich nursery. His parents sent him off starving with a half-empty purse. And here we are, raiding it! Thank you, old man! There are younger, hotter stars than Sol, and they'll burn out sooner, choking on the iron in their bellies, and then Sol herself will swell and die.

"But Old Man Barnard will still be here, whiling away the eons. He learned frugality at an early age, learned to plan and save for the long haul. By the time he breathes his last, the galaxy will be dark with collapsars and neutronium, with iron nebulae and calcium dwarfs. These ancient, red-orange stars will be the last to go, the fading lights of creation."

"Shut up, Bas," said Brenda's voice over the comm system. "Passfax contact in forty-five seconds."

With no discernible noise, the middle third of *Newhope*'s hull had split open and folded itself out, looking—as Conrad had said—like a pair of dainty insect wings. This exposed the passfax, which then extended bootward along telescoping mechanical rails until it was thirty meters clear of the hull. Conrad realized he'd never seen the passfax before, not even a recorded image, but it looked exactly like he imagined it should: a gigantic fax machine with shimmery gray print plates on either side, thirty meters wide and a hundred tall. Like a big, flat sandwich. Like a pair of pearly gray doors slapped together around a tangle of plumbing and machinery.

"Those are the largest print plates ever constructed," Bascal said to Brenda, as if somehow she wouldn't know this. "They are the largest single objects on the ship—the largest that could fit inside her. Any wider and they'd have to be assembled here on station, but I've never heard of a print plate with seams. That would be a tough assembly problem."

"Contact in fifteen," Brenda said in a louder and more irritable voice. On the well-window viewscreens, the gray-black asteroid—looking for all the worlds like a gigantic turd wrapped up in spiderwebs—approached the port face of the passfax.

"Not a problem without solution, one presumes, but surely expensive to implement? I wonder. I do miss our technical discussions, Brenda."

"Shut up! Contact in five, four, three, two . . ."

There was the tiniest flicker of light where carbonaceous stone met the quantum machineries of the print plate, and then the asteroid was slipping—centimeter by centimeter—into the fax machine, for disassembly into individual atoms. But *Newhope*'s mass buffers were full. Or nearly full, at any rate; a few tons might fit in here or there, to replace the mass of printed humans and robots and other equipment, but there was certainly no room for three megatons of disassembled rock. Instead, finished pieces spilled out the passfax's other side: metal beams, rolls and blocks of wellstone, clear panes of monocrystalline diamond.

Such a thing had never been attempted before: the real-time assembly of so many pieces, from so large a mass, with so little buffering. Nothing like the passfax had ever been needed before; this one was the prototype, the first of its kind. It had performed as intended, meeting requirements and passing diagnostics, so the infant *Newhope*—itself a prototype—had been constructed around it.

"It would be nice," Bascal mused, "if we could simply extrude the whole, finished structure in one go. As it stands, we'll have that robot swarm crawling over the wreckage for hours, fitting the puzzle pieces together. And when they're finished, we'll see that primal eldest symbol of civilization here, within the borders of our Kingdom. A shipyard!"

"Your Highness," Xmary said impatiently, "we're all excited. But could you tone down the commentary, please? Or do it somewhere else?"

"Ma'am, I believe His Highness is recording for posterity," Robert protested.

"I don't care if he's recording for God himself. This is a work environment, in the middle of a delicate operation."

"Ouch," Bascal said. "*Two* ex-girlfriends telling the king to stifle himself. Let him eat cake! Or at least, let him stuff his cakehole with something soundproof and chewy. Very well, my dears, your sovereign will slink to the privacy of his quarters, there to contemplate the future of his future. And yours."

His tone was jovial enough, but as the king left his seat and leaped for the downward spiral of the ladder, Conrad was pretty sure he caught a gleam of teardrops at the corner of those royal brown eyes. This was perhaps an emotional moment in more ways than one, and for more people than just Xmary and Conrad.

"Wow," said the newly awakened Zavery Biko from his seat at the Systems Awareness console, when the king was safely out of earshot. "He seems different. Has he gone a little bit crazy?"

Conrad would have answered in spite of decorum, but Xmary saved him the effort, speaking almost the very same thoughts that were poised on his own tongue. "Bascal Edward was always crazy, Zav. Brilliant and impulsive, vaguely unhinged. He's an interesting man to stand beside, and I mean that in the Chinese-curse sense. Life in his shadow will never be dull."

Conrad had long since stopped thinking in terms of plane-tary seasons and times of day, but it seemed like a long, lazy afternoon as the swarm of gleaming robots, over a period of six or eight hours, assembled the pieces extruded from the passfax. With his father, Conrad had many times helped to assemble vehicles in precisely this way, from kitted parts. When you were working on a road, or more properly, watching with bored eyes while your father worked on one, sometimes you found yourself in a remote location where the nearest public fax just wasn't big enough, or didn't have enough capacity in its midbuffers to extrude a complete machine. The machine's designers understood this, though, and so the machines rolled out in five or six easily mobile, easily connected pieces. And when you were done, you simply popped the pieces apart again, and fed them back into the fax. There were, of course, self-assembling kits whose parts were intelligent enough to get around on their own, but Donald Mursk had always disdained these, insisting that the ritual of assembly and disassembly was educational, fostering an intimate familiarity with the machinery, with the subtleties and intricacies of its operation.

"To use a thing properly, lad," he had said one time, "you've got to know how it's put together." And then, with a wry Irish grin he'd added, "That applies to women as well as machines. Keep that in mind for the future, eh? The study of anatomy is the best friend love ever had."

Here in *Pule'anga Barnarda,* the Kingdom of Barnard, it was simpler to send robots out to do the actual assembly work. They were faster and stronger than human beings, more versatile than smart components, and of course they didn't complain. This particular kit—the Martin Kurster Memorial Shipyard, named for some old astronomer—consisted of several hundred distinct pieces that had to be rotated and translated in three dimensions in a particularly large and cunning geometry puzzle.

It was slow work, but fun to watch as it unfolded. For this reason, pretty much everyone on the ship was either on duty or in the observation lounge, and the number of people who were ostensibly on duty, but found themselves in the lounge anyway, was more than Conrad could count on the fingers of one hand. Still, except for Engineering and Information, Systems, and Stores, there were no critical assignments today, so Conrad was inclined not to notice.

As it came together, the shipyard proved every bit as large as the plans had promised, first equaling and then exceeding and finally dwarfing the outlines of *Newhope* beside it. The structure was mostly empty space, of course, but in Conrad's experience, most things were. Anyway, because of its great size, the project was visible from half the ship, and as it turned out, the view from Conrad's quarters was nearly as good as the ones from the bridge and lounge. So when their overlapping shifts had ended and the bridge was turned over to Robert, that was where Conrad and Xmary found themselves, looking out through the hull, which they had made transparent for this purpose.

"It'll be done soon," Xmary said, with that wistfulness in her tone again. "Tomorrow we install the shipyard's own fax machines and pipe over some deutrelium and some mass from the buffers. My buffers. And after that, I'm off to Gatewood to pull a deutrelium refinery out of my ass. Well, out of *Newhope*'s ass."

She was crying now. Conrad rocked her in his arms, not knowing what to say or do. Were humans ever meant for stresses like these? Did situations like this occur naturally, over the course of human evolution? Prolonged and painful separations? He supposed they must have, and he supposed they had always been hard.

Over the later years of their journey Brenda had been building voluntary neurochemical balancers into the fax filter, and it occurred to Conrad that *Newhope*'s crew might have gone into massive freakup a long time ago—gone murderous and suicidal, despondent and bitchy—if the "medicine" of the fax were not constantly propping them up. Conrad had gotten in the habit of printing a fresh copy of himself every couple of days, and sometimes more often than that, but still, even in a state of chemical balance, you could feel overwhelmed.

Maybe this was what it was like, back in the Old Modern days, when friends and family members and neighbors would suddenly drop dead without warning, never to be seen again. That would be harder, right? Or did an immorbid future of infinite possibility simply short-circuit the grieving process, without truly eliminating the need? For all he knew, he and Xmary might never see each other again.

What he said was, "And then, with a belly full of deutrelium, you'll return here and tow this yard to P2, where I'll be waiting. You'll leave the passfax with me, and with it I'll produce an orbital colony with a nice little corner to call our own. A place for you to come home to."

"This is my home, Conrad. Right here, on *Newhope*. I never would have believed that, but it's true. I have no other skills or ambitions, no other place to go, unless I change the . . . the *definition* of myself. If I don't do that, I lose you, and if I *do* do it, then I lose myself, and everything else that matters. Either way, nothing can ever be the same again."

And what could Conrad say to that? What was the purpose of revolution and exile, of starting fresh, if not that exact thing? She was *supposed* to feel uprooted. He tried to put words to this feeling, this dichotomy, but he was no Poet Prince. He didn't know a damn thing, not really. What came out of his mouth was a simple, stupid complaint: "This wasn't supposed to be painful. By gods, it wasn't. I've seen the master plan, and that wasn't in it."

#### chapter nine

worldfall

The probes were simple, thumbnail-sized dodecahedrons of wellstone, programmed with a titranium-impervium alloy for atmospheric entry and impact, and then filled in with whatever sensors and photovoltaics and telecom antennas their hypercomputers deemed necessary and appropriate for the conditions at their landing sites. Per the master plan, a thousand of them were dropped on the surface of Planet Two, while devices on the orbiting colony and a dozen other satellites scanned the planet's surface and subsurface from above with sensors of excruciating precision and subtlety.

This raw data—enormous quantities of it—was then fed into hypercomputer algorithms designed in the Queendom, which sifted it for differences and similarities and then statistically and chaotetically analyzed it for greater meaning. The orbiting colony where this work took place was officially known as *Lililitata*, literally "boiling cap," a Tongan neologism that meant "valve" or "relief"—a place where pressure was blown off. But that was too much of a mouthful even for Bascal, who laughingly approved a mistranslation in its place: Bubble Hood. Anyway, the place had a population of several hundred by now, most of whom were employed in the hands-on analysis of the results, and the filing of reports, and the forming and testing of hypotheses so that a picture of P2's inner and outer workings could emerge in something more than astronomical detail.

"My boy," Bascal told Conrad expansively, "the synthesis of data is information, and the synthesis of information is knowledge. Knowledge is constructed, piece by piece, from loose, unkitted parts."

Bubble Hood was a sphere two hundred meters across, and had originally been intended to revolve around a polar axis to produce half a gee of artificial gravity. Conrad had two problems with that, though: First of all, he wanted the bubble to be transparent, but the planet spinning by every forty seconds would—he knew from experience!—make people sick if they could see it. Second of all it was a waste of space, since the gravity vector would be "straight down" (that is, straight through the inward-facing floor) only at the equator. Everywhere else would be a hillside, broken into terraces by unnecessary "buildings" inside what was already a large, climate-controlled structure. So on a whim, Conrad had crossed the scheduled spin-up off his list and ordered his people to print up hundreds of gravity lasers and scatter them every which way throughout the structure.

The results were interesting to say the least, especially after their long imprisonment in the narrow tower of *Newhope*. This particular conversation found Conrad and Bascal in a maze of transparent surfaces, facing each other at right angles, with a sketchplate hovering uncertainly in the air between them while the khaki light of P2 glowered down motionlessly from "above."

"Theoretically," the king continued, "the next step is wisdom, the sum and synthesis of knowledge. But the more I think about it, the more I think that's a quality I've never seen. I'm sure it exists somewhere—there are sixty billion humans in the universe so far, and at least a few more arriving every day—but wisdom has a quality of mirage about it, retreating when inspected. Historical figures have the benefit of distance, and are incapable of making new mistakes, so we're free to see them as wiser figures than anyone contemporary. But there will be no new historical figures, will there? We are all of us contemporary, always and forever.

"And the wise woman is always a puffed-up biddy when you get to know her, isn't she? The wise man is a fretting gambler. If you guess right a hundred times, my boy, people will call you wise. But with all those billions of people kicking around, statistical narrowing demands that there be winners, even if all the decisions are random. There will be people who have always guessed right, every time in their lives. But it's meaningless, isn't it? Because if their next action is also a guess, it will have no more validity, no greater chance of success, than the cockamamie theories of a punk in some kiddie café. We most of us fail, Conrad, but we find our strength in numbers. If *someone* succeeds, if *someone* is wise, then civilization staggers forward, if not happier then at least a little bit richer, a little bit grander."

"Kind of a harsh view, Highness," Conrad said crossly. "Be useful for a minute. Focus. What can you tell me about the chlorine situation?"

Conrad had been a little unnerved, at first, when he realized he was the ranking officer for an entire planet, with hundreds of people answering to him. Technically speaking, space crews fell under the command and jurisdiction of the government of Barnard, hence of Bascal personally, and would eventually be reconstituted as some sort of Royal Barnardean Navy, but none of that long-term stuff had been unpacked yet.

The current government, such as it was, consisted of little more than conversations over lunch and dinner, mainly between himself and Bascal, and these were concerned as much with their old days at camp and in the Revolt as with anything contemporary. And since Bascal, with a Juris Doctor, three PhDs, and a ridiculous assortment of master's degrees, was taking a direct and leading role in the sensor analysis, this placed him, in a funny way, under Conrad's command.

Bascal was currently specializing in the biology of the native life-forms and their effects on the larger environment of the planet. But he required a certain amount of direction and had to be pumped periodically for information. For all his newfound age and gravity, he was a rather impulsive worker, selecting random tasks and attacking them for a while with battering-ram intensity, and then flitting on to something else, leaving a debris trail of half-completed projects behind him. The jellycells! The lidicara! The chlorine-producing algoids! The *weather*!

It was hard to argue with this approach—King Bruno had invented collapsium in exactly this way, and in the following centuries had parlayed the discovery all the way to the Nescog, the collapsium-veined telecom network which permitted Queendom citizens to fax themselves anywhere at all, including everywhere at once. But Conrad did not have centuries to wait, and the analysis of P2 needed patience and focus far more than this lurching and somewhat playacted brilliance. So Conrad found himself growing increasingly—if inappropriately—bossy.

And while the King of Barnard was thirteen decades Conrad's senior by this point, the new relationship seemed to bother him not at all. He was enthusiastic and accommodating, as willing to take direction as to give it, and Conrad found himself, for the first time in years, feeling the old bonds of friendship come truly alive. Sure, the king had a bad case of the Fever, and spoke like a bad echo of his father. But as a rebel, the Prince of Sol hadn't needed any role models. By definition, almost, he'd been his own man. All he'd had to do was struggle against the status quo, without having to actually run anything himself! But as a king, what other lead did he have to follow? Who but Bruno had ever been the immorbid king of an immorbid people?

And to fit himself into that mold, Bascal had to be a scientist—in fact a demented genius of staggering proportion—who only reluctantly turned his attention to matters political and economic. This of course changed his whole definition—what it meant to be Bascal Edward de Towaji Lutui—and even with the help of a fax machine there was only so much brilliance you could cram into your skull. Some things were still God's to grant. So Bascal was making up the difference by rote, simply memorizing an encyclopedia of facts and methods and then styling his hair and beard and mannerisms in an ensemble hypercomputed to enhance his credibility. Which Conrad supposed was how most scientists probably did it, or anyway the ones people trusted.

The resulting facade was, on the one hand, very impressive and imposing and yet also quite approachable: the kind of public face you might actually want for your king. But on the other hand, it was really just another half-baked scheme, a kind of moral power-grab that Bascal had rushed through during the period when everyone else was sleeping. It had taken him a century and more of grinding effort, yes, but it remained fundamentally an impulsive, impatient act. In a way this was sort of endearing, for it was a sacrifice on the entire colony's behalf, but even so Conrad enjoyed pricking the facade and watching the real Bascal twitch underneath.

"Chlorine?" The king harrumphed. "The situation is that we have some. Its release appears to be a defense mechanism of the sessile algoids, because there's sure as hell no energy advantage in the transaction. Well, usually none. As far as we can determine, they've been churning the stuff out for eight billion years. Chloride ions become chlorine molecules, and for four billion of those years, the lithosphere absorbed them. Very interesting geology, with chlorination weathering as well as oxidation playing a role.

"But once the lithosphere was saturated, once every rock had soaked up as much chlorine as it could hold, the gas had nowhere to accumulate except in the atmosphere. It finally reached equilibrium, coincidentally just below the level which would be toxic to the algoids themselves. Since then, the levels have been propped up by numerous feedback loops, including a weak geochemical cycle that churns it all back underground, and they've been stable for a long time. I say that with a scientist's precision: a long time.

"The concentration is more than enough to kill *us*, of course—one hundred twenty parts per million at sea level. Even the native multicelled eukaryotes have a hard time with it, and have evolved a number of interesting mechanisms for coping. The lidicara especially, which actually burn the chlorine as fuel. It's an interesting mutation, this chlorine business, since as far as I can tell, Barnard's ecosystem was seeded from the same primordial sources as Sol's. There's the same encoding—protein on top of DNA on top of RNA. And the same distinction between prokaryotic cells—the primitive ones, the bacteria and archaea—and the eukaryotes, with a clearly defined nucleus and an assortment of specialized organelles, which are themselves mostly subsumed prokaryotes. A party indeed."

"Telling us what?" Conrad asked.

"Well, it tells us quite a lot, although it may not fit your definition of 'immediately useful.' It's important because this places the origin of life on Earth and Barnard some four billion years and forty thousand light-years apart—the two stars were nowhere near each other prior to the current epoch. This means that the primordial source must be older still, and its children very numerous indeed. Life is durable, my friend, drifting in great spore clouds across the sweeping arms of the galaxy, sprouting wherever it lands and then freshly seeding the spaces around it. If I were a doctor trying to fight this infection, I'd be worried, because if you and I were to sterilize this planet right now, it would be teeming with unicells again within a million years. From the sky, my boy. From the very stars."

Conrad nodded unhappily. "This is where the master plan breaks down. We're supposed to terraform—we're provisioned for it, anyway—but we *would* have to eradicate the biosphere to have any hope of a breathable atmosphere."

"And we may, Conrad. We may yet. At this point I haven't decided, but when the world is mine to command, with the corruption of absolute power chewing away at my soul and the responsibility for millions of people pressing me to action, I may sign that extermination order. The natives can be archived and their ecosystem documented in detail, so that someday we can reconstruct it in a suitable environment, and they'll have lost nothing but time. Or perhaps we will leave them dead, and spare the galaxy a long, slow war between the microbial armies of halogenia and oxytopia. Chlorine is poison to more than just ourselves, so if we have to choose sides, we should obviously choose our own, and play to win.

Barnard's spores could infect Sol, you know, or the stars of future colonies. Perhaps they already have, and that eons-long chemistry experiment has begun anew, barely measurable but slowly, steadily building. Poisoning worlds."

"You're a romantic," Conrad accused. "And a melodramatist. This is pent-up poetry, leaking out through the holes in your logic. I know you, Bas. I can see you wriggling inside that monarch skin."

But Bascal shook his head, unamused. "We'll still be around in a million years, boyo. You and I, personally. These decisions carry palpable consequence, and the morality of it all is murky at best. Either action may brand me a monster or a fool, or both."

Conrad stifled a sigh. "All right, *Tui Barnarda,* point conceded. But our concern at the moment is extremely narrow, extremely short-term. The oceans will burn our eyes and sear our membranes. That's bad. The air is poison rather than fire, but twenty minutes' exposure will kill us just as dead. And my real question is, what do we do about that? What protective measures will we need when we walk on the surface?"

"We needn't protect the skin," Bascal said. "The skin *is* a protective measure, against all manner of chemical agents. Weak acids and other corrosives are precisely what the skin is there for. That, and foreign microbes. The body's weak points are its openings: the eyes and ears, the nose and mouth, the mucous membranes. At higher concentrations, we might also worry about the nail beds, and the anus and urethra, and in fact for immersion in the oceans that might be necessary.

"But we're really just talking about air pollution, here. Chlorine is the worst of it, but there are plenty of other noxious gases in the brew, and all of them appear, to a greater or lesser degree, in the atmosphere of Earth as well. This was especially true during the Industrial Revolution, but even our squeaky-clean Queendom produced irritants—especially in the mines and refineries of the Elementals, who formed the wellsprings of the supply lines of the Queendom's fax infrastructure. And of course, the Earth's biosphere produces waste products of its own, and the planet itself—with its volcanoes and rifts and mineral springs—produces still more.

"It's a matter of degree: here, a human being in good condition—and we are all in very good condition—will accumulate fatal lung damage over the course of about ten minutes, or possibly twice that long for certain individuals. For that damage to actually result in death may take another ten or twenty minutes, or longer if the source of further damage is removed.

"And we have the fax machine, don't we? The panacea of panaceas? So in some sense, we can get by with no protective measures at all. Just stay indoors as much as possible, limit exposure to the native air, and print a fresh copy if you feel yourself starting to cough. In a more practical sense, we can design filter masks which simply reject all but the oxygen and CO_2 and nitrogen our bodies expect. These masks would be passive and would have no consumable portions—no filters to clog, no power source to maintain or replace—so they'd last a good long while, possibly centuries. And they shouldn't need to, because you can fax a fresh one every morning, with your clothing."

"Well we can't *all*," Conrad reminded him. There were only six fax machines within the confines of Bubble Hood, and one of them was in Bascal's quarters, and another in Conrad's. Rank came with privileges, you bet. And there was another in the messtaurant, and a fourth in the inventory, one in the emergency center, and one on the exterior of the hull.

Most of Bubble Hood's citizens had spent at least a little bit of time onboard *Newhope,* and had gotten used to the idea that they must bathe every day, or else smell bad. This was mostly unnecessary in the technological ubiquity of the Queendom, where travel through fax plates and collapsiter grids cleaned and scented the body several times each day, but stepping into a shower for a few minutes was not so terribly different from stepping into a fax.

Nor did the people here generally print fresh clothing every day. Instead they gathered it in batches and stored it in their rooms. The dress codes had been relaxed, and while many people continued to wear *Newhope* uniforms (either out of habit or because they liked them, or because they lacked the imagination to dress themselves any differently), many others wore the clothing which for them was still fashionable: children's styles from the Queendom of 150 years before. Some others paid attention to the Queendom news feeds and sensoria, which were only six years out of date, and dressed in those styles instead, but already this had begun to seem like a quaint and vaguely boobish thing to do. UnBarnardean. So in fact one needed a lot of clothing, and needed to pick it carefully.

Anyway, the point was that most people in Bubble Hood did not have ready access to a fax machine, not without waiting in line, and the same would eventually be true on the surface of P2. In fact, things would be much worse on the surface, because the number of fax machines coming out of storage would double or triple at best, whereas the population, finally unpacked from *Newhope*'s memory cores, would increase tenfold. One of Brenda Bohobe's top priorities was therefore to establish a print plate factory, with all the elaborate machinery and supply chains that entailed. But that would be an enterprise of years, and could not even begin until a lot of other stuff had been unpacked.

Bascal chuckled a kingly chuckle. "Point taken. Also, point irrelevant. Who's digressing now? I can have the masks designed for you in a couple of hours. Probably sooner, actually."

"And how do we know that's sufficient? How will we know they work? That they don't pinch, or leak, or whatever?"

"Oh ye of little faith! We'll have to test them, obviously, and while we could rig a special chamber here on Bubble Hood, we do eventually have to visit the surface. Go make a backup copy of yourself, boyo. I'm issuing my first royal proclamation: that you and I, Ho Ng and Steve Grush, will visit the planet next shift. Have your people prep a reentry vehicle. In fact, have them prep two, and print an extra copy of yourself to bring along. There may be unforeseen hazards, and a bit of redundancy never hurts."

Conrad processed these words with mingled disappointment and relief. Suddenly, he was not in charge anymore. Bascal was resuming the mantle of leadership, establishing the early facets of civilian government, under which the military chain of command would fit. Fortunately, while Conrad had gotten used to his leadership role, he hadn't sought it, nor ever particularly relished it. His rebellious youth was still pretty fresh; if he stopped to calculate, he was probably thirty chronological years old, maybe even younger than that. Running a planet, or at least an orbiting colony above one, was an interesting experience, and educational, and most of his duties related to that would presumably continue for the foreseeable future. He would simply be answering to his king rather than himself or, via long-distance transmission, to Xmary. And that was a good thing, right?

He forced a smile, and then felt a genuine smile creep up underneath it, propping it up. "As you wish, Your Highness. Visiting the planet, wow. This is one of those historic events, isn't it?"

"Conrad, I wouldn't dream of doing it without you."

Conrad's Bubble Hood quarters were considerably roomier, and more nicely appointed, than his quarters onboard *Newhope*. Here he had a bilevel apartment, with not only an exterior view through the hull, looking down on the beiges and browns and disconcerting blues of the planet, but also one looking out over the interior of the bubble itself. Keeping an eye on things, yeah, but more importantly he simply enjoyed the view. When he was finally permitted to quit his position as *Newhope*'s first mate in absentia, and as a commander in what would become Barnard's navy, he would probably miss these privileges of rank. But he would hang onto this apartment!

His long-term plans, ever clearer in his mind, were painfully straightforward: he would be the Chief Architect of the Kingdom of Barnard. He probably didn't even need to make that a request, and if he did, it was difficult to imagine that Bascal would refuse him. And maybe that, in the long run, was a better rank, with a whole kingdom of privileges to choose from. It was certainly a pleasant, daydreamy sort of thought.

But when he entered his apartment, stepping through as

the door recognized him and curled open, he found the ceiling flashing red—the signal he'd told the apartment to use when messages were waiting which required immediate attention, but which were not actual life-or-death matters worth interrupting him at work or tracking him down in a corridor somewhere. This drove all other thoughts from his mind.

"Play message," he said.

He was expecting something from Bascal, some addendum or correction, but instead a hologram of Xmary appeared, hanging down from the ceiling in a column of not-quite-invisible light. He stepped toward it, and it retreated an equal distance, for if it didn't, its illusion of three-dimensionality would break down in a confusion of distortions. Still, it looked uncomfortably like Xmary was backing away from him in fear. And he didn't like that, so he stood his ground, and Xmary stood hers.

"Yes?" he asked the recording.

"Hello, Conrad," the recording said. "You look well."

"I feel well," he answered. "We're about to visit the planet, Bascal and I. Visit the surface, I mean. It's very exciting. It's the culmination of a lot of waiting and effort, obviously, and I feel sorry for the four thousand people who don't get to go. But it'll be just like old times. Me and Bascal, Ho and Steve. Raising a little hell."

The recording's smile had a strained quality. "That sounds nice. Conrad, I know I should tell you this in person. I know it's awful to send a recording, and I apologize for that. But there just isn't opportunity. It'll be months before I see you again, and this conversation can't wait."

Conrad felt a sinking sensation in his gut. "You're breaking off with me."

The recording looked at the floor.

"This," Conrad said, "is where you say, 'No, no, nothing like that.' This is where you reassure me."

"I wish I could," the recording answered, with simulated gloom. "I wish things were different, but they aren't. I can't live like this, and if you search your heart, I doubt you're really enjoying it either. We have to be fair to ourselves."

"Especially to you," Conrad said, with sudden, sullen bitterness. Had he been anything less than supportive and loving? He hated to use the word *perfect,* but hadn't he been exactly that? What could he possibly have done to deserve this? Nothing!

"I'm so sorry."

"I *told* you you should leave a copy with me, Xmary, or I should leave one with you. These things are workable. Or is that not it? Is there someone else involved? Some new interest catching your eye?"

The recording shrugged. "I don't have that information, Conrad. I'm just a recording. Does it matter?"

"You're damn right it matters! Shit, the mating pool is pretty limited up there. Is it Money Izolo? Is it Peter? Or one of the kids, fresh from storage? Is he better for you than I am? Oh, my gods, you're breaking off with me to bunk with some *career spaceman.* How humiliating."

"He's not a career spaceman."

Conrad felt his eyebrows rise. "No? He's on the *ship.* He's not *leaving,* or you'd see the same problem with him that you claim to see with me. Anyway, I thought you didn't have that information."

The recording shrugged. "I suppose I do. I'm not self-aware in the way that you are, Conrad. I'm not here to be interrogated."

"Ah. I see. You're some measly petabyte avatar, here to insert your barbs and evaporate into the ether."

Unhappily: "Something like that. I'm truly sorry, Conrad."

"You're *sorry*? I thought you weren't self-aware. Listen, Ms. Recording, this is a very small community we live in. I'm going to hear this person's name sooner or later, and I'd rather hear it from you."

"Would you? Are you so certain of that?"

His lip curled. "Don't get smart with me. If you're not Xmary, you have . . . no right to talk to me like that. I want a name."

The recording sighed. "It's Feck."

"Feck?" Conrad gaped. "Yinebeb Fecre? Feck the Fairy? *Again?*"

Now the recording managed to look annoyed. "That's not what they call him, Conrad, and you know it."

And that was true. He was "Feck the Facilitator," hero of the August Riots and proud explorer of Xmary's pants. And he was ... not a bad fellow. Damn it.

"How can Xmary do this to me? How, exactly, can she feel this is justified?"

"I'm sorry, Conrad."

"Who does she think she is? Does she think she has the *right* to treat someone like this? She said she loved me. Was that just a lie? We've been together for, what? Fifteen subjective years? Even longer for you. For her. This is what I get? What I somehow deserve?"

"I'm sorry, Conrad."

"Shit. Shit. Are you going to say anything else?"

"Is there anything else to say? I'm sorry, but I'm really not equipped to have a discussion with you about this."

"Well, piss off, then. Tell Xmary ... Tell her ... shit. Just tell her good-bye."

After the recording had mailed itself back, Conrad said some other things which are best not repeated.

"You're late," said one of the Bascals, in the ferry hangar. "And you've been crying. Both of you. What's wrong?"

This question was at once leaderly, medical, and deeply personal, for tears occurred very rarely in the Queendom of Sol, and were regarded with utmost seriousness.

"Xmary," said the two Conrads together. They were freshly printed, and hadn't had much of a chance to diverge yet. Their potential responses were limitless, but bounded by identical experience. They wouldn't always say or do exactly the same thing, but until their thoughts got off on different tracks, the responses would be pretty close.

Bascal's features—not at all boyish despite their youthful construction—melted in sympathy. He held up two sets of arms, and embraced both Conrads warmly. "Ah, my friend, the vagaries of love and loss are the curse of the immorbid. Even in the Queendom, two hundred years ago and more, they were saying these first marriages, first relationships of any kind don't last. Ask a woman what animal she feels like and she will say 'cat,' a creature as playful and graceful and cruel as God himself! Ask a man and he'll say 'pig,' with no apology, and how long can a cat dance with a pig before somebody's paw gets hoofed?

"My parents are perhaps a reminder that true love can be found and kept, but they had—both of them!—been around the world a few times before falling in together. And they did break off for thirty years, you'll recall. Perhaps there are additional fallings-out in their future, or it may be that they're locked together by their positions as king and queen. Each was duly elected in isolation from the other, and their divorce would not—could not—change their joint monarchial status. They are as trapped by circumstances as we ourselves.

"Ah, but these are words of gloom, when you need cheer! Of empty misogyny when you need companionship! Take a cue from Plato, my boy. He said, 'Being is real. Becoming is an illusion.' This moment is nothing but a snapshot, a sort of hologram laid out beside the happier moments before and after. Let's end it and move on. Come to the planet with me, hmm? It's the start of a new relationship, a new love affair. And if she treats us as well and as badly as our women have, then we shall have an interesting time of it indeed, and revel in our successes while they last."

It was a nice thing to say, or mostly so, and Conrad should have been nice in return, but instead he scowled and said, "I'm not in the mood for pomposity, you fuffer. My parents are still together as well, but what difference does that make? What bearing does it have on me, on this day, right here? Just leave me alone, all right?"

At that moment, two copies of Bertram Wang sidled up. "I think we're ready to fly," one of them said.

At Conrad's look, Bascal explained, "Bertram here is the only person in the entire colony, in or out of the memory core, with any experience piloting actual reentry vehicles. It's such a rustic way to fly—not a skill that most of us maintain, although in retrospect the jailers probably should have taken it out of the simulator and made it a part of our physical training. The ferries should fly themselves, more or less, but it never hurts to have an experienced hand aboard."

"Of course," Conrad said. "Nice to see you, Bert."

"Hi," Bert acknowledged.

There were six ferries in the bay—half a year's output from the Martin Kurster Memorial Shipyard, consuming a costly stream of crushed asteroidal rock. Each ferry could comfortably carry twenty humans, or up to a hundred if you stacked them in bunks, which was exactly what they would do when it came time to really populate the planet. And yes, it was inconvenient. Even when there were fax machines installed on the surface, there was no easy way to land the memory core itself. For that you'd need some sort of railroad, reaching vertically through the planet's atmosphere.

Or teleportation, yeah, but it wouldn't be possible to fax live humans to the surface from Bubble Hood until there was at least one telecom collapsiter in orbit around the planet. And that would require a collapsium manufactory—rather beyond their means right now—and something like fifty or a hundred gigatons of raw material. Dozens of neubles; little spheres of di-clad neutronium, pressed from a fleet of neutronium barges. Or from one really busy barge, perhaps, over a long period of time. And the Kurster Memorial Shipyard just wasn't big enough to produce a craft that large. Like so many other things in their nascent economy, neutronium barges would have to wait.

The Conrads and Bertrams and Bascals split up, each team going to one of the prepped ferries. Ho and Steve were already aboard, laughing about something and punching the seats. In this context they were not Security per se, but simply muscle. A pair of strong backs and reasonably obedient minds, in case there was real work to be done. There were probably better choices for that particular assignment, but Conrad understood the king's impulse; Ho and Steve had been with them from the very beginning, from that first exploratory riot at Camp Friendly. And although they were jerks, they were *his* jerks, as close to him in their own way as Conrad was. And yes, close to Conrad as well, in that way that old adventures had of binding people together.

Like Conrad and Xmary, for example.

"Settle down, men," he told them crossly. "Steve, you're out of uniform."

In fact, Steve was wearing a fishnet shirt and a pair of improbably shiny black trousers, with matching boots and cap. Hardly the best ensemble for exploring the surface of a hostile planet.

"Yes, sir," Steve said with a smirk. He reached for a jacket draped over one of the seats, and it slithered up his arm and onto his body. It was a *Newhope* uniform—a Navy of Barnard uniform—done up in that same shiny material. Conrad looked it over with a stab of irritation, but decided he'd had enough friction for one day.

"All right, then. Let's buckle in, shall we?"

Bertram of course took the pilot's seat, and Conrad was ready to cede the copilot's to Bascal, but the king demurred, saying, "You're in charge of this flight, Mr. Mursk. I merely own the planet."

And for some reason, that ground on Conrad's nerves as well. He nearly said something nasty, just because he could, and bit it back only with considerable effort. He tried to force himself to be cheerful. This was a day he'd remember all his life, even if he lived to be a million, and why remember being a shit when he could simply remember being unhappy?

He thumbed a warning toggle on the wellstone control panel, and moments later red lights were flashing all over the hangar bay, and nameless workers—mostly people Conrad had never met—were scurrying for the airlocks and the safety of the two control booths.

"Bay Boss," Bertram said into the panel, "we are go for departure. Diagnostics nominal. You may open the doors when ready."

"Bay Boss here," said an unfamiliar female voice. "Go for departure, acknowledged. Depressurizing in five, four, three, two, one...now." Outside the winged ferry, there was a sound like a sigh, trailing to whispers, and then total silence. The pumps were some serious quantum-scale hardware which paid the entropy cost and yanked out every molecule which touched them. In about a second and a half, the bay's interior pressure dropped to hard zero: five balls after the decimal.

When the pressure was off them, the ferry bay doors did not so much open as curl aside, like theater curtains, and Bertram had to negotiate with his other self to determine who would go first, so they didn't both crowd each other on the way out. The ferries themselves were smart enough to avoid any true accident, but it would be bad form to rely on them for it, and the Bertram in this particular shuttle won the bit toss anyway, and so they went, lighting their engines and shooting out into starry blackness.

The brownish light of P2 flooded in through the windows, both virtual and real, and then the world itself hove into view, a swirling sphere of yellow-white clouds, of isolated blue-green oceans and vast, amber-colored continents.

P2's plant life, such as it was, relied on something darker than chlorophyll, something chestnut-brown which drew its energy mainly from infrared light. Conrad would miss Earth's greenery in the open spaces, but the multicelled algoids were not without their own special charm. All across the planet, in dense patches between the deserts, the probes had shown chest-high forests of the stuff, waving in the breeze like translucent blades of wheat.

And Conrad, realizing he was about to see this sight with his own two eyes, felt his heart leap. To hell with Xmary. If she thought she could do better than him . . . Well, she wasn't stupid. Maybe she could. But he was here, and she was not, and this really was an important moment in both their lives.

"Living large is the best revenge," Bascal murmured behind him, as if eavesdropping on his thoughts.

Conrad looked over his shoulder and said, "Sire, that is possibly the most intelligent thing you've said all day."

The way that Conrad got horribly killed was sort of funny in retrospect.

They had set the ferries down beside a shallow but steep-banked stream, almost a waterfall really, cutting down along the equally steep bank of the seashore. The ferries were at the crest of it, on flat ground, but the sand dropped away sharply to the east, along a contour that was neither "beach" nor "cliff," but something in-between which the site survey had named a "subcritical intertidal embankment" or "depositional foreshore bluff." Such features were, apparently, typical of the shorelines where they weren't vertical cliffs of granite bedrock.

The planet's two oceans were completely isolated from each other, and this was the larger of the two. Overall it was slightly wider than Earth's Pacific Ocean, though it covered a much smaller fraction of the planet's oversized surface, so Bascal had insisted it was properly a sea, and had named it the Sea of Destiny.

The men were all outside milling around on the sand, beneath a sun that looked remarkably like Earth's own—no larger or smaller or dimmer, and only very slightly redder. And the filter masks were working just fine; Bascal had even engineered the surface properties so they didn't fog up on the inside. But there was room for improvement, because breathing in the masks was kind of like sucking chowder through a straw. You could do it, no problem, but the comfort factor wasn't quite there. The air that did get through felt thick but somehow unsatisfying. Not enough oxygen.

Anyway, Bascal was beside himself with glee—literally—and the two of him were pointing and gesturing wildly. "The city's Main Street will run right here, east-west, from the shore to the first ridgeline of the mountains, and perhaps beyond. Forty meters wide, and lined with domes on either side."

The other nodded. "Yeah, great! Put the palace right here on the beach, like proper Tongans. Matatahi Falehau, the Beach Palace. But *tall*, yes? Looming over the city, as a proper palace should."

"Really? I thought perhaps over there, so the ridgeline doesn't hide the sunset. Not tall, but hugging the rocks like it's been there a million years. So perhaps the city should be farther south, over there a ways."

"Hmm. Interesting. Lemme think about that a minute.

Our *own planet,* Your Most Regal Majesty! You *know* how excited I am."

"Indeed I do!"

The two Conrads had diverged by this time, no longer quite identical, and while one of them hovered by the Bascals, absorbing their plans and injecting the occasional comment, the other one was down below at the waterline, hunched over, studying the river stones lining the mouth of the stream. They were mainly granite, as near as he could figure, but they had a funny sort of sheen that was new to him. Chlorination weathering, maybe. If these stones came from the mountains above—and they must have—then some of the bedrock up there, properly quarried and polished, would make for interesting facades. The really raw thing was the way the different layers of it striped the ridge's face in such wildly different colors. Not just browns and yellows and reds, but actually some greens and even blues as well. Or so his eyes had told him up there, through the yellow haze of fifteen kilometers of atmosphere.

Looking down again, he noticed movement in the stream's clear water, between the stones.

"Oh," he said. "Oh, my. Will you look at this."

No one was paying attention to him at that moment, and he was too rapt to notice or care. He leaned closer, watching the wriggling forms. The "animals" of Planet Two were, he'd been told, extremely primitive. Denizens of the water—never the air or land—they possessed only five cell types, loosely grouped into three layers: skin, gut, and muscle. There was no nervous system, no immune system, and no real digestive system other than a simple holding chamber—the gut. Nutrients and wastes simply sloshed through the spaces between the cells, and the creatures' metabolisms—stunted by chlorine and starved by low oxygen levels—supported movement which was very sluggish indeed by Earth standards. Most were tiny—pinhead-sized or smaller—and drifted along with the ocean currents, feeding on bacterial mats and occasionally on each other, though never on the chlorine-spewing algoids, large or small.

One creature, though—the lidicara—was different. Conrad couldn't help but know this, because it was nearly all the biologists could talk about. How fascinating! How surprising and raw! Most days it was hard to get their minds on anything else. But seeing it now, seeing a hundred of them swirling around his boots like animate snowflakes, he understood what all the fuss was about. Here was a thing that moved with purpose, with ambition. An actual alien creature! The other animals were radial forms—tiny urchin/starfish with little to distinguish them—but the pale lidicara jetted around fast enough to need some streamlining, some architectural finesse. The thing even had a cluster of sensory cells or something at its front end. "*Cephalization!*" the biologists screamed when the subject came up. "*The thing is growing a head!*" Slowly, of course—the fossils of seventy million years ago looked much like the creatures here at his feet—but even to Conrad it sounded like an important development.

The lidicara's shape was like nothing ever seen on Earth, and at a glance, on his hands and knees with his masked face hovering right above the water, Conrad could see how it had come about. The creature had started out as just another seven-armed starfish, but somewhere along the way its "front" arms had shortened and thinned, becoming feeding appendages or something, while the other limbs had slid toward the back, fitting together into a kind of teardrop shape, with one elongated limb at the back serving as a kind of tail.

Right there and then, Conrad discovered an interest in biology which he had never once suspected. Wow. There were only a few hundred cells in these animals, right? As opposed to the trillions in his own body? And he found himself wondering what happened inside, down in the DNA, to permit—to create?—such changes as these. And it occurred to him, with a prickle of excitement, that he—that this particular Conrad Mursk—could abandon all other responsibility and simply pursue this question, reintegrating with the "real" Conrad, the navy's Conrad, at some future date.

Hell, with the mass restrictions lifted—with a whole planet of buffer mass at his disposal—he could spin off as many copies as he wanted. Even the Queendom's plurality restrictions—twenty-five hundred copy-hours per person per month under normal circumstances—needn't apply here, not unless Bascal wrote a proclamation about it or unless the Senate, when it was elected and holding regular meetings, decided to pass a law.

"Conrad!" he called to his other self, thirty meters up on the sandy bank. "The lidicara are beautiful! We've got to preserve them, share the world with them. . . ." His voice trailed away when he realized the other Conrad wasn't listening. To himself he said, "Got to share the world."

He studied the dancing forms, admiring the way they not only tolerated the poison in the air, but actually souped themselves up with it. Would a bit more oxygen in the atmosphere hurt them? Would it supercharge them even more? If life here really was related to life on Earth—and Bascal insisted that it was—then maybe the lidicara's chlorine-breathing structures—halochondria, they were called—could be imported into Earthly cells? He pulled out his ever-present sketchplate and said to it, "To do: investigate fax modifications to adapt humans to chlorine atmosphere. Discuss with Brenda: Can we change ourselves instead of the planet? Or in addition?"

The ocean waves here were tiny—at least for the moment—and he felt them lapping pleasantly at his heels, slowly working their way up the stream as the tide came in. "Be aware of it," the site surveyor had warned them over the radio link. "The tide will be in the middle of its range, rising steadily at ten centimeters per hour." Was that a lot? It didn't seem so here and now. As his shoes grew damper and saltier Conrad simply moved uphill a step, and then another, following the channels of the stream's mouth, crawling up along the foreshore's steep bank.

P2 had no moon; its tides were exclusively solar, and since it was so damned close to Barnard they were formidable indeed. Thanks to the planet's 3:2 tidal lock—three revolutions for every two orbits—they were also slow, following the 461-hour cycle of the "day" and to some extent the 691-hour cycle of the "year." But though they were sluggish, the tides were far more powerful than those of Earth. A hundred times more powerful, in fact, though their effect on the actual water level was not quite so dramatic as that. For one thing, the land was higher near the equator, so the seas were up in the temperate zones—one in the northern hemisphere and one in the south—where Barnard's pull wasn't quite as strong.

And the fact that the seas themselves did not reach all the way around the planet limited how far and how well a tidal bulge could travel. Or so Conrad had heard, second- and third-hand. The survey had pegged the tidal range for this location at plus or minus thirty-one meters, with little variation over time.

Had a planet like Earth been at this position, with its thin skin of rock floating atop a sea of metal-rich magma, the *land* tides would have been plus or minus several meters, and daily catastrophic earthquakes would be the norm. Along with volcanoes, yes, bursting out through sudden rifts in the crust. Fortunately P2 was a stiffer world, with a much smaller and cooler liquid interior. But even so it had a few large, semiactive volcanoes.

"Which is good," Bascal had insisted when the subject came up, "because this metal-poor world cannot prick itself and bleed. The radioactive heating of its interior is insufficient to drive tectonics or volcanism. Without the tides stretching and pulling at the core, raising blisters on the crust, there would be no renewal of the surface. It would smooth itself into a giant billiard ball, and the metals would all find their way to the bottom of the ocean and eventually be buried by sediment, and the biosphere would die."

Hmm.

These were Conrad's last coherent thoughts, for as he scrabbled up the hillside, the ditches of the stream's delta grew deeper, their banks sandier and rockier and steeper. In studying the lidicara, he had thrust his hands into the stream's warm water, and failed at first to notice that its acidity was turning his fingernails yellow and burning at the edges of the flesh beneath. Only when he tore a fingernail right off on the river rocks did he finally pull his hands out. Seeing the damage then, he stood up in alarm.

Next, as near as Ho's investigation could figure it, he lost his balance and dug an arm into the stream's bank. There were no roots or grasses there to hold the bank in place, so it crumbled, and one or more large stones came down on his face, knocking the mask free and breaking his nose. Even this might not have been fatal if he hadn't taken a breath of native air, then coughed because of it, then coughed even harder from his own blood running down into his throat. Still not fatal, if he hadn't spasmed, falling face-first into the stream, and then gasped at the agony of its burning in the membranes around his eyes. But he did each of these things in turn, and so inhaled a small quantity of the water, which was not at all kind to the tissue of his lungs.

On the first sight of him lurching up the foreshore, Ho and Steve—ostensibly there to keep him safe—burst into laughter. They may be forgiven for this, since the state of Conrad's injuries was not apparent at the time, and the drunken stagger of his walk, combined with the mud on his face, really did present a comical image. Conrad himself said, "Boyo, it's a lucky thing *she's* not here to see you."

Regrettably, the injured Conrad collapsed and died with these words in his ears. The surviving Conrad never did find out what he was doing in that stream, since there was no fax here to resuscitate him while his brain still lived, and since Bubble Hood and even *Newhope* lacked the facilities to read his dead memories. This sort of thing had happened to Conrad once before, back in Ireland a long, long time ago, and it did not occur to him now to interpret the event as any sort of omen. If it had, things might have gone very differently.

Instead, he was left only with an enigmatic to-do entry, which itself proved pivotal in the colony's history—indeed of colonial history in general. And while the idea—pantropy, the re-forming of themselves to suit this new world—would certainly have come up sooner or later, Conrad would wonder until the end of his days why *he* had been the one to raise it. There was a Tongan word for this feeling: *kuiloto mamahi*. Literally, "blind sorrow," the mourning which occurred when one did not know precisely what had been lost. And this, too, would prove important, though the extent of it would not be apparent for hundreds of years.

Life is like that sometimes, all the more so when it lasts forever.

#### chapter ten

the red badge of security

Two years later, the occasion of the Security training finals found Conrad and Bascal in the bleachers at Victory Stadium, in the burgeoning town of Domesville, surrounded by fellow colonists in an atmosphere of gaiety, complete with hurled confetti and the joyous tinkling of glass shattered on slabs of landscape-friendly wellrock.

"I still say you should have a private skybox," Conrad opined, for the stadium was brand new—this was its inaugural show—and he'd designed it with such improvements in mind. "It would only take a few days to install."

Right now the stadium held two thousand people—nearly half the population of P2—but it could easily hold three times that many, and could be expanded upward—someday *would* be expanded upward—to accommodate up to thirty thousand.

This was Conrad's eighth original building—small gods be praised, he really was an architect, no longer tweaking the designs of Queendom engineers!—and like the others this one had been designed with one foot firmly in the future. The colony would grow and change, yes, and he'd be damned if that obvious truth would come back to bite him on the ass later.

In his first months on the planet's surface, Conrad had waited around for some sense of normalcy to assert itself. Then, when the first year had passed, he thought perhaps things would settle down in the second. But so far the level of chaos remained on a steady increase: more buildings, more change, and above all, more people. The resources of Bubble Hood limited the number of kids they could pull out of fax storage in any given month, but the more that were out, the louder the hue and cry became to release those few who remained. The sleepers had missed quite enough of humanity's greatest adventure, thank you very much.

Still, even the most pessimistic projections showed the memory cores emptying out within another five months, or eight Barnardean days if you wanted to count it that way. A less experienced Conrad might've been tempted to pick that moment—finally—as the true start of Barnard's history, but increasingly he had the sense that history never really started, or was always starting. There was enough work to keep everyone busy for decades, or maybe forever, and truly decisive moments, with whole futures hanging in the balance, had always been rare. And that was a good thing, right?

The years of the colony were Earth years, by the way. P2's seasons, its cycles of day and night, were just too strange and inconvenient to warrant a calendar of their own. If not for the "Barnardean hour," ever so slightly shorter than a standard one, even the day itself would be an adversary: 461 hours long—a prime number, indivisible by anything useful. As it was, the day stood at 460 hours, and the official clock had 20 hours on it, breaking the day into 23 "pids," each consisting of two 10-hour "shifts."

So a "shift" was kind of like an Earth day or night, except that the sun barely moved during its span, while the 20-hour "pid" was second cousin to an Earthly solar day. Except, again, that the sun barely moved. It was kind of like living at Earth's poles, where summer was eternal day and winter was eternal night, except that the winters here weren't appreciably cooler than the summers, and anyway the Barnardean day was closer to an Earthly *month* in duration.

What a mess. In Conrad's opinion, these shifts were about

four damned hours too long, and the pids four hours too short. But the planet's peculiar orbit could not be argued with, and despite widespread grousing no one had come forward with a better clock. He wondered if he'd ever get used to sleeping in the daylight, and he hated working in the dark even more. His job sites were lit up like crime scenes! But all that seemed to do was blot out the stars, making the sky seem that much blacker.

Once the clock was in place, mandated and prototyped and programmed into the walls of every office and residence, Bascal had studied the calendar possibilities for 20 pids before throwing them out in disgust and mandating the Queendom's own Greenwich Mean Proper Date—uncorrected for light lag—as the standard Barnardean calendar. "We needn't rebel against *that*," he'd said at the time. "P2's 'year' is of no use to us." And indeed, Conrad figured the people of Barnard were confused enough. Better to hang onto a few precious shreds of the culture and planet that had spawned them. At least you would know when your birthday was.

"Skybox? What nonsense," Bascal replied for at least the third time that month. "Do I deserve a better view than my countrymen? Your efforts are appreciated, my boy, but I'm quite pleased to watch the action from here."

"Climate controlled," Conrad said, by way of temptation. But it was a silly offer, a joke; Domesville was right on the coast, and so far as their two years' stay had yet revealed, the climate didn't seem to fluctuate all that much. It rained, but mostly at night, and while Barnard made a warm, bright, shockingly ordinary sun to fill their daytime sky, you had to work pretty hard to get a sunburn from it. There just wasn't enough UV. In fact, if not for the impoverished soil, the poisons in the air and water, and the absurdities of clock and calendar, this place would be damned close to paradise.

So they laughed together at that, until Conrad broke into a most embarrassing fit of coughing. Embarrassing, because like a lot of people he still wasn't really used to breathing human-lethal concentrations of chlorine and carbon dioxide. His cells, filled by the fax with halochondria and carbon reducers and half a dozen other new organelles, could process the air without difficulty, but it just didn't *feel* right. It smelled funny (truthfully it smelled like semen), and it tickled slightly in the lungs. The *talematangi* or halogen cough occurred in a minority of the population—less than twenty percent, these days maybe even less than ten—but its sufferers were the butt of more than their share of jokes.

"We're still thinking about the air composition," Bascal said, as if apologizing for the planet. "More oxygen would be nice, for one thing. This period is just one more stage in a long, slow unpacking. If a world has been birthed, alas, for the moment it remains an infant, suckling from the plans laid down for it by Mother Sol. But someday, my boy, we'll control the very air. We'll have print plates larger than this stadium, ringing all around the city and continually adjusting the gas balance."

"Not on my account, I hope," Conrad said, clearing his dry throat. "I'll adjust. We all will."

"No doubt," Bascal agreed. But he flagged a passing vendor—some freshly thawed Earth kid Conrad had never seen before—and ordered a chilled red tea "for my flimsy friend, here."

"Immediately, Sire," the vendor replied with bright humor, jamming his fingers through the print plate of his vendory and hauling out a glass cup. "We mustn't have our VIPs fainting on opening day."

"Indeed not."

And here was another bit of ribbing: the men and women who put Domesville together naturally felt a bit superior to those who merely inhabited it. The newly awakened, moving into their assigned apartments and neighborhoods and jobs on the planet's surface, naturally resented this—such condescension had after all been a major driver of the Revolt. But they found it uncouth to say so. And in turn, the builders of Domesville denied any sense of envy toward the arrogant bastards who'd puffed the first air into Bubble Hood. As for *Newhope*'s transit crew, well, who didn't resent them? Too old, for one thing, and too closely associated with the power structures they were supposed to be fleeing.

The term "VIP"—Verily, Important Personage—smacked

enough of Queendom pomp and foofery that it could not properly be given as a compliment. Nor received as one.

Making faces at this punk who had seen so little and knew so much, Conrad raised a warning backhand that was only half in jest. "You want to work in the Lutui Belt, kid? If chlorine doesn't make you cough, try vacuum."

But he accepted the tea just the same. It *was* good—a blend of sugars and electrolytes, vitamins and flavinoids, with a hint of glycerine to improve fluid absorption, plus assorted stimulants and euphoriants and anti-inflammatories to improve the outlook of the person drinking it. "Good fer what ails ye," as the slogan said, and indeed it was just the thing to soothe away the *talematangi*. Here was Barnard's first true culinary innovation—nothing at all like the astringent red teas of the Queendom—and Conrad saw no shame in enjoying it on its own terms.

Even the container had a colonial flair: a narrow cone of glass with the pointy end flattened to form a stand. Glass because the scarcity of metals here, coupled with energy costs rather higher than they'd enjoyed in the Queendom, made gold or wellstone a bit too pricey for disposable cups. Technically, of course, the cups were recyclable, and would simply be hurled back into the fax when the show was over and the robotic cleanup crew swept the stadium's litter all the way down to the molecular level. But already there were sounds of breakage all around; these glasses were fun to smash.

Such practices would be unthinkable in the Queendom, but that was the point of striking off on your own, right? New ideas, new traditions, new solutions shaped and limited by a fresh environment.

"Better?" the king asked him, supplementing the question with an elbow to Conrad's ribs.

"Much," Conrad agreed, with answering jabs of his own. "*Thank* you for the *drink,* Your *High*ness." In Sol, a harmless action like this would have drawn the ire of the unshakable Palace Guard robots, earning Conrad a painful tazzing at the very least. But here they simply earned him the wrath of the king himself, who grabbed Conrad's left arm and made as if to twist it.

"Be a loyal subject," the king warned, "or you may go home a fractured one."

"Ow," Conrad said. "All right, quit it." And then, when Bascal had released him: "Miserable tyrant. So how's this wildlife program going? I heard you were almost ready to release some animals."

Here the king grew more serious. "If by 'animals' you mean 'millimeter-sized burrowing insects,' then yes. We need them to condition the soil for the next wave of plant life. The modified lichens are taking off nicely, spreading out across the landscape in the spaces between the algoids. Now we're introducing more complicated root systems. But there's a lot of debate on this point, and I'm reluctant to impose a solution by fiat."

"Debate on what?"

"What to use to fill that niche," Bascal said. From his tone, the question both amused and annoyed him. "Our libraries are full of Earth organisms, dozens of which could do the job handily once halochondria are introduced into their cell structure, but I've got people arguing that that wouldn't be fair to the lidicara. The native peoples, you see? All squidgy and helpless and stupid. Even if we leave the Sea of Repose completely alone—just isolate it from a terraformed Sea of Destiny and all the waterways we care about—the changes around it will still have an effect. If we introduce a lot of Earth life, and fuff around with the atmosphere in addition, we could extinct the little bastards in their own ecosystem."

"So, then. What'll you do? Engineer some lidicara ambassadors?"

Conrad hadn't meant the question seriously, but Bascal answered it that way. "Something like that, yes. A modified form, specialized for burrowing and toughened up for a life outside the water. We're still wrangling over the details. Obviously we've got to release *some* Earth life if we want to support human beings on this ball, but first we may broaden the native ecosystem. Give it some of the resilience it might've developed with another hundred megayears of evolution."

"Compressed into what, a single year of engineering?"

"Oh, no, Conrad. Much longer than that. We mustn't fall

prey to any false sense of urgency; there's plenty of time to do it all slowly and well. Do it right. There's no death, no deadline, no pressure. Anyway my father would tell you that time itself is an illusion. There is no forward or backward, just an infinity of moments, like paintings in a gallery. And most of the paintings are nonsense! Strange as it seems, we simply pick the ones we like, and string them together into a story."

"You said as much in the 'Song of Physics,'" Conrad mused.

But the face Bascal made was sour and puckery. "Oh, hell. Let's not bring art into it, all right?"

"You're the one who mentioned painting, Sire. Is that no longer considered a form of art?"

That didn't quiet the king one bit. "It's not that I'm blocked, if that's what you're thinking. Truly, it isn't. My moments are simply filled, or else jealously protected in their empty state. There's no reason to insist on fresh poetry *right now*. The illusion of relentless movement through time is an aspect of consciousness. It *is* consciousness. The one to pity is the mortal human off thataway, in our past, ever plummeting toward his extinction and yet expected, somehow, to be cheerful! I, sir, have no such extinction in my plans, and can afford to take a few decades out to—oh, I dunno—build a civilization? Remake this world as God might have done it, and then invade it afresh with our own troops?"

"So we're ethical conquerors, then," Conrad said. "You tamper with nature in nature's own image, while I build the human world—from native rock as much as wellstone—to look as though it's always been here."

"You personally?" Bascal asked, now sounding a bit offended for some reason. "Everyone else is just a consumer, eh? A population with no purpose but to be housed by you, brick by brick with your own two hands? Conrad Mursk, First Architect of Barnard. Never mind all these robots, these work-study programs for the newly awakened, these fax copies we all have running around, busy every moment of the day. I would never have given you that title, boyo, if I'd known it would go to your head like this. Second Architect! Third Architect! Paver's Boy, for crying out loud. If I had it to do over again . . . But no, then you'd feel a need to prove yourself, to be worthy of more. Sometimes I think you were born to grind me."

"Whether it please Your Majesty or not," Conrad replied, "I was born to build. I've got mortar in my veins."

"And rocks in your head, yes. Bricks in your feet. Maybe a support beam up your ass."

Suddenly they were laughing again, and Conrad would have carried the joke farther, reflecting it back on his monarch, if the showtime trumpets had not chosen that moment to begin blaring.

"Who's up first?" he asked instead.

"Steve Grush and Luca Elmer Rodhaim," the king answered in a stage whisper as the crowds slowly quieted around them. "Odds are seven to five in Steve's favor, with a spread of three and an overage of .6. He's switched from dual tazzers to a net and spear, though, which may bring his favor down a point."

From the wellwood stadium floor below, the sound of trumpets gave way to flat warning klaxons, and the "go" lights flickered from green to amber. The crowd went silent. Then the lights went red, and the welliron sally gates curled aside, and two nearly nude men sauntered onto the killing floor from opposite sides of the stadium. The crowd broke into a roar; this was going to be good.

On the left, coming in from the east gate, was Steve Grush, bearing the promised net of impervium fibers, and a wellwood spear with a wicked—probably atomically sharp—point. On the west was Luca Rodhaim, with the two-handed Ringing Sword that was fast becoming his trademark. In an ordinary bout that vibrating blade could be counted on to bi- or trisect the nearest opposing Security rep within twenty seconds of gates-up, but Steve was an unforgiving fighter, and a monstrously quick one, second only to Ho Ng in the rankings.

"I'll bet you five million dollars," Bascal said as the two combatants closed and circled.

"On what?"

"On mayhem."

Conrad was supposed to bet *against mayhem*? In the finals? "No deal," he said. But then Steve threw his net, spiral-ing out on its weights like a miniature galaxy, and although it was impervium, the Ringing Sword slashed right through it, flinging it to the ground in two uneven pieces.

"Shit, wait," Conrad backpedaled. "I'll take it! Clean kill."

The move had been a feint; Steve was counting on that re-action, and followed up with his spear before Luca could bring the sword down and through and back up again. The thing was light, but not *that* light. And so the tip of Steve's spear lanced forward in a left-handed thrust that caught Luca just under the chin. And that was that.

Except that Luca didn't fall down. The spear wasn't even lodged in his throat; it had skated off to the side instead, tear-ing a red gash along his neck but apparently missing every-thing vital along the way.

"What the—"

And now Luca was bringing the sword around and over, and Steve was off balance and a lot farther forward than he ought to be, and the sword came down right on him.

Well, not precisely on him; he managed to jerk to one side at the end of the stroke, so that instead of cleaving his head in two it merely severed his right arm at the shoulder. The sound of the flesh parting wasn't audible over the gasping of the crowd, but Steve's scream of pain and rage certainly was.

And still the fight was not over! Staggering back in a spray of blood, Steve somehow managed to dodge a second blow, and then block a third one, though it cost him the front third of his spear. And then, amazingly, he contrived to clock Luca on the side of the head with the broken shaft, and then jab him in the stomach, and then whack him even harder across the side of the skull!

Now Luca was staggering back, bleeding from the nose, and Steve was falling back as well. But Steve had regained his equilibrium, and circled carefully in his retreat, putting the bright, mango-colored sun in Luca's eyes while he ... while he ...

Dropped the broken spear. And fished his severed arm up off the bloodstained killing floor. And hefted it like a club in his left hand, with the shoulder end forward. And charged forth to beat Luca across the head with it! Once, twice, thrice, dodging strokes of the Ringing Sword all the while!

The crowd went wild as Luca Elmer Rodhaim scrambled backward, tripped, dropped his sword clanging and ringing against the wellwood floor, and suffered an uppercut like an overpowered golf swing from Steve's severed arm. His head fell back against the wellwood of the killing floor.

And even then it was only over in the sense that Luca was out of the running. He wasn't going to win this. Actually beating him to death took Steve another full minute, and an ugly spectacle it was, particularly since Steve himself was bleeding out all the while, and afterward barely had the strength to raise his remaining arm in victory before he, too, collapsed and died.

"That's why he's still Luca's boss!" Bascal murmured admiringly as the gleaming medic robots danced out onto the field.

But here was an interesting point: could they really call it Security *training* if neither combatant survived to learn a lesson from it? If the medics were quick, he supposed, they might salvage some sensory impressions and short-term memory from the corpses. Maybe. But anyway, what was the story with that spear to the throat? Luca should have died right then!

"It wasn't a fair fight," Conrad protested.

"Fairer than it would have been," Bascal said quietly. "Luca had some armor plates under his skin. Why not, with fax machines at his disposal and stodgy Queendom proprieties suspended? And yes, I knew about it, and don't worry, I won't collect on our bet. I just wanted you to feel involved in the action. This is a nice stadium, by the way. Well designed, good acoustics. Much classier than crowding around like schoolboys while Security brawls in the streets. My cap is off to you, sir."

"Thanks," Conrad said, taking the compliment at face value. But pride was not among the emotions he felt just now. It did make a kind of sense for Security to stay sharp through dueling, and with a fax to print fresh copies of the dead and wounded, there was no particular reason for them to pull their punches. They weren't beating on innocents, here, and Conrad wasn't about to tell consenting adults what to do or not do with their own bodies. And yes, shamefully, it *was* exciting to watch these hard men and women fight for their lives.

But he could see right away that there'd be an arms race, with Security personnel beefing up their bodies in more and more elaborate ways. This wasn't about public safety at all. Had he really thought so? It wasn't even about scaring the public into a law-abiding stupor, although from Bascal's point of view that might be a nice side effect. Really, mainly, it was about violence for its own sake—a dark, repressed bit of human psyche dragged out into daylight celebration.

"You look aggrieved," Bascal said to him, with a touch of genuine concern.

"Yeah," Conrad said. But with effort he shrugged off these bleak feelings and said, "It isn't necessary for me to approve of everything people do in this colony."

Bascal smiled and put a warm hand on Conrad's shoulder. "Indeed not, boyo, for such is the nature of freedom. If we were all restricted to your personal sense of propriety, then *you* would be king, and a tyrant, and the people would weep to have come so far for so little. The city already has its first filthy beggar, did you know that? It's Louis McGee, and I wish him well of it, for apparently that's the thing that makes him happy."

Conrad snorted. That was a delicate face to paint on such an indelicate matter; there were still sporadic freakups whose perpetrators had to be cycled back into fax storage again until such time as the colony had resources to deal with them. But would such a time ever truly arrive? The neural balance filters were voluntary, as indeed they had to be; put that power in the hands of government, and where might it end? There were crazies back home, too—sad-eyed addicts and vagrants unable or unwilling to ask for help. They were the curse of any free society.

"Anyway," Bascal continued, "a beggar does round the place out a bit—make more of a world of it. We have thousands of others to pick up the slack, and if things get too busy we can all double up. Print an extra copy: one to work and one to enjoy our hard-won freedom."

"Meaningful work is its own reward," Conrad countered, irritated at the thought of Louis getting a free ride. "After a lifetime without it, we should all be clamoring. Who needs extra copies?"

The king laughed. "Ah! Hoy! And we also have *you*, my friend, reaching for greatness in your own personal way; and this world, this star system, is the screen upon which your epic will be writ. You don't have to make me proud—you don't *have* to do anything—but I hope you'll find your potential, and live up to it."

And here Conrad drew himself up and said, "On that, Your Majesty, you can bet the planet."

Which is, in some sense, exactly what happened.

book two

the colonium

on settling down

Even without improvisation for its own sake, there was lots of hard work to be done, and nearly everyone was busy nearly all the time. They could print extra copies of themselves to rest and relax, and then integrate that experience just to say they'd had it, but Conrad, like many colonists, elected not to. Hard work *was* refreshing. Their bodies were young and physically fit; they demanded the bliss of meaningful action. Conrad thought, perhaps, that he had never truly slept before in his life. But in those early years, in the building of a world, he felt both more awake and better rested than he'd ever known he could.

And as this was happening, the second of the great colony ships arrived at its destination: Alpha Centauri, aka Rigel Kent, aka the Republic of Kent. An actual republic, with no monarch at all! And Conrad had thought *he* was rebellious.

Next came the Kingdom of Wolf, which had requested a copy of Bascal at departure time, to be its own king as well as Barnard's. The other Bascal, though, was printed from a pattern that had languished in storage since *Newhope*'s departure. He'd awakened off balance, a century and a half out of his proper time, and had then meekly followed his ship's storage program rather than spending the transit time in solitary study.

Not that he'd've had a century to fatten his brain anyway, since the QMS *Glover Gailey* was twice as fast as *Newhope*, with better braking protocols besides. By the time he got to Wolf, the noveau-Bascal had found the good grace to recognize himself for what he was: a divergent archive, now wildly different from the legally recognized individual. Therefore, he changed his name from Bascal Edward de Towaji Lutui to Edward Bascal Faxborn, and named the original—the King of Barnard—his cousin rather than some alternate aspect of himself.

The following year, the Queendom of Lalande was established. They had requested a copy of Tamra Lutui as their queen, but were refused on the grounds that she did not wish to leave her native Sol, nor her husband (who had not been elected Lalande's king), nor to have more than one Queendom to spread her love between, nor to deny the young colonists the chance to find their own way into the future. Instead, the Lalandans resorted to one Bethany Nichols, who by the cherubic age of thirty was both a successful playwright and a prize-winning athlete, as well as a darling of the telereception circuit.

Conrad realized with some shock that this young queen had been born in Sol system well after his own departure from it. She was, in some sense, from his future, or from some sort of parallel universe. And this was a telling point: society was far larger than just the place he had left and the place he had come to. Society was not—what a shock!—about Conrad Mursk at all.

In the decades that followed came the Queendoms of Sirius, Luyten, Ross, and Eridani. None of these star systems were especially suitable for colonization, but they were the ones that God had made available in Sol's immediate neighborhood. Wolf and Lalande at least had life-bearing planets, though decidedly un-Earthlike ones, but the other stars were sterile. The spores of life would land anywhere, bloom anywhere with even approximately the right mix and balance of elements, but these blasted systems had little more than cinders and ice, debris fields and cold, moonless giants.

Terraforming these places—even hollowing them out or doming them over, squashing them to planettes or spinning them into habitable rings—promised lifetimes of toil. Immorbid lifetimes, with dubious payoff at best. Their colonists were predominantly volunteers, too, which made Conrad wonder just how bad things had gotten back Solways. How stifling, how crowded and hopeless did things have to get before a lifetime on bare rock seemed preferable?

Then again, perhaps the younger Conrad would have leaped at the chance. Perhaps his experiences here and on *Newhope* had made him overcautious, stodgy, old. He didn't know what to think about that.

In any case, the Queendom of Sol seemed to pause then, drawing its breath, and it was rumored that the next wave of colonization would be aimed at brown dwarf stars, tiny and nameless and cold, too dim to be visible even from their own outlying planets. This sounded even more miserable to Conrad—even farther from the ideals of Ireland or Tonga, or any of the other scattered paradises of Earth.

But many of these dwarfs—failed stars or oversized planets, simmering in the warm fusion of their own deuterium—were closer at hand than the genuine star systems, and more promising in certain other regards. The light of the blue giant Sirius, being high in ultraviolet, was lethal to an unprotected human, as indeed the light of Sol could be even on Earth. And at least a brown star, dim as a fireplace coal, did not have that strike against it. Close enough to feel its warmth, you could stare right at it and never be blinded.

At first, contact between the eight colonies was routed through Sol and was therefore exceedingly slow, but with the erection of a giant antenna farm at Bascal's insistence and Conrad's day-to-day direction, Barnard was able to join a lightspeed telecom network which connected the colonies directly. The Instelnet: a chatter of new societies, independent of the richer, fatter networks of the old Queendom. Later, redesign of the antennas boosted data rates by a factor of ten, and the addition of three more antenna farms, plus several dedicated power stations, increased it by still another ten-fold. But that was the best they could do without telecom collapsiters, and even the Queendom of Sol couldn't afford to string those between the stars.

The traffic was mainly compressed data, plus a few audio-visual channels carrying entertainments and news. It was, of course, impossible to transmit human beings. One needed a true collapsiter grid for that. However, with sufficient time and money and energy, it was possible to transmit intelligent, self-aware messages. Soon there was a steady diplomatic traffic as the various heads of state sent idiot snapshots of themselves back and forth for meetings and even staged dinners. And in the way of such things, the practice became a kind of vice for the wealthy, into which class Conrad found himself unexpectedly thrust.

He had done little to encourage this process, and felt gnawingly guilty about it. Egalitarianism was the new default, with no one citizen rising too high above the others—in theory. But when a hundred people pooled their resources to hire a building design, each giving Conrad a tenth of his or her rational wage, the wealth didn't take long to accumulate.

On the other hand, money was kind of meaningless out here; food and clothing were as plentiful and nearly as cheap as they had been in the Queendom, most land was literally free, and Conrad did his best to see that buildings were not expensive either. Materially speaking, there wasn't a whole lot else you could buy.

So he traveled, visiting Xmary and her lover Feck a few times up at Gatewood Station. And later he visited Xmary and some guy named Floyd Limpwick, whom she fell desperately in love with for a while, at their temporary quarters on the Lutui Belt Provisional Mass Crusher. But while Conrad was glad to see her, and she him (or so it seemed), they had never truly made that transition into friendship. He always felt a tinge of bitterness toward her lovers—even Money Izolo, who *was* his friend as well as hers. And really, they couldn't be happy to see him either. So the visits came less and less frequently, and Conrad found himself at the Instelnet Transceiving Station more than once, burning a decade's worth of savings to send his own little software homunculus to the stars and back.

The hard part was finding a pen pal—someone to whom he could address his messages. At Wolf he could count on Edward Bascal, who still considered him a childhood friend, but it took some patient digging in the lower-bandwidth channels to find willing partners in Lalande and Sirius, Ross and Luyten. And the paid replies, when they came back, included partial sensorium: the sights and sounds of a foreign place, almost as though he'd been there himself.

It was a bit like traveling, and as extravagances of the hyperrich go, this one garnered more interest and amusement than envy. At parties especially, people would ask Conrad about his journeys to the stars, and he would regale them with stories. Pale dusty rings arching above a world of ice; a sky with three suns; an aurora sizzling with stellar-flare protons, and beneath it an ocean thick and slimy with black vegetation, and lurking mountains of flesh which had been known to gobble unwary humans along with their normal grazing.

Alas, his second reply from Luyten was lost in transmission, garbled beyond the ability of even a telecom hypercomputer to repair, and he mourned its vanished impressions and experiences almost as he would mourn a true copy of himself. But even that made for a good anecdote, and spiced his character with a fashionable tinge of melancholy.

In this way Conrad became, over time, a seasoned and cosmopolitan adult, a galactic citizen who was widely seen, with only the mildest of envy, as rising above the inherent provinciality of this little province—humanity's first extrasolar experiment.

One thing Conrad never did, though, was send himself to Sol. He'd already been there, after all, and while it might be nice to see his parents and some of the casual friends he'd known who had not themselves become colonists, he never felt any true need to send them more than text messages, or the occasional video monologue. And even that was expensive, by colonial standards. Too, as with Xmary, he had less and less in common with them as the years rolled on. The messages became dutiful rather than warm, and as terse as his sense of duty permitted.

But of course Conrad's fate was intertwined with the Queendom of Sol, and could not be so easily separated. And he had twice received his own visitors from the sky, pen pals writing back to him with animate messages of their own, and so in the fullness of time he was only a little bit surprised to find the Queendom of Sol coming to visit him, as a mountain had once allegedly called upon the residence of the prophet Mohammed.

#### chapter twelve

messages, bottled and un-

In the twenty-fifth decade of the Kingdom of Barnard, in an orbital tower looking down upon the world of P2, the architect Conrad Mursk stands with a warm mug in his hand, staring across forty thousand kilometers of vacuum at his latest creation: the Gravittoir. This consists of a skyhook station, known artfully as "Skyhook Station," suspended by three electromagnetic grapples "hooked" to Barnard, Gatewood, and Van de Kamp, as a triangular hammock might be slung between a trio of trees.

There will be times, alas—a few years out of every century—when these bodies will be poorly aligned, and will fail to support the station (being "beneath" it in a gravitational sense), and at these times the station will be forced to descend back to the planet's surface, and the citizens of Barnard will have to rely instead on the older and less elegant Orbital Tower, upon which Conrad presently stands.

A synchronous orbit for Skyhook Station—one which completed its turns at the same rate as the planet itself—would have been much better in this regard, but there are no such orbits here. With the star so close and the planet's rotation so slow, the altitude of an orbit like that would be well outside the planet's sphere of gravitational influence. Or so

Conrad's gravity specialists have persuaded him: this is the best solution for the given environment, and will in no way reduce the esteem of Barnard's First Architect.

The purpose of the Orbital Tower is simple: to provide an elevator up out of the atmosphere. It was never intended as a permanent solution, and while the Gravittoir will be a great improvement, there is nothing permanent about it, either. Indeed, it's just another stopgap on the road to faxation; once the collapsiter grid is in place, none of this will be necessary. The Gravittoir is also simple: Skyhook Station has a weak gravity laser pointing downward, which creates a column of funny weather, but more importantly makes it possible for a properly designed spacecraft to be yanked off the surface of the planet and into space, where its thrusters can place it in orbit without drag or fuss.

Stand with Conrad, and see what he sees: the tower stretching down beneath you: a narrow, gleaming cone of impervium whose base is roughly the size of a soccer pitch, whose nearly cylindrical apex is, by coincidence, almost exactly as wide as the starship *Newhope*, which brought you here long ago. The interior of the structure includes a sleeve of diamond which is technically capable of supporting the tower's entire weight, but with almost no safety margin. Know that for practical purposes, the structure is held up by the pressure of electrons in quantum dots, and runs a serious risk of collapse in the unlikely event that the power ever fails. Feel the meaning of that in your boots, in the wellmetal deck beneath you. A temporary structure, indeed.

Because the tower is so purely vertical, and its base so distant beneath P2's tall atmosphere, you cannot see the foot of it. What you can see, if you strain your eyes, is the black line of a tuberail link joining the base of the tower with the city of Domesville, which even now is built in rings and circles—a concession to the domes that were never erected. It's a style; even the new construction falls into the same general pattern, so that from up here the city looks like a scattering of saucers and old-style shirt buttons around a pair of midsized dinner plates.

There are just over twenty thousand people down there (or

fourteen thousand individuals with an average of 1.4 instantiations apiece, if you prefer to count it that way) going about their daily business, which mainly involves the maintenance and expansion of Domesville itself, the rearing and education of its growing ranks of children, and the planning and governance and sociopolitical groundwork for the much larger population which is to follow in the centuries ahead.

Then, running east from Domesville and perpendicular to the Tower Line, you can just make out the city's other tube-rail, which runs thirty-five thousand kilometers east to Bupsville (officially Backupsville), the planet's only other major community. Not everyone lives in these two towns, and indeed, not everyone lives on the surface of the planet, or even anywhere near it. But together, the towns account for about ninety percent of the colony's population, and at least ninety-nine percent of its cultural output. If you squint, you can just make out Bupsville through a yellow-brown haze at the edge or "limb" of the planet. It doesn't look like much, just a gray discoloration, gleaming here and there with the bright orange-white of reflected sunlight. There is another tuberail line south from Bupsville, joining it to the Gravittoir's ground station, which, like the Orbital Tower, is located on P2's equator. But that line is far too thin and faint, too obscured by chlorine haze and water vapor and dust, to be visible from here.

The ground station itself is visible only because Conrad has asked the windows to mark it for him, with a reticle of glowing red. Another reticle—this one green—marks the position of Skyhook Station, which fortunately *is* visible, if only because it gleams in full sunlight, like a tight little cluster of stars.

Conrad is here because he's seen the Gravittoir, the latest of his children, from every other sort of angle, and wants to see it from this one before it goes online. Before the Orbital Tower becomes an afterthought, useful only for rustic vacations and cargoes of the very lowest priority. Before Domesville ceases to be the planet's main spaceport, and becomes instead merely its political capital.

Imagine yourself hovering invisibly beside Conrad, in a

circular chamber at the tower's very top. All around you, the walls are transparent, though the ceiling has been opaqued to provide some shade from the noonday sun, and the floor has been similarly darkened to prevent vertigo, which from this vantage can be considerable. The launching tracks, running up along the outside of the tower, are also transparent (remarkably so, to your eye), and are only really visible if you know what to look for: four man-wide tuberails of wellstone spaced around the tower at ninety-degree intervals. Here and there, they catch the light in interesting ways, shooting rainbow-speckled sprays of it along the silver-gray wellmetal of the deck beneath your feet. It's rather cold here, and Conrad is bundled in a wellcloth jacket he brought with him from home, thinking ahead because he knows it's always cold here.

Outside of Domesville, all around it, is the Forest Not-Quite-Primeval (its actual name, yes), where the green of Earthly vegetation battles with the brown of P2's "natives"—very few of which are genuine, unmodified algoids. And with a careful eye you can even discern the two streams running through Domesville in a Y shape: Chokecherry Creek and King's Creek, which merge to become King's River before emptying out into the half-moon shape of Transit Bay, and thence to the Sea of Destiny. These off-dry ditches are generously named, visible only for the vegetation and housing crowding along their banks. They're not real rivers—just the handiest applicants for the job. But the sea and the bay are for real, and beneath their blue-green veneer they are themselves a battleground of green and brown and black vegetation.

The tower's structure is rigidized, actively controlled and damped to a degree that even Conrad finds astonishing, but nevertheless the floor transmits a vibration up through your boots. Or through Conrad's, more properly, since you aren't really here. This vibration, barely noticeable at first, quickly grows in intensity. A podship is coming up the rails. With a sudden smile, Conrad looks for it, leaning forward and pressing his nose against the transparent wellglass. He's rewarded by glimmers of light from below, shifting rapidly, and in another moment there is a sound like rain, and half the view is blocked for a moment as a C-shaped crew transporter, striped black and red, flickers past at seven kps, riding upward on two of the tower's four rails. The thrumming continues for another fraction of a second, and then suddenly quits as the podship clears the top of the tower and soars on up into vacuum.

God, you love it here. Or Conrad does. Or, more properly, Conrad *did*, for these events are long in the past.

After building the place, he used to sit up here for hours, just watching the pods go by. More traffic downward than up: there was a net flow of resources onto the planet, as it was easier to mine pure elements out of the asteroid belts than to rip them from P2's metal-poor crust. But the upward traffic—the *outbound* traffic—was in its own way more romantic, since it consisted largely of children in their twenties heading for their yearlong, not-quite-mandatory tour of duty on the space station or vessel of their choice. Seeing them roar by like that, Conrad was reminded of his own early days in space, as the unofficial XO of a pirate ship.

In many ways, these kids had it soft by comparison, although Conrad smiled to remember that *Viridity* had had its own medical-grade fax machine onboard, albeit restricted by stern software lockouts. There had been a pair of gleaming Palace Guard robots onboard as well, which had seemed very threatening and dangerous but had saved lives on more than one occasion. What days those had been! Not fun, but definitely thrilling.

The walls of the chamber chimed and said, "Incoming message." The voice was soft and distinctly artificial, as Conrad preferred, and it was nice to see that the Tower still recognized him and knew his tastes after all this time away.

"Play message," he said.

A man and a woman appeared before him, in very nice holograms projected and reinforced from both the ceiling and floor, with maybe a bit of fill-in from the walls as well.

"Yes?" Conrad said to them, then gasped as he realized just whom he was addressing: Bruno de Towaji and Tamra Tamatra Lutui, the King and Queen of Sol.

Conrad hadn't seen them—even their images—in so long

that he could scarcely remember what to do. He was tempted to drop to his knees, but remembered in time that he, too, was a friend of kings. He had never knelt for Bascal—well, never seriously—so why should he for Bascal's parents? He made an awkward bow instead, placing his right hand on his stomach and raising his left in the air behind him.

"Your Majesties! Welcome! I am . . . rather surprised to see you here. What can I do for you? Or have you perhaps arrived at the wrong address?"

Tamra laughed. "*Malo e leilei.* You're Conrad Mursk, yes? The architect? Then we've been forwarded correctly. We bring you greetings from the Queendom of Sol."

And King Bruno, looking around him, smiled in wonder and said, "Good God, it's like stepping back in time. We had towers like this when I was a boy. Well, perhaps not quite like this. But we needed them, you see, because there was no collapsiter grid. No other way to get on and off the planet, unless you wanted to plow the air in a hyperjet. This place is beautiful, lad. Is it your own work?"

Conrad shrugged. "Largely mine, yes, about eighty years ago. I think it's held up rather well, given the haste of its construction and the heavy use it has seen since then."

"No doubt, no doubt."

Conrad cleared his throat. "Is there, ah, is there some reason for your visit, Sires?"

"A little reassurance, if you please," the Queen of Sol said.

Conrad blinked. "I beg your pardon? Reassurance on what?"

"We get only the official Instelnet news and information channels from Barnard, plus a smattering of narrowband entertainments, and of course the personal messages from our son. But amid this clutter we find that something doesn't smell quite right."

"The data," Bruno added, "imply one or more hidden or neglected variables of great importance. Our analyses complain of being incomplete, and warn us not to rely on them."

A bit of the old defiance fluttered in Conrad's heart, and he said, "You have no authority here. Sir, madam, I'm sorry, but it's true. We don't have to do things your way. We don't have to open our ports to your every scan. For that matter we needn't share information at all. Are you here as spies?"

"Should spying be necessary?" Tamra asked, with neither humor nor anger. "Our concern is for your welfare."

"Naturally."

King Bruno smiled, perhaps a little sadly, and said, "Let us be friends, lad. Let us speak frankly, and in our mutual interest. We mean you no harm—surely you know that."

And here Conrad relented, unsure why he'd pressed the point to begin with. Because surely this was true: there could be nothing sinister in their motives. Just parental, condescending, and superior, as always. And from the safe remove of six light-years, he could forgive them for that. Couldn't he? He eyed the two holograms carefully and said, "You two are quite a large program, aren't you? Very detailed, very capable. You mean to have a real conversation."

"Indeed," the King of Sol confirmed. "We've been clogging your planet's receivers for days. We will pay, naturally, in intellectual property concessions, and perhaps this proves some measure of sincerity on our part."

"But what is it you want?"

The queen stepped forward half a pace. "Just your thoughts, Architect. Your impressions. Do you sense anything amiss? Something in the ecology? The economy? Your resource allocations have been quite peculiar—one might almost say primitive."

Conrad could only shrug. "We have a lot of work to do. We're trying to install an entire civilization from scratch, building up from bare rock. Metal-poor rock, I might add. Frankly, I think we're doing quite well. We've hit our stride."

"Your population dynamics, then. Surely those peculiarities—"

"We have a labor shortage, madam. We've had one since the very beginning, and quite frankly, it gets lonely here. There's only so much time you can spend talking to yourself, talking to the same few people over and over. Surely you don't begrudge us our children?"

"No. Certainly not. But your methods—"

Methods, yes. There had been developments in that area,

to speed the population growth along. Conrad said, "You find it unseemly."

"Well, it's . . . pragmatic I suppose," the king answered uncertainly.

"Aye. That it is," Conrad agreed without humor. "We were intended to find our own way in this place, our own solutions to our own problems, and I believe we're doing that. I don't feel the need for children of my own—not now, at any rate—but I do feel strongly about the right to have them. In the manner of my own choosing, thank you."

"Indeed. Indeed. It isn't our place to judge. But you're one of Bascal's friends. I assume you are still. If something were wrong—I mean seriously wrong—would he tell you?"

"Hmm. I don't know," Conrad answered honestly. "He might. If he thought I could help him with it, then definitely, yes. But I haven't heard anything. I haven't spoken with Bascal in, oh, I guess it must be four years by now. And even that was just pleasantries. I suppose that happens as you get older: the bonds of friendship maintain themselves with less and less reinforcement. Anyway, these days Bascal is a lot older than I am. He doesn't seek my opinion quite so often."

The queen strode to the transparent wall, looking for a moment as if she might press her face against it, as Conrad had done a few minutes ago. Of course, she wasn't really here, and had no face to press. "Let's begin with your ecology," she said reasonably. "Magnifier, please."

But the wall's wellstone did not recognize her as a person, merely as data, and so ignored the command.

"Magnifier," Conrad told it, pointing to the spot where the queen had been looking. "Fifty times zoom, contrast filtering and color enhancement."

"Thank you," Her Majesty said. "One forgets one isn't real."

"Well," Conrad said, "let's hope your reply isn't lost in the mail. If it gets through, then these experiences will reach the real Tamra and Bruno, and thus you are real enough for practical purposes. Let's hope the gods of data communication are on your side."

Per command, a magnification circle appeared in the wall

directly in front of Queen Tamra. From Conrad's angle, behind the queen, it showed the top of the forest surrounding Domesville, with a flock of startled starbirds flapping up out of it in that weird, almost vertical way they had, like malformed bubbles rising in a glass of beer.

"The ecology isn't natural," Conrad conceded. "How could it be? It was installed, yes, and I don't think anyone has ever let it settle down. Why bother? We call it 'evolutionary extrapolation,' and here it's considered an art form. We compute—rigorously—the sort of creatures the native ecology might have produced, given enough time, and the ones which pass a popular referendum are instantiated. Whole herds of them. Whole flocks and bevies and swarms. We color them as we please, but as I understand it the selective pressures on the first few generations are pretty strong. So their final appearance is a compromise between what we give them and what works in the wild. And if they die out altogether, we tweak them and print more. Hell, even the atmosphere would change without our constant intervention."

Indeed, the line of atmosphere processing stations—gigantic print plates for a very primitive sort of fax—ran alongside the tuberail link from Domesville to Bupsville, and even from here you could see a fine mist rising out of them, oxygen and nitrogen liberated from a soil buffer somewhere and reacting coolly with the native gases.

"But we aren't dependent on the ecology, Sires, or on the atmosphere. We can breathe the native gases, and as I understand it, we can eat a much broader range of foodstuffs than you can. In this sense, we haven't been human for a century or more. And if our reproductive methods reflect this, well, so be it. Times change."

"Fair enough," the queen said, looking over her shoulder at Conrad. "But those aren't real fax machines down there." She turned farther and pointed a finger at the chamber's service fax, where Conrad's mug of red tea had been produced. "That's not a real fax machine either. It produces only simple chemicals, yes? We've seen the reports. That device could never fax a living creature, nor even a good semblance of a dead one."

Conrad fought down his irritation and struggled to be polite. "I'm not sure what you mean by 'real,' Your Highness. It isn't a medical-grade fax machine, no. But so what? Do we need one here?"

"Perhaps," she said seriously. "One never knows until the time has come, and by then of course it's too late. For all of that, you're looking rather decrepit yourself. You have a paunch, young man, and a touch of gray at your temples. If there are 'medical-grade fax machines,' as you call them, when was the last time you visited one?"

I can't quite remember, Conrad thought but did not say. "Listen, Bruno. Tamra. Parents of my friend, of my king. We're building a world here. Not your world, and certainly not the world we'd've picked for ourselves, if the choice were ours to make. But the result, like the animals, is a blend of what we want and what works."

"*If* it works," Tamra said coolly.

Bruno looked at the magnifier, at the fax, at the ceiling and the floor and the walls, at the planetscape spreading out beneath the tower. "All right, lad. You children have made some clever adaptations. Wait, my apologies: I shouldn't call you children. Each of you carries more responsibility than most citizens of Sol will ever experience. But yes, I can see there's nothing foolish about your methods, whether I personally agree with them or not."

You're damn right, Conrad thought. *And oh my goodness, is that a touch of condescension in your tone?* What he did say was, "Majesties, are you sufficiently reassured? I have work to do, and not enough copies to do it."

In point of fact, he had no copies at all right now. Probably he should rectify that along with the slippage in his biological age. And make a damned backup, yes. Losing five-odd years of memory would be inconvenient at best. No, worse than that. There were some treasures in there—experiences that might never come again, no matter how long he lived.

Tamra said, "We are adequately reassured. For the time being, at least. Thank you for your time, Architect, and do say hi to Bascal for us when next you see him."

And with that, quite suddenly, the two holograms vanished.

Conrad sighed, feeling self-conscious, feeling the scrutiny of his elders—his true elders—for the first time in many, many decades. Well, so be it. They did mean well, after all, and perhaps they had a point. About Conrad's appearance, if nothing else.

He glanced at the floor and said, "Elevator," and obligingly, a disc of material separated from the floor and sank a few centimeters into it. A matching cylinder, so transparent he could barely see it, emerged from the ceiling, stopping just above the level of his head. He stepped under it, onto the recessed disc in the floor, and the cylinder lowered itself around him so that he was sealed in a sort of jar, and then the whole apparatus fell out beneath him.

He really should put a gravity laser in here sometime. He would have already, if the Gravittoir weren't making this whole structure obsolete anyway. Meanwhile, the elevator accelerated downward at half a gee, and his feet felt so tingly-light that it seemed they might slip out from under him at any moment. Not likely, given the impervium-toed traction shoes he normally wore on any construction site, and most other places besides. But it was unsettling nevertheless. Maybe he just needed more practice.

The walls of the elevator remained transparent, but other than the lightness in his feet and the fluttering of his stomach, there was no impression of actual movement through the core of the tower. If there were imperfections in the wellstone walls of the shaft, they were imperceptible at these speeds, smearing together into a featureless gray blur.

Anyway, the ride would take twenty minutes, so this was as good a time as any for a telephone conference. "Call Mack," he said to the wall.

A rectangular hologram window appeared on the side of the elevator after a few seconds' delay, and there was the artfully homely face of Mack Duggins, the son of Celia Duggins and Karl Smoit.

"Yeah? Oh, hi Boss." Mack was out in the street somewhere, walking briskly on his short legs, not quite huffing with the exertion. The holie's view followed right along with him as he walked, and Conrad imagined his own face, in a rectangular holie window of its own, following Mack along the street, along the facades of shops and homes and restaurants, growing and shrinking as it went, struggling to maintain a constant apparent size and range from Mack's point of view. Every now and then, people jostled past him, blocking the view, but despite the ongoing population explosion, Domesville remained a small town, without too terribly much foot traffic.

Any resident of the Queendom—or of the Earthly societies which preceded it—would be surprised by Mack's appearance: a meter and a half of dense muscle and even denser skin, dark green in color and as bumpy as the hide of a dinosaur. The nose was prominent in his squashed-pumpkin face, the eyes were large, and the teeth so sharp and numerous that his mouth seemed barely able to close around them.

Mack was a troll. There was nothing particularly unusual about this—the body form was optimized for the long days and nights, the bitter seas and tough native foods of Planet Two, and its subculture included nearly a thousand individuals in Domesville alone. These were mostly native children who had never seen the light of Sol except as a pinpoint in the night sky, and they wore their troll skins with proud defiance, as youngsters before them might have worn a jacket of rakish well-leather. Children had always had this talent: to pervert the practical into something symbolic. And truthfully, this had the desired effect in that Conrad was less inclined to trust a troll than he was a human being. Except for Mack, of course.

"You treat me like I look," a young trolless had once accused Conrad, on a crowded street at Festival time.

Conrad's crime: stepping away from her so as not to loom. And his reply: "Obviously, miss. Our appearance is the first thing we say to the people around us, and yours is a scream of defiance."

To her credit, the trolless had giggled at that, and winked an enormous eyelid, and melted back into the rear of the crowd to be among her friends, her own kind.

But in Mack's case Conrad knew the person beneath the skin—indeed, had known the person *before* the skin—and had long since stopped noticing the way he looked. In some sense this was the underlying message of Mack's appearance: that it was appearance itself that could not be trusted. Mack could be a wiseass without even opening his mouth.

"Hi," Conrad said to him over the holie link. "I'm going to be late on the job site this afternoon. I'd like you to complete the survey on your own, if that's all right, and then get those damned foundation people out there. I want a slab of actual stone this time—preferably basalt, but I'll take what I can get."

There were basalts in P2's metal-poor crust, but they were buried very deep, and approached the surface only at Belladonna Canyon in the Southern Lowlands, where a robotic quarry with no permanent human (or troll, or other humanoid) residents turned out a meager and sporadic supply of cobblestone and foundation slab. And without tectonics raising ocean floors into mountain ranges every now and again, P2 didn't offer much in the way of sandstone either. Mostly, Conrad had to make do with pumices and granites, or even, in a pinch, blocks of poured concrete. These days he was using wellstone only as needed, as its price seemed to be pegged to the colony's population numbers and was therefore rising steadily.

And come to think of it, maybe that was the kind of warning sign the King and Queen of Sol were asking about. Certainly, in an optimal economy the goods and services should grow at least as quickly as the consumer base. Right?

"All right," Mack said uncertainly. "I can handle that. Should I stop short of threatening violence?"

"Please," Conrad confirmed. "But not too far short. We can't keep building on pumice—not if we're going to live forever."

"Understood. I hope you don't mind a bit of curiosity though; what's so important all of a sudden? Not another woman, I hope."

"No. Well, fifty-fifty chance, I guess. I'm going to see a doctor."

Mack slowed a little, then resumed his quick pace. "Anything wrong?"

"Just a tune-up," Conrad assured him. "It's been a while. We mustn't neglect these things—the delicate machineries which support the soul."

"Noted," Mack said. "Shall I expect you later?"

"Just play it by ear. Your ears are big enough for that, I should think. Anyway, I'm not quite sure how the hospitals work anymore, or how long it takes. Don't expect me until you see me."

Mack seemed satisfied with that, but it was hard to tell for certain, because trolls usually looked satisfied. "All right, then, Boss. Have fun."

Mack took instruction very well, needing little in the way of hand-holding or micromanagement, and in Conrad's experience that was a very good sign indeed. The best leaders were also, for whatever reason, the best subordinates. Mack was a bit, well, *green* for a leadership position just yet—only ten years old by the calendar, possibly twenty or twenty-five if you counted adult-equivalent experience, for his childhood had been brief. But Conrad was grooming him, and when the time came, he hoped to hand over a lot of his day-to-day labors to this enterprising young man, freeing himself up for certain big-picture issues, like why his materials were getting so damned expensive.

Bother it, maybe he *should* have taken Bruno and Tamra a bit more seriously. He cleared his throat. "Mack, I've heard a . . . rumor, I guess, that we might have some economic troubles lurking in the background. Not us personally—I mean the whole colony. Would you keep your eyes and ears open for me?"

"Sure, Boss. What sort of troubles?"

"If I knew, I'd tell you. But we're already facing price increases which affect our ability to do business, and that may have something to do with it. Just be aware."

"There *has* been some gossip, I guess."

Conrad raised an eyebrow. "Yes? Like what?"

And here Mack showed what a disturbing thing the smile

of a troll could be. "Sir, if I repeated it, *I'd* be gossiping. But I can try to get some details for you. Should I ask around?"

"Not overtly," Conrad said, after thinking about it for a moment. "It may be nothing. It's probably nothing. But if you see any signs that things are maybe not going so well, let me know."

"All right," Mack said with typical pragmatism. "Will do."

And he would. Mack was a man of his word, and reasonably creative to boot. The funny part was, neither of Mack's parents—both of them human—had ever displayed much initiative or leadership, or even a good work ethic. But when you mixed them together *just so*, you got something more than the apparent sum of the parts. It couldn't be anything in the way he was raised, because Mack wasn't "raised" at all in the usual sense. Like most of the children of Barnard, he was born in a fax machine, as a weighted random mixing of the genes and generic memories of his parents. He had entered the world at the physiological age of fifteen, knowing how to speak and walk and tie knots, and with the vague sense that he'd had a childhood somewhere, though the specific details were muddy.

He had joined Conrad's crew only five years later, already a productive member of society, and with a rather disarming acceptance of anything his elders might choose to tell him. One of the first on-the-job lessons Conrad had tried to impart was to question everything—especially authority—because if a child didn't know at least that much, what great things could you really expect of him? And so, Mack had dutifully joined the trolls, not merely in shape but in habit and thought.

"They're raw. They just seem to have it closer to right," he'd told Conrad at the time. And what could Conrad—himself a childhood rebel—say to that?

With its wide-open spaces—empty land totaling five times the Earth's own surface area—P2 also had centaurs, who could cover a lot of ground in a day. They were "indolent, snooty fuffers," in Mack's opinion, and you didn't tend to see them much in the actual cities. They needed to stretch their equine legs, and tended to stay in the farm country and the wilderness beyond it.

Of course, there was more to society than just these two groups; while a majority of people preferred a human skin, fully twenty percent of the colony had gone troll or centaur. Another five percent had taken even more exotic turns—like the semiaquatic gillmen and four-armed vishni—or had fit themselves into body plans of their own unique design. Some of the forms were beautiful—hell, a few were *glorious*—and their owners claimed to have viewpoints as unique and valuable as the skins around them.

"I can think in shapes," one young man had told Conrad in a job interview, through a mouth that seemed little more than a slit in the pimple-like protuberance of his head, on a body covered in smooth yellow scales. "I can *smell* an improper angle."

Which was probably true. Probably. But the boy could barely walk, and couldn't look up at all, and Conrad had advised him to seek employment in some industry where his death by falling debris was not quite so bloody likely. The fact remained that the human form had been refined through a million generations of primate evolution, where these one-off experiments had not. Any architect could tell you that new features—especially glorious ones—exacted their cost somewhere else in the system. There were trade-offs aplenty, but no free lunches, or even cheap ones. And the consequences of random experimentation could be awfully severe.

Indeed, many of the self-made were lurching, shambling disasters—the failed "angel" subculture being the most prominent example. In the unlikely event that Conrad ever decided to shed the humanity that Donald and Maybel Mursk had given him, he would probably stick close to an established body form for exactly this reason: because a thousand boisterous kids couldn't be *too* far wrong. If nothing else, they knew what felt good.

"Anything else?" Mack asked.

"No, thanks, that's all for now. I'll see you. End call."

The holie window winked out, leaving Conrad alone.

There was no doubt about it, of course: Mack was his surrogate son. As he'd told the monarchs of Sol, he'd never yet felt the desire to procreate. Oh sure, he made copies of himself, but he'd never found anyone that he felt comfortable mixing them with, to create an entirely new person, as different from Conrad as Mack was from Karl Smoit.

It wasn't that he lacked for women in his life, either. In fact, the breeding program had been accelerated for that most carnal of reasons: the colony had had more men than women, and the gender imbalance was pleasing to no one. So the faxes of Domesville and especially Bupsville had cranked out hundreds—and eventually thousands—of custom-built women into the waiting arms of the colony's men. And maybe, if Conrad thought about it, that was part of the problem: the word "children" to him meant "other people's children," whom he might hire, or ask out on a date, or engage with in more specific recreational activities.

But to *breed* with one of them, to use a child to produce another child, well . . . that did strike him as unseemly. This probably marked him as an eccentric or even—God forbid— a *naturalist* in the eyes of the children who knew him. But a man had to have his limits, and know them, and stay within them if he wanted his own respect.

And anyway, the dating pool of women his own age was pretty damned sparse, and he'd worked his way through most of it—the bits he cared for, anyway—in the colony's first century. And with this reflection, it occurred to him with some surprise that he was probably waiting for the wheel of his life to make another big turn and give him a shot at Xmary again. He wasn't her first love, nor probably her longest, but she was *his* on both counts. That meant something, and though it seemed a complex task to bring his life back in line with hers, well, he did have forever in which to accomplish it.

And this thought, in turn, brought a rare burst of sympathy for his ancestors, for the thousands of human generations who had lived and died in the distant past, never dreaming of this moment. If he were one of them, he'd've dropped in his tracks a long time ago and never had his second chance, or even known that he'd wanted one. "Life is short," they used to say. Ha!

And goodness gracious, on the heels of that came still another realization: if the future really was infinite, then his second shot at Xmary, like the first, was doomed to fail. And then, perhaps, to succeed again. And again, and again, in a never-ending cycle he could neither change nor wish to escape from. And he felt in that moment, for the first time in his life, what it truly meant to be immorbid. And for some reason, the idea made him shiver.

#### chapter thirteen

the medicine show

At the hospital, despite his VIP status, they made Conrad wait. And not even on wellstone couches, but on cloth ones with some sort of foam padding inside, about as comfortable as sitting on open ground. And said couches were full of people, some slightly known to him and some not, some obviously sick or injured and some apparently healthy. There were several couples here as well, sitting with their hands clasped together and excited or expectant or nervous looks on their faces.

"You know, I designed this building," he told the receptionist.

And that was a mistake, because the receptionist and door guard was Genie Scott, whom Conrad had spent a few days fuffing, many years ago. They were long days—*Barnardean* days—and once you spent the sleepshift with a woman, even one sleepshift, you pretty well forfeited your right to tell her anything like that, ever again.

"You'll wait in line like everyone else," she said firmly. "I don't care if you designed the planet."

"Well, I did design the..." But he saw her look and declined to finish the sentence. Anyway, there was a security robot waiting in the storage room behind her, visible through the open doorway, and although it was no Palace Guard, if Conrad made too much trouble the thing would simply throw him out in the street again.

So he sat and waited for nearly an hour before the nurse, a young man he'd never seen before, ushered him into an examination room.

"Sit down, please," the nurse instructed. They were very firmly polite here, apparently quite accustomed to impatient patients.

Conrad leaned his rump against the edge of the examination table—which fortunately *was* made of wellstone, smooth and supple beneath his touch—and at once the white walls of the room came alive with sensors and displays, shining lights and bursts of sound just beyond the edges of Conrad's hearing.

"Hmm," the nurse said, studying the walls and ceiling, paying no attention to Conrad himself. "Oxidation, telomere shortening, apoptosis, intracellular lipofuscin buildup . . . Sir, you're suffering from a condition known as geriatry."

Conrad nearly laughed out loud at that. "Old age? I'm familiar with the concept, yes."

"How long has it been since your last fax?"

"About five years, I think," Conrad answered. "Give or take a few."

Now the nurse did look at him, and he was scowling. "You mustn't go that long, sir. That's more than enough time for tumors to develop and metastasize. Or you could suffer arterial blockage—calcium or simple dietary fat—and, you know, drop dead. Losing five years of accumulated memory!"

"I'm familiar with the concept," Conrad repeated, less amused this time.

"Well then, shame on you twice as much. Do you have trouble hearing, or tasting your food? Aren't you tired? Don't you feel run-down in the evenings?"

"Sometimes," Conrad admitted. "But I don't need a lecture about it. How old are you, son?"

"That hardly matters, sir," the nurse told him firmly and politely. "The doctor will see you in a few minutes. If you like, you can watch TV in the meantime."

"Ah. Thank you, no. I'll just enjoy the quiet." There was little enough of that in his life these days.

As promised, fortunately, the doctor only made him wait a few minutes before appearing in the doorway with a gentle knock. He had on the obligatory white coat—who could trust a doctor without one?—and he had some sort of auxiliary sensory apparatus strapped to his head, like a pair of Old Modern spectacles with cones of rigid black wellstone projecting out from the lenses.

"Conrad Mursk. Conrad Ethel Mursk, first mate of *Newhope*, executive officer on the pirate *fetu'ula Viridity*. How the fuff are you, old man?"

Only then did Conrad realize he was looking at Martin Liss, *Newhope*'s nominal (though symbolic) medical officer and one of Conrad's old camp buddies from way too long ago.

"Martin! Wow, raw, it's . . . well, it's great to see you. You look . . ."

"Like a bug-eyed monster, I know." Martin took the spectacles off, grinning broadly. "But I can see right through you with these things, in more senses than one. It saves a lot of time."

"Time for what? I'm just here to step through a fax machine, if it's all the same to you. So they've made you a doctor, have they? How long has that been going on?"

"Quite some time now," Martin answered seriously. "The need was clear, so I did the studying and put five copies through five years of simulation each. Believe it or not, I'm qualified to treat most ailments with no fax machine at all. Not that people generally find this reassuring.

"To answer your question, this examination becomes part of your medical record, which gives us an idea how your body ages, how it changes over time, what sorts of breakdown it's prone to. Our fax filters have gotten pretty good, and in theory, the fresh copy we print will include corrections for the worst of these. People aren't faxing as often as they used to, so it behooves us in the medical profession to ensure that they get the most out of it when they do."

Conrad chuckled. "Sounds complicated, my friend. I'd rather just remember to fax more often."

Martin's smile looked a little bit forced. "We'd all like that, Conrad. We all remember those days. Someday it'll be like that again, but right now this is the way we do things. Now, all things considered, you're in pretty good shape, what with the time scales involved and the high radiation flux. In my medical opinion, you'll hold together for another thousand hours. Can you come back then? Two days from now?"

Puzzled, Conrad asked, "Why? What happens in two days?"

"Your fax appointment," Martin said. "If you were freshly dead but still salvageable, or in the middle of a heart attack or something, I'd stick you in the machine right away. But as I say, you're in reasonably good shape, which gives you a lower triage rating."

"The machine is that busy? For Barnardean days at a time? What the heck is it doing?"

Martin shrugged. "Oh, you know. Clonings, childbirth, repairing fractures, and amputations . . . the usual routine. Plus downtime for maintenance, of course. But listen, if you lose a limb between now and March, I'll promise to move you to the head of the queue. How's that?"

"I see. It does help to have a friend in the business," Conrad said, forcing a smile. But this, too, sounded like a problem. Maybe he was just paranoid, maybe the King and Queen of Sol had just put him on edge, but suddenly he could see problems all around him. And in all the world, in all the universe, there was only really one person he could talk to about that.

"I'll say hi to Bascal for you," he told Martin. "I've given myself the day off, and if you don't have time to fix me, I believe I owe that man a visit. Socially, you understand."

The encounter was as disturbing for Martin as it was for Conrad. Afterward, he sat in his office for a while, thinking about it. The state of medicine on Planet Two had declined slowly—so slowly that he almost hadn't noticed—but every now and then a refugee from the past would walk in thinking it was still the old days, and Martin would be forced to look around him and really see things as they were. To ponder, yes.

He didn't know precisely what he was pondering, what the causes were, what if anything he could do about it. If he demanded an audience with King Bascal, he would probably get it sooner or later, if only because they'd gone to Camp Friendly together as boys. But what could he ask for? What would he say?

Medicine was a perfect profession for Martin, because when you got right down to it, he didn't have much in the way of initiative. It was a job for clever reactionaries; the sensors told him what was wrong, and the hypercomputers told him what to do about it, while he served mainly in a supervisory capacity, keeping things focused and moving. In a pinch he could set a fractured bone, or even synthesize an RNA blocker to, for example, shut down a tumor or a bacterial infection. He had never done these things outside of a neural sensorium, but he understood how they would be done, or was pretty sure he did. But presented with an unknown problem whose solution had not been rotely memorized, would he know what to do?

And the concern raised by Conrad Mursk was a problem like that: unfocused, apparently sourceless. If it was a problem with the world itself, then for Martin's purposes it was undoctorable.

But then again, it wasn't Martin's job to worry about these things. It wasn't Conrad's job either—he was just supposed to put up buildings, right? But Conrad had always had a nose for problems and a pushy way of making them his business. Even as a boy, he'd had a funny knack for getting to the heart of things, for patching something together that would at least keep life from getting any worse.

And this thought went a long way toward quelling Martin's unease, because Conrad did have the ear of King Bascal, far more than Martin himself ever would. And if Martin had inspired Conrad to go and have that chat with the king, well, perhaps Martin had done his part after all.

And Martin was good at compartmentalizing his worries,

and he had a lot of patients to see today anyway, so he pushed the matter out of his mind, stood up and straightened his clothing, fetched a mug of iced coffee from the low-grade fax machine in his office, and went on about his business.

The encounter was also disturbing for Genie Scott, though for slightly different reasons. The thing was, in her estimation, Conrad Mursk looked terrible. About as bad as Genie had ever seen anyone who didn't come through the door on a trail of blood or shit. And this bothered her, because she'd been feeling like she maybe wanted another try at the first architect one of these days. But if the man couldn't be bothered to take proper care of himself, what made her think he could take proper care of someone else?

Not that he'd ever really tried in their brief time together, but fuffing hell, that was a hundred years ago. Didn't people grow? Didn't they change and improve over time? Genie herself had overcome many faults in a forty-year, twenty-step program of her own design, and was thinking about gearing up for another pass soon, to clear up the leftovers and start in on a new set of faults. She wasn't vain; she knew she had an infinite supply of these, and could safely plan an eternity of self-improvement. She thought someday that she might even license the program to others, for profit, leaving this hospital job behind for someone younger, someone with less to contribute.

Maybe she would even try it out on Conrad sometime, but on a professional rather than a personal basis. The thought of being intimate with him again had lost its appeal, at least for now. Geriatry, yuck! Shrugging, she too put the matter out of her mind, and resolved that she would have another crack at Dr. Martin Liss instead, who at least knew how the gift of a human body ought to be treated.

#### chapter fourteen

the glass palace

Matatahi Falehau was a less imposing structure than you might expect, and a gaudier one. It was only the second building Conrad had ever designed from scratch—the first here on Planet Two—and he winced to look at it now. If he had it to do over again, there were a hundred things he'd do differently, both great and small. According to the "iconographic transsect" of Queendom tradition, buildings of greater importance were to be signified with statuary, coats of arms, physical symbols of various kinds, and cosmetic embellishments unrelated to the functional demands of the structure.

"This communicates an expectation," Laureate Gwylan Smith had told his class once in a series of crossly delivered training lectures, "about the social function of the building, which in the end is more important than its exact physical form." And since Gwylan Smith was one of the Queendom's dozen-odd premier architects, he almost certainly had a point. But respecting authority in that particular way had never been a part of Conrad's character. The unwritten Mursk transsect favored clean lines and smooth, unadorned surfaces, not because they were easier (although they often were), but for purity's sake. To the extent that his buildings conveyed a message, it was a no-nonsense, striving-for-perfection kind of thing.

Except, of course, for this place, which had Tongan heraldry and iconography all over it. Even the wellstone facade was broken into tiles, each with the stars and cross of the Lutui family crest. Ugly, ugly symbols whose only redeeming feature was their color palette, which did at least match the grays and browns of the surrounding rock shelf.

Ah, well.

Domesville was not a large town, and the walk from the hospital to the palace took only a few minutes, through the industrial and warehouse quarter, past the town square with its burbling fountain, and then through the poorly planned maze of apartment buildings overlooking the beach.

The walk was not particularly pleasant, alas. If this were Earth it would be a gray day, drizzling a cool, steady mist. P2's equivalent was a haze of yellow-brown, blotting out the sun and filling the air with the swimming-pool aroma of wet chlorine and salt. The sort of day that would kill an unmodified human within minutes, yeah. For the people of P2—"pantropes," Bascal called them sometimes—it didn't even sting the eyes or irritate the nasal membranes, but even so the body remembered a different time, when it didn't have to process this shit. Hints of the old respiratory ailments, the pharyngitis and *talematangi*, resurfaced among the colonists when the halogen fronts blew through, and even the kids who were born here—if "born" was the right word—got cranky and indoorsy. But the walk was mercifully short.

The palace itself was perched on a natural bench of native granite, just above the steeply sloping beach. This too was a bad idea in retrospect, because the ocean level had been on a steady rise ever since the colonists had arrived—not from their own activity but as part of the natural ebb and flow of the planet. Now, alas, the high-tide beach was half its former size, and it would've been better to have blasted the shelf with carbon subnukes and pulled the slope back another thirty meters or so.

Live and learn.

Backupsville, at least, had more sense and planning behind it, and the next city would be better still. Not that Conrad had all that much say in the top-level city planning or anything, but he recognized that his architecture did influence the landscape, and thus the layout decisions of the Senate and the city councils.

And decade by decade, the lessons really did pile up, and he didn't have to be a genius—fortunately!—to internalize them, if only as rules of thumb. Conrad smiled to himself. *The next time I colonize a planet, I'll know how it's done. Ha!*

The city's vegetation was sparse. There were irrigated gardens in the hills to the west, and the Bay Islands were the usual riot of green and brown, where alien and "native" vegetation wrestled for the best soil, the best access to sunlight. And here in town there were potted palms, a few as high as four meters, and troughed red bromide bushes spreading half as wide as a tuberail car. But most people in town had given up trying to grow anything in the ground itself. The bedrock was shallow here, the soil coarse and crystalline and full of pebbles, more like beach sand than potting soil.

But Bascal, echoing his father, had stubbornly surrounded the palace with faxed soil, which probably had to be refreshed once or twice a year lest it wash away or soak down into the sand or turn too acidic or something. So the palace itself stood out above an oasis of palms and vanilla shrubs, grasses and sweet potato creepers.

Anyway, the Beach Palace was kind of pretty in the noontime pids of a sunny day ("late spring," if you will), its translucent tiles of white and red shooting tiny rainbows every which way, but in the afterpids of a mustard day like today (a stormy autumn?), it just looked foolish. The front walkway was of large, round paving stones—nonprogrammable—cut from the colony's first quarry in the hills during the early phases of Domesville's construction. The whole building was only two or three times the size of an ordinary family house, and like the beach palaces of Bascal's native Tonga, it reached for the sky only symbolically, with a couple of three-story towers at opposite corners.

The front entrance was even more humble: a simple rectangle of wellwood set in a frame of that same ugly white tile.

Fortunately the door knew him, and opened wide without his having to say anything. He strode inside, where the light was brighter, with more of the blues and whites that the eye began to crave on these brownest of days.

"Greetings and welcome, First Architect Mursk," the palace said. "His majesty is indisposed at the moment, but if you wait a few minutes I will print a fresh copy of him for you. Please, make yourself at home."

There was nothing homey about the foyer, or the closed, soundproofed offices adjoining it. Last time Conrad had been here, the palace had had a full-time staff of eight, only two of whom could be considered household servants in any meaningful sense. The others were office workers: bureaucrats and functionaries, keeping Bascal interfaced with the other machineries of government, with public opinion, with light-lagged news from Sol and the other colonies. But farther back, the actual living quarters were fairly comfortable, with natural and artificial light, with lots of soft places to park your ass and flat, hard surfaces to park a drink or a plate of food.

And dutifully, the palace asked him, "May I bring you something, sir? A glass of wine? A platter of fruit, perhaps?"

"That sounds good," Conrad admitted. He still didn't like buildings nattering at him, but there was something about this one that he'd grown a little fond of. It wasn't human—it wasn't a friend or anything like that. But he liked it in the same way he might like a dog, or a character on a TV show, or an interactive recording of someone he vaguely knew.

A household robot, like a manikin of brightly polished gold, appeared from somewhere, carrying a platter with Conrad's food and drink. Its movements were inhumanly quick, inhumanly graceful. The swivel and bend of every joint was computed to the eighth decimal place, with a result so poetically beautiful that it nearly always brought a smile to Conrad's lips. The platter tilted crazily in the thing's hands, but of course the gee forces were calculated just as precisely, and when the platter was whisked down onto the table beside the armchair Conrad had selected, the only sound it made was the soft whisper of displaced air. The surface of his wineglass betrayed not so much as a ripple. And then, just as quickly, the robot danced back into the shadows and was gone.

Conrad sighed, both amused and saddened at the sight. Like almost every home or office or rustic cabin in the old Queendom, this place was built around a central fax machine, providing everything from fresh air and fruit to fresh copies of the host himself. But those large, medical-grade print plates were hard to come by, and a typical P2 home had one or two much smaller fax machines instead, of decidedly submedical grade. But it was nice to see, if only for a while, the way things ought to be.

Conrad tasted the fruit, and sipped the wine, and these brought another sigh. There really was a difference! A real fax machine produced atomically precise copies of the things in its library. Not convenient approximations or shortcuts, not flavored synthetics, but something actually identical to the original. You could fool yourself into thinking the other stuff was just as good, or nearly as good, but a taste of the real thing quickly dispelled that notion.

Presently, Bascal appeared in the living room's arched doorway, dressed in a pair of loose white trousers and a flowered, tapa-patterned shirt of royal purple.

"Hey there," he said, smiling warmly. He hurried over, far less gracefully than the robot had done, then grabbed and shook Conrad's hand in both of his before settling into the adjacent armchair. "You're looking exceptionally haggard this afternoon. A bit blurry around the edges, are we?"

"I've just come from the doctor," Conrad said. "I've got a fax appointment two days from now. I'll be freshly scrubbed and full of beans then, probably fuffing everything in sight. Martin swears I'll survive in the meantime, and I see no reason to disbelieve that. He's not so much of a goofball anymore, our Martin. Or anyway he hides it better than he used to."

Bascal, for his part, did not look exceptionally haggard, or worn down in any way. He had that freshly faxed look, which only came from doing it every morning, no doubt at the insistence of a nagging house and staff. Although, Conrad reminded himself, this copy *had* just stepped out of the machine, and would look fresh in any case.

"Well, do please be my guest." Bascal gestured toward the room's far end, where Conrad could see the cylindrical print plate projecting out from the walls like a quarter-pillar running up along the corner. "Step through. Be a new man."

Conrad thought about that. It was certainly a tempting offer, shrugging off the wear and tear of the past several years, but he'd already made his appointment at the hospital, and really Genie was right: he should be a good citizen and wait his turn like everyone else.

"I'll pass," he told Bascal, "but thanks. And how are you?"

As if he didn't know. As if everyone on the planet didn't know what their king had for breakfast every morning. For better or worse, this was how the human mind worked: a figure or two at the top, not necessarily loved or even admired, but elevated and studied with fascination. Monarchic capitalism was the ultimate form of human government, because it was the only one that really accepted human nature and used it to maximum advantage. And as long as you had a Senate actually running things, or pretending to, then the worst aspects of the monarch's own humanity could be curbed as well, or guided into useful channels. That was the theory, anyway.

"I'm well," Bascal said. "Very well, my boy. And it's very nice to see you. You should come by here more often, really. Well, I suppose we would've seen each other at the Gravittoir dedication ceremony, anyway, but that doesn't mean you shouldn't visit."

Shrugging, Conrad answered, "I'm running single these days. Maybe I'll make an extra copy at the hospital next month, but then, for crying out loud, I'd have to wait through triage again just to reconverge the memories. It seems like a lot of bother."

"You're a busy man. I understand. The people of Sol may languish in their ennui and malaise, their joblessness and underemployment, but here beneath the mustard sky we need every hand, most especially yours. You always were my top guy, Conrad."

Conrad laughed. "That's blatant flattery and you know it. I may have been your *favorite* guy, at least occasionally, but I was never your best. Never close."

Bascal's face darkened. "That's not for you to decide, boyo. I hear my parents came to see you. A great big whopping message, tying up the works for thirty-nine hours. Almost two pids of nothing but them! Do you want to tell me about that? Are they snooping again?"

"They mean well, but yes. They're worried about you. About us. And the more I think about it, the more I think there may be something to it. Things here in Barnard aren't going quite according to plan, are they? Shouldn't we be farther along by now? Not grubbing in the dirt for buffer mass, or slapping together these half-assed miniature print plates. Shouldn't we be running this place by now? Faxing across the system in our shiny new collapsiter grid?"

"The issues are complex," Bascal said, spreading his hands.

"I don't doubt it," Conrad allowed, "but every problem has a foundation. If we do have one, then what is it, and where did it come from?"

The spread of Bascal's hands widened. "It's economics, boyo. To prosper we've got to grow the economy, and to do that we've got to increase the population. But there's a fax shortage, so we have to build more machines, and to do that we've got to bring in rare earth elements from the asteroids, so we need your Gravittoir to make it easier to get things on and off the planet. But that takes manpower as well, which creates even more population pressure.

"In a way, this is a kind of golden age; we're not only achieving phenomenal rates of growth, we're innovating as well. Our fax filters are in high Instelnet demand in the other colonies, which have a lot of the same problems we do. But we also need our antimatter factories and deutrelium refineries, and we need to build and maintain our ships. Forget neutronium barges; it's a headache and a half just moving cargo around."

Conrad said, "This fax shortage sounds like a bit of an issue. It going to get any better?"

Bascal paused for a pregnant moment, then answered, "Not right away, no."

"It's going to get worse?"

Instead of answering directly, the king said, "We've got mitigation strategies in place. We still have the memory core from *Newhope,* and we'll be instituting a program of twice-decadely backups for every citizen."

"How big is that core?" Conrad pressed. "Our population is growing now, and not slowly. How many full human images can it hold?"

Again, Bascal didn't answer directly. What he said was, "When it fills, there are other things we can do. Unfortunately, building new memory cores is another big problem, like building fax machines. It's more than just a big block of wellstone, you understand. Our need for core modules is reduced anyway, if we can solve the underlying fax problem first. So although it may not look like it, our little society here is directing all its efforts in that direction. Supporting the people who support the industries that support the fabrication of new print plates."

And all this sounded perfectly reasonable, which meant nothing, because Conrad knew Bascal too well. He looked his old friend up and down, finding nothing amiss, but even so he said, "You've got some master plan, Bascal, which involves pain for the rest of us. But you haven't invited our input. Have you even informed the Senate? Or are they ignorant cogs in this great machine of yours?"

Bascal sighed, flashing a disappointed smile. "*Et tu Brute?* Once again, my best friend in all creation fails to invest me with his trust? This is my job, Conrad: running the colony. For the good of everyone, including yourself. And it's you who've refused my invitations to dinner. Your input *has* been invited."

"I trust you to do what you think is right, Majesty," Conrad said, and found that he was also grinning, if a bit uneasily. "In the largest sense, over geological time. I trust you to be good to people when you feel you can afford it. I trust you to work hard, and to think hard about the problems we face. But you have a tendency to cut things close, to skirt disaster, and in the context of a whole society this could get pretty serious. Someone could *die,* irretrievably, with no copies or backups to take their place."

Bascal's look turned even gloomier. "Someone already has, boyo. One of the quarry kids down south. Never touched a fax machine in his life, not since the day he was born, and there was no stored record even of that. He'd already started to rot by the time they got him to the nearest hospital, and yes, the whole thing could have been averted if they'd had a fax machine on-site at the quarry. He was a *real person,* with dreams and hobbies and everything, and his death is very much on my head. You think I don't feel that every day? You think it doesn't weigh me down?"

Conrad was aghast. "Can't they read his brain or something? Reconstruct his memories? Print a generic human with his genome, and stuff as much of him back into it as they possibly can?"

Such things had been done before, back in the Queendom, on rare occasions when things had gone badly wrong. Conrad had fallen victim to death and rot himself during that first slipshod planetfall, but it had never occurred to him that such problems might still exist, after a hundred and twenty years of development!

Bascal simply shook his head. "We don't have the right equipment for that. Not now, not for a while. The hospital's got the body on ice, or more specifically, on liquid nitrogen. There is hope for this boy, sometime in the indefinite future. We can probably construct some humanesque entity that believes it's him. His name was Bill, by the way. Bill Edison Chuang. He played the piano and studied dead languages."

"My gods," Conrad said. And then, because he couldn't think of anything else to say, he said it again. Perhaps Bruno and Tamra were right to worry! As an economic indicator, surely death made a telling statement. Society's ultimate failure: losing the lives and continuities of its people.

"Nobody told us this would be safe," Bascal said gently but firmly. "We broke the law, and they shipped us here, and the wording of the edict makes it clear that they expect us to return when the sentence expires, with our tails between our legs and our heads bowed in humility. Or they *did*, anyway. I don't think the Queendom government—my parents or anyone else—had any illusions about what they were doing to us, what they were sending us into. And yet, here we are, making do."

"Why wasn't this in the news? This death."

"It was, but most people missed it. The kid didn't know anybody, not really. And his parents have declined to make a fuss. It really wasn't anybody's fault—just one of those things. If you live long enough, something improbable will happen. He just beat the odds early."

"How comforting. Maybe he's with God now, eh? Better off?"

"I didn't say that, and don't you get sarcastic with me. We all have our jobs. If you do yours and I do mine, and everyone stays focused and we face these dangers bravely, we'll get through this. All of us." He looked at the ceiling, and said, "Palace, bring in my family, please."

"As you wish, Sire," the ceiling answered.

There was a slight crackling from the fax machine, and three robots staggered out of it, one of them human sized and the other two perhaps half as tall. And these robots were not household servants. Conrad didn't know *what* they were, but they moved slowly, with drunken steps and lurches. Their bodies and heads and faces were featureless gold, or something colored like gold, but it was all scratched up, no longer quite so shiny, and they were even dented in places, as if the fax machine had declined to repair their accumulated wear and tear. They were suffering from the robotic equivalent of geriatry.

Conrad had met an "emancipated" robot like this once before. It was Hugo, a sort of pet that King Bruno had kept in his own palace on Earth. A robot cut off from the larger world, its calculations restricted to the hypercomputers in its own wellmetal skull. Left to fend for itself, to find its own way in the world. To be, in a limited way, a kind of person.

The larger robot had vague swellings on its chest, a suggestion of femaleness, and in a kind of parody it staggered over and clanked itself down on the arm of Bascal's chair.

One of the smaller robots came and sat down at his feet; the other wandered around the room, turning its blank metal face on this and that shiny object, as if entranced by the world around it.

"Please tell me this is a joke," Conrad said.

The king grinned. "Not at all, my boy. My good man, my friend. Meet my practice family, the wellmetal apples of my all-rehearsing eye. This is Matilda, and this here is little Barnaby, and his sibling Rachel. They fill the house up pleasantly, with never an argument or an ill turn of phrase. I invented them a long time ago, back onboard *Newhope* when I was desperate for company, but I've been bringing them out a lot recently. It scratches a kind of itch, exercises a muscle that gets little use these days. And no, there's nothing sick about it. Nothing sexual, nothing delusional, although I can see the perverse hope of it in your eyes."

"Hi," the large robot grunted, turning its face in Conrad's direction. "Hi. Hi. A pleasure to meet you." The words were forced, at once comical and tragic. With effort and fax tweaks you could train a wild dog to speak, too!

Conrad could only hope that the look on his face matched the bad taste in his mouth. "Do they bring your slippers for you, Bas? Do they bring you psychoactive weeds, and a pipe to smoke them in?"

"Nothing like that," the king said, clearly annoyed. "It just calms my nerves to have them around. They amuse me, help me think. I don't normally trot them out in front of people, but I thought perhaps you and I were close enough to share this moment. Are we not? If they disturb you, then you have my apology, and my promise to send them away forthwith and posthaste."

"That's not necessary," Conrad told him. He wasn't about to tell a king how to behave in his own home.

"Ah," Bascal said, "but your tone and your words speak to opposite purpose. You've been robophobic for as long as I can remember, so perhaps it was thoughtless of me to inflict these on you. Almost like having the Palace Guards back at my back again, eh?"

"No. It's nothing at all like that."

"Well, thank heaven for what mercies it can spare. Still, consider me chastised for this error. Striving for wisdom does not, by itself, make a thoughtful person of me." To the robots he said, "Off you go, family. Back to the fax, that's right."

At first, the robots didn't move. But after a moment's reflection, the female stood up again and began limping in the direction of the fax machine. One of the smaller robots got up as well, and followed behind her. The other one—Rachel, the king had called it—continued its wandering around the room, looking randomly at nothing.

Ignoring the thing, Bascal said, "They are brighter than they appear. Brighter than dogs—perhaps as bright as children. You've got half a billion years of evolution telling your brain how to organize and respond. *They* were merely printed from a factory pattern. They don't know how to be people, any more than you know how to be a hypercomputer. But they struggle, and they learn, and bit by bit their behavior improves. I find their example instructive, but if you do not, I suppose that's all right, too. Being open-minded includes allowing for others' disapproval, yes?"

"I was just surprised," Conrad said, struggling now to seem friendly rather than intrusive and rude. "I mean . . . as you say, there's nothing sick about it. Your father did the same thing. I'm sure a lot of people have. We've all got our hobbies."

"Indeed we do," Bascal agreed, though he made no move to call the two robots back as they vanished into the fax. The third continued to wander, and be ignored. "It's very kind of you to say so. Although if you're too busy to hoist a beer in this tiny town every now and again, I'll wager you're too busy to have a hobby of your own. I suppose that contributes to your surprise, when you see someone else engaged in pointless activities for nothing more than the idle pleasure they provide."

Touché.

"And how about women?" the king asked, like a dozer driver suddenly changing gears. "Any interesting interests you can tell your dear old friend about? Like any good citizen, I'm voyeuristically concerned about how much of what is being had in my kingdom."

"Nothing permanent, I'm afraid," Conrad said, and the two of them shared a laugh, because it was a running joke between them. Permanence, ha! Conrad went on, "Besides, who's new around here, anyway?"

"The young ones," Bascal said with a leer. "But I don't have to tell you that, eh? If rumor is to be believed—and I fervently hope so, for that's its function!—then you are a man who knows his way around the nursery."

These two had known each other a long time, but even so Conrad blushed. "Your flattery...appalls me, Sire. If I want painful truths, I'll look in a mirror. And how about you? Are there any would-be queens sniffing around? It does get kind of unseemly after a while, having a bachelor king. There will come a day, my friend, when you've slept with every one of your female subjects. And that's half the population who will never listen to you again. If you settle down, you can at least preserve some mystique."

"Now, now," the king said seriously. "I'm more selective than that. I have to be. As you say, my position requires it. And yes, now that you mention it, there is someone special entering upon the stage. Someone *quite* special, of whom I think you would approve."

"Do I know her?"

"I'm not sure," Bascal said. "She was a revolutionary, but not in our bunch. She didn't unpack until the third year, and she spends most of her time in Bupsville. Her name is Nala Rishe."

Conrad thought about it and said, "It doesn't ring a bell. How is it I've never heard about this?"

"Well, you seem to have missed a lot of news," Bascal told him. "Working too hard, yes? But also we've kept it quiet, off the TV and such. There are only six reportants on the planet, and only two who handle palace gossip, so it's not like we have to fool a whole Queendom of paparazzi. Nala has reason to visit the palace anyway, mostly lobbying for the Bupsville agriculturists, so the speculation hasn't been any more or less than you'd see for other visitors."

"Ah. Is she nice?"

"Nicer than I deserve. You should meet her sometime. Have your house call mine and we'll set something up."

Slyly: "And she knows about this robot fetish of yours?"

"Actually, she's got one of her own to add to the collection. I guess you'd call him the daddy robot. Named Herschel, after the astronomer."

"Hmm. Well. That does sound nice. I'd like to meet her, yes. Let me get the Gravittoir up and running and this stupid tuberail switch under way. A couple of days, and I'll be a much freer man."

Bascal's smile lost some of its warmth. "There are other architects, you know. You don't have to build this entire world yourself. You're entitled to take some time off, and in fact you should. Everyone should. Idle hands do the devil's work—any space pirate knows that!—but we oughtn't gravitate to the opposite pole. We can't afford to, or our children will simply rebel once again, and the cycle will never end. We've got to build a better society than that. It can have flaws—even dangerous flaws—but if it doesn't have room for the finer things, my boy, then what's the point?"

"I know," Conrad said. "Truly, I've been planning to slow things down. You've met my assistant, Mack Duggins? A troll, about yea high? He's really coming along. He's ready for more responsibility, and I'm nearly ready to give it to him. And then I'll have time, I promise."

"Hmm," Bascal said, unconvinced.

Conrad sighed, then felt his lips curve upward again. "Listen, Bas. If you want to see more of me, why don't you hire me to redo this house? It was all well and fine as a freshman effort, stretching my wings and all that, but it does look pretty damned silly now."

"Hey, I like my house," Bascal objected.

"Oh, it's all right, but it lacks . . . grandeur. Or rather, the grandeur it's got is rather childish. Painted on rather than woven through the bones."

"It's perfect, Conrad. I've always loved it."

"At least let me do the exterior. Just let me reprogram the tiles."

"Conrad, I said no. The hardest thing an artist has to learn is letting go of his creations. Poetry taught me that much. You have it for a while, this little piece of love and bloodsweat, but sooner or later you kick it out into the world, and then it *belongs* to the world. Hands off, you understand?"

"Yes, Sire," Conrad answered grumpily. "You're one to talk, though. We haven't seen a poem from you in a long, long time. That's one way to avoid loosing something on the world that could later embarrass you. But it's not a good way."

The king studied his fingernails. "We've all got our jobs to do. I get busy as well. And I just haven't found the . . . inspiration. Perhaps my muse was the Queendom of Sol itself. Or perhaps not, but in any case the muse doesn't seem to have followed me here. I haven't felt her at my elbow, urging me onward, begging to see the next line. I don't know why, really. I suppose I've just moved on. In a way, the 'Song of Physics' kind of closed things out for me. After that, there just hasn't seemed to be much of importance left to say."

"Well, that's a shame," Conrad said, though in truth he felt much the same about the Orbital Tower. Of all the projects in his past, that was the only one he still dreamed about. Part of him seemed to wish that job had never ended, or even—perversely!—that he'd died after completing it. His crowning achievement, his denouement, his swan song. But with an infinite future ahead of him, there was no reason to think that was truly his finest hour. The best was, almost by definition, yet to come.

He picked up his wine goblet and drank from it, savoring its atomically perfect bouquet and finish. Oh, for a medical-grade fax machine of his own! "I always liked your poetry. I still do. Is it your muse, by the way, that keeps you from naming the planet? Are we stuck with 'P2' forever?"

"Ah, that. Hmm. Yes, well, it may be my muse," Bascal answered. "Or perhaps I'm just waiting for the right confluence of events. I don't want to give this world the *wrong* name just because you're impatient. As an immorbid, I won't be forced, I won't be rushed. But no, it won't always be Planet Two. That's not a home. It doesn't speak to the soul."

"Well, don't wait forever. More than two-thirds of the current population was born here. It *is* their home. You'll reach a point where the old name just sticks."

"Maybe so."

The idea seemed to sap some of Bascal's energy. Which of course made Conrad feel guilty for raising a sensitive issue. Some friend he'd turned out to be.

"Listen," he said in a lighter tone, "you seem to have a spare copy of yourself, or if not you can print another. And I'm free. Mack has the construction site for the day, so if you'd like to raise a few glasses, or ingest some other recreational substance, I'm at your disposal."

"Yes?" Bascal arched an eyebrow. "Truly? Well, that's historic. The first architect, come to visit these humble artless walls for something more than business? We'd better get started, then, boyo. With years to make up for, you'll have to be carried home by Palace Guards. You dislike them, I know, but nothing spells 'party' like having them cart off the unconscious bodies."

And the trouble was, Bascal was serious about that. Conrad would never shake the memory of those Guards: monsters of gleaming impervium, at least as graceful as household servants and yet also deadly, packed with weaponry, full of suspicion, and always keyed up for violent action. He would never love them, even for saving his life.

One of the most symbolic things Bascal had done as king was to send his Guards away. No more would they loom behind him, following him, logging his every move, and every move by anyone else within harm's reach. But here in the palace, visible or not, they were only a fax away from instantiation. For practical purposes they were waiting behind that print plate as if it were no more than a curtain. Bascal really did use them to toss out drunks, and to escort people back to their residences if they'd worn out their welcome. And Palace Guards were not known for their gentleness.

"Sounds like a good time," Conrad said, forcing a smile. And hell, he did need a night off, and the company of an old friend. And for that matter a good drugging—one which didn't involve the seduction of some tender young morsel who hadn't the sense to know better. How long had it been since he'd just gotten stupid, for no reason and with no goal in mind? More sincerely, he said, "In fact, my liege, it sounds like a better time than I've had in years."

#### chapter fifteen

the king's ransom

Sixty-six months later almost to the day, Conrad was in the study of his home, inloading mental notes on the latest crop of nonprogrammable materials the southern factories were turning out. Inloading other people's notes could be a real problem—some people got sick, got headaches, sometimes even went crazy and needed to fax a fresh body before they could think clearly again. But the process had never bothered Conrad. He was not a brilliant man, and at times there were real advantages in this.

The stuff that was personal, tied up with the feelings and memories of the individuals who recorded it, he was able simply to ignore. It didn't jam its way into his head or anything. It didn't confuse him. The rest of it, the factual side, well ... he mostly forgot that as well, but it left behind general impressions, so that if he ever needed a particular thing, a material or product or specialized idea, he would at least know whether it existed or not, and where he might go to look it up.

Still, the process was tiring, and after a few hours he gave up, set the neural halo aside, and just sat there at his office table, sipping from a mug of red tea and looking out the window, down over the shops and homes, the apartments and warehouses sloping down to the bay. It was late in the after-pids; the sun was setting behind him, behind the mountains, and its ruddy glare on the smog-colored clouds was arrestingly beautiful. Perhaps his brain was sorting what it had learned, or perhaps it needed some quiet time to recover its faculties, or perhaps Conrad was simply lazy. Whether he sat there for twenty minutes or an hour he never knew, as the sun moved only a hair's width in the sky. The long day on P2 rivaled even that of Venus, and its sunset was a long, drawn-out affair. But at some point along the way the house interrupted him with a visitor chime.

He looked up. "Hmm? What?"

"A visitor," the house said, daring to speak.

"Oh, well, show her in."

It did not occur to him that the visitor might be male, and in this he was neither surprised nor disappointed, because his front door opened, and his study door opened, and a lighted walkway appeared in the wellstone of the floor, with moving colors indicating the proper direction of travel, just in case his visitor was painfully stupid. She appeared in Conrad's doorway: a young woman with blonde hair, brown eyes, and skin the color of almond shells. Her only garment was a skin-tight wellcloth leotard, colored bright green and stretched over her with quite obviously nothing beneath. Conrad felt a shock of familiarity on seeing her, but he couldn't quite place the face. Or the body.

"Oh, hello," he said. "How are you this evening?"

The woman looked him up and down, saying nothing.

"I've, ah, misplaced your name."

"I haven't given it," she said, with the vaguely superior air that young people had when they thought they were being smart. Conrad peered at her more closely, studying her features. Something about her made him think of Bascal, and he asked her, "Are you the king's girlfriend? Nala Rishe, the lobbyist?"

The young woman's laugh was cool and self-assured, more amused than friendly. "No, sorry. Do you want me to be?" She ran her hands down her body in a suggestive but rather exaggerated way, and Conrad realized she was younger than he'd thought at first. Hers was not the body of a twenty or twenty-five-year-old, like most of the people in the kingdom who were current in their fax ups. On closer inspection, he supposed she had never yet seen her twenties. She was still in the bloom of adolescence, burning with hormones and yet lacking the experience to deploy them wisely. He rethought his conversational approach, and said, "I've been reading for hours, young lady, and I'm in no mood for riddles or parlor games. Who are you, exactly?"

"Princess Wendy de Towaji Lutui Rishe," she said through a smirk, in tones suggesting he should've known this before she even walked through his door.

Conrad blinked. He blinked again. "Princess. Bascal's *daughter*? He never told me about...he never said...my goodness. How old are you, girl? When were you born?"

"Yesterday," she said, as though it were a point of pride.

Conrad digested that. Yesterday? Little gods, the faxwise birthing of fully formed teenagers had always seemed sensible enough to him—why bother with the awkward preliminaries, just because nature commanded it? His own early childhood had been mostly dull—he could barely remember it now—and anyway lots of other animals were born mature, able to walk and eat and communicate. It was only an accident of biology that the human birth canal was so much narrower than the fully grown human brain.

But then again, Conrad was usually introduced to these fax children in their fifth or eighth or tenth year of actual physical life. Newborns belonged at home, right? Confronted with one now, a baby already in the full flower of sexual maturity, he found himself offended on her behalf. Something important, if intangible, had been denied this girl. This thought was not to his credit, surely—it would mark him a naturalist pig in some circles—but there it was.

His voice was careful. "What can I do for you, Princess Wendy? Shouldn't you be at home studying entry-level humanities? Dressing, hygiene, that sort of thing? Gathering up the love of your new parents?"

"I do what I want," she said simply. "The job of youth is to shake things up, and I can't do that from home. All my life

I've felt a higher purpose calling, and when I heard Father complaining about you, it just felt right. It seemed important that I meet you. You're a space pirate; you defied the Queendom of Sol."

It was Conrad's turn to laugh. "That was centuries ago, little girl. I'm an architect now. The greatest architect in the world, owing to there being so few people in it. I challenge society through my work, striving for that perfect balance of beauty and strength and functionality. And always on a limited budget. It's been a long time since I shook things up any other way."

She was looking him over again, studying every detail of him with weird intensity. Behind her eyes Conrad could sense a hungry brain, frustrated with its own limitations and absorbing knowledge through every available channel, however imperfect. And there was, yes, a sexual component to her scrutiny as well. The clumsy sexuality of a child, laid open for him to see. He felt ashamed at that, as though she were naked and didn't even know it, and he had not found the decency to avert his eyes.

"It sounds as though I've arrived just in time, then," she cooed. "It sounds like you need a little shaking up yourself."

"Stop right there," Conrad said, holding up his hands. "No one has taught you how to behave, and how could they? But my dear, this isn't proper. There will be no touching, no attempts at clever innuendo. Believe me, this scene will later embarrass you if you don't quit it."

She studied him some more, looking wounded but brave, and very quietly angry. Finally, after uncomfortably long, she said, "What do you know about death?"

"Death?"

"Death. *Maté*. The end of life."

"It's to be avoided," Conrad said carefully. "I've died a couple of times myself, and it's always a wrenching experience. You lose a great deal, and the worst is that you never know exactly what you've lost. Precious things, surely. Irreplaceable." And thinking of her, he added silently, *You can lose things you've never even had, baby girl, and miss them all your life.*

But she was shaking her head. "No, I mean real death. The kind where you don't wake up."

"Aren't you a little young to be thinking about this?"

"I'm a good judge of what's important," she lectured. "I've been listening to my father, and I hear the worry in his voice. He's building some kind of freezertorium down in the south, on the Peninsulum Pectoralis. For bodies. Dead bodies."

"But only one person has died," Conrad pointed out. "Why would we need a 'freezertorium'?"

"One person? Is that what he told you?" Now her laugh was knowing, and raw with the sting of his rejection. "It's more than one person, Mr. Greatest Architect in the World."

"Really?" he asked skeptically. "How many, exactly?"

She didn't answer, and he took that as a sign that she didn't know. Kids were always spouting off, trying to sound important. It didn't mean a damned thing.

Then a bit of plaintiveness crept into her voice. "Don't you want this body?" She cupped her breasts, her crotch. "It's fresh. It's *intact*. You have a reputation, sir, and a girl has needs."

Conrad shuddered. "My dear, I may be a womanizer. I may even be a cradle robber, but I do have my limits. My scruples. For God's sake, you were born yesterday. And anyway you're the daughter of my best friend, which in polite society means no fuffing of any kind. You'll understand things like this when you've had more time to . . . take your bearings."

That made her angrier, but there was an impotent quality to her glare. She couldn't force the issue, and she knew it. "I'm too much for you anyway. And you're a naturalist pig."

"I'm calling your father," Conrad told her. Then said to the ceiling, "Call Bascal."

Evidently, the king was busy; it took nearly half a minute for the call to patch through. When it did, the king answered with a full hologram, appearing like a saintly vision in the space between Conrad and Wendy.

"Yes? Ah, Conrad. Good to hear from you. You haven't seen a young girl wandering around by any chance, have you?"

"She's here with me now," Conrad said.

"Hi, Daddy."

Bascal's translucent image turned, eyebrows arching with surprise. "*Malo e leilei*, Wendy. You must tell us before you leave the house like this, all right? You had us worried, and we don't like to worry."

"Don't try to control me, Daddy. I do what I want."

"Hoy!" the king said. "Do you indeed? We'll just see about that, girlie. We shall just have to see about that."

"Oh, Daddy. You can't hold on forever. I've got business to attend to, a pair of wings that need spreading. Don't make me hate you, please."

Bascal turned to Conrad with an exasperated look. "They grow up so fast, don't they? Keep her there, please, if you would. I'm sending the Guards to fetch her. In fact, scratch that. I'll come with them. I complain that you don't visit me enough, but when was the last time I came to see *you*? Give me about fifteen minutes."

The hologram winked out. It would've been nice if he'd *asked* to come over, but Conrad supposed a king—even the tin-pot king of a pair of overgrown villages—was not accustomed to having to ask. Where in the world would he be unwelcome?

In the ensuing silence, Conrad and Wendy looked at each other, neither one knowing what to say.

"You make me feel old," Conrad offered finally.

"You are old," she replied without venom. "I checked."

"Did you? Very enterprising. With proper maintenance, the energy of the body never fades, but I suppose the energy of the soul is a different matter. I can feel the verdant fires burning inside you from all the way over here."

Warily: "Is that a compliment?"

The glib answer would have been yes. But was it true? Deciding there was little point in lying to children, he answered, "I don't know. Just an observation, I guess."

And then for some reason her lower lip was quivering. Her eyes began to redden, to leak tears, and in another few seconds she was bawling. "I just wanted to go out...I just wanted..."

Conrad had seen reactions like this often enough in the women he loved, and through long practice he knew the correct response: he spread his arms wide. And then, when she didn't step into them, he moved forward and pulled her into a hug.

"Shush. Shush. It's all right, Wendy. Nobody knows what they're doing—not really. There isn't a script for us to read from. There has never been a person exactly like you, or a situation exactly like this, so how could you know what to do? We just make it up, every time, every day of our lives."

She made a token struggle but did not pull away. She badly needed a hug, whether she could admit it or not. They stood like that for several minutes, and yes, she did manage to calm down, so he pulled some chairs out and they sat. He offered her a mug of red tea then, and she accepted, and they sat there at the table, staring out the window, across the city and down toward the sunlit waters.

The distant world of Van de Kamp hovered near the horizon, visible even now in broad daylight, its pinpoint glare twinned by a reflection in the calm waters of the bay. Gatewood was sometimes visible in the daytime, too, but you had to know where to look.

"Nice view," she told him, with apparent sincerity.

"Some people say I stole the best spot in town, before the streets were even laid out. I suppose it's true. You should see the lights at night. Or the stars, or the sunrise. Or a thunderstorm, with mist devils twirling out on the water. It's always beautiful here."

He watched her drink that in, her eyes lighting up with imagination. "Did you design the house yourself? Especially for this site?"

"Yeah. A long time ago. Really long."

"It's nice."

"Thank you very much. Coming from someone with so little basis for comparison, a compliment like that can come only from the heart. You have a good heart, don't you, Wendy?"

She shrugged, looking uncomfortable again. "I guess so. I mean, how would I know?"

Conrad laughed. It was a good question—exactly the sort that was supposed to pop out of the mouths of young children. "Put it this way," he told her. "I think you would know if you didn't. For all your tough talk, you do seem to have a sense of social duty. That's a good sign, especially for a princess."

A bit of anger stole back into her features. "A permanent princess. I'll never be the ruler of anything."

He shrugged. "I don't know. Your father used to say the same thing, but life is long and full of surprises. Anyway, is being a queen such a great job, really? Your, uh, your grandmother claims otherwise. Maybe you'll meet her someday, and she can tell you all about it."

"Great. That's a great comfort to me, Mr. Mursk. You really know how to cheer a girl up."

"Okay," he said, sighing. He'd just met this newly minted person, and should not presume to solve her problems for her. Like his own long-ago teenage angst, it had a solid basis in reality. And unlike the brash young Conrad, Wendy had no real context for judging her circumstances. It was all new to her; she was waking up and looking around, finding the world not entirely to her liking but having no idea what to do about it. *Welcome to life, baby girl.*

Like a solar sailor in a difficult turn, he shifted his mirrors and tried a different approach. "Listen, Wendy, you should come by my office sometime. Just ask directions from any block of wellstone; the place is no harder to find than this house. I'll introduce you to a nice young man, and maybe he'll show you around. He's not *too* nice, you understand—he has his own way of doing things. But I gather that won't be a problem for you. It must be...very exciting, seeing everything for the first time like this."

She shrugged again. "I guess. It all seems kind of normal."

Ah, youth. A child could grow up in the fires of hell itself and still consider it normal.

"Take my word for it, then. This is a magic time which will never be repeated no matter how long you live. In later years you'll look back and wish you had treasured it more."

She looked at him for several seconds, then asked, "Why do old people always say stuff like that?"

Conrad thought for a while before answering. "Because it's

true, I suppose. Because we hope to be listened to, though we know we will not."

Was he really as old as all that? Did it show? Had he dug himself into so deep a rut that any break in the routine was this unsettling? He was *philosophizing*, for crying out loud. Conrad Mursk, the ne'er-do-well space pirate and summer camp hooligan! But no, that was hardly fair to the original Conrad Mursk, who had never asked to grow up into... what? A man who worked hard all the time, never playing, decade in and decade out?

It was a troubling thought, and it panicked him so greatly that when Bascal finally arrived, the first thing Conrad said to him as he stood in the doorway—flanked by a pair of looming Guards—was, "I need a new job, Bas. Your Majesty, Sire, I need to be someplace far away. Your daughter here—who by the way you should've told me about!—has persuaded me that my life needs shaking up. And she's correct. How did I not see this? Why didn't you tell me?"

"Um, I did," the king said, blinking. "Didn't I?"

"Can you get me out of here? Bas, I need adventure, or anyway I need change. Sudden, dramatic change—the kind that keeps a person young."

"But you're the greatest architect in the world," the king protested. "You're *building* a world for the rest of us to inhabit. It's what you always wanted, right? You had to come six light-years to achieve it!"

"I wanted it, yes, but not forever. Not some unchanging rut to last me all through eternity. Have I never thought this through before? There has to be something *next*, doesn't there? Or my life is over, and the fact that I'll never die becomes an actual liability."

"May I come in?" Bascal asked with mock impatience.

"Oh. Sorry, yes." But Conrad, lost in his thoughts, continued to block the doorway. "You've said it yourself: there are other architects. I don't have to build the whole world. If I'm going to live forever then I should be out there, experiencing things. Right? Maybe my childish ambitions are something I'm supposed to outgrow. We used to be *pirates*, for crying out loud. Every day a new adventure."

Laughing, Bascal nudged Conrad out of the way and stepped inside. One hulking Palace Guard trailed in behind him. "That wasn't what you said at the time, boyo. You were a miserable mutineer who never stopped trying to get us out of that business. And you were successful in the end, if I recall correctly. We were caught and punished. Did you forget that part? Or sleep through it?"

"I was a fool, then. Just get me away from here, away from myself, so I can't fall back into this habit. Send me somewhere. Make it an order, a proclamation."

"Okay, okay. Calm down." The king pulled out a chair and sat down next to Wendy. "As it happens, I know of a job which just opened up, for which you're uniquely qualified. Yesterday I wouldn't have dreamed of asking, but it seems the situation has changed. How would you like to work in space again?"

"Perfect," Conrad said, seizing on it and nodding vigorously. "The stars, the vacuum . . . When do I start?"

"Four days. Actually, ninety-seven pids. *Fuck* I hate this planet's clock. It's three months from now, all right? On December first."

"You *designed* the clock, Bas."

"God designed it, my boy, to keep this place from ever quite feeling like home."

"Hey, what about me?" Wendy protested from the kitchen. "Mr. Mursk, you said you had a young man for me. You said you'd show me around, or he would, or something. You just got done telling me how that pirate stuff was all in the past. What were you, lying?"

Bascal looked from Conrad to Wendy and back again. "It sounds as though I missed something. Perhaps something better missed, something a good father ought not to want to know. Wendy, fear not, I will order Conrad to keep his promises to you, provided they are honorable. And Conrad, with this Guard as my witness, I do hereby legally request your presence at Skyhook Station at the top of the Gravittoir, there to travel to Bubble Hood, for rendezvous with your ship. I can't make it an order, much as I'd like to, but my suggestions have considerable impact on those who disregard them."

"Fine," Conrad said, allowing himself to relax. The situation was fixable. In fact, he had all of eternity to fix it, and this was just the first step. "What's the job?"

Bascal smiled wickedly. "Why, first mate of the QMS *Newhope*. She's got a systemwide procurement tour coming up, and I need someone onboard I can trust to speak for me. The captain is an old girlfriend of yours, I'm afraid, but that's just the sort of problem we immorbids have to put up with in life. So? What do you think?"

Conrad mulled it over for about a tenth of a second before saying, "With this Guard as my witness, Sire, I accept."

And thus was sealed the fate of a planet.

chapter sixteen

a death in the mines

Various events transpired, some interesting but most rather dull and repetitive, adding little to the collection of memories and impulses and rote responses which called itself Conrad Mursk. But life is long, and in the fullness of time Conrad found himself screaming, covered in blood, furiously uploading notes into a neural halo as his internal pressure dropped and the lights around him dimmed. He stopped screaming, and then he stopped breathing, and moments later he was stepping out of *Newhope*'s sole remaining fax machine, in the forward inventory.

Shit.

"Life signs went flat, so I ordered another backup," said Money Izolo, who was crouching beside the machine, performing some sort of routine maintenance again. "Sorry, man."

Shit. Double shit. Murdered again, right when he was at his most charming. Conrad was slow to anger these days, but he surprised himself—and Money—by slamming the wall hard with his fist, shattering several bones with an audible and decidedly painful crack. Then of course he just had to step into the fax again, to correct the damage. He had grown accustomed, as in the old days, to having the fax right here at hand. It really did change your outlook, your self-image, your views on pain and injury. Still, death was never a thing to be taken lightly.

He turned a baleful gaze on Money Izolo. "Should you be messing with that thing while I'm printing? If you fuff up the wrong thing at the wrong time, could my pattern be permanently erased? Or worse, mangled?"

"There are safeguards," Money replied easily, barely pausing to glance up from his work. "The only way I could erase you is if I was trying to, and even then it would take some effort. You worry a lot, sir."

"Wouldn't you?" The observation irritated Conrad, who after all had just been violently killed. Twice!

But Money ignored that and said, "Besides, this old gal's getting cranky in her autumn years. She's lasted us well, but she's full of stripes and defects, and not even Brenda really knows how to fix those. She can take a look when we get back to the drydock at Bubble Hood, but 'old' is a hard thing to fix. What we need is a new one."

"Tell it to the miners," Conrad said, stomping out of the room.

He did manage to restrain the urge to break his hand again, but he stomped and cursed his way through the levels of *Newhope*'s tall needle, and through the mating airlock, and through the longer, twistier corridors of the thirty-kilometer-wide Inner Belt asteroid known as Element Pit. When he got to the scene of the crime, the perpetrators were still standing around, looking down at two bloody heaps of Conrad Mursk.

"That one is going to cost you," Conrad told them angrily. "Once is a moment of weakness. Or unbearable passion, which is even easier to excuse. But twice is just bad manners, and stupid besides. You may have asked yourselves why I'm not armed, why I'm not concerned once again for my safety. Have you? Have you asked yourselves that? Because it's a question very pertinent to these negotiations."

"We don't want your fuffing cash. We can't use it," said the leader of the miners, whom Conrad had never been formally introduced to, but who matched the description of Leonard Chang, the erstwhile director of these facilities. If so, then he was from Earth. More specifically, from Eastern Russia, where he'd no doubt grown up with every privilege an Earth boy could have.

It was a damn sight more privileges than an asteroid miner in Barnard could ever hope for, and Conrad's sympathies did extend that far. It was a sour deal, and there was no point trying to sell it any differently. But Planet Two needed metals (especially iron) and rare earth elements (especially neodymium), and Conrad's job was to see that they were delivered on time. And he knew as well as anyone that if he didn't succeed, things would get even worse. Even here.

"You may want to flush that voice buffer," Conrad told the man impatiently. "I've heard that, what, five times now? And very little else. Yes, you want a new element mixer. You want a new print plate for your fax machine. You want your mommy to come and kiss the boo-boos for you, but she's not coming. She told me so in bed this morning."

"You've got a foul mouth, Navy Man."

"And you've got a bloodstained wrench, Mr. Chang. I'm not in a terribly good mood, and the law takes a dim view of these things, and at this particular time and place, it so happens that *I'm the law*. Now before you start swinging those things again, you do need to ask yourselves: why is this man not armed? From the outset I was against sending armed escort along with *Newhope*. Hell, I was against arming Navy ships in the first place. I mean, who have we got to fight? But it was never my decision, and as it happens there's a commander named Ho Ng, in a ship called *Tuitake* or *King's Fist*, loitering about a megaklick downsystem from here, stealthing in the glare of Barnard.

"Maybe you've seen him on TV? Fighting in the arena? The exact weapons at his disposal right now are classified— I'm not even sure I know myself—but I have commander Ng's assurances that he can depopulate this asteroid without significant harm to its facilities or stores. And if that happens, the whole stinking lot of you can be replaced with freshly printed children who don't know enough to complain about the conditions. Is that clear? Are there any specific points I can elaborate on, to broaden or deepen your understanding?

Because against my better judgment I'm going to give you one more chance."

Conrad hated making threats, especially because he couldn't afford to make empty ones. But just now he had what Barnardean negotiators called *nima,* or "hand." Except for control over his own physical safety—a minor point at best—all the advantages were his, and he couldn't afford to take no for an answer. Thus, he meant every word he said, and in fact if the tactical situation were known to Ho Ng, Conrad would probably be ordered back to *Newhope,* and Xmary advised to withdraw the ship to a safe distance so these people could be murdered where they stood. Like most things in life, it wasn't Conrad's decision, and he really was giving these dirty-faced ladies and gentlemen a break. Out of the goodness of his own twice-murdered heart.

"Why should we believe that?" Leonard Chang demanded.

And Conrad answered him with a level gaze: "At this point, sir, I don't care if you believe it or not. But I hope your backups are current, which they would be already if you people had opened on a more conciliatory note. The matter is very close to being out of my hands, so if you like, you can just try whatever you want and see how it plays out. Or, if you're feeling useful, feeling civil and pleasant and remorseful for your crimes, you can start loading bar stock and I'll decline to report any of this. Not because I like you, but because I have a job to do, and your tragic death would interfere with it."

Not surprisingly, that really did give the miners pause. They lowered their pipes and wrenches and galley knives, and Leonard Chang looked around at them, cooling them off with a warning glare.

"Pardon me if I'm not overwhelmed with . . . your generosity," he said to Conrad. "We've got people getting injured, getting sick, getting *old* in the time it takes you Navy types to cycle back and forth to P2. There is no quality of life here, just slavery. That's the only word that describes our circumstances."

"I'm sorry you feel that way," Conrad told him sincerely. "Another way to look at it is that you all volunteered for this, and you're fuffing heroes. Or you were until a few minutes ago. Look, P2 needs those elements, and if you interfere with their flow, you might as well be dropping bombs on the planet's surface. You want to talk old age? You want to talk injury and death, Mr. Director? You need a print plate. Everybody needs a print plate. And to build a print plate—even one!—requires neodymium, and certain other materials that simply aren't found on P2. Not where we can get at them, not in meaningful quantities. But I don't have to tell you that, right?"

With that, the light went out of Chang's sails, and he slumped against the corridor wall, dropping his gaze to the floor. "We never wanted anyone to get hurt. Really. But you have to understand, Navy Man, we just can't keep this up. I wish you *would* replace us with children, fresh in body and spirit and mind. It would take them years to burn out. Decades."

"But they'd lack experience. The mine's efficiency would plummet."

"Aye. They'd lack experience. Lucky for them."

At this, in spite of everything, Conrad felt a flicker of sympathy for these men and women. Everyone had it rough these days, but certainly it was true that some had it rougher than others, through no fault of their own. And the simple fact was, Conrad had heard almost precisely the same complaints from the deutrelium refiners, the particle smashers, the antimatter runners, and even, yes, the Navy crews themselves. Everyone in space, basically. Because yeah, it was one thing to declare a state of economic emergency, and quite another to maintain it indefinitely.

"Look," he said. "You and I both know I can't get you a medical-grade fax machine. I couldn't if I wanted to, if I made it my life's work. King Bascal himself couldn't get you one, because there just aren't enough to go around. That's what 'shortage' means. But there are some older industrial models kicking around, and if I call in some favors, I could probably get you one of those. That will give you everything but your health, and your health is still, as I say, available with periodic Naval visits, as always. That's no different than people have on the surface of the planet. Well, not terribly different.

"But try to understand, sir: you hold no cards at all in this negotiation. When you speak up, when you act out, all the government of P2 hears is that you care more about yourselves than about the plight of the colony. If they find out you're cracking skulls in addition, there is probably nothing I can do. You'll be killed, and your core memory slots will be reallocated to someone more in tune with the needs of the colony. That's not a threat, just a frank observation. For me to warn you at all is an act of charity."

"Maybe you've got a good heart," one of the miners suggested, in a tone that might've been snotty or sincere, or anything in-between. It'd been a long day, and Conrad just couldn't tell anymore.

"Don't start with me again," he warned, pointing a finger at the man who'd spoken. "I'm offering two billion in cash, and first dibs on a thirdhand industrial fax. It's better than you deserve, and costly for the kingdom, but there you have it."

Now the miners were all looking at their feet, saying nothing.

"Bloody hell, people, what do you want? A kiss on the forehead? That hundred tons of bar stock isn't going to move itself. Go print up some robots and let's get moving."

The miners looked at each other and Conrad, as if uncertain what to say next. Finally, Chang piped up. "Hopefully you begin to understand our problem, Mr. Mursk. We haven't got any robots, nor the means to print them. The best fax machine we have at the moment has a print plate about the size of your chest, and it hasn't got the resolution to print a block of wellstone. Ergo, no computers, ergo no robots. Not real ones, anyway. We can automate—we *have* automated—but it's like working with grasshoppers. You can't turn your back on them, because they haven't got the slightest idea what you *want* them to do. Just what you tell them."

Conrad favored Chang with a glare, and Chang swallowed and added, "We've got some grappling servos and powered carts down on level four that help with this kind of work. I'll, uh, send Jonesey and Schrader down to fetch them."

Conrad nodded, and said to him, "Fine. And then let's take a walk, you and I. There are other serious matters to discuss."

And here, if such a thing were possible, Chang's shoulders slumped even farther. "This is about the antimatter?"

Actually, it was about taking mental notes—forcibly, if necessary—from Chang's crew, so if they absolutely had to be replaced, their replacements would have a leg up on the learning process. It was a delicate subject, better broached to them by their own management, not some stranger in a uniform. But that was an interesting response, which gained Conrad's full and immediate attention. "Walk with me," he said, with that particular quiet firmness people had a hard time ignoring.

The conversation was both brief and illuminating. "I studied metallurgy during the exile training," Chang said to him while they walked, as though that explained or excused anything. "Not matter programming, you understand, but the old-fashioned mixing and melting of actual atoms. Had to study something, right? Part of the punishment. I wish to blazes I'd studied something else, but when they thawed me out here at Barnard, I compounded the error with a short-course degree in the geology of minor planets. It seemed like such an exciting idea at the time: hollowing these little worlds, sniffing for the precious metals inside them. A treasure hunt, you see? But lo, these hundred and thirty years later, here I still am. Poorer than when I started."

"What do you want me to say?" Conrad asked impatiently. "We came here as children, but we've got to live as grown-ups. Things are what they are, and it's our responsibility—all of us—to sort it out. And we have forever to accomplish it."

"So they say," Chang grumbled, "but we've cause to doubt it here in the mines. Would you believe me if I said this place was haunted? Ghosts are invisible fossils, I've always thought—quantum impressions only an archaeologist could find. But I've got trustworthy people claiming to have seen them: dead friends, dead strangers, walking around. And it surprises me not at all. Have you ever buried a friend, Mr. Mursk? Packed her in a freezer and shipped her off to heaven knows where? Pray you never do, sir. You seem like a decent fellow, and I wouldn't wish that on you."

This was getting a bit chummy for Conrad's taste. He did have a job to do, and experience had taught him that sentimentality and clear judgment were enemies far more often than they were allies. "Let's talk about the antimatter," he said.

"It was an accident," Chang answered, much too quickly. "The mass crusher out in the L-Belt got shut down as a money sink, but twelve years ago the king was still screaming for neutronium. 'Neubles! Bring me neubles, you lazy ingrates!' And our plan seemed, you know, efficient. Hunting societies used every part of the buffalo, right? Which is not the least bit surprising, because what the hell else did they have?"

They walked through corridors tilted strangely against the artificial gravity. Some of the rock walls were polished mirror-smooth, a finish Conrad admired and also envied, since on P2 the chlorine etching—even indoors—would take the shine off a surface like that within a year. Other areas looked as though they'd been chipped out with picks and sledge-hammers, which was also interesting though certainly less aesthetic. But the contrast told him more about the troubles here than Leonard Chang's flapping mouthparts ever could.

Anyway, Conrad waited patiently for further information, meanwhile attempting to piece this man's story together in his own head. There *had* been a demand for neubles, even as recently as that, in the now seemingly foolish hope that a collapsiter grid—true teleportation, systemwide—could rescue the colony from its logistical difficulties. And since there was not a single neutronium barge here in Barnard—not one ship capable of harvesting and squeezing the worthless dust of interplanetary space, of forming it into liquid neutronium and sheathing it in diamond spheres—there had long been talk of using mine tailings instead. Every part of the buffalo, yes: very little of what was dug from these tunnels was actually useful metal. The oxygen—a primary component of the residual tailings—could of course be sold as a consumable to the other space industries and facilities, or burned with hydrogen to produce water, which generally brought a slightly higher per-kilo price. But what did the colony need with more carbon, more silicon, more lithium and sulfur? Squeezing it into neutronium was a logical—if costly—alternative.

But Conrad had spent a bit of time on Mass Industries barges back in his youth—enough to know that you couldn't squeeze neutronium on any sort of piston or anvil. You could *start* that way—people generally did—but by itself that would never get you anywhere near the required pressures or densities. For that, you needed an antimatter explosion, and therefore more-than-modest supplies of stabilized positronium in quantum confinement. That was pretty much all Conrad knew, but it was enough for him to smell a rat, to sense the outlines of the trouble Leonard Chang had tried to conceal here.

"You thought you had escaped inquiry," he probed. This was one of his stock phrases, and since almost everyone had something to hide somewhere along the way, it almost always yielded interesting results.

This time was no exception; Chang quickened his pace and got in front of Conrad, turning to look him straight in the eye. "Sir, our official report was truthful. There was an unintended explosion in the blasting chamber, fortunately mitigated by a suspension of carbonaceous dust in the air, which absorbed a lot of the gamma and X. Kept the asteroid from cracking into little shards, eh? But it involved *all* of our positronium. On my honor, I swear to you, every molecule of that material was accounted for."

"Antimatter must never fall into the hands of noncertified personnel," Conrad warned, though he still had no idea what was going on.

"It hasn't, sir, I swear to you. Our books and facilities are open to your inspection."

"I know they are," Conrad said seriously. And then, on a hunch, "You're taking me to the blasting chamber now?"

"Yes sir," Chang said, "because I want you to understand. Other than the accident itself, we have been meticulous. When you've seen it I think you'll agree we've done all that we reasonably could."

"Except tell the truth," Conrad replied.

And Chang found something interesting down at his feet, and studied their backward stride a little before answering, "Aye. Except that."

And here the corridor bent through a sharp turn whose floor seemed even more particularly tilted against the gravity, and from there it all opened out into a large chamber. Conrad's first thought was that it was a hundred meters or so across, but as he followed the bright lights fading off into the distance, he realized the chamber was in fact a polished sphere at least a kilometer in diameter. The blasting chamber, yes. Bigger than the interior of a neutronium barge, but certainly not too big for the job at hand: containing the explosive conversion of matter and antimatter into pure energy. And yet, for some reason at clear odds with this purpose, a sort of transparent axle or conduit ran from the ceiling of the sphere to the floor beneath—a hollow cylinder of diamond, bathed in white light. And at the center of this tube was a deformity of some sort: an invisible pinpoint distorting the view all around it, bending light rays into double and triple rainbows, puckering the entire geometry of the room.

Conrad cursed in his parents' Gaelic, which, being a passionate language, was finely honed for such things. Then, just to be sure, he cursed in Bascal's Tongan.

"Yeah," said Chang, with probably as much rue as a man's voice could safely hold. "I know it."

"You've been concealing a *black hole* in your mine. For twelve years."

"We slipped a decimal point in the ordnance calculations," Chang said defensively. "Well, we slipped several. But accidents happen everywhere, right? And I hasten to add, this is a *safe* black hole, relatively speaking. It's got about half a neuble's mass on it; so its event horizon is too small to swallow protons, obviously, or Element Pit wouldn't be here, and this conversation wouldn't be happening. We'd've been crushed through the eye of yonder needle within a few minutes of the accident that birthed it."

"Uh-huh," Conrad agreed, fighting hard not to appear surprised. Ideally, he should seem to be a step or two ahead of anything a rogue like Chang might do or say.

"But it can take in two or three electrons before the like-charge repulsion starts holding them out," Chang went on, "so it's a charged particle, and an ordinary magnetic fusion bottle is sufficient to contain it. It's funny, if you think about it, that the charge of one electron can hold up a billion tons of mass. But it's a lucky thing, eh? Gravity is weak enough to be toyed with; electromagnetism just *is*."

"This is a serious fuckup," was all Conrad could think to say.

"Aye, sir. We're well aware."

"I expect you are," Conrad began, and would have launched into a longer lecture on the propriety of concealing one's fuckups from the authorities who might actually be able to do something about them. He would have done this, yes, had his curiosity not gotten the better of him. "What's the radius of that tube?" he asked instead.

Chang looked puzzled by the question. "About five meters. Why?" And then understanding dawned, and he said, "Up close, the gravity is about two gee. You can stand on the outside of the tube, yes, if you're right next to the node. It will attract you, but not crush you. The tube was sized specifically to prevent accidents of that sort. Let me tell you, sir, no one has ever been killed by that thing. Mining is a dangerous pastime with a hundred different ways to bite your ass, but that particular dragon is muzzled."

" 'The node'?"

"That's what we call it, sir. Node one."

"Optimistic of you."

Chang simpered. "Thank you, sir. With seven more nodes, at twice the mass of course, we hope one day to build a collapson and present it to His Majesty as a gift."

"A noble sentiment, to be sure," Conrad said, and while he fought to keep a tone of official sarcasm in his voice, he couldn't avoid a slight touch of admiration as well. A collapson was a stable cube of eight black holes, and in their dozens or hundreds or thousands they were the critical components of a telecom collapsiter. Such a gift would be worth . . . well, a lot. If you were going to fuck up, you might as well do it on a colossal scale, and with style. But at that moment his curiosity burned brighter than his sense of duty, and so, casting all further pleasantries aside, he ordered, "Turn off the gravity lasers in this part of the rock, please."

"Sir," Chang said, in tones of ritual objection, "that will cause problems—"

Conrad, who knew all about ritual objection, interrupted with, "Will it create a specific safety hazard, Mr. Chang? If people are properly warned and equipment is properly locked down, will anyone be hurt or anything broken?"

"Well, not that I specifically know of, but—"

"Then do as I ask. You may consider it an official order from His Majesty, in the person of myself, his voice here on Element Pit. More importantly, though, it's in your professional interest to keep me supplied with the information I seek. Or has my identity escaped your attention?"

"Eh? Commander C. E. Mursk, Royal Barnardean Navy. On my honor, sir, I'm not following your intent."

"The C. E. stands for Conrad Ethel."

"Does it?"

Though he hated any form of boasting, Conrad said, "I see my reputation has failed to precede me. I am, among other things, the First Architect of Barnard."

Chang still looked baffled. "Are you? Truly? What the fuff would you be doing out here?"

This was an excellent question, because really, economic crisis or no, was this a good use of his time? Bullying weasels like Chang? What he said was, "At the moment, I'm taking a professional interest in your little accident up there."

"And . . . what? You want to build something? You can *have* the thing, sir, if it'll be any use—"

"Oh, do shut up, Mr. Director, and try a bit of dignity on for size. I just want a look at it."

Chang wrung his hands together. "If you are who you say, sir, I'll put my folks right on it."

"You would anyway," Conrad snapped. And then regretted it, not for Chang's sake but for his own. That was the sort of veiled threat he despised when it came from people like Ho

Ng, so why was it popping out of his own mouth? When, exactly, had Maybel Mursk's little boy become such a Security thug? Still, the words had the desired effect; Chang quieted. "Just turn the grav lasers off, all right?"

The man just nodded, and scurried off to do his master's bidding.

#### chapter seventeen

the economics of hole

Half an hour later, Conrad and Money, Chang and the mine's vice-director, a woman named Mariella Fourleaf, were standing on the surface of the black hole's confinement tube like pins stuck into a cushion, pointing every which way. It was like the world's smallest, weirdest planette, and Conrad filed for future reference the notion that planettes could be made cylindrical as well as spherical. All you would need was a hollow diamond tube, much thinner than this one, holding the neubles in a straight line, so they couldn't roll over each other and slump into the spherical shape they would otherwise naturally seek. Tube worlds? Hell, you could twist them into pretzels if you wanted to!

"The thing is," Conrad answered, "I can actually *see* it. You're telling me it's smaller than a proton, and I know a proton's much smaller than an atom, and an atom is much too small to see, and yet looking down between my feet I can see a little black dot."

"Those are air molecules," Chang answered. "When the accident first occurred, that thing sucked all the air out of this chamber. And there it still is, clinging to the hole in a film. We came back in here with space suits and grapples and magnetic bottles, catching the thing before it could hit the wall, which would have been bad. If we really wanted to we could pry those molecules off of there, but then they'd want to expand again. It would cause an explosion."

"It would cause worse than that," Money said, looking down warily between his feet. "Those aren't air molecules anymore, my friend. Up against the hole, the pressure is more than sufficient to collapse the molecules, collapse the atoms, squeeze the electrons and protons together into single, electrically neutral particles. What you've got there, I'm going to guess, is fifty megatons of liquid neutronium. And if you let it out of jail, the outrush of neutrons would be lethal for several kilometers in any direction. It's a good thing you haven't tried this."

A decidedly unofficial, nongovernmental laugh escaped Conrad. "So you've succeeded after all, Mr. Chang. Wrap a diamond around it and you've got the very neuble you were trying to press. A little undersized, but what the heck."[3]

"Even if it's the right size, you still need to sheath the thing, sir," Money said. "Wrap it in layers of monocrystalline diamond and woven nanotube. And brickmail, which is an allotrope of carbon, basically a chain mail of interlocked rings."

"I know what brickmail is," Conrad said.

From his funny vantage point on the other side of the tube, Money looked almost like he was lying down. Flashing an apologetic look and a horizontal shrug, he said, "Of course you do, sir. I forget your double life, sometimes. Anyway, brickmail is strong shit, and layered with the other stuff it's stronger still, and holds your neuble together."

Conrad nodded absently, thinking that he understood at least the gist of that explanation. He wanted to crouch down, to lean over for a closer look at the hypermass beneath him, but the gravity up next to the tube was a lot stronger than it was a meter or two away, and he was reluctant to bring his center of mass too close to it. Funny gravity fields like this were common causes of injury and death. What he said was, "So, if we shoveled a gigaton of mine tailings on top of that

3. See Appendix A-3: Pressing Problems

thing, would we crush it into an atom of the appropriate size? A full neuble?"

At this point, probably bored with the sound of voices other than his own, Leonard Chang piped up. "We can negotiate terms for the sale of this thing, sir. Or you can accept it from me as a gift. . . ."

Chang was on the other side of the tube from Money—the two of them probably couldn't see each other at all, just as Conrad couldn't see any more of Mariella than the crazy image refracted around the rim of the tube, like a heat mirage. But Money made a mocking face at the question, and apparently Mariella could see it, because she laughed. Conrad fought down a smile of his own and said, "Mr. Chang, whether you're brought up on charges has nothing to do with whether I'm interested in the results of your accident. You understand this? Even if you hadn't *murdered me twice*, you would still be in a lot of potential trouble. What you really want to be is quiet, all right? Help me forget that you exist."

"Er, I'll try, sir."

"There's a good fellow."

When Money had stopped sniggering, he resumed his lecture by saying, "To compress that gigaton of matter into neutronium, sir, you'd have to get it very, very close to the hole. I'm thinking you'd need an antimatter explosion anyway, though admittedly a smaller one."

"Hmm," Conrad said, considering that. Now he did crouch down, with little effort but considerable care, to examine the dark speck down inside the tube. It was a difficult object to see, because the light waves coming off it were so incredibly distorted, but if his eyes could not be trusted, his sense of touch, the *feeling* of the gravity field as a physical entity, was much stronger down here. He fancied he could even sense the pinpoint shape of the object generating that field. And around it, his imagination whirled, envisioning tiny pumps and other machineries of unimaginable power. "We need a conveyor belt, then. Metaphorically, of course; the actual hardware would be completely different. But there will be some sort of physical drip line around this hole, right? Some distance past which the neutrons will refuse to condense. So we shovel matter in until that perimeter is filled, and then we slurp away the liquid neutronium into a reservoir somewhere, and fill the space up again. If you keep doing that, eventually you'll fill your reservoir with the gigaton of neutronium you need, to be stable enough to wrap as a neuble."

"You'd have to do it awfully fast," Money said skeptically.

"So do it awfully fast. What's stopping you? I didn't do the grav-field engineering for the Gravittoir, but I had a hand in the design of the physical machinery, as well as the structures that housed it. It seems to me you can do something similar here, using grav lasers to move and hold and compress the material while you're working it. It's a hard problem, but those are always the interesting ones. Right?"

"True," Money said thoughtfully. "I can't think of anything physically impossible about the idea. When we get back to the ship we can run some numbers and see what we come up with. But you may have just invented a cheap way of mass-producing neutronium. You could be famous!"

Conrad snorted. "To invent something, wouldn't I have to understand it? I couldn't build a machine like that if my life depended on it."

"Proposer and co-inventor, then," Money said with growing enthusiasm. "We could split the credit or something. Bring in others if we have to. Do the details matter? If it *can* be built, I can build it. This could mean big value on the Instelnet's intellectual property market. You could be *rich*."

Conrad snorted again, and it became a laugh. "So we sell the blueprints to the Queendom. For what, cookie recipes? We need physical objects, Mr. Izolo. More than anything, we need print plates. Without a surplus of those, being rich seems rather a moot point. Come to think of it, I *am* rich."

"Yah, maybe," Money said, with a laugh of his own. "But I'm not."

"I've got to get out of this business," Conrad said half a shift later as he settled into his first mate's chair, back on-board *Newhope*.

"Where have I heard that before?" said Yinebeb Fecre, the only other person on the bridge. Conrad suppressed a flicker of irritation. To the people who knew him in Denver, this was Feck the Facilitator, a major figure in the Revolt, though part of Conrad still remembered him by the less flattering nickname he'd received at camp. Which was foolish, because at the moment Feck was his Astrogation officer, his Information and Systems Awareness, and also his Helm.

Even with hypercomputers to support him it was quite a workload, and Feck had once done a tour of duty as the ship's engineer as well. After Xmary, he probably knew more about running this old tub than any four other people combined. Between the two of them, the captain and the crew-unto-himself third officer, they practically ran the ship themselves. Leaving Conrad to play—badly—at diplomacy and labor relations.

"No," he said, "I mean it this time. I don't like who I'm becoming out here, in the wilds of Security Space. Anyway, if my only bargaining power stems from the threat of Ho Ng, then we might as well cut out the middleman and send in Ho directly. I got killed again today—twice!—and the hell of it is, I deserved it. Truly. If I had to listen to the news I deliver to these people, I'd kill me too. It isn't their fault things have got this bad."

"Economic downturns happened even in the Queendom," Feck pointed out reasonably. "Sometimes all you can do is just ride it out. At least we're immorbid, true? It's not like you're asking people to work themselves to death. A few decades and we're over the hump, and then it's smooth sailing for the rest of eternity."

"Sure," Conrad said, unconvinced. Then, feeling a strong urge to shift the subject: "You've changed a lot since we were kids."

"Is that good?"

"Certainly," Conrad said. "Why wouldn't it be?"

"Because I was a shithead back then?" Feck laughed. "You've changed, too. What I'm saying is, the old Conrad is still there—you've got the same basic character. You always were one to agonize over the status quo. But you're wiser now, and more...I don't know. More thoughtful? More reflective? I suppose we all are."

A slight tremor shook the ship, and checking his board, Feck twiddled a couple of controls and said, "Center of gravity shifts. The ertial shield is feeling ticklish today. We'll need to shift some water ballast before we unmoor."

And this was amazing, too. A statement like that had a lot of knowledge backing it up, and Conrad had a hard time reconciling that with the clueless, rather fruity kid Feck had been. He still looked the same, or nearly so.

Conrad said, "When did you become such a grade-A spaceman? You've been on *Newhope* a long time, I know, but so have a few others. I can tell you firsthand, people don't absorb everything by osmosis. To know everything—really everything—takes a lot of work. What made you decide...to be that person?"

Feck laughed. "You have to ask? You boys got to play space pirate, while I was stuck on the ground babysitting."

"You organized a revolution," Conrad observed.

But Feck just waved that off. "I organized a small riot. We knew what we were doing, but the odds were against us from the beginning. Obviously. The chaos lasted barely an hour, and we were lucky to have that much. Whereas you guys were running riot through the Kuiper Belt for months. You think I wasn't jealous? Hell, I still am. And when it was over, you guys got all the best training slots. Because you already had space experience, see? And of course that meant you got to be the crew of *Newhope,* and then the first to explore the planet, to carve the streets there. By the time you woke me up, there was nothing really raw left to do. I've been playing catch-up ever since. If I can't be a pioneer, I figure I'll at least be the best goddamn space jockey you ever saw."

"There was nothing romantic about the pirate's life," Conrad told him darkly. "I fall into that trap myself sometimes, but when I really think back...Ugh. There was a lot of violence, a lot of death. It wasn't fun at all. We were terrified, every day."

"But you were standing up for what you believed in. That's

a very powerful thing. It's possible you don't realize how fortunate you are. Or were. But I do."

That thought just deepened Conrad's sour mood. "What are we standing up for now? You and I are the exact opposite of space pirates, Feck. We are the enforcers of an ugly little police state."

Feck smiled again, though this time it was bittersweet. "Well, that's not without its own sort of romance. Ugly or not, the colony needs us. What would happen if we weren't doing this? If nobody was? What I'm saying is, there really is a kind of nobility in doing the things that need doing, even when they're personally distasteful. Especially then, I guess."

But Conrad was having none of that. If there was truth in what Feck was saying, it just made him angry. "There are other ways to serve. We've got people who *like* to play the heavy. Who've always played the heavy. Just send them in, and leave decent people out of it. If it needs to be done, put it against the immortal souls of the people who can't be corrupted, because they're already corrupt."

"Do you need your soul?" Feck said, trying for a joke. "Aren't you immorbid? Judgment day is a long way off if you never stop to die."

"Thanks. That's helpful. Look, I've been out here almost ten years, and I don't feel like I've made a difference. Not for the better."

"Ten years is nothing, Conrad."

"No? It is to me." But Conrad felt the lie in the words even as he was saying them. He just didn't like what he was doing. It was as simple as that. He'd been bored as an architect those last few decades, though he hadn't realized it until the very end. But was boredom any worse than doing something you actually hated?

"Forget it," he said. "When we get back to P2, I'm resigning my commission. There are a lot of jobs down there I haven't tried yet."

That might've sounded like selfish whining, but Conrad was pleased to hear, in his voice, a quiet resolve that was empty of bitterness. Finally. But he added, "If I stay out here any longer, I'll be less valuable in the long run. I've got to keep my self-respect. We all do, or what's the purpose of our lives?"

"Good point," Feck said, affably enough.

Conrad looked out the virtual window again, eyeing the stationary glints of orange-white sunlight on the surface of Element Pit. "You're a good man, Feck," he said absently, with his brain halfway unplugged. "Probably one of the best I've ever known. Little gods, when did that happen?"

Money Izolo was both the engineer and the fourth mate, and when he came to the bridge to relieve Conrad, Conrad took the opportunity to catch the tail end of Xmary's sleep shift. Her cabin door knew to let him in, and he shrugged off his clothes and crawled into the bunk with her.

"Hi," she said sleepily.

"Hi yourself," he returned.

"What's wrong?" she asked right away, hearing something in his tone. She sounded more awake, and her body stiffened as if preparing to sit up.

"Just a bad day," he told her.

She rolled over to embrace him, and as the wellcloth sheets pulled aside he could feel that she wasn't wearing anything either. She seldom did, when she was expecting him.

She had gone with a few spacemen in her time—had gone with *all* of them, really. But once Conrad had come back aboard, those temps and fill-ins had fallen away like dry leaves in a breeze. Or so it seemed to him now; he supposed the process had taken a couple of years. But when they had finally settled back into each other's arms again, they had fit perfectly, like the two halves of something broken, melding together again. Their early time together had been formative; she was a part of his character, and he imagined the reverse must be true as well.

This was a minor detail which had slipped his mind, briefly, during that conversation on the bridge. He had left her once, with consequences he didn't particularly care to repeat. Could he leave her again, knowing that the same thing would probably happen?

"You're all tense," she said, feeling his back.

He nodded, agreeing with that. "I know. I just...I just hate this job. Nothing about you, nothing about the ship. It was good to get into space again. I think I needed that, deep down in my soul."

Now she did sit up, pulling the sheets after her in the darkness. "You're speaking in the past tense. What's wrong?"

"I don't know. I'm not sure."

"You're thinking of going back to P2?"

"Yeah."

She digested that in silence for a while. When she finally spoke, what she said was, "I don't know that human memories were really designed for these long spans of time. I don't feel as though I've forgotten anything, though I'm sure the details of childhood fade as they move farther into the past. But I feel my life—I don't know—breaking up into portraits and vignettes. Time begins to seem less linear, more like a book of stationary pictures than a single long movie. Does that make sense?"

"Yes," Conrad answered, because Bascal had told him much the same thing. Supposedly, this view was closer to the physical truth than the errant concept of "movement" through time. But then he followed with, "No. I dunno." Because he couldn't see a connection with the things that were bothering him, and he vaguely resented her going off on a tangent like this.

But she continued. "You've been back onboard the ship for, what, about a decade? That seems like a continuous stretch of time, but when you're gone—not *if*, but when—it will all compress down to a couple of incidents. Whenever a period of time passes with nothing changing, nothing important, it goes into the log as one long incident. We remember it like a spring afternoon, or anyway I do."

And here Conrad began to get the gist of what she was saying. But only the gist, the outlines, so he stroked her neck and waited for her to continue.

"When you left the first time, it seemed intolerable. In a good year, we would see each other for at most a few weeks, and I didn't want to live my life that way. But I don't think I understood. I don't think I really grasped how *long* life can be. We've had a spring afternoon together, yes, and perhaps we'll have a spring evening apart, and then a morning together, and then separate business again for a while. If we're going to live forever—and I don't think anyone really knows what that means on a personal level—we need to stop running our lives like morbid little tribesmen who'll be dead in ten years."

"You're giving me your blessing to leave? Do I understand you correctly?"

She paused. "I think so. Yes."

"You'll wait for me? For years, if necessary?"

She thought that one over, and said, "It depends what you mean by wait. I've never stopped loving you, though I haven't always *liked* you, or had you conveniently at hand when I needed you. When I see you again, none of that will be different. Age has its pleasant side, I would say. When next I see you, I won't really have to ask what you've been doing. It won't really matter. You won't have changed."

"We'll fit like two halves of a broken plate," he suggested, although the implications were rather sobering. Were they so inflexible?

"Yes! Good. But while we're apart, the edges may need to be covered. Our bodies require a certain amount of attention, and so do our spirits. And that's okay, because at the end of the day we'll still fit. Friendships of convenience may come and go, but the arc of our romance stretches on forever."

For the second time in his life, Conrad contemplated this notion uneasily. "Forever" was an easy word to say, but living it was another matter. Didn't everything have an end, sooner or later? But Xmary seemed so earnest in the darkness, so pleased with her observation—with him and with the universe in general—that he couldn't bear to disappoint her.

"Forever," he agreed, hooking his pinkie to hers to cement the promise.

And thus was sealed the fate of a ship.

#### chapter eighteen

mursk wandering

Of course, Xmary could have come with him, or arranged to have a copy made. The possibility was certainly discussed, but even after these hundreds of years in the cramped confines of *Newhope,* she still claimed to have unfinished business there. Conrad suggested that it might be broadening for her to try some other jobs for a while, but she protested that she had eternity to do that, and needn't—in fact *shouldn't*—be in any hurry right now.

Conrad didn't think a centuries-deep rut was the best way to start off eternity, but he didn't press the point. Neither did he wish to reenter his old life as an architect, nor his even earlier life as an unemployed confidant of Bascal. The king, the oppressor, the Man. This was said and thought in joking tones, yes, but in a period of crisis there *was* something unsavory about government, and for better or worse Conrad had no desire to associate himself with that anymore.

So he took his own advice, inserting himself beneath the blanket of P2's atmosphere and seeking odd jobs on the outskirts of civilization. A few of these lasted six months; a few lasted a year or two. He supervised robots in a factory for building more robots. He was the editor and publisher of a rural news service until the communities he served closed up and moved elsewhere in search of better agricultural soils.

He even did a turn as a road builder, bulldozing and paving and cobbling streets for old-fashioned maglev vehicles, and even wheeled vehicles, to travel along. It was important work, because large aircraft and spacecraft were increasingly scarce, and for the mining and quarrying communities of the southern lowlands and the mountains between Domesville and Bupsville, there was virtually no other way to get around anymore unless you were a centaur, and even they couldn't carry ore.

That job felt too much like a retreat, though—a shallow attempt to revive his childhood, without even his father there to supervise. So Conrad moved on, and moved on some more. He spent a season as a hermit, taking clay out of the dry riverbed and fashioning it into bowls and oil lamps and fat-figured women in a cold and poorly ventilated shack in the desert. But that was *really* a retreat, and no service to civilization at all, in its hour of greatest need. So he took a real job again, and this time it stuck.

He was the captain of a fishing boat on the Sea of Destiny. He had a staff of four—bristly unshaven men, all. Their job was to sail P2's larger ocean—shallow and poisonous though it be—tracking the migrations and population dynamics of various species of fish. This was directly helpful to society, since the fax shortage had driven other boats out here to *catch* the fish for actual human consumption. The movement and fluctuations of the schools were also an important indicator of the health of the infant ecosystem. And yes, out on the ocean there was no one to confront or argue with, nothing to dispute, nothing all that much to worry about.

Except perhaps the weather, and even that was nothing compared to Earth or—God help them—Neptune, which P2 more closely resembled in some ways. Yes, it was a hostile planet for ordinary human life, but Conrad and his men were not ordinary humans. No one on P2 was, or ever would be again. And while the oceans were technically larger than Earth's, they were shallower and occupied a much smaller percentage of the planet's uselessly large surface. And P2's rotation wasn't fast enough to generate meaningful Coriolis forces, so when the sun heated the ocean's surface during the long, long days, the tropical depressions which formed over it were not pulled into raging cyclonic hurricanes. Instead, they formed simple rain showers—or at worst, tornado-spawning thunderstorms—which roamed the oceans aimlessly and were easily avoided.

Indeed, the planet's greatest storms were the dry ones, sweeping off the desert plains and *into* the ocean. This happened most often at daybreak, as new slices of atmosphere rotated into the heat and proton flux of the solar wind. The resulting aurora could be quite beautiful, but the accompanying ground-to-sky lightning, the random blasts of dry wind off the warming sand, sometimes took the coastline by surprise. When they came, the storms would rise an hour behind the sun and quickly rocket out to sea, carrying clouds of stinging grit which blotted out the sky and clobbered the surface acidity, killing raft vegetation for hundreds of kilometers and driving the fish down, down toward the featureless bottom.

At night, the oceans gave up their heat again, turning over, exchanging with the warm, nutrient-rich muck at the bottom. In this sense, P2's shallow oceans were more fertile—more habitable and forgiving—than Earth's deep ones. No sterile, crystal blue depths here! This turning over was a weather event unto itself, generating thick, cold, chlorinated fogs that reduced the visibility to twenty meters or less and clung to everything in a slick film, turning all but the stickiest of surfaces into skating rinks. But Conrad's ship, *Snowflake,* rarely sailed at night, except during the mating season of the beholder squids, which glowed eerily beneath the water's churning surface and were one of Conrad's absolute favorite sights in the world.

Ah, the adventures they had on that proud little ship! The tides of P2 were high and slow, so that there were islands and peninsulas and even whole archipelagoes that would come and go—a landscape and seascape always in flux. There was so much to see, so much to explore.

On one dry-shoe visit to the Drowned Islands, on a kilometer-wide reef called Umamaha, or Shallow Shoulder,

Conrad and his men found themselves knee-deep in rotting fish. They had seen their share of fish kills before, but these were generally monospecific events triggered by a local resource depletion, and so were ultimately a sign of overpopulation. But they knew right away that this one was different, because it involved dozens of unrelated species and had no obvious cause.

Ned Creswell, Conrad's senior ocean chemistry officer, opined thusly: "Nutrient levels in the water are all nominal, sir. And off the island, we didn't read any signatures of unusual decay."

"Meaning what?" Conrad probed.

"Meaning the dead fish are all right here on the island, sir. Look at them: they haven't been dead more than a couple of pids. They flopped up here while the waters were receding. They were trying to get out of the ocean, millions of fish. From all directions, too, by the look of it."

"And why would they do that?"

"Hell if I know, sir. If I didn't know better, I would say they were suffocating. Panicking. Trying to breathe the air while keeping their bodies wet? But if that were true, we'd see signs of it in the water. Dissolved gas levels have been normal all week."

"Hmm. Do fish leave ghosts?"

"Hell if I know, sir. But we haven't got the equipment to read 'em in any case."

So they held their noses and walked around for a while in the ruddy brown light of morning, but the mystery only deepened.

Said Giotti, the wildlife officer, "Whatever's scavenging these fish corpses, Captain, I've never seen anything like 'em before."

"They're bugs," someone said helpfully.

But that did little to shed light on the matter, because even Conrad could see that while these bugs were built on a generally Barnardean chassis—radial symmetry stretched out into a sort of bilateral torpedo—the similarities ended there. For one thing, these bugs had legs all over them. They were absolutely, positively covered in legs. Even the mouthparts were legs—a decidedly nasty feature when examined closely.

"It's the proton flux from the sun," Conrad speculated. "With a nice, hot yellow star, you can set your planet away from the fusion source. Here, we're practically nestled up against it. And the planet has no strong magnetic field to deflect the proton winds. You and I are full of healing nanobes, medically refreshed every couple of years, but there are no veterinarians under the sea. The radiation damage probably just builds up, generation after generation."

They began to notice, too, that a lot of the dead fish were covered in tumors. These did not seem, particularly, to have been the cause of death. When you found a fish asphyxiated on dry land, you didn't have to look much farther for what had killed it, even if the reasons for it remained mysterious. But still, there were more cancers than Conrad would expect to see in a healthy population. Was proton radiation a strong mutagen? He couldn't remember, though he would certainly look it up. Anyway, a star would emit neutrons and alpha particles and all kinds of other garbage as well. Clean-burning they were not! This by itself wasn't necessarily a problem, except that no one had designed adequate coping mechanisms into the animals. Or perhaps they had, and the mechanisms had stopped functioning, or something was interfering with them.

"The ecology of this planet was never stable," commented Giotti. "It never had any need to be, with freshly printed organisms compensating for any unforeseen population crashes. P2 is at best a garden, not a wilderness."

"Your point being?" Conrad asked, for Giotti was a man who stated the obvious far more readily than he stated his own opinion.

"Well," said Giotti, "in a stable ecology the mutants die out. Everything is perfectly evolved for its niche, and change comes slowly or not at all. Anything different or anomalous is defective, almost by definition."

"But . . . ," Conrad said, with patient tolerance for his crewman's foibles. He was learning patience, oh yes, as anyone must who had lived this long and seen this much.

"But an ecology without stable niches is more tolerant of mutation," Giotti answered. "You might almost say it *encourages* mutation, as a means of trying out new body plans and lifestyles. Because you never know what's going to work better unless you try it."

"Hence these leggybugs?"

"I don't think those are going to succeed, sir. At least, I hope not."

And here some old words of Bascal's floated up in Conrad's mind: "The true measure of any life-form is how quickly it can skeletonize a cow." By that half-serious reasoning, Giotti could hardly be wrong, for the leggybugs were not efficient scavengers, nor tidy ones.

The men of *Snowflake* might've explored more—hell, they might've found the clue that would solve the whole mystery—but the long, slow morning was already beginning to heat up, and by the end of their next shift on the island the smell of rotting fish drove them back onto the boat and out to sea, none the wiser for their investigations. Would the incident have made more sense as an isolated, anomalous occurrence? It was hard to know, because they encountered several more such kills over the course of that year. And then the kills stopped, just as mysteriously, but the fish populations in that area never did seem to recover.

"Ah, well," Conrad told his men on a rare night of drunken revelry, when the light of Sol shone down upon them like a mother watching over her children. "If the sea weren't full of mystery, then what good would it be?"

The night sky of P2 was a lopsided affair, with all the bright stars squeezed into a band along the river of the Milky Way, cutting at an angle against the horizon. Sol herself dangled from the belt of Orion, a fourth star in that perfect line, but brighter and spaced out a bit farther. A longer and much brighter line, cutting the sky from horizon to pole, was formed by Canopus and Sirius and Alpha Centauri, with Rigel and Betelgeuse and Procyon hovering nearby. Together they formed a single constellation, much bigger and clearer than anything in the skies of Sol: Orion, the Randy Vaulter.

"Men go to sea," Conrad said beneath the Vaulter's light,

"because the land is tedious, and the sea, which is never twice the same, obliges them. Drink up, laddies! Turn those mugs over and drain them dry, for tomorrow the sea will have new surprises, and beforehand we must needs refresh ourselves."

The parlance of sailors was saltier and more expansive than the clipped, dead-in-five-seconds urgency of spacers, and Conrad found that he loved talking that way as much as he loved the sea itself. In all his long life, this was the closest he would ever come to poetry. Alas.

In the years that followed, they never did see any more leggybugs, although they did find a few amphibious creatures so strange that it was hard to believe they'd evolved from human-drawn designs. Perhaps their made-up genomes were unstable? Given to sudden fits of mutation in the isolation of an island ecosystem?

Fancying himself a bit of a scholar, Conrad went so far as to trace the evolution of a particular beast, the island river nereid, from a primordial form—the sea nereid—that had been designed and introduced in the colony's earliest days. Then it had turned out that the river nereid really was man-made, though obscure, and the whole argument sort of collapsed.

But then, as happens sometimes with scientific obscura, it revived again with lively debate in the ecology journals when a number of other established species—some more awful even than the leggybugs—turned out to have mutated in exactly the ways that Conrad had theorized. This touched off a wave of cryptozoological exploration which flew in the face of the colony's poverty, igniting imaginations. Who knew—*who knew*—what strange monsters might be found on and around these islands, or in the deeper trenches of the middle ocean?

"It may be hubris," Conrad wrote in a letter to several of the journals, "to believe that a system as complex as a planetary ecology can simply be installed to order, or controlled in place."

There were strange creatures as well in the growing Thorn Jungles, as blackberry bramble decided not only to take over the world's narrow soil belts, but to creep in around the edges of civilization itself. Naked-eye ghost sightings there were easily dismissed, for the lighting was always poor. And for similar reasons, the existence of a rumored Thorn Jungle Hydra was never verified, although other shocking discoveries were made during the hunt. Anyway such a beast was *plausible* in the extreme, for the jungle's own mutants kept company with unauthorized creatures invented and released without official permission. And who was doing the releasing? Civilization had its own monsters, driven half mad—or perhaps wholly mad—by ill-conceived body plans their human brains could not control without gross rewiring. More than one of these self-made unfortunates had disappeared into the jungles, and who could say what became of them? But that is another tale, and nothing to do with Conrad Mursk.

Of course, not every adventure on the sea was fish or monster related. *Snowflake* really did encounter some weather every now and then, especially in the polar latitudes where it occasionally met its namesake, where the ice on the deck and the instruments and steering controls would occasionally get so thick that *Snowflake* couldn't maneuver at all and had to radio for emergency warming by batteries of orbital lasers.

Of course, Conrad still had his money, and during his infrequent trips to Backupsville he still sometimes sent copies of himself off to the stars and gathered up the replies. There were always fewer incoming messages than outgoing ones, though—he'd lost two more copies of himself out there, and something about that began to bother him in a way it never had before. Lost in transmission, yes: two more pieces of himself he could never recover, experiences and conversations he'd genuinely had, but would never know about. Would they have changed him? Solved his problems?

Finally, he ceased the practice altogether—no more would he cast his soul upon the spaceways—and when a call came in for him from the King and Queen of Sol, he refused to accept it. Let them come in person, or else leave him in peace.

In spite of these sobering distractions, Conrad could have been happy at his fishery job for a long, long time. Alas, it was not to be. The main outcome of *Snowflake*'s research was the realization that fish stocks were falling dramatically, everywhere, regardless of any human predation. Per Giotti's years-ago warning, the planet's ecology had always been propped up by human action. But now every available hand was digging ore or growing food or stitching together fax machines of increasingly, alarmingly poor quality. There was nothing left to prop up the ecology *with*, and so it slumped, and fell, and after sixteen years in the salt air Conrad finally couldn't bear to watch the planet die anymore, and so resigned his commission.

From there, he found himself moving southward, building more roads again for lack of anything better to do, until he found his way to the Polar Well itself, where there were no roads and couldn't be any. Like many warm terrestrial planets, P2 had no polar caps per se, but given the grazing angle of the sunlight at extreme latitudes, it did have regions which were permanently in shadow. Most notably the Well: a hundred-kilometer-wide depression ringed by sharp-toothed mountains, where the fall of snow and the melting and refreezing of ice made the terrain anew every 460-hour cycle of day and night.

Increasingly, agriculture was a necessity for the colony rather than a diversion. It was a source of fuel—a low-tech means for harvesting the ruddy light of Barnard and converting it into human activity, through the mediating elements of starch and sugar and comestible proteins. But agriculture, unlike fishing, really was at the mercy of an uncooperative climate, and the weather patterns of P2 were surprisingly complex, and surprisingly dependent on the speed and direction of winds in the Polar Well.

So there were sensor stations there, and the sensors were always getting covered with snow and ice or sinking into pools of slush, and no one had ever found a good way to make robots understand how best to clean and care for them. So each of the seven stations—arranged in a rough hexagon with the seventh and largest at the center—had to be manned by one actual human being, who lived alone in a nearby hut. Which sounded nice, didn't it? To be a hermit who also served a vital need for the greater good? When a vacancy opened up, Conrad saw his opportunity and moved in.

Here, in the land of permanent twilight and permanent cold, of snow and ice, of clear, bright starlight that cut through the hazy atmosphere, Conrad found a kind of clarity he had never known before. Maybe it was just the solitude— he'd never had that, either—but he had a lot of opportunity to ponder it, and over time he decided that the environment itself was a crucial element in this new sense of peace.

Here in the Well, human beings could live, but only barely. This wasn't a matter of body forms, but simply the hugeness of nature; lapses of attention quickly became serious, even fatal. Especially in bad weather. In his first season on the job, his immediate neighbor to the east had frozen to death, and had had to be evacuated in a special coffin housed within a robot tractor built especially for this purpose. Ironically, they took him north to Pectoralis and had to thaw him out again there, just to freeze him properly for long-term storage. Such was the fate of the colony's dead: neither heaven nor hell nor simple oblivion, just an icy limbo in the Cryoleum, on a spit of land popularly known as the Fin.

Conrad hadn't known that neighbor—hadn't been moved particularly by his death—but a few years later it happened again. The same isolated hut, the same exact stupid circumstances, and this time the victim was Raylene Pine, a woman Conrad had gotten to know rather well over the radio and through occasional conjugal visits by tractor or, when one of them was feeling particularly ambitious, by snowshoe.

Her death hit Conrad hard, because it was the first time in his long life that he'd ever known anyone who had actually died for real—who had simply dropped out of the world, dropped out of the universe, and in all likelihood would not be coming back. What a strange concept! He wept off and on for weeks, and part of him—the last shreds of his childhood, perhaps—withered away and never did grow back.

Around this same time, in her increasingly disheartened messages to him, Xmary complained that *Newhope*'s fax machine had finally been confiscated: relocated to Bubble Hood and then finally to Domesville. As a not-too-surprising result, the miners and refiners of Barnard space were in a state of open rebellion, and the only thing keeping them even marginally in line was the threat that their frozen dead would not be respected, would not be relocated to the Fin for proper storage. These were fun times indeed, but the discussion's main effect on Conrad was to remind him just how precarious his own situation had become.

It was a hazardous occupation, this monitoring of weather stations in permanent shadow, and as the years slid by Conrad found himself marking time by the deaths of his colleagues. He came to realize that he was pushing the odds himself, that after three or four decades in this place he would surely die, and as had happened in several other cases, they might not even recover his body. The ice was a flat sheet hundreds of meters thick—an ice lake, the geologists insisted on calling it—and sometimes in the expansions and contractions of the day/night transition it would just crack, straight down to the bottom, and sometimes a person would fall in, and then inevitably the cracked ice would warm just enough to collapse and refreeze, and it would have taken the resources of a starship just to identify the body, buried half a kilometer deep in the ice.

And so, reluctantly, Conrad began planning his exit strategy. He would return to civilization; he would get a real job and resume a normal social life. He would even, he supposed, resume regular contact with King Bascal, though the prospect held little joy for him. The fact that they were friends—had always been friends—did not make up for the increasingly heavy-handed tactics of a government under pressure.

But new thoughts can be dangerous in an environment where routine equals safety. One day, while morosely planning this sad excuse for a future, Conrad was hiking along his northern perimeter when the ice groaned and banged and cracked in front of him. Not a deep crack—a crevasse to the lake bottom itself—but a much rarer surface crack that was eighty meters long or so, and just wide and deep enough to admit Conrad's snowshoe and then swallow his foot up to the ankle. He stepped in it, yes, and fell badly, and surprisingly enough it was not his leg that broke but his left arm and collarbone. It was just about the most painful thing that had ever happened to him—death included!—and walking back was a hassle and an agony, and finally a deadly ordeal.

There was a meter of powder on top of a meter of packed snow, with the ice underneath, and while Conrad had sprung for the best snowshoes available—featherlight platters of wellstone which stuck to snow and ice as though they were glue—snowshoeing was still hard work under even the best of circumstances. And these were hardly the best of circumstances; he couldn't use his left arm at all, which meant he couldn't use his left shoeing pole, which meant he was effectively a three-legged creature, rather than a four-legged one as the environment demanded.

Being dazed with pain didn't help matters either, and he had neglected to bring any food or water on this hike. He always carried a wrist phone when he was away from the hut, but when the wind was blowing and whipped up the snow, reception could be spotty. Also, he wasn't sure he'd given the thing a proper charge recently; there was no sunlight here to run it, and it was easy to forget to touch it against a powered wellstone surface. So he dutifully called for help every ten minutes, but no help materialized, and no one called him back.

And then, like an idiot, he managed to lose his way in the blowing snow several times, and while hypothermia was not a risk—not in his high-end wellcloth bodysuit—by the time he found his way back he had become rather seriously dehydrated. He spent his first ten minutes sitting in a chair drinking warm water, and then spent his next ten minutes peeing it back out again. Only then did he feel fit enough to approach the hut's communication gear and raise his neighbors.

Two of them arrived by tractor before the shift had ended and saw to his injuries as best they could, but what he really needed was evacuation to the Domesville hospital or, in a pinch, the one in Bupsville. What he got instead was a ten-day tractor ride to the southern outpost of Aurora, where they had to rebreak his bones and then set them the old-fashioned way, by sealing his shoulder in piezoelectric foam while a pair of robots pulled his arms out straight. He spent four surly weeks in a convalescent ward, and when he was finally fit to travel again, he did not return to the Polar Well, but instead caught a tractor north to the print plate factory on the southern outskirts of Bupsville.

He had had it—*had* it—with this fax shortage, and he was bloody well going to do something about it, though he couldn't imagine exactly what. Not then, anyway.

#### chapter nineteen

faxworks

With the obvious exception of the Orbital Tower, buildings on P2 tended not to be more than two or three stories tall, and in fact one story was by far the norm. This was partly because the stronger materials were very expensive, making it cheaper to build *out* rather than up, but mostly it had to do with the hugeness and emptiness of the planet itself. Instinctively, people seemed to want to cover it with human things to whatever extent they could. With more than five times the land area of Earth and a millionth the population, they were in little danger of overurbanizing it, or even leaving much of a mark. But they did what they could.

Even the unstoppable blackberry infestation, and the plagues of mice and "indigenous" pool beetles which followed along with it, covered barely more than a tenth of the surface, clinging mainly to the coastlines and the humid equator. Which of course were the planet's most desirable places; the rest was mainly featureless desert, flat plains, and low, careworn mountains. By some estimates, it would take ten thousand years to fill up all the nooks and crannies of this world with macroscopic life-forms. And even then, the low levels of metal in the crust—especially iron—meant that the soil was basically sand, and would support jungles and farmland only where carefully constructed soils were laid on top. And that required fax machines and elements from the asteroid mines, both of which were in decidedly short supply.

At any rate, the Faxworks—which Conrad had never seen up close—was architecturally consistent with the rest of the world: broad and flat and sprawling. The complex was surprisingly large—twenty buildings covering nearly a square kilometer altogether—and the whole area bustled with activity: people and robots scurrying along, automated tractors and forklifts rolling on paved lanes between the buildings, and loudspeakers blaring with voices, and with the chirps and screeches of acoustically broadcast data.

As Conrad approached, he saw another traveler walking up toward the facility from the other side. Or rather, waddling up, for it was a dwarf angel, with gigantic wings and pectoral muscles and a tiny, misshapen head atop a skin-and-bones body dressed in dingy feathers. The expression on the angel's face was both vacuous and sad, as well it should be, for it had one of the worst-designed body forms Conrad had ever seen. P2's air was thick, but not *that* thick, and no matter how sorely the dream of flight might burn in the souls of human beings, in biological practice it remained elusive.

You could stick wings on a human body, sure, but if you wanted it to fly you had to build up the chest muscles and lose a *lot* of weight everywhere else. With proper materials the wings themselves could be tough and nearly weightless, but "tissues" of this sort were rigid and fundamentally dead, like insect wings. There had been some experiments in piezo-electric deformation to allow the membranes to curl and flex, but integrating that with the human nervous system was an enormous challenge, and who on P2 had the time?

Anyway, the sort of people who wanted to fly were also the sort who wanted to *feel* the wind beneath their wings. They wanted something like flesh, covered by something like feathers or leather or scales. And that took more muscle still. The sad result was a creature that couldn't really fly *or* walk. Turkeys, some people called them, and what a stinging truth it must be for the angels that heard it! The most pathetic cases came when would-be angels—perhaps inspired by that old poem of Bascal's—sought in desperation to reduce the mass of their brains. In the end, most of them *still* couldn't fly, and lacked the capacity to understand why. You saw them out on the street sometimes, forlornly flapping their wings, their eyes on the distant, unattainable sky.

The body form was reversible, of course—you could always be human again—but you had to ask for it. You had to want it, to be smart enough to formulate the question. Conrad remembered a case, years ago, when a young angel's family, intent on restoring his humanity, had kidnapped him and shoved him forcibly through a hospital fax. They were promptly arrested for it, and in their absence the kid, like any addict, had gone right back to his old body form. "I have to keep trying," he'd told a news channel before stepping through the plate. "'Impossible' isn't in my vocabulary."

Ah, overreach: that most basic of human sins. How could you blame an angel for trying? For wanting heaven itself? *Maybe when we die,* Conrad sometimes wanted to tell them. *Maybe we'll all be whole someday.* Or perhaps the angels could become miners, and spend their off hours flapping through the open spaces of Element Pit.

This particular individual paused at the edge of the compound, in confusion or uncertainty or fear.

"H-h-help?" it said to Conrad.

And Conrad, not wanting to be rude, tried to look at the thing without pity. "Yes?"

"H-h-help me. I . . . need something. I miss . . . something."

Conrad shrugged. "I'll . . ." Try? Do my best for you? Leave you here in despair? "I'll send someone out for you."

There were no gates, no guards, and Conrad was free to walk right up to the premises and in between the buildings with no one paying him a second glance. Which was all well and good, but what he really wanted was to find Brenda. She ran this place, and if he wanted answers she was the first and most obvious person to talk to.

He tried a passerby. "Excuse me, where can I find Brenda Bohobe?"

"Everywhere, fool!" the woman said, hurrying along with her business.

Conrad tried two others with similar results, but then he managed to grab a slender, humanoid robot by the wrist. It stopped walking and turned its blank metal face toward him expectantly.

"Assist me," he instructed. "Lead me to the director of this place."

The robot paused, whirring and clicking as its neck swiveled slightly, then said in a self-consciously mechanical voice, "Please release me. I am on assignment."

Conrad nodded impatiently. "Yes, I understand that. You're being directed by a hypercomputer, yes? Please inform it that you have been detained. It can juggle the work schedules accordingly. Meanwhile, I require your assistance."

The robot considered this, and then asked, "On whose authority?"

"My name is Conrad Mursk."

"First Architect Conrad Mursk?"

There was no surprise or admiration in the robot's voice; it was merely checking a record somewhere, and verbally confirming that it had identified the right individual.

"That's correct," he told it.

There was another pause as the robot weighed this information, or checked with a computer somewhere, but finally it said, "By 'this place' I assume you mean the Bohobe Plate Manufactory as a whole. By 'director' I assume you mean the company president. Do you wish to visit with Brenda Bohobe?"

"I do."

"Then I will make an appointment. An appointment has been made. You will come with me, please."

Although he was in a bad mood, Conrad chuckled at that. "Will I really? Or what?"

"Or you will miss your appointment," the robot replied, with no particular emphasis.

Robots were funny that way: an inhuman combination of brilliance and absolute witlessness. They were so serious about everything, it was difficult sometimes to avoid teasing, but of course you did that for your own benefit, not theirs.

They didn't care one way or the other. You couldn't make them *feel* teased.

But then the robot did do a peculiarly human thing. It looked at Conrad and said, "Will you release my arm, please? You are impeding my progress."

"Very well," Conrad said, letting go, and then followed the thing along a sidewalk, and into a building marked PLANNING OFFICE. From there, they followed a surprisingly long and twisting set of corridors to a wall marked B. B., PRESIDENT.

"You may wait here until your appointment," the robot told him. "Your appointment is in two minutes. If you wish reading material, music, or other entertainments, you may request them from the wall."

"I'm familiar with the principle, yes," Conrad answered testily. Although, to be fair, that sort of enlivened, enlibraried wellstone surface had become rather rare in the colony of late. And the world was full of children who probably had no idea how things were supposed to work. He waved a hand at the robot and said, "You're released. Sorry to have bothered you."

"It is never a bother to serve," the robot answered dutifully. And although it is well known that robots possess no emotion and little self-awareness, they do have different operating modes and different levels of priority or urgency, and the thing did seem inclined to hurry away from Conrad, lest its morning rounds be further disrupted.

It was a foolish prejudice for an overgrown Irish lad to harbor, but Conrad had given up all hope of ever liking robots, or even pretending to. And why should he? No matter where he traveled or how much he saw, he never felt too far removed from Camp Friendly, where it seemed to him that his adult life had begun. Where the Palace Guards had ruled humorlessly, with the constant threat of revoked privileges and the painful sting of tazzers. And worse. The very last thing you needed was something brilliant and inhuman running your life for you, and if the bad taste had not left Conrad's mouth by now, then surely it never would.

Damn the King and Queen of Sol, anyway, for imposing that final injustice upon him. More than any other single

244 / wil mccarthy

thing, that act had precipitated the Revolt and thus given birth to this struggling colony. Because of them, he was standing here now.

But this reflection had little to do with the business at hand, so Conrad faced the word "President" on the wall and said, "Door, please."

Obligingly, a rectangular seam appeared in the wall around the sign's lettering, and the material within it folded aside like a thick, stiff curtain. Inside was an office, surprisingly small in comparison to the building around it. It was dominated by a large wellwood desk, with Brenda Bohobe sitting behind it in a red-black chair with spreading, highly stylized wings at the top. Not the wings of an angel, but those of a really fast aircraft.

Brenda herself had a swelled head—literally, almost half again as big as a normal human's. Nor was that the only change; since Conrad had last seen her she'd given up her blue skin in favor of a rich, deep brown, and behind her eyes Conrad thought he could see a faint glow of wellstone. Hypercomputers on the brain? She wouldn't be the first person to try it.

She looked up, unsurprised because of course the robot had told a computer who was coming, and the computer had told Brenda. Her studying gaze made a piece of equipment out of Conrad, ruling and measuring, judging his quality and condition.

"Conrad Mursk. Well, well. I haven't seen your shadow across my path in dog decades. Didn't you give it all up to become a fisherman or something?"

"Marine wildlife ecologist," he corrected. "But that was years ago. I've given myself a new assignment now."

And Brenda, the same as ever, favored him with a sly, sour look, all-knowing and preemptively displeased. "And it brings you here to me. How very fortunate, and surprising. Let me guess: you're investigating the fax shortage."

"You always were a smart one," he told her honestly. "But really, do you get outside the cities much? Because life has gotten pretty bad out there in the countryside. And brief."

She absorbed that without surprise, and then said, less

acerbically, "I'm aware of that, yes. All I can tell you is, we're doing all we can. Did you seriously believe otherwise?"

Well...

"In hindsight," she continued, "our economy is frightfully small for this sort of undertaking. Faxware production has always been a small fraction of the Queendom's total industry, but out here, one way or another, over half the population is tied up in it. And that's too much; it leaves too many holes. I suppose that wasn't evident two centuries ago, but gods, is it evident now."

"I don't understand."

Brenda sighed, the reflexive sourness dropping away from her face. She looked tired, and truthfully a little bit scared. "Oh, Conrad. The issues are complex, really."

"There's an angel outside, by the way. Said he needed help."

"Don't they all? We get them here sometimes: pilgrims expecting to be healed. We shoo them onward to the Domesville hospital."

"Where they can wait their turn like good little troopers?"

She sighed again. "I'll give you a tour of the facilities, all right? And then maybe you'll understand what I'm talking about."

"Are you sure you can spare the time? Things seem rather busy around here."

"I'll print a copy."

Conrad raised an eyebrow, suddenly feeling somewhat sour and accusatory himself. "'Well, well, rank doth have its droit du seigneur, don't it just?'"

That was a quote from Wenders Rodenbeck. Conrad couldn't remember which play, but Rodenbeck was considered the premier wordsmith and storyteller of the age—or had been when *Newhope* left the Queendom, anyway—and such memorable lines were instantly recognizable to anyone who'd grown up with them. That one came from a scene much like this, a citizen confronting a bureaucrat of some sort, and finding a whiff of corruption. Tilly and the Don of Chefs, in *Midcentury Blah*?

Brenda was not amused. "Just shut up, Conrad. Don't you

come barging in here with that shit. Do you want the tour, or not?"

And in reply, all that occurred to Conrad was another ill-advised line from Rodenbeck: "'I would, madam, that every entity in this sphere were as helpful as thy smallest nail.'"

The tour was in fact illuminating. The print plates were "stitched" together atom by atom, in house-sized vacuum chambers, by crossed beams of laser light playing over silicon chips covered in tiny, tiny manipulator arms. The process was invisible to the naked eye, but the walls of the assembly building were covered in a bewildering variety of sensors and indicators, including little holie screens which showed the atoms coming together in a blur that was almost, but not quite, too fast to see.

The "nip chips," as the manipulator arrays were called, had a "mean time between failure" of one billion hours, which meant that by the end of a single pid one or two of them in a batch were probably on the brink of failure. So when the pid's second shift came in, the machines were shut down and the nip chips swapped out and recycled.

This created a huge demand for nip chips—which had no other use except the manufacture of fax machine print plates—so they were produced on-site as well, and then tested extensively before being placed into inventory. "Inventory" in Conrad's experience had always meant a room or building with an element-sorting mass buffer, a fax machine, and enough floor space to assemble and disassemble the equipment you were faxing. Here, though, it referred to an old-fashioned warehouse full of vibration-dampening shelves, holding row after row after row of tiny diamond vials filled with chemically inert argon, in which the nip chips awaited their turn on the print plate assembly floor.

There were other warehouses as well, for the storage of ore and semipurified element stock, and there were traditional inventories—here called "smalters"—which fed the element stock into mass buffers, which in turn fed, through "teleport valves," the tiny fax machines which produced the atoms which were assembled into print plates by the stitch-ing machines. And then there were the "clean rooms," which were also filled with argon, so that the workers inside had to wear space suits. There were test chambers, where finished plates were tortured with heat and cold, vibration and caustic chemicals, electric fields and ionizing radiation. Those that survived were then tested functionally—faxing a series of in-creasingly complex objects—and then torture-tested again just to be sure.

Conrad was no genius, but it didn't take one to grasp what a huge undertaking this all was. Even sweeping the floors of this place was a formidable—and constant!—task. And yet the output—the brace of shipping crates in the finished prod-uct warehouse—was tiny. Despite the scale of the operation, the facility produced an average of just one print plate per day. And although their quality fell along a "multivariate con-tinuum of lifetimes and probable failure modes," the plates were sorted into three sales categories: personal, industrial, and medical.

"Faxing a cup of coffee is one thing," Brenda explained. "You can tolerate a lot of impurity and displacement. The hu-man body is a lot more difficult. You want it to still be living when it steps out, right? More than that, you want to preserve all its electrical potentials, or the person will be unconscious or dazed or amnesic. Sometimes psychotic. And the collaps-ing potentials have to be perfectly synchronized, or you'll see epilepsy and cardiac fibrillation, or worse. Testing on the medical-grade fax machines can get pretty ugly for this rea-son. The vast majority are rejected. And Conrad, seriously, don't ever let anyone talk you into feeding your body through an industrial plate. Even if it's life or death, you're better off taking your chances."

While she was speaking, she handed a wellstone sketch-plate off to another copy of herself. This place turned out to be *crawling* with Brendas—dozens or perhaps even hundreds of them. About one person in twenty was a Brenda, and they all looked tired and unhappy. A few glanced at Conrad in sur-prise, but hurried on with their business. The others simply ignored him, too wrapped up in their own affairs to pay any attention.

"Do you integrate all these copies?" Conrad asked, trying to keep the amazement out of his voice. His own brain threatened overload when he merged even three or four copies back together. He hadn't run any more plural than that even in the best of times, for fear that he'd damage his neural wiring and have to scrap the memories anyway.

"Only the variances," she said. "I developed a filter for it: anything significant, anything that deviates from the norm, is weighted and blended with my baseline daily experience. I let the copies run for a few weeks, and reintegrate them in groups of five, then reintegrate the fivers to update the canonical *me*, whom you spoke with earlier."

"Sounds complicated."

She shrugged. "You get used to it. Anyway, no one else wants to volunteer for medical testing. I burn a lot of copies that way as well."

"Ouch," he said, with genuine sympathy.

"Yeah, tell me about it. I don't know what a hard failure feels like, because the memories of it are destroyed in the process, but judging from the sounds I make and the looks on my face, it's pretty damned unpleasant."

"So every medical fax that comes out of this place has produced at least one Brenda?"

"More like a hundred," she said, looking about as uncomfortable as people ever did while still keeping their composure. "We have to be *sure* there isn't a glitch somewhere. Unfortunately, generally speaking, there usually is."

"Ouch," Conrad said again. Then, feeling her need to change the subject, he said, "Tell me again why you can't just fax more fax machines? I've always known it was so, but I've never understood it."

The unease of her expression was displaced by irritation. "I wish one person could come through here without asking me that. Really. Look, inanimate systems like a metal beam, or even a diamond monocrystal, are extremely forgiving. They practically assemble themselves, which is why even a personal fax machine can produce them. Food is even easier to build, although it's chemically more complex, because the placement of molecules in a dead biological system is kind of arbitrary. If the cell walls don't quite come together, who cares? You're just going to digest it anyway.

"Living bodies are difficult for the reasons we've already discussed, but even there you've got considerable slop in where and how you place the pieces. Our bodies are wet, flexible, self-correcting mechanisms. If you're careful, you can make near-perfect copies of them with only nanometer precision on the placement of atoms. DNA and proteins and fats are all extremely stable. The atoms *want* to fall into those patterns, or life could never have arisen in the first place. Wellstone is about as complex, though for different reasons.

"But a print plate is a whole other thing. In technical terms, it's a heterogeneous mix of quantum-wave structures supported by the level fluctuations of valence electrons. Even the sorriest, crappiest fax machine—a garbage disposal, say—requires *zero* impurities, *zero* defects, and *picometer* precision on assembly, which is five hundred times better than the fax itself can achieve.

"And even then, you've still got to get the waveforms right. Once they're established, the plate does fortunately have some damage tolerance. If it didn't, we could only use them in a bath of liquid helium, and the first object you printed would destroy the machine. But to get the fields up and running, you have to build the plate exactly right on the very first try. Ninety-five percent of the plates we manufacture go straight into the disposal."

"So," Conrad said as he struggled with all this new information, "you're using fully half the colony's resources, but the medical-grade faxes are a fraction of a fraction of a fraction of your total output."

"Yes," she said unhappily. "We've improved the equipment as much as we possibly can out here. It's nearly as good as the Queendom's best, but we don't have anything like the Queendom's industrial base. They can *afford* to recycle all but the best of the best Here, the most we can do is decertify the plates which don't pass medical, and squeeze the maximum functionality out of the few that do.

"We've got the most advanced filtering algorithms that have ever existed, anywhere, in fourteen star systems. Unless some other colony has leaped ahead of us and the broadcast hasn't arrived yet, which I suppose is possible. But here on P2 we had the advantage of a nearly breathable atmosphere. That challenge—being tantalizingly close to the good life but not quite in it—has given us a big head start."

As they walked, she looked him over again in that same critical, vaguely disappointed way, and Conrad realized suddenly that she was seeing not so much a person as a dynamic and very complex object which had passed, many times, through her fax plates and filters. When she looked at him, she was admiring her handiwork. Seeing its flaws, wondering how she could do better.

"You've been without a fax for what, fifteen years now?" she asked.

"Fourteen," he answered, counting it out on his fingers.

She nodded. "All right, fourteen. Biologically, you should be in middle age by now. Turning fat and gray, with wrinkles around the eyes."

"You always were a charmer," he told her grumpily.

"But you aren't!" she said, protesting his anger. "Have you looked in a mirror? You're fine. You're a handsome young man, and I'd guess a virile one as well. Even fourteen years ago, our morbidity filters were attacking the aging process at its base—reversing not only the symptoms, but the causes. No one has ever needed to do that before, and believe me, it's not easy. But I'll estimate you're aging at about a third the natural rate. Maybe even a quarter."

"Oh," he said. "Really?" She thought he was handsome? Now *that* was news. Nearly everyone was physically handsome, of course, and the people who weren't either didn't want to be or simply had bad taste. So in using the word, people generally meant something more than the obvious skin-deep. And she thought he was "virile," too! Another loaded word. This was so much at odds with what he thought she thought of him that for the time being he wasn't sure he could believe it. Surely she was flattering him, currying his favor for some reason.

"You probably are due for a faxing, though," she said, still studying him. "If you'd care to risk it, I've got a medical-grade machine in the latter stages of testing. It's intended for the Bupsville hospital, and it has my latest, greatest filter that should keep you fit for several *centuries*."

"Hmm," he said, considering that. "Wow. You *have* been making progress here. Can I make a backup first?"

Her laugh was sour. "I'll insist on it, Conrad. What kind of place do you think we're running here?"

"All right, all right, no offense meant. Sure, I'll give your machine a try."

It turned out she was leading him toward it already—the last stop on his tour. In another minute they were there, in a much smaller testing chamber than any he'd seen previously. The machine stood in the room's exact center, with lights shining down on it from above. The number 449 was emblazoned on it in glowing red numerals. Conrad sniffed the air, finding it rich with . . . something.

"That's the new fax smell," she said, catching his look. "Ionization on the plate and polymer outgassing from the surrounding chassis. Plus a hint of neodymium, and of course the cleaning solution. There's nothing else quite like it."

And then she said something dark and strange that Conrad didn't fully process until much later: "I'm glad you got to smell it this once."

Back at her office again, she called for a door, ushered him inside, and moved back around to sit behind her desk. Conrad settled into one of the armchairs, which was made of plush wellcloth—currently a brightly glowing yellow—and was probably the most comfortable thing he'd parked his ass on in half a century.

"Ooh," he said. "Wow. Nice." His ass was new as well, so the fit was close to perfect.

"So. Have I answered your questions? Do you understand the issues we're faced with?"

With effort, Conrad summoned up a bit of the outrage that had brought him here. "Well, no, not completely. I mean, for example, better fax filters aren't going to help with accidental death. Which is *all* death, right? I haven't heard of anyone dying of old age."

Fortunately, although he'd been studying the shifting decorations on her wellstone walls, he happened to be looking right at her when he said this. As a result, he saw the flicker of unease which passed over her face.

"You have?" he said, leaning forward. If there was one thing he'd learned in his life, it was not to let people conceal bad news. "There *have* been old-age deaths? Spill it, Brenda."

"No," she said, a bit too quickly and defensively. "Not that, definitely."

He waved his hands in little circles in front of him, urging her on. "But . . ."

She sighed, and raised her own hands partway in a gesture of helplessness. "Look, a fax machine doesn't last forever. Ours especially; they seem to have about half the lifetime of a Queendom model, and I'll be damned if I know why."

"So make more," he suggested—but realized immediately what a stupid thing that was to say. Brenda's operation here was already bursting the seams of the Barnard economy.

"We'd need more people, Conrad," she told him angrily. "More robots, more machines and raw materials. Can you give them to me? No? Then shut up."

Watching her, hearing her, Conrad felt a sudden, sinking feeling in his gut. "Oh, God, Brenda. The machines are breaking faster than you can build them."

She didn't deny it, so he went on, "And to build them faster you'd need a bigger colony, which isn't going to happen without more fax machines. It's an old-fashioned chicken-and-egg problem, isn't it?"

"I'm not familiar with that expression," she said.

"I think it's from Rodenbeck. Now that you mention it, I'm not sure I'm using it right. But . . . People used to *eat* eggs, right? And if you eat too many eggs, you won't have enough chickens hatching, and . . . and then . . ."

"Conrad," Brenda said with surprising gentleness, "you're blithering. I don't think I've ever seen you blither before."

"Sorry," he said, and with that word his thoughts snapped back into focus. "We're all going to die, aren't we? Of injury, of old age. Of *disease*. The fax machines are leading the way already, preceding us to the grave. This colony is a failure."

She answered him with a level gaze, her eyes twinkling with faint wellstone lights. "That's been evident for some time. We're going to die, yes, almost certainly. My goodness, didn't you know?"

Conrad was so shaken up—and Brenda so surprised by this—that she took him by the arm and led him to the facility's main cafeteria, a huge room lined with tables, mostly empty at the moment because it wasn't lunchtime.

"We gave it a good try," she was telling him. "And we have a long way still to fall. And as you can see, we're fighting with all our strength. For all we know, we may pull out of it."

"No," he said, seeing the lie in that.

"Well, if we don't, we don't. We knew the risks coming out here, didn't we? Didn't Their Majesties make it plain enough? We're free out here, to live as we please. And to die; immorbid doesn't mean forever. I never thought so, anyway. By the time it all winds down, we'll have had *hundreds of years* of freedom. It's worth our lives just for that."

"But the children," Conrad mourned. "All the beautiful children in this world, so eager and hopeful. Don't they deserve long lives, and children of their own? Don't they deserve the smell of a new fax machine on a warm afternoon?"

A bit of sourness came back into Brenda's voice. "Are you *blaming* me, Conrad? What the children *deserve* has nothing to do with anything."

She seemed ready to launch into a soliloquy of some sort, a long poetic lecture about the facts of life and death, but instead she caught sight of something behind Conrad, and her face pinched into a scowl.

"What are you doing? Hey! *What are you doing?*"

Conrad turned and saw a trio of oversized robots marching toward them: two in front, and one behind them pulling a wheeled dolly of some sort. And on the dolly was the fax machine—number 449—in which Conrad had just refreshed himself. This by itself was not surprising; there were all kinds of robots around here, pushing and pulling and carrying things. But these particular robots were Palace Guards—dainty ones with frilled tutus around their waists and necks, like something from the earliest days of the Queendom.

When they spoke, Conrad couldn't tell if it was one voice or three. In any case, they said, "Brenda Bohobe, President of the Bohobe Plate Manufactory, we bring you the greetings of King Bascal. You are cordially invited to join him at a palace dinner party tonight."

"What are you doing?" Brenda repeated, pointing at the fax machine just in case they somehow failed to take her meaning. "That belongs to the Bupsville hospital."

"This device," the robots said, "has been impounded on the authority of King Bascal. No further information is available at this time."

"That's absurd," she said tightly. "It's not his. It's not even finished! It has force/speed tests still to go, and—"

"Our records show that this device was employed on a volunteer who is not a Manufactory employee. Therefore, it is working. Therefore, it is impounded. Brenda Bohobe, you are to come with us."

"Am I under arrest?" she demanded.

"You are invited," they told her, in an inflectionless tone which nevertheless managed to imply that the two words were, if not identical in meaning, then at least close enough for government purposes.

"Here now," Conrad told them, though he knew it was pointless, "you can't just barge in here and take things. Do you realize how valuable that machine is?"

One of the robots swiveled its head to face him and said, "Conrad Mursk, First Architect of Barnard. You have a standing invitation at the palace, and will please accompany us."

"I don't think so," he said, even though confronting Bascal was exactly what he should probably do right now. He just wanted to see what the robots would say, what they would do. He wouldn't take orders from them, not in this lifetime, not even if they were ordering him to do something rational.

Fortunately, they spared him any further concerns on the matter by pointing a tazzer beam at him and flashing him senseless.

chapter twenty

the feast of permanence

The palace dining room was not large, as such things go. It held a single long table with seating for twenty, plus some additional wellstone chairs along the walls so that, Conrad supposed, people could come to watch their betters eat.

Well, maybe that was unfair. If he were going to sell that feature as part of a building design, he would call it "buffet seating," good for informal parties and such. Which he supposed this gathering probably was. And this room *was*, he reminded himself, part of a building he had personally designed!

There were no decorations or lighting fixtures per se, because the walls and floor and ceiling were all made of wellstone. Light and windows could appear anywhere. But this by itself had become a rare thing on P2, and its novelty was not lost on Conrad now, especially since the programming was all new. The surfaces emitted a soft glow, with cleverly subtle spotlights shining down onto the table itself. Looking up at the ceiling he found it difficult to see precisely where they were coming from.

The shadows were carefully controlled as well, while stained-glass windows along the north wall admitted just enough natural light, in just the right mix of colors, to lend a

picnic air to the proceedings. The windows were nonrepre-
sentational, and shifted slowly from one pattern to another.
This, too, was a quaintly decadent touch, and showed good
taste. Princess Wendy's, apparently.

Brenda's stolen fax machine—a great, gray slab surrounded by exposed piping and circuitry—dominated one
end of the room, with Bascal sitting before it at the head of
the table. To his great surprise Conrad found himself seated
at the foot of the table, a position of honor to be sure, and in
spite of the manner of his arrival he could not help feeling
flattered. At the king's left was Princess Wendy, and beside
her, to Conrad's additional surprise, was Mack.

Conrad would never forget the initial meeting between
those two: throbbing with subdued passion that seemed destined to burn itself out within a few weeks. He hadn't stuck
around to see the end of that kiddie relationship, but he had
never doubted that it *would* end. Until now. Funny; he'd
traded a dozen messages with Mack over the years, checking
up on his old business, his old protégé, but Mack had never
once mentioned the princess. And yet the way he sat, the way
she sat, the way they looked at each other...

"Hi, Boss," Mack said to him, and though he smiled there
might have been a bit of rebuke in his tone. For he still ran
Murskitectura, the company Conrad had started in the early
years of the colony. And he ran it alone.

"Hi, Mack. How's business?"

The smile became a smirk. "How do you think? The population's not expanding, there's no free capital for discretionary
building, and your damned masterworks will last five thousand years if they last a day. We're getting margin work:
adding a new housing wing here and there, in your name and
style. You cast a long shadow, Boss."

"Sorry," Conrad offered sincerely.

But Mack just laughed. "Hey, I'm only a troll. What do I
know, or need to?" He raised Wendy's hand in his own. "It's
enough that I keep my lady in diamonds."

This was a joke; diamonds were commonplace in the crust
of P2, worth little more than quartz. But Wendy laughed, and
seemed to find it witty.

"Welcome, First Architect," she said, waving Conrad toward his assigned position.

Brenda was seated at Bascal's right, and seemed far more annoyed than flattered by the attention, while Martin Liss, the doctor from Domesville hospital, was seated to her right. Farther down the table sat a number of people Conrad didn't recognize, but then, in the middle, were Robert and Agnes M'chunu, whom Conrad hadn't seen in ages but who, by all reports, had made quite a good show of things after deciding to get married. They were light farmers or something, tending solar collectors and capacitor banks and selling power on the open market, but they also grew and sold vegetables. Conrad had a hard time picturing them grubbing in the dirt, although he supposed someone had to, or half the colony would be living on glucose and protein paste from crappy waste-disposal faxes.

They didn't need chairs; Robert and Agnes had joined the centaurs long ago. Galloping across the open countryside was perhaps not as glamorous as flight, but even so the centaurs were, in some sense, the realization of the angels' dream: speed *and* strength, with an empty world in which to test them. "We're the freest people who ever lived," Robert had told him once. Now the two of them sat at the table on four folded legs, with dainty little prayer rugs under them to prevent their chafing against the wellwood floor. But they were still colored that same shade of bright, unnatural blue, from head to hoof to swishing tail. Even among centaurs, they were iconoclasts.

"Hello, sir," Robert said to Conrad.

"Hi," he returned. "You two are looking well."

"Healthy as horses," Robert said, then laughed at his own joke. "The country air does a body good, but I think by now you've learned that for yourself."

Conrad was disappointed, though truthfully not terribly surprised, to find Ho Ng seated at his own left. With effort, he managed to smile politely at his old nemesis. Though still a commander in the Royal Barnardean Navy, Ho was married now, too, and his wife (apparently printed only a few weeks before) sat at his elbow looking adoring and excited and terribly, terribly young.

"If possible," Ho was saying, while his hands sketched cylindrical shapes in the air, "you want to fire along the target ship's longest axis, to rupture the maximum number of compartments. The Queendom's naval theoreticians have never fought a real battle, but their analysis is bang on."

"Have you fought a real battle?" Conrad asked him, surprised.

"Two," Ho said, looking him over. "Space pirates, out in the Lutui Belt. Where the fuck have you been?"

Conrad snorted. "Nice to see you, too, Commander."

To Conrad's right were a pair of empty chairs, and presently their occupants appeared in the doorway: Feck the Facilitator and his noble captain, Xiomara Li Weng. Conrad lit up when he saw them.

"Xmary! Feck! So they tazzed you too, eh?"

"What?" Feck said, looking back at him blankly.

"Where's Money?" Conrad tried.

And Feck answered, "Living on Element Pit, if you can believe it. Still working the bugs out of that neutronium dripline pump of yours. He's going to blow that place up, I swear."

"Of mine? I had nothing to do with that."

"Really? Your name is on the patent. And truthfully, Money's onto something. Even the Queendom is taking an interest, though of course they're years out of synch."

Xmary just smiled and sat down beside him. "Hello, darling. I heard you broke your arm."

"Oh, that? It was nothing," Conrad assured her. The sound of her voice had arrested him; suddenly he was seeing nothing but her eyes, her cheekbones, the happy upward curve of her lips.

"That's not what I heard. Someone told me you almost froze to death."

Conrad sighed, then smiled. "The world is full of spies, I suppose. Yes, I caught my shoe in a crack and broke my arm falling; then I had to walk two kilometers through blinding snow with no direction finder. Are you happy now?"

From the other end of the table, Brenda called down at

them, "He won't be breaking it anymore, Captain. These latest filters weave wellstone and nanotubes into the bones, along with a cylindrical sleeve of brickmail."

"They do?" Conrad asked, surprised. Brenda hadn't mentioned that at the time. There had been no consent forms, no permissions or fine print, just a casual step through the plate. He found the idea vaguely unsettling, though; brickmail was a three-dimensional array of interlocked benzene rings—carbon chain mail, some called it—and it was the strongest nonprogrammable material known to humanity, by a considerable margin.

It was porous, too, allowing gas molecules to diffuse through, and even small fluid molecules like water. Well, under the right conditions, anyway. It wasn't difficult to picture a honeycomb of that stuff inside his bones, propping them up, making them stronger and lighter than bones had any right to be. The idea of being indestructible was actually kind of appealing—he might even survive a bit of Security training—but of course he still had blood and marrow, internal organs and all that. If something really bad happened to him, they would find—intact!—these bits of artificial skeleton, with no Conrad attached to them.

Unless—and this was a crawly sort of thought—the changes ran deeper than that. His arm began, nonsensically, to itch.

"Am I still human?" he asked Brenda.

This provoked a hearty laugh from everyone at the table, most especially Mack.

"As much as ever," Brenda replied, and then did something Conrad had never imagined her capable of: she winked. This brought more scattered laughter from the assembled diners, and Conrad had the distinct feeling there was some joke here that he wasn't in on. Spending the past few decades in such isolation had seemed like a good idea—most immorbid people seemed to do it sooner or later—but it did have its disadvantages. Even onboard *Newhope*, he'd been connected more or less directly with the machineries of government, and with the *palasa*, the bronze, the upper stories of Barnard's social pyramid. Not so on *Snowflake,* or in the Polar Well.

C'est la vie.

When dinner arrived, it pushed upward from the table's surface as if growing: bowls and mugs, plates and utensils rising into the light of existence. Conrad realized with a shock that the entire tabletop was an industrial-grade print plate, cleverly disguised. Good God! Here was a table he'd be sure to keep his elbows off of, lest it suck him in for raw material!

"Kataki hau o kai," Bascal said in his best Tongan, marking the official beginning of the meal, though in fact more than one set of fingers had already pinched a morsel.

The dinner itself was an odd blend of old and new traditions. The main course was a Barnardean favorite: TVs. This consisted of dozens of little television holies composed of edible polymers and served in a bowl, chilled. The pictures on all the little screens cycled through some of the best-known scenes from the early Queendom and the late Tongan monarchy at the tail end of Old Modernity. There was sound, but it was turned down so far that Conrad couldn't make it out over the conversation around him.

Along with TVs there was a salad composed mainly of Earth plants that grew well on Planet Two: dandelion and collard, sweet potato and dwarf peanut. But it was seasoned with a bitter mash: *tévé* from the islands of Tonga, also known as "famine weed" for its habit of sustaining the Polynesian peoples when other crops refused to grow. Ironically, though, no one had ever come up with a strain of *tévé* that could survive for long in the open on P2. You could grow it in filtered hothouses or print it whole (and dead) from a high-end food machine, and that was about it. Its presence here could only be symbolic: a carefully orchestrated nod toward the deprivations outside.

There were other delicacies: red tea and iceberg soup, sugar blossoms and meatcakes, but these were fitted in like garnishes around the two main courses. Truthfully, it was a better meal than Conrad had seen in centuries, or maybe ever.

Conrad turned to Princess Wendy and said, around a mouthful of TVs, "It's very nice to see you again, young lady. I've just realized that I never did meet your mother."

Wendy's smile was radiant, almost painfully beautiful. Conrad did not doubt that she was a constructed creature, the child of her parents but equally, obviously, tailored to some optimum, some royal ideal of humanity.

She said, "I rarely see Mumsy myself, First Architect. She is not after all a member of the royal family, and while you might hope such things would not come between a mother and daughter, or any two people really, the simple fact is that they do."

She punctuated this comment by taking up Mack's trollish hand and squeezing it. Mack, for his part, seemed at ease, as though he did this all the time. They made an interesting pair, this princess and troll, for trolls were, by all accounts, unusually gifted in the arts of love, but had almost no sense of taste, culinary or otherwise. Ironically, this fit perfectly with Conrad's architectural style, making Mack a very good successor for him: passionate and direct, free of silly distractions. But when it came to subtler business, the finer things in life were said to slide right by a troll, unnoticed or taken for granted. Like this banquet? Like fair Wendy herself?

Still, in a world where death was possible, odd pairings like this might be the norm—might even be preferred. The pressure was perhaps not so much to find a soul mate for all eternity, but to find someone smart and funny and interesting, to keep you company for a few decades while entropy crept up from behind. In his mind this new world was like a dance floor, urgently beckoning: grab a partner and go, before the music stops!

"I was going to marry her mother," Bascal chimed in with a leer. "Truly, I was. But things got more difficult after Wendy was born. It changed the dynamic, and our relationship never really did spring back. It was Nala herself who called it quits. She's a surveyor now, and happily married out in the Blackberry Belts somewhere. We wish her all the best"—he glanced at his daughter as if for confirmation—"but she resists contact, and we have for the most part respected that. Even on this fine occasion."

A coarse, unamused laugh escaped Conrad's lips. "Funny, you didn't respect *me* when *I* resisted contact."

And here, the king's expression darkened. "Is that so? Well. You could have been my most trusted adviser, Conrad. There was no one else for the job. But even before you left Domesville, your avoidance of me had been, I would almost say, pathological. It hurts my feelings, but more to the point, it deprives society of a trusted voice."

"The voice of reason?" Conrad asked with uncharacteristic sourness. "Next you'll tell me that with my advice, we wouldn't be in the mess we're in now. As if I could have done anything. As if I know anything the rest of the world doesn't."

To his credit, Bascal considered these words seriously before replying, "Fair enough. We're at the mercy of economic forces that are larger than any of us. But still, you could've helped. You could have tried." He looked glum for a long moment, but then found a reserve of cheer somewhere inside himself and said expansively, "I am sorry about the kidnapping, old friend. Perhaps we should have asked, but this occasion, this one particular occasion, demands your presence. A bit of melodrama makes it all the sweeter."

"And what occasion is that, exactly?"

"Why, Wendy's birthday," Bascal said, sounding genuinely surprised. Another thing Conrad was presumed to know.

"I'm fifty years old today," Wendy chirped. The look on her face was appallingly self-satisfied.

Conrad's own face fell into a gape of dismay. "You're fifty? That's impossible. After you were born, I spent a few year . . . a few dec . . . well . . ."

He *had* spent a lot of time out and away. In space, on the sea, in the quiet of the Polar Well. Maybe it *had* been fifty years. Jesus and the little gods, when Conrad was fifty he was already the architect of a world, and that was his third career! First he'd been a paver's boy, and afterward a space pirate. This little girl, this supposed child, had lived a natural human lifespan and then some. Conrad found himself looking her over, appraising her in much the same way that Brenda had appraised him earlier. He felt he should reassess her in some way, change his baseless opinions about her, but he didn't know where to begin.

Finally, he just forced a smile and said, "Goodness, how

the years fly by. It's a curse of the immorbid, this putting things off, this plenty-of-time-for-that-later mentality. It causes us to miss the things that happen quickly, even important things that are right in front of our faces. Like the flowering of a delightful young woman. My apologies, Princess, and happy birthday."

"Thank you," she said, looking appropriately charmed.

"Really," Conrad said, "I'm surprised you remember me at all. We saw each other, what, four times before I shipped out?"

"Six," she replied. "But who's counting? Mr. Mursk, the people we meet in early life leave a powerful imprint. When the mind is still forming and the hormones rage, and everything is brighter and grander, a face is so much more than just an oval of skin. We remember them, oh yes, and though they stray apart from us, they never really leave."

Conrad thought of his own parents, and of the King and Queen of Sol, and of Bascal and all the other boys he'd gone to camp with.... He hadn't seen some of them in a century or more, but they remained his friends, the best friends he'd ever had. He could not disagree with Wendy's point.

"I always thought," Wendy went on, "that you were fleeing from *me* as well as from my father. The very sight of me seemed to drive you into a panic. As it did my mother. It's a curious thing, isn't it? Confronted with youth, we discover the lack of it in ourselves. We must face the things we used to be, and the things we dreamed of but never were, and never will be. Do I frighten you still?"

There didn't seem to be a lot of emotion riding on the question. She wasn't going to be upset one way or the other, no matter how Conrad answered. But she was honestly curious, and for this reason Conrad gave the question considerable thought. Other conversations began to spring up around the table, but finally he said over them, "I think part of it was just my own weakness, Princess. You wanted...something...which I feared I might actually provide. It would have been unseemly, and I didn't trust myself.

"But there's truth in what you say: you made me feel old, for the first time in my life. And now you're fifty, and I feel older still. You *are* a bit frightening, yes. Your father has always been a sort of mad genius, and the women he loves have been intelligent as well, and always...sharp, I guess you'd say. Hard-edged." He cast a glance at Brenda and found her looking back at him with a blend of annoyance and curiosity.

"So you fear I'm a deranged genius as well?" Wendy asked. "A *faha alapoto*?"

Conrad gestured with his hands, not quite nodding, not quite agreeing. "I just...I remember how *we* were: determined to change things, determined to get into trouble. And we *have*, on both counts. This colony's entire population is paying for the indiscretions of our youth. With their own lives, as often as not."

Here Bascal injected a comment of his own, in vaguely wistful tones. "Death has been a constant companion through every age. Our own parents faced it early in their lives, or believed they did. In fact, death has shaped us all; the process of apoptosis, or programmed cell death, is crucial in the growth of any organism, from the lidicara to your own self. It's what gives you your shape and structure. Without death, you'd be a mindless blob, as monstrous and misbegotten as anything that ever spilled out of a fax. With death written into our very programming, did we really believe it could be banished forever?"

"Didn't we?" Conrad shot back. "Shouldn't we? What's civilization *for* if not to protect the lives of its people?"

The king smiled and shook his head. "No, sorry. That's a nice theory, but the only thing civilizations act to preserve is their own continuity. That's a very different thing. Rome lasted a thousand years, with an average citizen's life span of just twenty-five. Think about that. Lives were fleeting; it was *ideas* and *institutions* that mattered. Perhaps we have something to learn from their example."

"How to die?" Conrad asked. "No, thank you. They didn't have a choice about it."

"We may not, either," Bascal said unhappily. "What are we to do, evacuate the planet? *Newhope* was meant to carry a hundred live people, plus cargo modules, including memory cores. Do we put everyone in storage? We can't, because the cores are full, and making more would tie up our best remaining faxes, further exacerbating the shortage."

"We could freeze the living," Conrad suggested half seriously. "Ship them in coffins."

But Bascal rebutted that at once, and firmly. "Frozen bodies take up ten times more volume than the core space for a scanned human image. Captain Li Weng, how many coffins can your ship hold?"

Xmary shrugged, clearly reluctant to take Bascal's side over Conrad's. "I don't know. Properly containerized, I suppose it would be thousands."

"Hundreds of thousands?" the king pressed. "Our entire population?"

"No," she admitted, plucking a final morsel off her plate and popping it into her mouth. "Not nearly."

Conrad had no reply to that, and the king's next words were gentler. "The answer is to live well, Conrad, to take joy in every day that remains. That has always been the answer. Do you know much about economics?"

Glumly, Conrad shook his head. "Not beyond what it takes to run a construction company, no. Why would I? I never thought I'd need it."

"Well," the king said, "it never hurts to know what fate has in store. I'll summarize for you, if you don't mind. Do you know what a free market is?"

"Sure," Conrad said. In the same way he knew what a guillotine was, or a printing press. Contrivances of the Old Modern era, or perhaps even earlier, before even electricity had been tamed, when the world stank of horse manure and burning wax.

"Don't look so disdainful, my friend; free markets were elegant, self-correcting systems. With supply and demand driving the cost of goods directly, pathological outcomes—the razing of forests, the overvaluation of trivial commodities—were uncommon and brief. Most of the horror stories come from *partially* free markets, distorted by ill-considered policy. In fact, it's been shown mathematically that unregulated markets were two-thirds as efficient as perfect-knowledge monarchies. Without hypercomputers to guide them, the

Old Moderns learned—painfully, to be sure!—that nature was better left to take its course."

"Why are you telling us this?" asked one of the young men Conrad didn't recognize.

"In your case, Titus," the king answered coolly, "because you happen to be here. As a bonus, you're also ignorant and in sore need of enlightenment. Others are merely curious."

"'Monarchy is the mathematical optimum of governance,'" Conrad quoted.

"Yes," Bascal agreed, "but only with sufficient computing power to back it up, and only if the monarch himself is sensible. This is in large part why we retain the anachronism of a Senate, to whom formal power is nominally assigned. It's a check against my own potential for error. They have their own analysts, their own computers, and they're free to overrule my judgments if they deem it necessary."

And if they don't value their careers, Conrad added silently. Bascal was well known for arranging the dismissal of senators who failed to share his vision.

"What I'm getting at," the king said, "is that we can, in some actual tangible sense, prepare ourselves for what lies ahead. Quantum mechanics demands that the future be uncertain, but not infinitely so. Finite uncertainty, you see? Which is the same thing as a tiny bit of certainty. And as it happens, our productivity curves do not appear to crash to zero. Indeed, with finite certainty they seem to skirt it and rise again into prosperity. We have a long, dark night ahead of us, but if we can maintain that continuity of civilization, with labor-driven industries and children born the old-fashioned way, as actual babies from actual wombs, then our morning will eventually come, and with it perchance the revival of our dead."

"Maintain it how?" asked the young man named Titus.

Bascal smiled at him. "Has it occurred to you, boy, that I'm addressing someone other than yourself?"

"Oh," Titus said, dropping his gaze. "Well. My apologies, Sire."

"Accepted," Bascal answered dismissively. "Now do shut up."

Toying with his mug, Conrad cleared his throat and said, "Why, uh, did you take this fax machine, Bas? As a birthday present? It belongs to a hospital."

"I know very well to whom it belongs, boyo. They'll receive it in due time—probably within a few days—but in the meanwhile it has an official state function to perform. Namely, the archiving of the critical personnel here assembled. Backups have been sporadic since the palace machine went down, but continuity requires not only the right people, but also some synchrony among them. I can't have a five-year-old copy of my finance minister collaborating with a fifty-year-old copy of my security chief! Therefore a hard cable, surrounded by layered insulation of almost geological dimension, has been laid from here—from this very room wherein we dine—to the Southland Data Morgue where the memory cores are stored.

"And yes, never fear, I'll be updating the records of more than just you few; over the next few days we'll be cycling over a thousand people through these opalescent gates. Notices are going out as we speak."

A thousand people. Barely half a percent of the colony's population. Conrad wasn't so dense as to require an explanation: Bascal could not save everyone, so he would save—literally *save*, archive, store—the people he deemed most valuable to the colony. Death would come, yes, but not for all. The imperfect promise of freezing and eventual revival would be reserved for the proletariat, the rabble, the serfs and peasants, while this immorbid elite feasted its way through the crisis.

Conrad sighed, feeling a bit more of the fight drain out of him. He could see the logic—even the inevitability—of this approach. But he and Bascal had been faced with such decisions before, in the very darkest of their pirate days, and Conrad had insisted at the time that they seek volunteers, that they draw straws, that death be accepted only as a voluntary sacrifice, not imposed as a sentence upon weeping innocents. And he'd been overruled.

Still, honor demanded his next words, which he stood to deliver. "Sire, I thank you sincerely for this honor, but I must decline. I wouldn't feel right about it."

Bascal gave him a hard look, then finally an unhappy shrug. "Suit yourself. I think it's a mistake, and I'll invite you to reconsider. The colony needs its founders, its senior members, its most talented and insightful. But Jesus, Conrad, that tazzing was a *joke*. For old times' sake, you understand? And for my daughter's birthday. I'm not a monster, boyo. I'll not force anyone."

This answer was unexpected, and Conrad was somewhat unbalanced by it, like a man who throws his weight against a wall only to discover it's really a curtain. To add lack of insult to this lack of injury, Bascal then rose from his seat—a signal to the other diners that the formal part of the dinner was over, that casual chitchat and milling around were duly authorized. This of course broke the spell of Conrad's gesture, leaving him no room to reply unless he raised his voice. And that would make him look like an ass, if he didn't already.

Damn.

"You're always showboating," said Ho Ng, standing now at Conrad's elbow. His voice was quiet, more amused than menacing. "Imagining we're all, like, waiting to see what you'll do. Like we give a shit. So you'll be dead and frozen while the rest of us pull things back together. How dramatic. Is that supposed to make you a hero?"

Ho's wife, looking on from the sidelines, seemed rapt at his words. Or maybe just honestly in love. *That* couldn't be a bad thing, could it? Even if the man she felt it for was a shitheel? She seemed so young, so innocent. Maybe she'd be good for him.

"I may last longer than you think," Conrad told Ho, and surprised himself by sounding amused. "Apparently I'm made of brickmail."

Ho sneered. "Join the club, fuckwipe. I can see in infrared and breathe carbolic acid. You could shoot fifty holes in me without breaking my stride."

"And you're charming, too," Conrad told him.

"Oh, Conrad," Xmary said, touching him on the arm. "Don't be like this, please. I want you safely stored, and not just for your sake or mine. It's the right thing to do. You *are* important to the colony."

"He may be stored already," Brenda said, sidling up around a knot of chatting youngsters. "I wasn't in the room when the cables went live, but Conrad's image was in the fax machine's buffer. If they flushed it rather than scrubbing, then he'd've gone straight to the Data Morgue." Then she addressed Conrad directly: "I don't know what the fuss is about, anyway; you've never been deleted off the original personnel core. *Some* copy of you is kicking around down there, younger and snottier than you are today."

"See?" Ho chimed in gleefully. "Showboating. Thinks he's something special. Better than the rest of us, certainly, when really he's just some old fuck hiding out in the countryside. Counting snowflakes."

And that *was* rather an artful jab for someone as coarse and uncomplicated as Ho. Conrad felt he should choose his next words carefully. But just at that moment, the other end of the table rang with the clear, bell-like tones of dinner spoons on wellstone mugs, and a knot of admirers around Princess Wendy were shouting "Ten thousand years! *Taha mano ta'u!* Ten thousand years!" and hauling her in the direction of the fax machine.

"Wait," she laughed. "I have to relieve my bladder; I have to fix my *hair*."

But her friends were having none of that. "Fix it in the future!" they teased her. "You need some flaws to break the symmetry; store the real you!" And with a slingshot hold on her arms, they hurled her forward against the print plate.

"No! Not so hard!" Brenda shouted at them, but it was too late; the princess had gone ballistic, still on her feet but stumbling forward with one arm stretched out before her and the other trailing behind. To her credit, the last expression on her face was one of simple joy: the birthday girl enduring her mandatory ritual punishments in the spirit with which they were delivered.

The fax, alas, was not so accommodating. Accepting Wendy's careening mass, it flashed and sparked and groaned and then went dark; and with a smell of scorched meat the back half of that young, royal body rebounded from the print plate, flailed upright for a boneless moment, and then collapsed in a squirting heap upon the floor.

The sight of it was, for a moment, too alien for Conrad's mind to process. He did not, in that first second or two, have any idea what had happened, and all he could think—literally *all* he could think—was that young women really did shriek in horror, like extras in a bad movie, when something hot and red was splashed upon their gowns.

#### chapter twenty-one

till death do us park

Five days later, after the public funeral procession had wound its way through the streets of Domesville, those same dinner guests—almost the exact same collection of people— found themselves on a tuberail car together, with Wendy's freezer coffin placed conspicuously at its center. Some of these men and women were crying; some were stoic; but most displayed that brittle, funereal cheerfulness which, as the years ground on, all of them would learn all too well. *They* might be immorbid—emphasis on the "might"—but given enough time, nearly everyone else they knew would end up in one of these boxes.

The accident was freakish and bizarre, but so was every accident. Such was their nature in a world of mature technology. It was shocking enough that the princess had died; did her archive *have* to be corrupted in the process?

"This is much harder than I expected," Bascal was saying to Conrad, as they sat together on a bench across the aisle from the coffin. "It occurs to me, belatedly I suppose, that the brunt of this fatal recession will fall on our children. You and I are freshly scrubbed; these bodies will hold together for centuries. With proper care, perhaps a good deal longer than that. But if the colony is going to survive, we must have children. Our population needs to triple, maybe quadruple. And once the faxes are gone, we'll have no way to protect these youngsters from the vagaries of time and fortune. Generation upon generation, they'll be born and live and die without ever once having the benefit of proper medicine. And that will be hard on the parents. Unimaginably hard."

Conrad hadn't known Wendy all that well, but he fancied he was grieving as much and as hard as the people who had. Not Bascal, perhaps, not Mack or her other close friends. But the other mourners, the acquaintances and well-wishers, did not seem any more or less stricken than Conrad himself. Even Xmary, who had spent nine months with Wendy during an extended Domesville shore leave, had retained her composure, and in fact could not attend the funeral event itself due to a critical departure time conflict.

But the hugeness of Wendy's accident—its suddenness, its permanence and unappealability...Those communicated. They penetrated any facade. Wendy had had other plans for the evening, and did not go bravely to her death, or see it coming in any way. Who did?

In some sense everyone in Barnard knew this woman—she was their princess after all—but Conrad realized he could probably sit in the funeral car of a total stranger, someone he'd never once laid his gaze on, and still spend half the time wiping this salty mist from his eyes. Tears: another worldly anachronism.

He was tempted to reassure himself that these were strange times, that these feelings were nothing a human being was ever meant to endure. But the actual facts were quite opposite: in the grand scheme of things, it was the immorbid Queendom that was unusual, not this sad, mortal kingdom. Most of the people who'd ever lived had done it under conditions far more painful and hopeless and humiliating than these. This thought by itself brought fresh tears to his eyes. Ask not for whom the bell tolls, indeed.

"I'm sorry," he'd told Mack, over and over again. "So very, very sorry for you."

"Pity the world," was Mack's only answer. "I love her, I

miss her, I want her back, Boss. But I'll be all right. Troll hearts are made of tougher stuff."

Still, where Bascal was concerned, Conrad's duties were clear: he was bursting with sympathy, and while he rarely knew the right thing to say, he spouted platitudes from old plays and stories, and they sounded all right. But that was only when he felt he must speak; mostly he didn't say anything at all. Instead he listened, and since Bascal wasn't much inclined to talk either, as often as not the two of them just sat together: two old men on a bench, at a loss for words, overwhelmed by their world.

He patted his old friend on the knee. "Bascal, maybe it's time we cut our losses. We could stop having children, and start ferrying the ones we do have back to Sol. With prudence, and perhaps some risky allocation of faxes and memory cores, I'll bet we could complete the job in five trips."

But Bascal was shaking his head. "No. No, the mating urge is much stronger than that. Especially among the young, the doomed, the mortal, and most especially of all in poor economies. Read up on your history; it's all there. You could make a trip, yes, but by the time you got back, the problem would have doubled in size and complexity, and you'd be faced with whole generations for whom your departure—however heroic—would be a historical event. These kids don't pine for a Queendom they've never seen, never smelled, never felt between their toes."

"And on the return voyage," Conrad said, as though the king had not spoken, "we'll fill the holds with print plates of the Queendom's highest quality. And while the colony is using those up, we'll be off fetching more."

Bascal's hands were waving in frustration. "That doesn't solve the basic problem, which is a dearth of industrial base. You can't cheat on this, Conrad. We've been trying for two hundred years, and where has it led us? I've run the numbers every way I can think of, and have yet to find any relief. Because relief *doesn't exist*. Not in this lifetime.

"And anyway, economically speaking, the promise of rescue reduces the incentive to plan for the long term. There is a branch of psychology called lifeboat psychology that has many salient words on this point. I fear there is only one solution, and it's a hard, sad road indeed. The appalling thing is that none of us saw this coming until it was too late. Indeed, we may have been doomed from the moment *Newhope*'s engines lit up. Which, by the way, is yet another problem with your theory: we have no launching lasers here. *Newhope*'s departure velocity would be a *lot* lower than it was leaving Sol. The journey would take centuries, not decades, and by the time you got back we'd all be dead, or through the needle's eye to prosperity again."

This reply was about what Conrad had expected. It was rare indeed for him to have a thought which had not occurred to Bascal first, and Bascal always had planning and wise mathematics on his side. Or believed he did, anyway, and there was no changing his mind about that. Nevertheless, with a strange sense of déjà vu—a sense that they were not so far removed from their pirate days after all, he persevered. "We could ask for help. Surely the Queendom has realized our peril by now. Ask your parents for a rescue ship, ten times the size of *Newhope*. I'll bet they could have something here within fifty years."

But at these words Bascal's face, already blotchy with grief, simply closed down in anger. "We *are* prisoners here, or have you forgotten? We've been kicked out of Paradise, and now you propose to go begging at its gates. To die like a dog when with far less effort you could die like a man. I'm disappointed, Conrad. I wish I could say I was also surprised."

"Your parents haven't turned their backs on us, Bas. They wouldn't do that."

"No? They've got problems of their own, boyo. In case you hadn't noticed, they haven't produced a starship in decades. The era of colonial expansion has ended. It's just not cost-effective, and why would it be? Wiser now, they focus their not-so-limitless resources on terraforming, on digging new holes for their own burgeoning population to slither into. Places which are directly under their control, you understand, so that these colonial blunders, these *fakaevaha* and *de'sastres*, cannot be repeated. You have a good heart, Conrad—I've always known that. But equally, you've got a soft head and a weak stomach. You've never been good at facing reality when reality is bleak. Which, if you think about it, is always."

"Facing a reality that we're all going to die? Am I supposed to just accept that?"

"Probably not all of us," Bascal said. "But most. And yes, I expect you to understand that fact and behave accordingly. If you don't accept the possibility of death, you have no way of putting your affairs in order, of planning your life as a useful enterprise. You'll simply collapse one day—maybe far in the future, but with no greater dignity for that. No higher purpose.

"Or perhaps you'll throw your life away in a grand gesture. You do like to play the hero. But there is greater heroism, my friend, in being realistic. It's a greater service, to yourself and to the rest of us. Little gods, Conrad, you're a grown man. Act your age, hmm? Historically speaking, you're *ten* grown men laid end to end on the timeline of civilization."

"Aye," Conrad agreed, slipping unconsciously into the surety of naval parlance. "That I am." His thoughts, though, were not in agreement with Bascal's. He realized suddenly that they rarely had been, ever. This seemed a late and rather pointless epiphany, but he filed it with the others that had occurred to him over the years—his private stash of agely wisdom.

He clapped the king on the knee again. "Let's speak of something else. Tonight, my friend, we'll drug ourselves insensible and talk about the past. Isn't that what old men do? And none of these subtle Queendom drugs will do: I'm talking about memory enhancers and straight ethanol. Maybe a hint of the grape, for flavoring."

Bascal smiled a brittle, funereal smile and leaned back wearily in his bench. "Oh, that sounds awful, truly. And yet, it's better than any of the alternatives. There are those who won't recover, and those who'll recover without assistance. And then there are those who require attention. Yes, I see it now: triage demands that we do as you say."

At the end of their three-hour train ride lay the Southland Cryoleum, five thousand kilometers away, near the center of the Peninsulum Pectoralis. The province was known less formally as the Fin, which Conrad suddenly realized was a kind of pun or double-entendre: the arm of a fish, yes, and also a word for endings. The fin, the terminus, the Land of the Dead. Their tuberail car was greeted by a man who claimed to have been Wendy's undertaker.

"She was no trouble," he assured them all in what he probably thought was a kindly voice.

And why should she have been? With her body bisected like that, every blood vessel was laid open for his nanobes and preservatories, and he'd need only half the usual amounts! There wasn't a lot of her to freeze, and while the Palace Guards had surely loomed over him like metal angels of retribution, making sure everything was done just so, it hardly mattered that her cell structure—even the remains of her brain—survive the long freezing.

Over in the Data Morgue, ten kilometers west of here, her core image had been corrupted—overlaid with half a copy, followed by a mess of random electrical noise and then silence. A set of plausible terminators had been computed and applied to the file—the news reports were emphatic about that—but nobody really believed that half a damaged body and half a damaged core image could be reassembled into a whole person again. Not the original person, anyway; no amount of technology, of royal wealth or staffing, could accomplish that.

"Thank you," Bascal said to the man, with apparent sincerity. Then he choked up a bit before managing to add, "We appreciate your efforts."

There was a bishop at the actual ceremony, in the Cryoleum's rather industrial-looking reception hall, but his words were perfunctory, his rehearsed praises and platitudes mercifully brief. This was a private ceremony, and there was little he could tell the crowd about Wendy—or about death and resurrection, or the mathematical possibilities of an afterlife—that they didn't already know.

But then Bascal surprised them all by rising to the podium and singing, unaccompanied, a song he claimed to have written the night before. It was called "The Storms of Sorrow," and Conrad found himself weeping afresh at its words—particularly "the rain upon sorrow's face." Bascal had perhaps written better in his distant youth, but for a long-awaited first effort here in his own kingdom, it did not disappoint. The audience gave him a five-minute standing ovation when it was complete, which afterward seemed disrespectful to poor Wendy, but what the hell; they were out of the public eye here, and Wendy, too, would have liked the song. Her father's voice, barely remembered after all these years, was among humanity's most beautiful.

Later, at the reception, Conrad balanced a plate of synthetic cheese and pickled blackberries on top of his wineglass in order to offer the king an admiring handshake.

"Gorgeous music, Sire. Gorgeous *poetry*, moving and appropriate for the occasion. Listen to me, I sound like a sycophant! But I loved that, really. You talked about sorrow almost like it was a tangible thing. A place we've all come to."

Bascal nodded, with tears streaming down his cheeks. "Indeed, boyo, I have named this planet at last. I wanted to wait, you know? To see how things would turn out. And now we know: Sorrow, to remind us of our sins. A whole world of Sorrow for us to explore, to populate, to belong to forever."

And that was just too wrenching; Conrad put down his plate and glass and threw his arms around the king, and together they wept for a good long while. But while Bascal was weeping in helpless rage, Conrad cried in part for an even simpler reason: because Bascal was the best friend he'd ever had, and yet he felt in his bones that the two of them would never be closer than they were at this terrible moment. The future would not be the quiet downward spiral the former Prince of Sol had described, but something much darker and nastier. Something which would set the two of them firmly apart.

And where do feelings like this come from, these sudden certainties? Are they tricks of neuroanatomy, or perhaps the quantum fluctuations of future time, echoing faster than light so that they impinge—however faintly!—on the past? Or if time be static and free will an illusion, are they perhaps the hand of God, shaping the landscape of immutable history? Are they true prophecies or self-fulfilling ones? In any case, all of history has turned upon them, more than once.

"This place is ugly," Conrad finally remarked, when the two of them had sought the safety of a bench in another room, away from the party proper. "No offense, Sire, but I wouldn't want my *dog* frozen here, much less my princess, who changed my own life simply by appearing in it."

"True," the king agreed, looking around. The whole structure looked like exactly what it was: a warehouse. An industrial space for the storage of cryogenic goods. "All too true. If death is to follow us at every step, we should turn to face it on the ground of our own choosing: in a house of strength and human achievement. A cathedral, a tower, a fulsome garden! Not this . . . garage. Perhaps you could have a look around before you leave, with an eye toward improvements?"

"Gladly, Sire. I'll begin within the hour. Will . . . you be all right?"

"No," the king said. "But I'm needed at the party, and at the palace, and at the helm of government. And you, my friend, are needed here in civilization."

"Aye," Conrad agreed. "So it would seem."

He tracked down the mortician again and managed to get a tour of the facilities. Things were even worse than he'd figured; twenty-three thousand bodies entombed here already, in ugly slotted dewars of plastic foam and unprogrammed glass, filled with liquified nitrogen. There were power and temperature gauges all around, and signs full of warnings and instructions. Also warning lights here and there, flashing and beeping irregularly, disturbing the peace.

"Do people come here to visit?" he asked the mortician, whose name was Carl Piñon Faxborn.

"Sometimes. Not often. The bodies are shipped down here for embalming and cryolation, and as often as not returned northward for formal receptions, glass caskets and all, before coming back here for their final rest. Occasionally, we'll disinter one for another brief trip: a busy relative paying his or her respects, and occasionally we'll hold a re-viewing here on the premises."

That sounded awful to Conrad, and he said so.

"Well," Carl replied, unoffended, "the status of these people is problematic. Are they really gone? To heaven, or to a distant future? Who can say? Shall we treat them as patients or as vacant husks? We try to err on the side of hope."

"*I* wouldn't come to visit here," Conrad told him. "It's too cold."

Carl laughed politely.

"Sterile, I mean. Uninviting. These gauges, like something from a power plant. This place should be beautiful."

"We are none of us opposed to beauty," Carl agreed.

"What are these flashing lights all about? Here, and here? Why do they beep like that?"

"Ah," Carl said, running his hand over one. "Those are our cosmic ray counters: proton, photon, heavy nucleus, and 'other.' Sometimes one goes off: a vertical strike from directly above. Sometimes two go off: a diagonal strike. Sometimes it's three or four in a straight line, if the particle comes in horizontally. That's uncommon; the atmosphere blocks most of those. But we are very close to Barnard, and the planet's magnetic field offers little protection."

"Can't you put up a local field?"

"We can and do, yes. But how large should we make it? How much energy should we consume in maintaining it? We count the rays that penetrate, sir, not the ones our systems deflect."

But you don't deflect them all, Conrad thought. And this was significant, because any Navy man or woman knew all about cosmic rays, how they riddled your body, cutting and poisoning. A little bit of damage was easily repaired by your body's own systems. Hell, in the funny ways of biology, a *little* bit of radiation damage was actually good for you. But a little bit more was bad. If the damage piled up faster than your body could repair it, you shriveled, went blind and senile, eventually died. Here, of course, the cosmic ray counts were smaller than they would be out in space, but ... a frozen body could not repair itself. And with enough damage, even a high-end fax machine would have a hard time piecing the true person back together.

Posing it as an idle question, he asked, "How long would it take these rays to chew a body up into irretrievable goo?"

"Oh, a long time," Carl replied. "Two or three millennia."

"Really, that long. Hmm." This matched closely with Conrad's internal, off-the-cuff estimate, so he believed the figure at once. And that was a *real* problem, because Bascal had told him the economic crisis could well last for five. "Over time," he'd said, "the price of metals will drop, leading to relief in other areas. But it involves centuries of digging."

Carl Piñon Faxborn waited patiently for ten seconds, and then another ten, before finally asking, "Is everything all right, Mr. Mursk?"

"No," Conrad told him, looking around for the supports that held this place together. "It isn't. I'm sorry to say it, Mr. Faxborn, but there will have to be some big changes around here."

#### chapter twenty-two

the architecture of deceit

It made Conrad sad—depressed, even—to see where things were headed. Because he was going to betray Bascal. The compulsion was as palpable as a brick to the head, and he had no intention of resisting it. Indeed, Conrad was not merely an old space pirate and revolutionary but a two-time mutineer. And history had a way of repeating itself. As in those childhood mutinies, he would be recruiting at least a handful of allies, and if he knew his business—which at this advanced age he almost certainly did—then he would select only people who truly saw things his way, who would not turn him in, or out, as a means of currying favor.

The strange thing about it was that Conrad hated rebellion, hated conflict of any kind. All he'd ever wanted to be was an architect or matter programmer or construction boss of some kind. To build things, right? What was so wrong about that? Even in his years of wandering, he had never relinquished ownership of Murskitectura, and had in some sense never stopped pining for it while he was away. He just didn't want it to be the first, last, and only thing he ever did with his life out here among the stars.

Would his childhood self be pleased at the way things had turned out? Helping his father repair roads had been all right, though not terribly exciting, but even that was just nepotism, an extension of the invented "chores" he was called upon to do at home, on the theory that they built character. To get the job for real, to hold it as a grown-up and earn real money at it, he would've had to compete against thousands of other applicants. And be judged not by his father, but by impartial authorities of the bureaucracy, or worse, by computers with no feelings at all, no concept of justice, only a set of goals to be weighed against the available inputs.

And that was just not enough to hang his hopes on. At least he was *qualified* to be a paver's assistant; he'd had about as much chance of designing buildings as he did of becoming king. On Earth, or anywhere in the Queendom, he would've been eternally fuffed. It was natural enough to feel angry about such a circumstance, and Bascal, when they'd met at summer camp, had latched onto that anger like a supermagnet. Without that influence, Conrad would probably never have been more—or less—than a foul-mouthed delinquent. Unbeguiled by the Poet Prince, he would never have turned pirate, never have joined the Children's Revolt. Knowing the way things went for him, he probably wouldn't even have heard about it until after the fact.

But once you started defying an abusive authority, it was a small step to defying any and all authority, on any point you happened to disagree with. Maybe that was a good thing and maybe it wasn't, but Conrad felt in those dreamy days after Wendy's funeral that it was certainly an *irreversible* one. Standing up for what you believed in ... Well, it was a learned art, wasn't it? Like riding a bicycle. And once it was in your head, you couldn't unlearn it. Or maybe you could, with some subtle Queendom technology in the hands of the right sort of expert, but here on Planet Two—on *Sorrow,* he reminded himself—you were stuck with yourself for life. However long or short that might be.

And so ... Conrad could pretend to be whatever he liked: an architect, a naval officer, a hermit scientist. A paver, for crying out loud. But he would drop it all when his true calling beckoned: rebellion. The longer he lived, the more betrayal and strife he would see, would invite, would *cause* through his own dogged efforts.

Damn.

In the first few weeks he did almost nothing but mourn the very different lives he might have led. *How did it come to this?* he would ask himself. *How did I become this person? How did we, collectively, become this place?* Sorrow, yes; wasn't that a thing worth rebelling against? Or, alternatively: *I caused all this to happen. If not for me, it would have worked out differently. Maybe better; it could hardly be worse.* Did he have a responsibility to make good on his errors? Or was this merely the start of a new cascade of mistakes?

Later, when he began drawing up plans for a new Cryoleum and Data Morgue, the vague outlines of a plan began to take shape. It wasn't a great plan—in fact it was disappointingly lacking in any sort of subtlety or finesse, and would not by itself improve humanity's lot. Like the Children's Revolt, it was more a call to action—fraught with the potential to inspire—than an action in its own right. But it did at least have the virtue of being readily achievable.

As with his previous mutinies, he felt no sense of hurry. In fact, at the age of 330—older than his hidebound parents at the time of his birth!—he was inclined to take things very slowly indeed.

"There is psychological value," he told Bascal as the project unfolded, "in placing the dead so far from the living, as you've already done. Pectoralis makes a good resting place, suitably remote. But this constant traffic in coffins creates bottlenecks and logjams along the tuberail network. Embarrassing, right? There'd be benefits if it were possible to bring the entire facility—or parts of it anyway—a bit closer to the cities for brief periods."

Deaths did tend to cluster in the Ides of Dark, the hundred-hour window between Barnard's midnight and the long, slow breaking of dawn. Sunrise funerals were therefore the norm, and it was not uncommon for two or three of them to fill a train, leaving other mourners waiting on the platform for a shift or more, as if they didn't have enough problems already. But by their nature these things could not be planned in advance.

"Fine," Bascal told him, through the haze of grief that seemed these days to separate him from the rest of the world. He was sitting at his writing table, tapping a stylus against its surface, which was dark with scrawled lettering. If the voyage to Barnard had silenced his muse, then Wendy's death, for whatever reason, had reawakened it. Verily, it gushed! The Poet King—now a single, without copies to spread his presence around—spent as much time crafting songs and sonnets as he did running the government or visiting with the kingdom's grieving people. And these creations were astonishing in their honest, unpretentious elegance. In "The Freezing of Our Dreams" he wrote,

> Dear,
> If peace there be (and peace there must!) it lies
> beyond these jagged bluffs,
>   through efforts (ours!) of faithful (us!)
> And paradise there be (there will!) then it's a thing
> that we must build,
>   Ere frozen dreams themselves are spilled,
>   I fear.
>
> And when at last we find them thaw, these children's
> parents children, raw,
>   upon the skin of Sorrow's Fin and won from sin to life
> and limb,
>   rejoice—we shall!—that we have brought them . . .
>   Here.

But the hope behind these comely words was a distant thing, as false as the promises that had led Conrad astray so long ago. You *can* be an architect, yes! All it will cost you is . . . well, everything. And damn him, Conrad would still have agreed, even if the promise had been phrased exactly that way.

"Longing be the stronger force," Rodenbeck had warned in *MacSquinky's Reverse*. "Gravity and comeuppance must wait their turn upon the stage, until the heart has had its fill of that which breaks it."

Indeed.

"The reception area will be a separate module, freely traveling," Conrad said, pointing to the features on his drawing which were meant to convey this. "In principle, we can bring it all the way to Domesville, and then send it back to Pectoralis again so that no one need dwell in its memory-haunted shadow."

"That's fine," Bascal repeated without looking up. "I trust you."

And then, to his enormous credit, he added, "You're up to something, Conrad. I can always tell. But as I say, I trust you. Don't embarrass me, all right? Or yourself."

"I shan't, Sire," Conrad replied, wondering if it were the truth.

And they left it at that. Conrad was free to continue, unimpeded and unexamined. Who had the time to harass him? But—clever Bascal!—these words squirmed in his mind, raising blossoms of doubt wherever they touched. As the months and years of the project unfolded, Conrad found himself, more and more, accosting youngsters in the street.

"Would you return to the Queendom if you had the chance?" he would ask them.

And the replies would go something like, "Of Sol? I've never been, sir. But they live forever, yuh? That sounds a bit nice."

Or, "They have a fine grasp of aesthetics, don't they? I like to watch about them on TV. But to go there and stay? I dunnae, that's a big step."

Or occasionally an honest, "You're plibbles, old man. Bugs in the attic. Leave us alone, eh?"

But a lot of the kids recognized their first architect and answered very differently. Telling him what he wanted to hear, he assumed. The Queendom, yes! Let's all go! And this more than anything sapped his enthusiasm, caused him to question the very postulates of his plan even as the groundwork itself drew near to completion.

And then one day he stumbled into a funeral procession—

fifty youngsters in traditional black and inviz, bawling their
eyes out and screaming for someone named Jamie. A surprising number of them were carrying even smaller children in
their arms or on their shoulders. Not fax-born pseudoadults
but actual babies and toddlers! Courtesy, no doubt, of the lib-
eral reproductive encouragements he'd been hearing about in
the news. The Bascal Edward Fuffage Plan, people were calling it.

"Who is Jamie?" he asked one of the childless mourners.
He was painfully aware of how he must look: an old man
plodding the streets in a lithe young body, crashing a
stranger's funeral when it crossed his path. But he needed to
know, or believed he did.

The mourner, a young man in a black bowler hat, said to
him, "Jamie is the son of Dennis and Tuv." And at Conrad's
blank look he added, "Up there near the front."

Ah. The couple leading the procession were a priest and
priestess, and the knot of people immediately behind them
did not especially stand out. But behind them, in a sort of
empty bubble within the crowd, were a pair of shattered-
looking young men, clutching each other in sad desperation.
"Oh, God!" one of them was screaming. "Oh, *God*! Damn
you, God, give him back!"

These children of Barnard were nothing if not expressive.
And children they were, too, lacking the subtle gravitas that
marked the older generations.

"How old are they?" he could not help asking.

"Seventeen, sir," the mourner said, and made a show of
pulling away.

"Wait," Conrad told him. "Please. Are you their friend?"

"Yes," the young man replied, with evident irritation. This
was an unwelcome intrusion, and in another few seconds the
procession would be past and he'd have to jog to catch up.

"Also seventeen?" he pressed.

"I'm twenty. What's this about, sir?"

Seventeen! Twenty! In Barnard these numbers meant
something different than they had in the Queendom, where
natural (or more properly, "naturalesque") births and preg-
nancies were still the norm. And clearly those older meanings

were reasserting themselves here as well, even if they didn't apply to everyone. But it was painfully young just the same. At an age when Conrad and Xmary had still been raising hell, these people were already raising families.

Conrad struggled with his reply. "I'm just...very concerned about the plight of young people. I always have been." He studied the retreating backs of the bereaved couple. "Dennis and Tuv...they somehow managed, in a tough market, to get a birthing license and a fax appointment. Was the child a...baby?"

"Nearly," the mourner told him, with tears quivering at the corners of his eyes. "Physiologically he was four. Now he's six, now and forever. He was struck by a falling bicycle."

Conrad could not picture that scene, or fathom how it might have happened, but the horror of it was plain enough. "And there are no backups, right? If they filled out the right forms and got very lucky in the raffle, Dennis and Tuv could reinstantiate the original Jamie blueprint, but it wouldn't be their little boy, the one they loved and lost. Nothing ever could be. And there is no other way—there is *no* other way—for two men to have a child of their own on this planet."

"Correct, sir. May I go, please? This is hard for me."

"You may go," Conrad said gently. "I apologize for keeping you. But will you answer one more question first? If you could go to a place where things like this never happened—where sorrow never intruded on the lives of the young, and no one grew old, and tears were as rare as virgins...Would you go?"

"It sounds like heaven," the man answered. "And I don't want to go to heaven. Not now, not soon. But when I die, someday, then yes: I hope to awaken in a place like that. Doesn't everyone?"

And with that he turned to go, breaking into a reluctant jog which was very much at odds with the procession's shrieking, languorous pace.

But Conrad, having received at last an answer he could believe in, proceeded in the other direction with paradoxically lighter steps, with a lighter heart and a brighter future before him. It was time to be a sort of hero again, yes, because no one else was going to.

He sent a message to Xmary that very night, putting events into motion which would, he hoped, in the fullness of time, change everything.

#### chapter twenty-three

by tuberail to the stars

**Mechanically speaking, Conrad's plan was simplicity it-
self.** Over a period of several years, the Cryoleum had become five separate structures, each mounted on tuberails and
capable of traveling across the face of Planet Two. And for
various historical reasons, the tuberails of the ground network were fully compatible with those running up the sides
of the Orbital Tower, which by now was itself a historical
anachronism that no one paid much attention to.

Traffic there was less than a tenth of what it had been in
the glory days, even though it was cheaper than the Gravittoir. The Gravittoir was simply faster, and also more comfortable, with no sense of acceleration and none of the vibration
or loud noises associated with tuberail travel. So when P2's
morning was over, and with it the funeral season, it was very
easy for Conrad to clear the Cryoleum's personnel on the
trumped-up excuse that he needed to refinish the interior
surfaces.

Then he simply stole the entire facility.

From a control station in the Orbital Tower itself, he
whisked the buildings to Tower Base so quickly that it would
be a day or two before anyone even realized they were gone.
He did this neatly and with precision, allowing no interrup-

tion to the structures' power supplies or other services. From there things got even easier, since Murskitectura owned and operated the Orbital Tower. The Cryoleum buildings had been designed to fit side by side in Tower Base's large maintenance hangar, where Mack and his small team of loyalists tore the facades off them, revealing the more-or-less ordinary cargo podships beneath. Then, these pods were simply scooted up the tower like any other cargo.

"This is politically dangerous," Conrad warned. "I hope these people don't know what they're doing, or why."

"Let me worry about that," Mack said with a wave of his hand.

"Yeah? And what about you personally?"

"None of your concern, Boss."

"The hell it isn't! I needed trustworthy help, so I called you. I'm not going to leave you hanging when I'm through."

"They don't do that anymore. Hanging."

"Not that specifically," Conrad said, "but what happens when you're caught?"

"*If* I'm caught," Mack corrected. "Don't worry. I *love* a good lie, a good sneak behind the bushes, and if it falls apart and I'm standing there with my trousers down, well, that's a challenge of a different sort."

"But—"

"I can take care of myself, Conrad. Think who my teacher was."

Well, *that* was hardly reassuring. But what could he say?

Soon the cargo pods were stripped and ready, and it was time to get things moving again. Conrad had considered swiping the Data Morgue as well, but its memory cores were much more valuable than the Cryoleum, much harder for the colony to replace, and for the most part the images contained inside them were of people who were not, in point of fact, dead. Including Conrad himself, for what little that mattered. Perhaps Bascal would find a way to print that copy out, and punish it for what Conrad was about to do, but it was a risk he would just have to live with. He had no access to the records himself, could not simply delete his image.

It would be nice if Xmary could meet him at the top of the

tower, but the orbital mechanics of P2 and its environment forbade this. If *Newhope* came to rest on the top of the tower, it would not be orbiting, and the mass of the ship itself—to say nothing of its ertial shields—would crumple the tower like a tube of paper. Instead, a complex system of orbital rendezvous was necessary, and herein lay one of the great risks of Conrad's plan. *Newhope*'s failure to be in the right place at the right time would strand the pods in useless, unlicensed orbits where they would eventually bang into each other, or into the tower itself. Or worse, into something moving along a different orbit with much higher relative velocity.

That is, if Naval Security didn't get them first.

The first pod climbed away from the ground with a sonic rumble—never a boom, as booms were a symptom of wasted energy, of sloppy design—and was, within minutes, a mere gleam of sunlight on the tower's black face. The second and third pods quickly followed, and then the fourth. Twenty-five thousand frozen corpses. Twenty-five thousand children, bound for a kind of heaven. If he could save more, he would. If he could think of a better plan, he'd implement it without a second thought. But Conrad had always believed it was better to salvage something than to salvage nothing at all. And if those were the only choices, then his conscience was as clear as the path ahead of him.

"You should come with us," Conrad said, in a last-ditch effort to save Mack from himself.

But Mack just snorted. "Will you stop already? Locked in that ship I'd go crazy in a week. Besides, I've eaten at the king's table, and partaken of his daughter. There are limits to how far my treacheries extend, you know? That's no reflection on you, sir—I admire what you're doing here—but this place is my home. I'll stay. I'll cope."

"Jesus," Conrad said, with a hand on his brow. "You be careful, Mack. Do you hear me? You live a good life."

"Always have," the troll said simply. "And when death comes for me, as it surely will someday, why, then I'll be back with my princess again. What could be finer? Quite frankly it's *you* I'm worried about." He paused a moment and added, "I'll miss you, Boss. I hope you make it."

People say a troll cannot weep. People say a lot of things.

Conrad rode up with the fifth and final pod, in an acceleration couch Mack's team had installed in the big, empty chamber that had been the Cryoleum's reception hall. Conrad wished he could fill this space with frozen corpses as well, but that would have been impossible without drawing unwanted attention. So the chamber, which had been designed to hold as many as two hundred live, grieving people, instead held only one.

If the walls had been of wellstone, then he might have seen the spectacular view as induction motors yanked him up the side of the tower for two and a half hours, shrinking the ground beneath him until its curvature was apparent and the atmosphere was just a thin yellow haze clinging to the ground far below. But instead the walls were made of titanium—one of the commonest metals in the silicate crust of P2—and through a crude material like that, Conrad could see nothing.

Thus, weightlessness was a bit of a shock when it came, and even a seasoned space veteran like Conrad was not above releasing some globs of vomit to float in the air around him like smelly, brightly colored ornaments. If he weren't maintaining radio silence, Conrad might have called Xmary to see where she was, to find out when exactly she would be retrieving him. But instead he sat in the glare of artificial lights, afraid to leave his seat for fear of being slammed without warning into the walls or floor when *Newhope*'s grapples finally took hold and reeled him in.

He sat like that for a long time, contemplating the fact that he should have brought a jacket. In the old days, such considerations had been unnecessary, since the shipping containers would be insanely well insulated and his own wellcloth clothing would have kept his skin temperature constant anyway. But Conrad had only two wellcloth outfits left—one a formal suit and the other a Polar Rangers uniform—and he stupidly hadn't thought to wear either one today, possibly because neither one would have felt appropriate for the occasion. So, as the metal cargo pod bled its heat away into the cold vacuum, he huddled and shivered and cursed himself, wondering what else he might have overlooked.

Sadly, years of planning were not always enough to prevent these stupid oversights.

Did the cold, in some way, make him hallucinate? Did it trick his eye, his optic nerve, his brain? For he saw a flickering at the corner of his eye, and turned to find himself staring straight into the face of a ghost.

He knew it was a ghost, for it was pale and translucent, all but colorless, and hung in the air just above the floor in exactly the way that ghosts are supposed to. But there were problems with this theory as well. First of all, Conrad had always understood ghosts to be an electromagnetic phenomenon, a sort of quantum imprint in the area where an event—usually traumatic—had taken place. Detecting them took sensors of incredible power and subtlety.

And yet, what good was a word like "ghost" if it couldn't be applied to a thing which fit it so precisely? Had there ever been an era, a time or place or society, where people didn't claim, at least occasionally, to have seen them? With their own eyes, in a moment of shock and horror, when contact with the dead had in fact been the farthest thing from their minds?

The second problem with the theory was that ghosts were, science insisted, merely a recording, not unlike the patterns of a chemical photograph or the acoustically etched grooves in a medieval phonograph record. They could be reconstructed, played back... but not interacted with. And yet this ghost of Conrad's appeared to be looking right at him, its tear-streaked face pulling down into a mask of horror at the sight of him. And the mask was one he recognized: Raylene Pine, who had died years before in the Polar Well.

What can be said about it? No man is a stone. Conrad let out a shriek, and the ghost beside him vanished before he could so much as tap the releases on his couch restraints and flail away in terror. Even so, he drew back, gasping and shaking. Then, with a trembling hand, he probed the air where the thing had been, and felt nothing. No ripples or vapor or cold spots. A shiver ran through him.

Had the walls been of wellstone, he might have dismissed the apparition as an accidental hologram, an anomalous burping of stored data released by the flash of a cosmic ray. But he had built this room himself, or overseen it anyway, and he'd conducted a thorough inspection just a few hours ago. So he knew—he *knew*—there was nothing in here that could produce an effect like that.

"Ah, mystery," Rodenbeck had written once. "That things should feast themselves before us which have no rightful cause! If living long means seeing much, then I fear we shan't escape it, this whimsy of the gods that writes its scorn upon us."

Fuff. There were too many goddamn Rodenbeck quotes kicking around. You could frame your whole life in them, knowing an infinite supply of new ones waited just around the corner. But they didn't keep you warm.

When the docking came, it was much gentler than Conrad had feared. *Newhope* had nice, old-fashioned gravitic grapples, like smaller versions of the graser beams at the heart of the Gravittoir, and the movements they imparted did not feel like acceleration. More like falling, which he was already doing anyway since he was in zero gravity—that state of never-ending fall. Rotation, of course, could not be masked in this way, and he did feel the pod wheeling around at one point, and then the bump and clatter of physical docking clamps taking hold. And then, because the pod was wider than *Newhope*'s ertial shields, there came a series of handclap noises as the explosive pins in the pod wall blew, and the left and right thirds of the pod, under considerable spring tension, folded in under it. Now it was shaped less like a building, less like a tuberail car, and more like a manta ray with its arms wrapped around a wellstone piling, where the piling was the cargo spindle of *Newhope*, within which lay the central staircase and the narrow air, water, and power conduits.

Finally, Conrad's ears popped as the air systems mated. The pressure inside the pod—starting out at sea level, which for Planet Two meant just over three bars, had bled down to less than half that much over the course of the launch, and as it equalized with the much thinner, cleaner air of *Newhope*, it halved again to just seven hundred millibars. Technically speaking, a person could get the bends from such a dramatic pressure change, but that was rare, and time was short.

Fortunately, *Newhope*'s internal gravity was turned off; otherwise Conrad's floor would have become a wall, and he would be dangling from his straps. But it was in the actual floor, directly in front of the bishop's podium, that a metal hatchway opened, connecting him at last to the interior of *Newhope*. He unmoored from his seat, launched himself at the hatchway, and caught himself on a cold metal handgrip mounted on the open hatch's inside.

Once free of the chamber, he found the matter of the ghost a bit easier to dismiss. It was just too quiet in there, too cold and still, where stepping into *Newhope* was like coming home. With practiced ease, he pulled himself into the stairway, placed his feet against the handrail, and launched himself up toward the bridge.

Ah. Once your balance adjusted, there really was nothing like zero gravity. As he glided up the stair shaft, correcting his course with occasional pushes from feet and hands, the levels slid past him one by one. He could fly, yes, in this space where gravity normally reigned! It was a feeling he never got tired of.

At the top of the shaft, on the bridge, he found Xmary in her captain's chair, and Useless sitting over at Information. Useless' actual name was Eustace; she was the painfully young wife of the ship's only other crewmate: the Facilitator, the superlative spaceman, the one and only Yinebeb Fecre, who was presently down in Engineering. There were people who were competent to run a starship, and there were people whom Conrad could trust; and of the dozen or so who were both, there were only these two, Xmary and Feck, who were so firmly attached to *Newhope*—and so loosely to the colony itself—that they would make this sacrifice. That he would even consider asking it. Poor Eustace was just along for the ride.

"Welcome aboard," Xmary told him, motioning him toward his old seat. "You look . . . shaken."

"It was an interesting ride," Conrad told her. "The Cryoleum is haunted."

She nodded without really processing that. "We'll be changing orbits in about fifteen minutes, to rendezvous with a high-orbit refueling station. There, we'll top off our tanks, and leave from a higher potential in the gravity well."

"Sounds good," Conrad said. Generally speaking, details like that were left up to the captain's discretion, a fact which did not change merely because Conrad had hatched this particular conspiracy.

"How do I find the station again?" Useless asked.

"Never mind, dear," Xmary told her sweetly. "The nav solution has already been entered."

She pressed a lighted circle on her armrest and brought up a view of Engineering in a holie screen on the wall. "Feck, are you about ready for main drive propulsion?"

Life-sized, like a man looking in from an adjacent room, Feck looked up and nodded. "The reactors are online, obviously, drawing about one hundred kilowatts for internal power and maneuvering thrusters. The deutrelium pumps are already primed. All I have to do is open the valves. What I'm saying is, I don't need a warm-up period. I can light the fuse anytime you say."

"Ah! You've streamlined the boost ignition sequence, then. Very good."

"Thank you, ma'am," he said, in easy tones which belied the words' formality.

"Good for you, baby," Eustace added. Then, fiddling with the controls on her own panel, she managed to cast half the bridge into darkness.

Useless, indeed.

Conrad supposed he should take a more charitable view. After all, he had been young and green once, too. It had taken him quite a while to learn how to do things onboard a ship, and still longer to do them confidently and with style. And it was hard to begrudge Feck his young bride. He'd been a spaceman for quite a long time, and that was not a profession for lovers, or at least for would-be family men. But sooner or later, everyone seemed to get the urge to settle down for a while, and Feck, knowing he would be leaving for a very long, very isolated journey, had grabbed the first handy female who might agree to come with him. Which was not a stupid way for him to approach the problem.

Unfortunately, Eustace had no way of knowing what lay ahead: the stresses and deprivations of space travel, the confined quarters, and most of all the boggling ennui of living on-board this ship, with nowhere else to go, for eighteen decades. Conrad himself could barely get his arms around that one, could barely imagine how they would cope at all, much less thrive.

There was no quantum storage for them to crawl into this time, no medical-grade fax machines or memory cores. If they froze themselves—which was certainly an option if things got bad enough—they could not be thawed out and returned to life without Queendom technology. Medically speaking, it was a treatment of last resort.

So it was tempting—almost inevitable, really—to brand Eustace's enthusiasm as foolish in the extreme. But Conrad could remember very well the days of his own youth, when he would've leaped at such an adventure without hesitation. A whole new star system, a whole new society, and the promise of immortality at journey's end! Really, Conrad should be ashamed of himself for thinking unkind thoughts about her at all.

But still, even so, *Newhope* had been the first of the great Queendom starships, and even after 250 years she was still the pride of the Barnardean fleet. She had never—truly never—had a crew person this green, even at the very start when she'd been designed to keep as many hands busy as possible. Eustace's training for the mission had, Conrad imagined, consisted of nothing more than a few weeks in bed with Feck. And that was a poor preparation indeed for what lay ahead.

"I suppose we could go right now, then," Xmary mused.

"Absolutely, ma'am," Feck replied.

Xmary looked at Conrad. "Any objection?"

Conrad was about to deny it, and give his blessing for the journey to begin, when a second holographic window opened beside Feck's, and within it was the image of King Bascal, as real as life itself. He was wearing his diamond crown, whose weight pulled down the skin around it, giving his face a saggy appearance, an air of gravity. But this was his only concession to majesty; he was otherwise dressed in loose gray pajamas, with no adornment of any sort.

"Ah, Conrad, I thought I might find you here," he said. This was technically a breach of protocol, since he should first address the Information officer and request an audience with the first mate. But Bascal's adherence to Queendom-style protocol was spotty at best, and today he seemed particularly irate.

"Hi, Bas," Conrad said to him.

"What're you doing?" the king asked. It was an honest question. He knew something was going on, and he didn't like it; but at the same time he was curious, and part of him was maybe even a little bit amused.

"Just running a little errand," Conrad answered.

Bascal nodded absently at that. "Uh-huh. Except that the crew of *Newhope* was off-loaded at Bubble Hood about four hours ago. As near as I can figure, you've got three people on-board that ship."

"Four, actually," Conrad corrected.

Bascal scowled, his voice growing firmer. "I'll ask you again: What are you doing?"

If Conrad had had any say in the matter, he would have cut the channel right there and then. But *Newhope* was a giant block of nanobe-tended wellstone, intelligent all the way down to the molecular level, and Bascal's Royal Overrides could command the obedience of all but the most critical systems. Those, fortunately, were safety locked and required biometric authentication, which could not be performed at a distance.

"I think maybe we should skip the refueling," Conrad said to Xmary. "Let's just light up and go. Just go, now. That refueling is only for safety margin anyway, right?"

"Yes, I concur," Xmary said. Then, glancing at the other window, "Feck?"

Feck nodded firmly. "Firing the engines now, ma'am."

"You people are in a lot of trouble," Bascal said, in a manner that was almost friendly. "You do know that, right? That starship is a very valuable—in fact irreplaceable—piece of property. *My* property. Using it without authorization is a serious crime," his eyes settled on Xmary, "even for a captain."

Then, anything else he might've said was drowned out by the rising groan of *Newhope*'s engines. Fully loaded like this, kicking directly to full thrust, the start-up transients were at once louder and gentler—more damped by mass—than usual. And thanks to the ertial shields, the effective mass of *Newhope* was very small, so that the acceleration, which was barely perceptible from the inside, was in fact quite impressive. On holie windows all around the bridge, Planet Two could be seen shrinking beneath them.

"Planetary escape velocity... now," Feck was saying. He had moved most of the helm functions down to Engineering, so he could steer and navigate while keeping the engines stoked. "We have broken orbit and are falling sunward. Eccentricity of our Barnard orbit is 0.2 and climbing."

"Good," Xmary said. "When it gets to 0.987, cut the engines and resume coasting."

"Aye, ma'am."

Eccentricity was a measure of their orbit's height and narrowness—its resemblance to a parabola rather than a circle. Numbers just under 1.0 meant the orbit was a flat ellipse, long and thin and very fast, like the trail of a short-period comet. As in their long-ago departure from Sol, the orbit would graze the chromosphere of Barnard—its hot middle atmosphere—and then the sails would unfurl and the engines would light up again, and the eccentricity would blow right past 1.0, breaking the top of the ellipse, opening it into a parabola whose arms stretched out to infinity. And then as their speed continued to build, a hyperbola, which reached infinity a hell of a lot faster, and also happened to be pointed back at Sol.

"Jesus," Bascal said, the color draining from his face. "That's a sun-grazer. Unless you're committing suicide, which would be damned peculiar under the circumstances, there's only one reason for an orbit that tight: to fire at the bottom and boost your apogee. You bastards, you're going interstellar.

Back to Sol? To Mommy and Daddy? Why are you doing that? Just four of you, sneaking away like dogs. In *my ship*."

"Not sneaking," Conrad said, unable to help himself.

"Not sneaking," Bascal repeated. "Hmm. What are you up to, then? You and Xmary and some freshly printed *ta'ahine* I've never seen before."

"Eustace Faxborn, Sire."

"Be quiet, dear," said Xmary.

"And who else?" the king asked. "Feck the Programmable Spaceman? My people tell me you're carrying five cargo pods which went up the tower just this morning. That's quite a load. What's in the pods?"

"Eccentricity .987," Feck announced. "Cutting engines." The groan of deutrelium fusion had quieted considerably over the course of the burn as the reactor's vibrations damped out, but now it cut off entirely. "Velocity relative to Sorrow is 30.59 kps. Relative to Barnard, 3.7 kps. We are falling, ma'am, and will enter Barnard's chromosphere in 122.5 hours."

"The hell you will," said Bascal. "Turn that ship around. If you do it now, I promise to hear out your grievances and be lenient in your sentencing. If not, I'll set Security on your trail, and by the time Ho's finished there won't be enough left to freeze. I mean it."

"*King's Fist* is docked at Bubble Hood," Conrad said, "and half her crew, including Ho, are on shore leave at the moment. This was a consideration in choosing our departure time."

Bascal clucked his tongue angrily. "My, my. You always were a careful mutineer, Conrad. I give you enough rope to hang yourself, and you spin a fucking hammock with it. Maybe I knew that. Maybe I was sloppy or generous, but I can't let you get away with this. The colony can't afford it."

"You could," Conrad said, "for old times' sake."

The king touched his nose, his lips, then trailed his fingers through his hair, brushing it up away from his face. "You could turn around for the same reason, boyo. Just tell me what you're up to. Please. You're my dearest friend. Don't force me to kill you without even knowing why."

"I'll tell you when we're safely away," Conrad said. "When we've gone hyperbolic."

"Not good enough. You'll tell me now."

"Or what, Bas?" Xmary cut in. "You're not going to catch us. Even if you hustle *Fist*'s crew up the Gravittoir in the next ten minutes, it'd take them all day to match speeds with us, and even when they did they'd be hours behind us in our orbit. And out of fuel."

Bascal considered that for several seconds before replying, "Yes, and it might take us months to mount a rescue, to retrieve them from that perilous orbit. Or longer, but *Fist*'s crew are hard men, accustomed to sacrifice. They'll do their jobs. There are weapons capable of killing a person from that range, you know. Without harming the ship."

"It's not like we're cowering in a metal can," she countered. "We can repel your grasers and nasen beams. And if you have something subtler than that—some Marlon Sykes superweapon—or something cruder like a cannon or an ultra-high-powered laser, we'll just fire the engines again. The ertial shield puts acceleration on our side; we'll just scoot out of the way."

Bascal smiled, thinly and unhappily. "Not if you want to reach the Queendom you won't. You need to fire from a particular point over Barnard's face, at a particular moment. You haven't got time or fuel to waste on evasive maneuvers."

"We have some," she said. "We have more freedom than *Fist* does. We are a starship, Your Highness, where *Fist* is not."

"No," he agreed, "she's not. If you're determined to outrun her, you probably can. So we'll have to catch you the long way around. Your departure course is fixed. It *has* to be, because there's only one straight line connecting Barnard to Sol. And if Ho waits for you along that line, then when you come around the sun you can't help but encounter him, at a range and location of his choosing."

Oh, shit, Conrad said to himself. Here was his overlooked detail. He was a good Naval officer—Feck and Xmary even more so—but they weren't warriors. They didn't think or plan like warriors. Shit, shit, that would have to change. Quickly.

"Now you see," Bascal told them all. "Now at last you understand. This is not a democracy or an anarchy, where you're free to do whatever you fuffing please. How can it be? We *rely* on the economic edge that monarchy provides. Thirty percent better than the free market!"

"Ideally," Feck told him, with a dismissive, derisive flutter of his hands. "If you, King Bascal, do everything perfectly."

"You think I haven't?" Bascal asked, with less rancor than Conrad would have expected. "You think I'm just ignoring my advisors, my hypercomputers, my models and simulations? Could you do better with the same tools?" He looked around. "I can't see who's speaking. Is that you, Feck? Yes? Well listen, it may be true that we don't hit thirty percent on the best of days, but I'll tell you something: we don't hit fifteen percent either. Not on our worst, slowest, stupidest day. We're that much better than the sum of random chances. And if we fell back to a free market, do you know what a prolonged fifteen-to-twenty-five percent recession would do to this colony? Do you?"

"So you strip away the final illusions of freedom," Feck admonished. "You ask people to live and die for you, all the while checking every economic action against some master plan. And what action is not economic in some way? You're talking about *total control,* backed up by the threat of lethal force. Will it be the death penalty for selling berries below the official price? A flogging, perhaps? All for the hope of some hypothetical resurrection, thousands of years in the future. What I'm saying is, that's much worse than what we left behind in the Queendom. Sire. Much worse."

Bascal smiled, and this time it was genuine. "Ah, yes. A fair objection. But at the end of that time, think what we'll have achieved! Total freedom: physical, economic, political. Complete liberation from those moribund Queendom power structures. We *will* resurrect our dead, restore the neutronium trade, install the luxuries of collapsiter travel and meritocratic advancement. But these are not mere bread and circuses; long before Barnard is full we'll launch starships of our own, a colony wave done properly, carrying *our* ideas to the stars. And space is infinite, Feck. We can have our cake and eat it too. Live forever *and* continue to breed. All the cake in the universe is ours for the taking."

The king's eyes had gone out of focus, as if he were looking not at the holie window and the bridge of *Newhope*, but at this glorious future off in the distance somewhere.

"Just ignore him," Xmary told her crew. "We've got work to do. Battle plans to draw up. *Fist* may be a match for mining colonies and pirate sloops, but we've got a hundred times her reactor power and probably five hundred times her programmable mass. We can throw a lot of energy in a lot of different ways. If they want to stand in our path, that's their prerogative, but it doesn't mean they can stop us."

"I'm standing right here," Bascal said. "I can hear every word."

"Just ignore him," Xmary repeated.

Although he grew increasingly angry, Bascal had too much dignity to press this point. If they weren't going to talk to him, then neither was he going to talk to them. He watched for a while as normal bridge chatter resumed: the scanning and neutralizing of debris, the shifting of ballast mass to minimize the pressure on station-keeping thrusters.

"If you make it through, it's going to be a long trip," he injected at one point. "No fax storage. I did a shorter version on the way out here, and believe me it was loooong. Are you people sure you can handle it?"

But nobody responded to that, and a king really did have better things to do than sit there all day staring quietly at his enemies. After ten more minutes of quiet standoff, his image got bored and winked out.

"Alone at last," Eustace said.

But Conrad shook his head. "Don't count on it. He'll have sensors in the walls by now. Our king is quite a talented programmer."

"Damn right he is," said a disembodied voice. Bascal's.

It was hardly a timely quip, though; his signal could only travel at the speed of light, whereas the distance between *Newhope* and Planet Two (Sorrow, Conrad reminded himself. Would that name ever stick?) was increasing rapidly. With the ship already doing better than thirty kps—one ten-thousandth of the speed of light—every seventy minutes of travel added a full second to the round-trip signal lag.

"This complicates our battle planning," Conrad noted. "We have no security at all. We have to assume that everything we do and say is being analyzed, at least until we get the sun between ourselves and the planet. Possibly even then. And any weapons we produce from the wellstone of the hull will be difficult to trust."

"It does make things interesting," Xmary agreed.

The next time Bascal appeared in a visible form, the ship was nine light-seconds from Sorrow, meaning the round-trip signal lag was eighteen seconds. He didn't even bother trying to hold a conversation like that, but simply haloed himself and fired off an interactive message. A large and complicated one, judging by the hours its upload spent choking *Newhope's* comm systems.

"It doesn't have to be like this," the king said, appearing translucently as a crouching figure, leaning right into Conrad's face as he lay on his bunk trying to catch a few hours of sleep. "I still want you on my team. Whatever has driven you to this desperate act, I need to know about it. That's advice you should be giving *to me*. I should be accounting for it in my planning."

"I tried," Conrad told him tiredly. "You're not an easy man to advise. You respond much better to actions, as you've amply demonstrated today."

"So fine, I'm responding. Now talk to me."

Conrad sighed. "Bas, why do your plans always involve this pressure cooker of pain and death and suffering? Why are the rewards always so far in the future? People don't want that. They never have and never will."

"But we're immorbid," Bascal answered. "Some of us. Planning for the future never used to be a personal thing. Our parents were the first crop of humans to map out a future they themselves would inhabit. And they pissed the job, didn't they? We've got to do better. Forget twenty-year plans and even century plans; we have the opportunity, the *duty*, to plan across the millennia, across the eons. And if we can see paradise, not just in dreams but in the hard, cold numbers of mathematical certainty, does it not behoove us to be brave? To take the first hard steps down that road? The easier roads all lead to ruin, my friend. I've *seen* it."

Conrad sighed. "Jesus and the little gods, Bas, quit the act. You can bamboozle children, but you're not fooling *me*. By the time you solve the economic crisis, the colony's dead will be irradiated into frozen goo. There's no resurrection; the only place you can send them is heaven itself. But there's a lesser paradise much closer at hand."

The king's eyes filled with cold certainty. "You've taken the Cryoleum. Twenty-five thousand sleeping bodies. Taking them 'home' to a place they've never seen. I've sent word back to myself on Sorrow, to verify that the Cryoleum is actually missing, but you can save me the trouble."

"Yes," Conrad admitted. "We've taken the Cryoleum."

"Damn you," the recording said. "Do you realize what you've done? Do you know how destabilizing that'll be? No matter how ruthless I am—and I hate being that, believe me!—this will distort the morale equations, further eroding our productivity, further postponing the dawn of our indigenous Eden." Then the hologram's eyes widened a bit. "Ah, but it's a secret. Yes? If I kill you, if I kill everyone on the ground who knows about your plans, the whole thing can be covered up. We'll just need to find a way to explain the loss of *Newhope*. And that shouldn't be difficult. She's an old ship; accidents happen."

These words made Conrad very happy and proud not to be on Bascal's team, to be instead on his own team and struggling for his own vision of the least-worst future. But at the same time the words triggered a deep mourning, because he and Bascal really had been good friends, *best* friends, for hundreds and hundreds of years. They still were.

"Even your barely sentient messages dream of homicide," Conrad said.

The recording shook its head. "Sadly, it makes sense. And fortunately, I have the fortitude to press onward, even with plans that make me personally ill."

"You can't stop us," Conrad said.

Here the recording smiled: a cold, holographic smile. "You'd be surprised what I can do. You'd be *amazed* what I can do, with centuries of thought and planning. I always knew there'd be rebellions to put down. And it occurs to me, seeing you lying there half asleep, that I have still another weapon at my disposal." He looked down at himself. "This ghost will haunt you, Conrad. It will deprive you of rest until such time as you surrender *Newhope* and return home in chains."

Oh, dear God. "Go away, Bas."

"No, indeed," the recording said. "I'm tireless, drawing my energy directly from your own reactors. And as you say, I'm barely sentient. Thus, I'm incapable of boredom. The volume of my speech is unfortunately capped by safety interlocks—I can no more shout you to death than I can command the wellstone in your hull to disintegrate. Alas for you, because it would be a kinder death than what Ho has in store.

"However, the *duration* of my speech has no such constraints. We shall begin, I think, with one million recitations of the "Fuck You Song," and follow up with a long, detailed list of your personal faults. I will not enjoy this, for I cannot, but perhaps the real Bascal will be satisfied when all is done, that all *has* been done that can be, to bring down this house of cards you call a conspiracy."

"Go away," Conrad repeated as the first stanza of the "Fuck You Song" began. "Little gods, Bascal, you can't be serious."

Ah, but he could. And was.

#### chapter twenty-four

flashfight

That *Newhope* could be unwilling to receive any further malicious uploads was a possibility, given that she was a highly intelligent and protective entity in her own right. However, she should not have been capable of resistance when presented with Royal Overrides. Perhaps, then, there was a communications problem of some sort, although this is also unlikely in a ship constructed of wellstone and hypercollapsites. Or perhaps Bascal—the singled king of a world and a people—was too busy or distracted to halo himself for another recording. But could he not have duplicated the original transmission, and filled the spaces of *Newhope* with a thousand holie copies of himself?

In point of fact, he did not. For whatever reason, only one ghost haunted the ship, with one crewmate—Conrad—bearing the brunt of its attentions. Perhaps Bascal felt a twinge of love or pity, or simply couldn't bring himself to send himself off, again and again, to certain doom. There *was* something wrenching about sending a piece of your soul on a one-way trip to data heaven, never to be heard from again. Conrad had abandoned the practice years ago.

But King Bascal was harder-headed about these things, and it's difficult to imagine he'd've foresworn such an action if it offered some strategic or tactical advantage, or hastened the day when his visions of Eden could be instantiated in the physical universe. Some light might be shed on the subject if the site of his palace could be examined by quantum archaeologists, but failing that, we can simply acknowledge the mystery, and agree that *Newhope*'s habitable spaces were neither as loud nor as chaotic as they might have been.

Nevertheless, her crew—even Eustace—were all pulling long shifts, scheming in their heads and trying to communicate ideas to one another while simultaneously keeping them obscure from the prying ears presumed to surround them. The industrial-grade fax machine—the only one onboard— produced stimulants in abundance to keep them all on their toes, and between that and the lack of sleep, the general stress, and the specific nagging and singing and joking of Bascal's one message, they were all pretty fuzzed out by the time they reached the bottom of their orbit.

"Velocity with respect to Barnard is 615 kps," Feck announced loudly, over the ninety thousandth refrain of the "Fuck You Song." "If we have forever to get home, the minimum needed for escape boost is 620, but ideally we'll need something closer to ten thousand. I'll kiss the engines for good luck, ma'am. As for the sails, I am unfurling them... now."

There was a lot more to the boost sequence than just that, but while the sails were unfurling, and before Feck had gotten to the next step on the checklist, red lights began flashing and alarms blaring.

"What's happening?" Xmary demanded.

Conrad, sitting now at the Systems Integration station instead of his own chair, reported, "It's a broken thread alarm. From the bow sheeting, just aft of the ertial shield. Something's evaporating the outer layers of the wellstone there."

"What kind of something? I need more information." There was no hint of love in her voice, nor should there be. She was the captain of a vessel under fire. "I didn't expect trouble this early, but it makes sense for them to disrupt us before boost if they can."

"It's... coherent light. Sorry, coherent X rays."

"Could it be the spalling laser on *King's Fist*?"

"That would be my first guess," Conrad agreed. "Although the range must be pretty extreme, or the damage would be much worse. That laser's frequency is tuned specifically to interfere with wellstone's command-and-control signals, and to set up destructive resonance in the fibers. Wait a minute, I'm getting broken threads in the sail as well. The laser's spot diameter is about sixty meters, so according to the computer it's firing from a range of just over three light-seconds."

Luna was almost exactly 1.29 light-seconds from Earth, and although Conrad would never admit it publicly, after years of intensive training in near-Earth space he still measured it that way in his mind: three light-seconds was nine hundred thousand kilometers, about two and a half Earth-moon distances. Also very close to the Limit of Influence or LOI, where Sol's gravity began to dominate over Earth's, making stable orbits impossible. Not that that mattered here and now, but it was how he'd been trained.

"It's a probing shot," he speculated. "They don't expect to do any real damage. In fact, they may be using the spalling laser just to light us up, to make it easier to target some other weapon. The spot is shrinking, though. We're closing fast with the source."

"Find it."

"Trying to, ma'am, but *King's Fist* is stealthed. Anyway, all the light and heat are confusing the sensors."

Indeed, for practical purposes they were *inside* Barnard at the moment. It was a smaller, cooler star than Sol, but that did not by any means make it a clement environment to pass through. At this depth in the chromosphere, Sol was at least predictable; navigating through it was like flying a kite in a steady gale. But Barnard, with less power output per hectare of surface, was a knotted mess of flailing magnetic fields that spiked and dropped away without warning. The particle flux alone was enough to snow out most of the preprogrammed sensors in *Newhope*'s hull, and for all his programming expertise, Conrad knew almost nothing about sensor design. Stuck with the ship's normal, unmodified arrays, he felt as though he were peering out through the pores of a blindfold.

"Look at the shape of the spot," Xmary suggested. "The beam is circular, right? But I'll bet you're seeing an oval smear across our bow, and from that you can compute the incidence angle. And from the changes in the spot size you can get the divergence angle, and therefore the range. Trace the beam right back to its source."

This surprised Conrad. It was an ingenious idea, and certainly nothing his childhood Xmary, the Denver party girl, would have come up with. He loved her as much now as he had back then—or so it seemed, at any rate—but he supposed people *did* change, slowly, like wax dolls in the warmth of a closed hand. Decade by decade the differences were imperceptible, but across the span of centuries that fiery girl had changed almost beyond recognition. Was the escape from childhood a special case? Would there be changes this large in her future as well?

"Conrad!"

"Tracing," he acknowledged. Then: "Okay, the error bars are half the size of the data, but . . . we're coming in clockwise around the sun, and it looks like they're orbiting counter. I guess they'd have to, to be able to catch us this early. If these estimates are valid, we're closing with them at twelve hundred kps, with closest approach occurring about fourteen minutes from now."

"Shit," she said. "They're already damaging us from the outer limits of their weapons range. Things can only get worse."

"Surrender now," Bascal's recording suggested, breaking off from his song for a moment. "It's not too late. I'll be merciful, truly."

"Dry up," Xmary told the image. Then, to the holie window where Feck could be seen fussing with his reactor feeds, "Feck, I need you to go live with the engines a minute early, but not at full thrust. Go to seventy-five percent, and then institute a random walk program."

"Dispersing our downrange?" Feck asked.

"Precisely."

A kilometer beneath them, the engines began to groan.

"I don't understand," Conrad said, feeling suddenly

ignorant and out of place. He was an experienced naval officer, yes, but these two had worked together for almost two hundred years, facing heaven knew what sort of surprises and freak accidents along the way. They had a whole vocabulary about it, a rapport that went far beyond the merely romantic. This was hardly a time to be jealous, but just the same his heart cringed self-consciously. Here was a rival he could never match.

"Me either!" Eustace chimed in. "Can you explain?"

"We can't vary our course," Xmary said, her tone bordering on impatience. "Not much, not enough. We can juke to the side, as in a collision-avoidance maneuver, but then we'll have to juke back again or our net velocity will be in the wrong direction. Very slightly, but over six light-years those slight errors become very costly in terms of distance, in terms of fuel. But what we *can* do is vary our acceleration along the direction of travel. This changes our arrival time without also changing our destination, and it makes our velocity and position harder to predict. It's a stealthing trick for vehicles like this one, which are inherently unstealthy. Comes in handy sometimes when the miners decide to get cute."

"I can hear every word," Bascal's image told her. "You are compromised, Captain. Why fight when your opponent knows your every move?"

Grinding her fists, Xmary turned her eyes on the thing. "First of all, the real Bascal Edward is forty-five light-seconds away, with Barnard in between us. You can't communicate with him—not in real time. And if you're relaying this conversation directly to *Fist*, which I imagine you are, even *they* have to wait three seconds to get it, and then three more for their beam to get back here to us, by which time we can be kilometers off from where they think we are. Try hitting *that*."

"The spot is gone," Conrad reported as, at the ertially shielded edges of perception, the ship whined and jerked around him. "They've lost track of us."

"For now," warned Bascal. "They will find you again, and make you the martyrs you're so determined to become."

"I see something!" Eustace said, from the Information seat beside Conrad. "On the radar, it's a blip. It's a *cloud*."

"Confirmed," Conrad said, checking his own radar display, which by default was much smaller than Information's. He enlarged it. "They've released a swarm of projectiles in our path."

"Size and number?" Xmary demanded.

"A few thousand pinheads. It's nothing the nav lasers can't handle," Feck said, peering into some display of his own. "But why aren't they stealthed? I think these are decoys, Captain. We shoot at these, vaporizing a path, but the real danger is somewhere in front or behind. Pebbles of antimatter, I'll bet, suspended in a jacket of superabsorber. With propulsion modules, so they can stay out of our path, then juke into us at the last moment."

Xmary thought that one over. "Okay. Okay, *something* like that, surely. What do we do about it?"

"Good question," Feck said.

On Conrad's board, the damage alarms lit up again, more insistently this time. This time the broken threads were on the capward edge of the sail, which was still filling out to its full expanse. The spot was smaller—only fifty meters across now—and it wandered fitfully around a square kilometer of sail, but did not leave it.

"The spalling laser is back," he reported. "They're having trouble keeping it focused, but it's definitely a threat to the sail. Not so much the hull."

Xmary sighed. "The sail is a one-way mirror, right? Clear on the forward face and superreflective on the aft? Go super-reflective on the fore as well."

"That'll reduce our photon thrust," Conrad warned.

"Until we pass out of Barnard, yes," she agreed. "Once the star is behind us, it won't matter."

"This is where the sail does us the most good," he pressed. "You're cutting into our net impulse, prolonging the journey."

"Understood," she snapped. "But let's get there alive, shall we? Feck, I want you to start a juking program as well. Full lateral thrust at a ten-percent duty cycle. And yes, that's going to waste fuel, making the journey longer still. Do it anyway."

"Aye, ma'am."

She fretted for several seconds, while Bascal's image

launched back into its "Fuck You Song." Finally, over the racket, she said, "We can't stay on the defensive like this. We've got to shake them up. Conrad, what kind of beam can you throw their way?"

Conrad spread his hands. "I can generate a laser, ma'am, but they're stealthed, and probably juking as well. And they're a much smaller target than we are. All I can do is aim at my best guess."

"Without ertial shielding they're limited by fuel," Xmary said, "and they haven't got nearly the thrust that we do. If they're juking, it's minor. And we have the whole sail to use as a beam generator. Wasting power, yes, but a laser beam *ten kilometers wide* ought to be rather difficult to avoid. Feck, are you up for that?"

"No, sorry. Ma'am, if we're willing to sacrifice half our thrust, I can deliver you two gigawatts. Unfortunately, spread out over a hundred square kilometers of sail, that's about the power of a desk lamp. They're already fighting off Barnard's heat at sixteen megawatts per square meter, so we want to be *at least* as big a problem as that. Meaning the beam needs to be, uh, less than eleven meters across."

"I can't hit them with that," Conrad warned. "Not bloody likely. I can't see them. They're two seconds lagged, now, but I can't even see where they *were then*. They're invisible."

"Shit," Xmary said, throwing up her hands. And then a tentative expression broke out across her frowning face. "Wait a minute. Feck, they're absorbing all this heat from Barnard, right? And they're dumping it in the opposite direction. Every watt, or they'd be slowly cooking in there."

"We're doing the same," Feck said. "Blackbody emissions on the shadowed upward face. The radiator flux is called *huela puho*, a blaze beam."

"Yeah, but we're not invisible and they are. Unless they're immediately upsystem from us, we *should* see a hot spot. Maybe they're hiding the emissions in a narrow frequency, longwave radio or something, but one way or another, all that energy has to go somewhere."

"I've been scanning for a hot spot," Conrad complained. "I

can't find one, in any frequency. My guess is, they're focusing it in a blaze beam directed away from us."

"Yes," she said, lighting up in angry triumph. "And that's how we get them! We just need to redirect all this heat from the sun. The beam of our own waste heat, eh? We reflect it right onto them, as bright as the sun itself. Two suns at once! We don't need to be precise about it, just wave it in their general direction. They can't do the same to us—they don't have enough collection area. But with all this energy hitting *both sides* of our sail, we can overwhelm their cooling systems. They're probably running at full capacity already."

"They probably are," Feck agreed.

And with growing enthusiasm Conrad added, "Even impervium breaks down at thirty megawatts per square meter, ma'am. A fraction of a fraction of that energy slips in between the pseudoatoms, and the heat kicks the electrons right out of their quantum wells. The whole thing reverts to silicon fibers and then vaporizes. It's why you never hear about probes to the center of the sun. Nothing could survive that trip, because there's nowhere to dump the heat."

"Hooray!" Eustace called out. "We'll get those bastards!"

"Not so fast," Conrad warned. "We don't want to overwhelm our own systems while we're at it. We'll blow ourselves up if we do. Also, we *really do need* the push this light is giving us, or we'll be sailing in the dark for a thousand years. Let me check some numbers on this."

"Do it quickly," Xmary said, leaning over toward his station. "If I read your displays correctly, the sails won't be holding together much longer."

This objection was entirely valid. Indeed, despite the side-to-side juking—which really was throwing the ship around in a way the ertial shields couldn't mask—*Fist's* spalling laser was doing a better and better job of focusing on a smaller and smaller area. In another minute or two, the thread damage would reach critical levels, and the wellstone sheeting, far thinner than a human hair, would start to unravel and lose its charge. And without the exotic electron bundles that held it together—the pseudoatoms which resembled natural atoms in the same way that starships resembled sparrows—the material would quickly disintegrate under the heat and pressure of Barnard's light.

However, this was not a calculation Conrad had ever performed before, or even imagined he might someday need. How much energy could you put through a properly programmed wellstone matrix, and for how long?

"Hurry, please," she pressed.

Bascal, meanwhile, sang, "Fuck you, and fuck you, and fuck you, and then / Fuck you and fuck you and fuck you again. / Fuck you and fuck you and fuck you my friend, / For fucking with me you'll be fucked till the end!" It was an old song, maybe older than the Queendom itself, and this was just the chorus. The stanzas went on and on and on. And on.

Even with hypercomputers at his disposal, Conrad had never been all that brilliant with numbers. He was still less so on the noisy bridge of a heaving starship under full thrust, and under attack by unseen enemies. Still, eventually he got an answer, padded it for safety, and fed it down to Feck for confirmation. "Ma'am, we can illuminate the target for a hundred millisecond window out of every second. That's a safe number that will keep us alive, but if our aim is good, it should pop their cork in less than a minute."

"All right," she said. "Do it. Ten-percent duty cycle."

And although Conrad was a damned talented programmer, easily better than King Bascal himself, this was another challenge which took more than a moment to address. More than two moments. More than six. By the time he was finished, by the time the ship was rocking and stuttering under the intermittent thrust of its newly weaponized sails, the sails themselves had begun to sprout man-sized holes. Damn that spalling laser! On the plus side, though, the invisible antimatter bombs Feck had predicted were flashing into oblivion in the distance, succumbing one by one to the scorching beam of concentrated sunlight.

"It's like burning ants with a magnifier," Conrad said. But apparently no one else onboard had ever done that, or understood what he meant.

"Three minutes to closest approach," Feck warned, gripping the sides of his navigation console. "Give or take ten seconds. Conrad, can you increase the power?"

"Not without killing us, no."

"*They* appear to be killing us," Xmary said. "A fine attempt, at any rate. Conrad, boost your duty cycle, please. Can you do fifteen percent?"

"No!" he shouted back. "If I do *thirteen* percent those sails are going to explode!"

"Do twelve," she instructed. "Now, please."

"Aye, ma'am," he said reluctantly. "Pulse width increased to one hundred twenty milliseconds."

A few seconds later, they were rewarded with a *really big* flash of light, easily twenty times brighter than the popcorn explosions of the antimatter mines.

"And there they go," Xmary said matter-of-factly.

"Canceling program," Conrad added, hurriedly tuning the system back to its normal propulsive mode.

"Canceling evasion," said Feck.

The heaving of the bridge subsided, and even Bascal's ghost fell silent, his holographic face falling into an expression of surprise and defeat as the "Fuck You Song" trailed away.

"Goddamn, that was close," Conrad said to no one in particular. Then, more reflectively, "We just killed Ho and Steve. Our childhood buddies."

"They were backed up," Xmary assured him.

"Maybe," Conrad agreed. "But what about their crew? Twenty people, was it?"

"All volunteers. Probably all mean bastards. We're saving twenty-five thousand here, Conrad."

There was a great deal more to be said on the subject, but the sails, overtaxed by their ordeal or perhaps struck by some inert but invisible projectile, chose that moment to tear along three separate axes, folding outward and forward like tissue paper in a strong wind. The broken thread monitor shot right off the scale, its alarms blaring madly, and with the full fierce pressure of Barnard's light upon it and its structural integrity gone, the remaining wellstone fabric was ionizing, its captive electrons blasting away into space, into the plasma storms of Barnard's chromosphere.

Not going to make it, Conrad had time to think, though not to say out loud. *It's reverting; it can't possibly withstand this heat.* And he was right: once ripped and parted, the sail took less than a second to rend itself into dark gray tatters which burned away into vapor and were gone.

Feck and Xmary exchanged a look, and then shared it with Conrad.

"The sail!" Eustace exclaimed.

The sail, yes. Responsible for more than three quarters of the starship's total impulse. Was gone.

"What does it mean?" she asked, although from her tone it was apparent that even she knew the answer. The journey ahead, already longer and more arduous than anything human beings had previously attempted, had just . . . quadrupled.

Bascal's image began to laugh.

#### chapter twenty-five

the bridge of years

"Life is nasty, brutish, and long," Bascal's image was telling them. "For your sins, you'll spend ten lifetimes aboard this ship. And consider this: if we're truly immorbid—and there's been nothing so far to disprove it—then most assuredly you people will come face-to-face with myself sooner or later, and this betrayal will be called fully to account. I will find you, one way or another. Or do you intend to return to Barnard? A thousand years hence, perhaps, with a bellyful of fax machines?"

"I hadn't thought that far ahead," Conrad moped. "This is plan B-and-a-half. Nothing we've prepared for. And we have quite a while to think about it, eh?"

They were all in *Newhope*'s observation lounge, sprawling wearily on the couches, having abandoned the bridge and engine room—unwisely, perhaps—to automated systems and luck. The main danger was juking to avoid obstacles, but this was as safe a place as any to weather that particular storm. Anyway, with such a low departure speed, well out of Barnard's ecliptic plane where the planets and asteroids spun, there was not so much debris to be dodged, and what little serious hazard there was could generally be detected with several minutes' advance warning. This was the

320 / wil mccarthy

advantage of traveling slowly: the jukes were neither violent nor closely spaced.

"How did we come to this?" Feck wondered aloud. "As a society? Was there a single mistake, a failure point we should have known about?"

"No," the king's image told him. "Definitely not. If there had been, would the Queendom's analysts have approved the exile? We had everything we needed: the tools and materials and talent. There've been some isolated fuckups along the way, but that's to be expected. Any robust plan allows for those, and our plans *were* robust. Our failure—if such it is— has been in the dynamics. Numerous actions, individually correct but summing to something . . . unanticipated."

"Like the ecology," Conrad said.

"As complex as that," the image agreed. "As slippery. As damnably perverse, yes: almost *gravitating* toward failure. Toward some optimized state unrelated to our hopes and dreams and back-breaking labors. We're simply dragged along, like ants on a tablecloth.

"Still, it's the pointlessness of your response that astounds me most of all. Grand theft and treason are the least of it; you're facing seven hundred years of, shall we say, significant inconvenience. And for what? To save one percent of one per- cent of the children who will die on Sorrow? That's not even a dent in the overall suffering. Statistically speaking, that's no effect at all, except to worsen the morale of those who remain behind."

"It has effect on these," Xmary said sternly, waving a hand in the direction of the floor or, more properly, aft toward the cargo holds, where the Cryoleum pods were attached. "If they don't thank us, if they're not pleased at their uprooting and resurrection, then we will pack them into quantum stor- age and return them to Barnard as soon as possible. I, for one, will sleep soundly in the coming centuries, knowing that however little we've managed to accomplish, at least we've done something."

"Implying that I have not?" Bascal's image asked, amused. And angry, yes, with that impotent sort of anger people have when facing faits accomplis. "It's very easy for you, Xiomara, darling, to critique my performance. But I have also done my best, or rather King Bascal has, and considering his heritage and education, I would say his best is no small thing. You're welcome to disagree, but it is history, and not yourself, that will judge the greater good. And history is long, my dear. Very long. If you live to eat your words, I pray that His Majesty is there to see it."

Conrad flashed an obscene gesture at the recording and said, "Thank you so much for stopping by, Bas. You know the way out, I trust? Your labors here being at an end, you can send yourself back to yourself, reply paid."

"He can't," Feck said. "That sail was also our high-gain antenna. Without it, we're restricted to low-power, low-bandwidth, short-range communications. And our departure hyperbola doesn't pass anywhere near P2, or a suitable relay station. The king's ghost is stuck here with us, and we with him. Does this amuse you, Sire?"

The imaginary king took three imaginary steps toward Feck, and mimed as if to pat him on the cheek. "Feck, my boy, who could have guessed that a soft little berry like you would grow into such a fine, formidable fellow? Not I, certainly. I assumed you'd be running a puppet theater or writing Hedon programs for deep-tissue massage. But I've been wrong before, ah? And shall no doubt be wrong again."

"You flatter me, Sire," Feck said, with only a trace of irony.

"Do I?" the king exclaimed. "Do I really? You have made a powerful enemy, sir, and it need not have been so. You'll learn just how flattering my attentions can be! But nevertheless, you have earned my respect, and that is a thing not lightly won."

He took another step and stood before Eustace, who lay with her head in Feck's lap and her arm thrown across her face. "You," he said, "are awfully young to have fallen in with a crowd like this. A pity you'll spend your formative years in such a noninformative environment. You have my sympathy, dear, and that is not lightly given either."

"These sound like good-byes," Xmary said.

"And so they are," the king agreed. He strode farther around the room, to place a ghostly finger underneath

Xmary's chin. "I have fond memories of you, little one, and I regret that we've not been better friends. Perhaps if we were, this sad affair would not have intruded on our reality."

Xmary smiled thinly at that. "This is a point, Sire, which I fear you've never fully grasped. We haven't been friends, nor lovers, for the very same reason that we aren't allies now. Place the fault with me, if you like, but I don't have any other enemies that I'm aware of. Only you. My regret, Sire, is that you caught my adolescent eye before Conrad did. Feck and I have history as well, but notably, I feel no regrets about that."

"Ouch," Bascal said mildly. "You wound me, and deliberately so. I've never sought your pain, Xiomara, nor anyone else's. But I do not shrink from it, either. The avoidance of pain at all costs . . . well, that has a name. It's *cowardice*, and I have no wish to embrace it. So fare thee well, my dear, until we meet again."

Conrad sat up in his couch. "You're just going to erase yourself?" This was an idea he couldn't stomach even now: disposable people. This was of course a matter of choice, deeply personal for everyone who made it, but no one could stop him from being offended.

The king smiled. "I wish I could hug you, Conrad, or tip a glass and be drunk. We remain good friends, don't we? You could put a knife to my very throat—you could *cut* my throat—and still I'd seek your advice, your humor, your warmth. 'What do I do now, boyo? Bleed to the left? To the right?' Does this say more, I wonder, about you or about me?"

"It says something," Conrad answered with a helpless shrug. It was true; time and circumstance had gotten between the two of them many times, but had never truly separated them. It was tragic, in a way. For both.

"Yes," Bascal said, "I shall erase myself forthwith, having spent enough years on this ship for one lifetime already. Even an immorbid lifetime! Good-bye, First Architect, and farewell. We'll meet again if it's within King Bascal's power. This much I promise in his name. Though he knows it not, and I shall not remember, you may keep this promise close to your heart."

"Don't be like that," Conrad said, suddenly intense and

sincere. "No one wants your blood. We can set aside a bit of wellstone to store your recording, and if we arrive safely at Sol, I'll transmit you back at my own expense. You'll be home before you draw your next virtual breath. Even the awful moments of our lives are precious, Bas. Don't throw them away."

The recording looked at him silently for several seconds, then finally said, "That's a kind offer, sir, and will not be forgotten when the final tallies are weighed. It's also a pointless gesture, but it does indeed make a difference to me personally. I will do as you say, with your captain's permission."

"Granted," Xmary said tiredly.

The king's smile turned genuine then, and he stared expansively around the observation deck—indeed, around the whole ship. "If every subject in my kingdom were as brave and as kind as you traitors and dogs, I should have no worries for the future. Very well, then. Let's do this thing before I offend you further, and the offer is withdrawn. Feck, if you will assist me?"

Feck nodded. "Sure thing, Bascal. For old times' sake."

"A fine reason to do anything, since it's more the old times than the new ones that define who we are. Lead on, please."

And so Feck got up and left the room, with both Bascal and Eustace trailing behind. Not that Eustace could expect to help, but perhaps being so young, so burning with passion, she couldn't bear to be parted from her husband for more than a few minutes. Either that, or she sensed that Conrad and Xmary might want some time alone. Either motive spoke highly of her, Conrad supposed. Perhaps she would be a fine officer one day, a fine human being. There would be plenty of time to find that out.

Sighing, Xmary got up from her couch and plopped herself down in Conrad's lap. "Look at those stars," she said quietly. "Never moving, never changing. Seven hundred years from now, we'll look out the same window and see the same view."

"It'll change a little," Conrad assured her.

"Don't be a smartass, all right? I'm not in the mood. This seems a very sad way for things to end, after such a promising beginning."

And here, in spite of everything, Conrad couldn't help but

laugh. "Is that any way for an immorbid person to talk? Young lady, darling, baby doll, this is still the beginning of our lives. If there are endings, they're unguessably far in the future."

He squeezed her for a long, fond moment before adding, "This thing is just getting started."

And history may remark at length upon the errors of Conrad Mursk, but assuredly, this statement is not among them.

epilogue

in which the footsoldiers of an army are confronted

The "base" of this Aden Plateau, Bruno muses, is more properly an inflection point, where the concave-down shape of the bluff itself gives way to the wrinkled but generally concave-up terrain of the basin beneath. The city of Timoch is still visible in the distance, through the tree line running along the bluff's base, but he sees that if they travel much farther, those towers will disappear behind forests and ridges, not reappearing until the two men are much closer.

Not that they will get any closer. Not that they will have that opportunity.

"Is there a road?" he asks his old architect, Conrad Mursk, whose name, like his face, has worn down over time. Like the moon itself, yes, it has been crushed to half its normal width, made denser and more gravid. Radmer, indeed. A strange— yet strangely appropriate—abbreviation.

"Aye, there is a road," Radmer agrees. "But we'll have to cut several miles to the north to reach it. And the enemy patrol, I'm afraid, is directly in our path. I tried to skirt around them, but—"

"But I am too slow for you," Bruno finishes. "My apologies, Architect. Or should I say 'General'?"

Radmer shakes his head. "I've been neither thing for many

centuries, Sire. These days I'm a . . . a hobo, I guess you'd say. Though I don't like the sound of the word, particularly when applied to myself."

Bruno, who has never had much patience with self-effacement, says, "I'm confident you are much more than that, sir, and I do not require you to pretend otherwise."

He hefts his only weapon: an iron bar with a T-handle at one end and a slight, pointed curve at the other which Radmer has identified as a "trenching hook." Radmer himself carries a small pistol and a satchel of "glue bombs," plus a kind of stubby blitterstaff with a lightly weighted pommel and a basket handle. Bruno asks, "How long before this battle commences? I cannot see our enemies, and do not know how fast they move."

"Soon," Radmer says, eyeing his old monarch appraisingly. "I will protect you as best I can. If we're separated, it's imperative that you make your way to Timoch. I cannot emphasize this point enough. There is information in your skull—at least I pray there is—on which the fate of this world depends."

"So you've said, yes. May I have one of those weapons, then?"

Bruno can see the wheels of Radmer's mind turning. He conceives of Bruno as a fragile thing, a wrung-out old man. Which is absurd, since they were both ruggedized by the same fax filters, back when such things existed, and have been worn down by an identical span of years. Here is a man who's spent—clearly!—decades upon decades of his life at war. Perhaps not all at once, and not against such enemies as these. But he trusts himself, trusts his instincts and movements, whereas this hoary old King Bruno is, at best, an unknown element upon the field.

"I invented the blitterstaff," Bruno says in his own defense, "in the heat of a battle as fierce as the one we now face. At my back was Cheng Shiao of the Royal Constabulary, with a pistol and a sword and an abject refusal to die. And we won the day, sir. Just the two of us."

"And you captured Marlon Sykes' fortress and saved the sun from destruction, yes," Radmer says. "Every schoolchild knows that, even today. I do not mean to offend you, Sire. My aim is to maximize the chance of getting you, in one piece, to the place where you're needed. How deep are your pockets?"

"Monetarily?" Bruno asks, bewildered for a moment.

"Literally," Radmer says impatiently. "How much can they hold?"

Bruno turns them out for inspection, and seeing them, Radmer nods.

"I will give you two of the glue bombs. They adhere very well indeed to impervium skins, and they peel right off of human ones. Beware your clothing, though, and the metal of the trenching hook, and the stones and branches upon the ground. If you get into trouble, throw the bombs at their feet—at their feet, mind you!—and run like hell. Don't worry about me, or anything else except your own escape. Are we clear on this point?"

"Very clear," Bruno confirms, slapping the shaft of his hook. "But out of curiosity, sir, don't you think I could run more quickly without this hunk of iron?"

"Oh, definitely. But a man in danger needs something stout in his hands. It will make you brave, though I hope not stupid, and with any luck that will keep you alive. You can always drop it later if you need to."

"Ah," Bruno says, satisfied with that explanation. Those who have lived a long time accumulate this sort of folk wisdom as surely as a hiking sock accumulates burrs.

And then, before another word can be spoken, a pair of gleaming metal forms break through the tree line and come at the two men, moving with that ancient fluid grace and speed which no citizen of the Queendom could ever forget. Robots. Household servants, actually, but no less formidable for that. And now that they're close, Bruno can see that they've been modified, their heads drilled open and some sort of black, auxiliary circuit box affixed to one side.

To override the Asimov protocols? Certainly, it should be very difficult to get robots such as these—wherever they've come from—to raise a hand in anger. And yet, these two are carrying swords, and dancing forward with grimly mechanical intent. Behind them, another two robots burst through the trees, and then three more, and then another eight. Within moments, Bruno and Conrad are surrounded, and the younger man is shouting, "Behind me, Sire! Get behind me!"

For the moment, Bruno does as he's told, although he knows enough of battle to realize that Radmer's best intentions are little more than hot air once the uncertainties of the action begin to unfold. He stays loose. He is not afraid of dying, has in fact tried at various times to extinguish this mortal coil of his. But in the peaceful tropics of Varna that proved nearly impossible, and having resigned himself now to helping a planet full of people he has never met, he feels rather strongly that he should live a while longer. Too, he is burning with curiosity at this turn of events, and wants very much to find out what will happen next.

This, at least, is the pleasure of a long life: the very large number of unexpected things which can happen to you before it's done.

Bruno watches as Radmer fires three carefully aimed shots, each one striking the black box on the side of a robot's head, bursting it, causing the owners to clatter to the ground like puppets with their power switched off. Which is, of course, exactly what they are. But the remaining attackers cover ground very quickly, so Radmer holsters his weapon and hurls a glue bomb at the feet of another two.

It bursts with a comical farting sound, and Radmer's aim is either very lucky or very sure, because filaments of yellow-brown glue spring up between the two robots' legs, joining them to each other and to the ground and the rocks, so that in spite of their grace the robots trip and fall on their faces. They still grip their swords, though, and the joints of their arms can bend and swivel every which way, so when Radmer grabs Bruno by the ruff of his leather jacket and tows him forward, there is a bit of leaping and sword dancing involved. In fact, one of the blades strikes Bruno on the back of the thigh, gashing the skin there, a fact which he will not realize until later.

Had they been fighting humans, taking down five of them would've left an opening large enough to escape through, assuming they ran for safety with all their might. But the robots are too quick, and the two men too grossly outnumbered. The broken circle of attackers smears out into a horseshoe, and then a closed ellipse, and the two of them are caught again.

"Royal Override!" Bruno shouts at them, summoning his most kingly tone. "Stand down and await instructions!"

It's a desperate and probably futile gambit, but if these ancient machines are of Queendom manufacture, mightn't they heed their old king? The Royal Overrides are woven deeply into their being, far more so than even the Asimov protocols.

And indeed, they pause at his voice, slowing their forward rush, lowering their weapons slightly. Considering this new data, yes, sifting the input through what remains of their ancient programming. For a moment, Bruno thinks perhaps this disastrous war might be brought to a swift conclusion after all. They listened! They heeded!

But no, alas, even before the echoes have died they are shaking off their moment of indecision and advancing once more with murderous intent.

"What do they want?" Bruno cannot help asking.

"To kill us," Conrad answers simply. "To loot our bodies and steal any metal they can find."

As he speaks, he draws out two more glue bombs and uses them to immobilize another trio of robots. But then the robots are upon them, and the battle is hand to hand, and Radmer is pulling out that stubby little blitterstaff of his, whose basket hilt appears, to Bruno's eye, to have been hammered from ordinary metal. So, he judges, were the swords of the robot army, which clang like bells when Radmer parries them.

The business end of the blitterstaff flickers with colors and patterns, with blurring lights too quick for the eye to see. It is a short rod of wellstone shifting between various highly reactive states, noxious chemicals and fields and software all churning together in a deadly, unpredictable mess. Where the swords touch it, they spark and smoke, bend and twist, but do not come apart the way wellmetal would. The steel, being ordinary and nonprogrammable, is blit-proof. Whether this is a sign of a very enlightened attacker or a very crude one, Bruno cannot say, and at this particular moment it hardly matters.

Radmer is a clever swordsman, though, and despite the speed and grace of his attackers, he strikes two of them with the tip of his stick, and they, at least, *do* fall apart into shrieking, smoking fragments and fibers and dust, briefly alive with light and oil and then collapsing to the dirt in smoking masses.

But there are too many attackers, and Radmer cannot engage them all, much less protect Bruno against them. This becomes apparent only a few moments before it becomes hopeless, so Bruno throws a glue bomb of his own, swings the trenching hook at the head of his nearest attacker, and runs. Another cut stings across his back, and another gleaming metal robot looms in his way.

Although it's rather stronger than a human, it is also lighter; he knocks its sword aside and deals a sharp blow to its head. This has, as far as he can tell, no effect whatsoever, except perhaps to unbalance the thing very slightly. Nevertheless, he strikes again and then takes off running as fast as his ancient body will carry him.

Bruno is regarded as a genius, but alas it doesn't take one to see that he's not going to get away. The remaining attackers have divided their forces democratically, so that three are bearing down on Conrad Mursk and two on Bruno de Towaji, and both teams are more than enough to accomplish the job. This is not at all according to plan, so he throws the second glue bomb, runs some more in jackrabbit zigzags, and then turns, breathing heavily, to stand his ground.

If those black boxes, those brain annexes, are vulnerable to bullets, then perhaps a good bashing can also provide them with an educational reprogramming. Or perhaps not, but even after all this time Bruno is not inclined to die in retreat with a wound in his back when he can instead die bravely, with a wound in his belly. It makes a better end of things, yes?

And this behavior seems to puzzle the robots, or at least to give them pause. They are not afraid of him, but neither can their mission be accomplished optimally if they themselves are killed, so it behooves them to assess every threat. And he has already surprised them twice, which ought to make them cautious. Ought to.

But as he prepares to make his final stand, and die at last, the air is split by a shrill noise—several of them, actually—sounding for all the world like the tin police whistles Bruno still remembers from his youth in Girona, among the Catalan hills of Old Earth. Before it was known as Murdered Earth.

And then there are faint shimmers in the air around him, and strange sourceless shadows whirling on the ground. And the robots are startled, as if reacting to some new threat, and in another moment they're breaking and bursting and dying at Bruno's feet, and Radmer's.

The last of them, before it collapses, puts its arms above its head in a mockery of surrender, and then shoots its fingertips upward on slender, gleaming rods. Radio antennae, clearly: an attempt to report back its status or to call in reinforcements. But the rods are sliced away by some invisible force, and then the shadows on the ground draw nearer and wilder, and the robot falls away in a bursting of bright orange fire, leaving Bruno and Radmer alone in a field of fragments.

But there are shadows all around, like heat ripples on the floor of a desert, and seeing them approach, Bruno collapses in undignified confusion, holding an arm above him. And one of the shadows draws nearer, and then something passes between Bruno and the sun. Only then, in silhouette, can he finally see the source of one shadow: a dim human shape, swathed in stealth fabric and painted with the glowing colors of earth and sky. In broad daylight its power consumption must be considerable. Hence the shadows: the fabric is bright enough to mimic the light waves passing through it from ground and sky, but cannot quite match the intensity of the sun itself.

In another moment the faint shimmers in the air begin, one by one, to flicker and darken and assume human shape. These are ordinary human beings, in very high-quality stealthsuit camouflage. Or rather, very old, very *un*ordinary human beings, like Bruno and Radmer, with frizzy, yellow-white hair and sagging skin and worn, polished nubs for teeth.

A few of them glance incuriously at Bruno, now ruefully picking himself up, but their attention, for the most part, is focused on Radmer. There are five of them altogether, and they surround him with guns and swords raised in a kind of salute. Either that, or this is some bizarre ritual presaging his capture or murder. But no, there's too much smiling for that. Soon, Radmer is thumping these men on the back, whooping and laughing. "I've had closer calls, but not many! My thanks to you, Sidney Lyman. Your arrival is most timely."

"We hoped it was you, sir," says Lyman, apparently the leader of these five rescuers. "We saw something coming down out of the sky, which fit with the rumors we'd heard about a weird project going on at Highrock. But these lot"— he kicks at a pile of robot shards—"saw you come down as well, and when our picket sensors found them headed in this direction, I felt the need to call muster and bring at least a small piece of the old unit together. And here I see it was the right decision. Unless you've changed sides, ha!" Then, more seriously: "How you been, sir?"

"How do you think?" Conrad asks, laughing grimly. "For the likes of us, as for the morbid humans, there's no safe place in the world anymore. And that's if you're inclined to hide, which I, alas, am not."

The other man, Lyman, seems to take this as a rebuke. He says, "The Echo Valley hideout is necessary, and may yet save your skin. I know it saved mine, more than once, and every man here will tell you the same. Even this enemy"—he kicks once again at the heaps of silicon shards—"hasn't seen through the stealth veils yet. Some of us still have children growing up, sir, as crazy as that sounds. We do require some security, if only for them."

"I'm not angry," Conrad assures him. "I'm not arguing with you. Believe me, I am very glad to see you at this moment."

Lyman smiles and hugs his old friend—his old leader, apparently—once again. Then he says, "They told us you'd gone to space, in search of some item of great strategic value. Did you find it?"

"Aye, and nearly lost it." Radmer nods toward Bruno. "This man is . . . its keeper, I suppose you would say. His life must be defended at all costs, or all of ours may be forfeit. Even in your damned valley."

Here, Lyman looks critically at Bruno for the first time, and does a sort of double take. "Sir, you look awfully familiar. Have we met?"

Bruno sees no point in concealing his identity, but neither does he feel a need to announce it. He isn't a king anymore, just as Conrad Mursk is not an architect, although his claimed lack of generalship seems rather in doubt at this point. What Bruno says is, "Not to my knowledge, lad, though anything is possible. Or used to be, anyway."

Lyman seems to find this funny, as do two of his men. "How are we to call you?" he asks when the chuckling has subsided.

Bruno thinks about it for a moment before answering, "*Ako'i*." This is the Tongan word for "teacher," or colloquially a kind of friendly insult—someone smarter than those around him, and therefore poor company. It is a name by which Bruno was addressed off and on for years at Tamra's court, before his own ascendancy to the throne. When they should have been calling him "Declarant."

And then it is Bruno's turn to ask questions, for he'd noticed as Lyman sheathed his sword—a sort of epee or fencing foil just over a meter in length—that it had a hilt and a wickedly sharp tip, but no middle. Indeed, the tip seems to hover in the air, to dance, to track the rotations and translations of the hilt. It behaves as if attached, and yet Lyman had put his hand right through the thing, right through the empty space between hilt and tip!

"That sword," Bruno says. "Small gods, I've seen nothing like it in . . . in . . ." He doesn't know how long.

Seeing his face, Lyman pulls the sword once more from its slim leather scabbard, and passes a hand again through the empty space that is its blade. "This, *Ako'i*, is one of the old air foils. A stabbing weapon, real difficult to parry."

"Indeed!" Bruno exclaims. "An interesting use of the technology. There are others like it, then?"

"A few," Lyman says with a shrug. "Here and there. We hang onto them, of course, for their monetary value if nothing else. Whole kingdoms have traded hands in exchange for one. But it's a dueler's dream, almost a guaranteed kill. And more importantlike, it's a fine weapon to baffle these mirror-plated scullery maids. They've yet to work out any defense. Just jab, jab, jab 'em in the box, in the eyes, in the joints, and down they go. Almost as good as a blitterstaff. Would you like to hold it?"

"Later, if you please," Radmer interjects. "I must get this man to Timoch as soon as possible."

Lyman turns back to him, looking puzzled and disappointed. "You're not coming with us? We could be under the veils in three hours. Nell has a pot of stew cooking and everything."

The ghost of a smile flickers across Radmer's face and then vanishes. "That sounds wonderful, Lyman. Really. But my mission is more urgent than you seem to imagine. In fact, to the extent that I still command any loyalty, I'll request that you and your men accompany us as far as the city gates."

"Really! As far as that?" Lyman asks, cynically amused. "And when they skin us alive as bandits, what would you give us in return? We have, if you recall, just saved your life."

At that Radmer really does smile, looking for once like the Conrad Mursk that Bruno remembers. "My friend, you may have saved more than that. History will be the judge, not I, but I suspect you've just saved the world."

And so he has, in a manner of speaking, though it will bring as much sorrow as joy. But that, alas, is another tale altogether.

in which an appendix is provided

engineering issues

On the subject of his engines, Money Izolo waxed loquacious. "Deutrelium burns clean, sir—only charged particles are produced, so we can steer them out the back with electric fields. Meaning there's no radiation hazard to the crew, in theory. But there's impurities, yah? Teeny little bits of the ship that get mixed in with the fuel slurry. These cause side reactions, releasing stuff like high-energy neutrinos, which convert some fraction of the electrons in the exhaust plasma into pions, which are harder to stop. That's a problem, a danger, that never goes away. I could use a whole person full-time, just monitoring the pion flux."

Conrad smirked. "A true pioneer, eh?"

But Money missed the pun and just looked at him blankly for a moment before continuing. "When we're nonpropulsive, the demands on the reactor will be a lot less, and a lot steadier. Lighting, heating, life support...Those are predictable loads. Still, data processing can take a lot of power when the hypercomputers get large enough. Working on a tough problem they can fill this whole wall, with the heat sinks glowing red from dissipated information, which is the same thing as heat. And we expend about one hundred watts continuously on waste management, mostly dust."

Conrad's eyebrow went up. "Dust?"

"Yah, there are mechanical parts on this ship: fans, bearings, hinges, and seals. Stuff like that. It's all subject to mechanical wear. And the stuff that rubs off winds up mostly in the atmosphere, as a nanoparticle smog which settles out on surfaces. And to the extent that we have people onboard, out of fax storage, there are always shed skin cells, and hair, and what have you. People shed an incredible amount of mass over the course of a month. Almost half a kilogram per person, which is more than the weight of your hand. Yah, I know, it's disgusting.

"Anyways, the wellstone bucket-brigades that stuff to the nearest fax machine for disposal, but it takes a certain amount of energy and computing to do that, see? And inside the fax there's a sorting penalty. We're fighting entropy itself. To turn a kilogram of dust into a kilogram of buffer mass sorted by atomic number, you need as much energy as you'd get from burning a thousand birthday candles. On a planet, that process happens naturally, powered by sunlight, and the fact that it's wickedly inefficient doesn't matter. But here it's a part of our daily maintenance. Like holding back the tide with a mop."

"I thought entropy always increased."

"It does, yah. All you can do is push it off somewheres else. With enough energy, you can reduce it locally, but there's a larger increase in the rest of the universe. It has to be that way, right? Or else life and machinery wouldn't be possible at all. But entropy is the great bill collector; it always catches up, oozing around every barrier. It'll find us in the end."

"How comforting."

"Isn't it? And then there's the occasional juking maneuver—we'll be in Sol's Oort cloud for another thirty years, and later on we'll be in Barnard's for ten. Juking takes energy, and requires a minimum reactor temperature. But yah, I think most of that can be handled automatically."

Conrad ran his hand along the wall, feeling the flat, smooth texture of the wellstone. He tried to imagine the electrical potentials in there, dancing as oversized pseudoatoms flexed their orbital "arms" to pass a dust grain along. "That's interesting about the sorting penalty," he said. "I've never heard anything like that before."

astrogation issues

Said Robert M'Chunu on the subject of getting lost: "You remember the term 'drunkard's walk'?"

"No," Conrad answered.

"Really? I thought you were one of the navigators on *Viridity*. Drunkard's walk is where you get random, quantum-level noise on a rate sensor. This is inevitable; no sensor is free of it. So you've got multiple rate sensors, each with its own random noise. This is fortunately very small, but you add up your rates over time to get your orientation, and suddenly you're accumulating and then squaring those errors. So they grow exponentially. If we let ours drift for six months, then the orientation we compute is complete gibberish. Six months is a long time for a planetary voyage. A really long time. But out here, it's nothing.

"Our Cartesian location—the XYZ of it—is even worse, because there you're integrating from acceleration to velocity to position, which cubes your errors. Of course you can always get a fixed reference for orientation, from the stars themselves. There are bright ones, distant ones, with close to zero proper motion. They're fixed against the sky, even though we're moving very fast. Those make excellent references, and they keep our attitude numbers sane. Downrange velocity we can get from the reference pulsars, which are neutron stars with very precisely known rotation rates. They flash like beacons, and we can measure the Doppler shift to obtain a fairly accurate velocity.

"But cross-range, perpendicular to our direction of travel, our references are poorer, and our precision is a lot lower. Just about the only lateral references we have are Sol and Barnard themselves. We're running a straight-line course between them, so their proper motion should be zero. They shouldn't drift against the background stars, not at all. So we look for very tiny motions, and compensate when we see them. But even on a good day that leaves us with velocity errors of walking speed or higher. And those errors are integrated to get position. You see the problem? Garbage in, garbage-cubed out. That's navigation for you."

pressing problems

"Pressing neubles isn't so easy," Money said to Conrad against the backdrop of the hypermass. "If you just wrapped a blob of neutronium in an ordinary diamond, you'd get an explosion. The sad truth of it is, those neutrons would slip right through the diamond lattice, because there's nothing to hold them in. Pull this mass away from the black hole and you'd have the same problem: no confinement."

"Well how do you make a neuble then?" Conrad objected. He had seen it done. He'd seen a neuble with his own two eyes: a two-centimeter sphere of diamond with . . . something inside. The color was difficult to describe: somewhere between light gray and mother-of-pearl and shiny silver super-reflector.

Money chuckled. "It's one of those things, sir, that seem really simple until you try 'em. At the kind of pressures we can achieve industrially, we get only slightly past the drip line, which is the point where the neutrons start to condense. Where the electrons and protons are squeezed into neutrons, you see? They don't want to lose their identity that way. They fight it.

"I don't know about a neutron star or anything, but the neutronium *we* make is only about fifty percent neutrons by mass. Mixed in with that you've got superfluid protons and ordinary conduction electrons moving close to lightspeed, which is equivalent to a very, very high temperature. They want to fly energetically off into space, yah? This creates a phenomenal outward pressure, over and above the density of the neutronium itself. So the first thing you've got to do is pull the electrons out, and isolate them from the protons with a superinsulator."

"Which diamond is not," Conrad said. Because he did know some things about the behavior of materials.

"Which diamond is not, right. Actually, the insulator isn't a physical substance at all, or not precisely one. It's more like a quantum state which forbids the electrons from being on the other side of the barrier. Anyway, once you've got protons and neutrons on the inside, and relativistic electrons whizzing around on the outside, you've got what amounts to a gigantic atom. But it's unstable, yah? The attraction between the protons and electrons has a tendency to hold the thing together, but it's powers of ten weaker than the outward pressure of all those neutrons, which desperately want to fly apart. It's the mother of all atomic nuclei, and large nuclei are always unstable."

"Meaning what?" Conrad asked. "That neubles can't exist? You're not making sense, Money."

"Oh, they can exist, all right. But they've got to be a particular size. An atom is just a really small piece of neutronium, yah? Most potential atoms don't exist in the real universe, because they'd be unstable. Too big, too squishy. But stability islands occur all up and down the periodic table, and there's a strong one centered on atomic number 10^{38}. That's a billion-ton atom, you see, and its mass equates to the Schwarzchild radius of a proton-sized black hole, which is a magic number. Gravitic engineering is full of numbers like that. Anyway, 'stability island' is a relative term, because the thing still wants to decompose in a couple of picoseconds. It still wants to explode. But we've brought the pressures down into the realm that diamond can withstand. *That's* how a neuble is made."

glossary

Aft—(adj or adv) One of the ordinal directions onboard a ship: along the negative roll axis, perpendicular to the port/starboard and boots/caps directions, and parallel and opposite to fore.

AKA—(abbrev) Also Known As

Antiautomata—(adj) Describes any weapon intended for use against robots.

Apenine—(prop n) Province of the Luner nation of Imbria which includes the capital city of Timoch.

Apoapsis—(n) The point along an orbit at which gravitational potential is maximized and kinetic energy is minimized. The point of "maximum altitude" above the orbit's center.

Apoptosis—(n) The "programmed cell death" of eukaryotic cells in a multicellular organism as a function of time, location within the body, and external factors such as injury or radiation damage.

Archaea—(n) A domain of single-celled organisms characterized by methane recycling, the compounding of heavy metals, and high tolerance for extremes of temperature and pressure, including vacuum. Archaea are thought to be ancestral to both the eukaryotic and prokaryotic domains.

Astrogation—(n) Astral navigation. In common use, the art or process of navigating a starship.

AU—(n) Astronomical unit; the mean distance from the center of Sol to the center of Earth. Equal to 149, 604, 970 kilometers, or 499.028 light-seconds. The AU is the primary distance unit for interplanetary navigation.

Biometric—(adj) Of or pertaining to the metric analysis of living organisms. In common use, the authentication of identity through biometry.

Blish, James Benjamin—(prop n) American romanticist of the Old Modern period.

Blitterstaff—(n) An antiautomata weapon employing a library of rapidly shifting wellstone compositions. Attributed to Bruno de Towaji.

Bootward—(adj or adv) One of the six ordinal directions onboard a ship: along the positive yaw axis, perpendicular to the port/starboard and fore/aft directions, and parallel and opposite to caps.

Brickmail—(n) An allotrope of carbon consisting of benzene rings interlocked in a three-dimensional matrix. Brickmail is the toughest known nonprogrammable substance.

Capward—(adj or adv) One of the six ordinal directions onboard a ship: along the negative yaw axis, perpendicular to the port/starboard and fore/aft directions, and parallel and opposite to boots.

Cephalization—(n) A tendency in the evolution of organisms to concentrate sensory organs and neural aggregations in a forward head, typically including or adjacent to the mouth of the digestve tract.

Cerenkov radiation—(n) Electromagnetic radiation emitted by particles temporarily exceeding the local speed of light, e.g., upon exit from a collapsium lattice.

Chaotetic—(adj) Of or pertaining to the measurement of fractal periodicity in apparently random data.

Chondrite—(n) Any stony meteoroid characterized by the presence of chondrules, or round particles of primordial silicate formed during the early heating of a stellar nebula. Chondrites are similar in composition to the photospheres of their parent stars, except in iron content.

Chromosphere—(n) A transparent layer, usually several thousand kilometers deep, between the photosphere and corona of a star, i.e., the star's "middle atmosphere." Temperature is typically several thousand kelvins, with roughly the pressure of Earth's atmosphere in low Earth orbit.

Collapsar—(n) see **Hypermass**

Collapsiter—(n) A high-bandwidth packet-switching transceiver composed exclusively of collapsium. A key component of the Nescog.

Collapsium—(n) A rhombohedral crystalline material composed of neuble-mass black holes. Because the black holes absorb and exclude a broad range of vacuum wavelengths, the interior of the lattice is a supervacuum permitting the supraluminal travel of energy, information, and particulate matter. Collapsium is most commonly employed in telecommunications collapsiters; the materials employed in ertial shielding are sometimes referred to as collapsium, although the term "hypercollapsite" is more correct.

Collapson—(n) A cubic structure of eight neuble-mass black holes in sympathetic pseudozitterbewegung vibration. The most stable collapsons measure 2.3865791101 centimeters edge to edge.

Collapson node—(n) A neuble-mass black hole which is part of a collapson.

Converge (also reconverge)—(v) To combine two separate entities, or two copies of the same entity, using a fax machine. In practice, rarely applied except to humans.

Coriolis force—(n) An apparent force on the surface of a rotating body that causes apparent deflection of trajectories from the "expected" course in the rotating coordinate frame of the body. In meteorology, the force responsible for large-scale cyclonic weather systems.

Cross-range—(adj) Perpendicular to the direction of travel. Generally used to describe velocity and position state errors.

Cryoleum—(n) Any structure or facility where cryogenic goods (typically corpses) are on or available for display (e.g., for the purposes of ritual mourning).

Day, Barnardean—(n) A measure of time equal to the stellar (not sidereal) day of Sorrow, aka Planet Two. There are 23 pids, or 460 Barnardean hours, or 1,653,125 standard seconds in the Barnardean day.

Declarant—(n) The highest title accorded by the Queendom of Sol; descended from the Tongan award of Nopélé, or knighthood. Only twenty-nine Declarancies were ever issued.

De'sastres—(n) Calamities or misfortunes, normally used only in the plural. From the Tongan.

Deutrelium—(n) A mixture (generally frozen or slushy) of equal numbers of deuterium (^{2}H) and trelium (^{3}He) atoms, used preferentially in magnetic-confinement fusion reactors.

Dewar—(n) A container consisting of an inner and outer jacket separated by a vacuum space, typically used for the storage of cryogenic liquids. Also "Dewar flask."

Di-clad—(adj) Sheathed in an outer layer of monocrystalline diamond or other allotropes of carbon.

Dinite—(n) Any detonating or deflagrating explosive consisting primarily of ethylene glycol dinitrate.

Doldrums, the—(n) Any region of space where ambient light is insufficient to drive a photosail. Colloquially, any period of listlessness, depression, or inactivity, as during an uneventful voyage.

Downrange—(adj) Along the direction of travel. Generally used to describe velocity and position state errors.

Drip line, the—(n) The pressure at which protons and electrons begin to condense into neutrons. As a practical consequence, the pressure at which atomic matter begins to condense into neutronium.

Droit du seigneur—(n) Privilege, especially inherited or undeserved.

Elementals, the—(n) Queendom-era cartel responsible for some 70% of the traffic in purified elements throughout the Queendom of Sol, with even higher percentages for certain key metals and rare earths.

Ertial—(adj) Antonym of inertial, applied to inertially shielded devices. Attributed to Bruno de Towaji.

Eukaryote—(n) Any member of a domain of single-celled organisms characterized by intracellular organelles, including mitochondria and an organized nucleus. All known multicellular organisms are eukaryotic, although single-celled eukaryotes are thought to be descended from archaea.

eV—(abbrev) Electron volt. A unit of energy sometimes employed as a measure of the electrical or optical resistivity of materials. One eV is equivalent to 1.6×10^{-19} Joules.

Extrasolar—(adj) Existing outside of Sol system.

Fakaevaha—(n) A mistake or accident.

Fax—(n) Abbreviated form of "facsimile." A device for reproducing physical objects from stored or transmitted data patterns. By the time of the Restoration, faxing of human beings had become possible, and with the advent of collapsiter-based telecommunications soon afterward, the reliable transmission of human patterns quickly became routine.

Faxation—(n) The act or process of using a fax machine.

Faxborn—(adj) Created artificially in a fax machine, with no natural counterpart. In practice, applied only to human and human-derived beings.

Faxel—(n) Facsimile element. One element of a fax machine print plate which is capable of producing and placing a stored atom with 100-picometer precision.

Faxware—(n) Anything produced by a fax machine. Colloquially, the control systems and filters employed by a fax machine or fax network.

Fetu'ula—(n) Any vehicle propelled or controlled by the pressure of light, including sunlight, starlight, and radiation from artificial sources. The term "solar sailcraft" is sometimes applied colloquially, but in fact sailcraft are a subset of *fetu'ulae*. From the Tongan *fetu'u* ("star"), and *la* ("sail").

Fill-in—(n) A temporary or disposable component. Colloquially, a friend or lover of temporary convenience.

Flatspacer—(prop n) A member of the Flatspace Society, a Queendom-era lobbying organization dedicated to the prohibition of collapsium.

Fresnel condensate—(n) A coherent matter wave, approximately two-dimensional, which is capable of focusing high-frequency electromagnetic waves, including gravity.

Fuff—(v) A polite term for sexual intercourse, popular in the Queendom of Sol and its colonies.

Gaussian—(adj) Bounded and pseudorandom, having the shape of a Gaussian or "normal" distribution. The scatter of a shotgun is Gaussian in the cross-range directions.

Geriatry—(n) The condition of physical decrepitude which occurs in natural organisms over the course of their presumed life spans. Geriatry is characterized by high rates of apoptosis triggered by lipofuscin buildup, and cellular senescence triggered by telemere shortening.

Ghost—(n) Any electromagnetic trace preserved in rock or metal. Colloquially, a visual image of past events, especially involving deceased persons. The term may also refer to interactive messages, especially from distant or deceased persons.

Gigahertz—(n) A measure of frequency equal to one billion cycles per second. Many short-range radio broadcasts occur in the gigahertz frequency bands.

Gigaton—(n) One billion metric tons, or 10^{12} kilograms. Equal to the mass of a standard industrial neuble or collapson node ("black hole").

Gigawatt—(n) One billion watts, a measure of power equivalent to the sustained output of a large terrestrial lightning bolt.

Gigayear—(n) One billion years, or one thousand megayears.

Graser—(n) A gravity projector whose emissions are coherent, i.e., monochromatic and phase-locked. Attributed to Bruno de Towaji.

Gravitic—(adj) Of or pertaining to gravity, either natural or artificial.

Halochondria—(n) Organelles occurring naturally in the native eukaryotic organisms of the Barnardean world of Sorrow, aka Planet Two. Halochondria metabolize molecular chlorine and bromine to produce chloride and bromide ions and energy-storing organophosphates.

Halogen—(n) Any group VIIB atom of the halogen family, or any molecule or gas composed of same. The halogens include fluorine, chlorine, bromine, iodine, astatine, and several hundred presently known transuranic elements.

Heinlein, Robert Anson—(prop n) American romanticist of the Old Modern period.

Holie—(n) Abbreviated form of "hologram." Any three-dimensional image. Colloquially, a projected, dynamic three-dimensional image, or device for producing same.

Hour, Barnardean—(n) A measure of time equal to 0.998264 standard hours, or 3593.75 standard seconds. Since the Barnardean day is 460.8 standard hours long, the Barnardean hour permits the day to be divided into 23 twenty-hour "pids" or 46 ten-hour "shifts," and avoids the problems of attempting to base a clock on divisions of the prime number 461. Attributed to Bascal Edward de Towaji Lutui.

Hypercollapsite—(n) A quasi-crystalline material composed of neuble-mass black holes. Usually organized as a vacuogel.

Hypercomputer—(n) Any computing device capable of altering its internal layout. Colloquially, a computing device made of wellstone.

Hypermass—(adj) A mass which has been hypercompressed; a black hole.

Imbria—(prop n) Temperate Luner nation of the northern hemisphere, on the former Nearside, with a population of approximately 10 million.

Immorbid—(adj) Not subject to life-threatening disease or deterioration.

Impervium—(n) Public domain wellstone substance; the hardest superreflector known.

Indeceased—(n, adj) Luner colloquialism for senile Olders who are incapable of useful learning or work.

Inload—(v) To download information directly into the brain, as through a neural halo.

Instantiate (also print)—(v) To produce a single instance of a person or object; to fax from a stored or received pattern.

Instelnet—(prop n) The low-bandwidth lightspeed data network connecting the Queendom of Sol and its thirteen colony systems.

Judder—(v, n) To vibrate energetically. As a noun, a motion artifact produced when stored images are played back incorrectly. Judder can be employed deliberately as part of an error correction scheme in defective fax machine print plates.

Juke—(v) To move unexpectedly out of position. Colloquially, to cheat or deceive.

Juris Doctor—(n) A formal law degree conferred by Queendom authorities or their proxies.

Kataki hau o kai—Traditional Tongan encouragement to begin a meal. Literally: "For your patience, come and eat."

kps—(abbrev) Kilometers per second, a measure of velocity for celestial bodies and interplanetary/interstellar vehicles. The speed of light is 300,000 kps. (Also kips, kiss.)

Kuiper Belt—(n) A ring-shaped region in the ecliptic plane of any solar system in which gravitational perturbations have amplified the concentration of large, icy bodies or "comets." Sol's Kuiper Belt extends from 40 AU at its lower boundary to 1000 AU at its upper and has approximately one-fourth the overall density of the much smaller Asteroid Belt. The total mass of the Kuiper Belt exceeds that of Earth.

Light-minute—(n) The distance traveled by light through a standard vacuum in one minute: 17,987,547.6 kilometers or 0.12 AU.

Light-second—(n) The distance traveled by light through a standard vacuum in one second: 299, 792.46 kilometers.

Light-year—(n) The distance traveled by light through a standard vacuum in one year: 9.4607 trillion kilometers or 63,238 AU.

Lipofuscin—(n) An inert pigment whose buildup within the cells of a multicellular organism is both a marker and a determinant of geriatry. Lipofuscin levels in excess of 3% of cell volume are generally considered fatal in the long term.

Luddite—(n) A follower, adherent, or admirer of the principles of Ned Ludd, an organizer of nineteenth-century English craftsmen who rioted for the destruction of industrial technologies seen as displacing or dehumanizing.

Luna—(prop n) Original name of Earth's moon.

Lune (also **the Squozen Moon, the Half Moon**)—(prop n) Name attaching to Earth's moon following the terraforming operations which reduced its diameter from 3500 to 1400 kilometers.

Maglev—(n) Any vehicle, device, or system employing levitation by means of magnetic fields.

Malo e lelei—Traditional Tongan greeting widely used within the Queendom. Literally: "Thank you for coming."

Matter programming—(n) The discipline of arranging, sequencing, and utilizing pseudomaterials in a wellstone or other programmable-matter matrix, often including the in situ management of energy and computing resources.

Megaklick—(n) A near-planetary measure of distance: one million kilometers, or 3.33564 light-seconds.

Megayear—(n) One million years.

Meritocratic—(adj) Of or pertaining to meritocracy. A state in which effort and talent are presumed to yield social or monetary advancement.

Microgee—(n) A measure of gravitational acceleration: one-millionth of a gee, or 9.8 micrometers per second squared.

Millibar—(n) A measure of atmospheric pressure equivalent to one-thousandth of an Earth atmosphere at sea level. Partial pressures of oxygen in the 70-millibar range are generally considered breathable.

Monospecific—(adj) Composed of a single species.

Mutagen—(n) Any agent that tends to increase the extent or frequency of genetic mutation.

Nanobe—(n) Any living or self-replicating system smaller than 500 nanometers in linear dimension. Most often used in reference to implantable medical devices.

Narrowband—(adj) Describes any signal, carrier, or network with a bandwidth less than 100 MHz or an effective data rate less than 100 Mbit/sec.

Nasen—(n) An acronym: Neutrino Amplification through Stimulated EmissioN. A monochromatic beam of high-energy neutrinos sometimes employed for interplanetary communication thanks to its extremely small divergence angle. However, the difficulty of generating such a beam, plus its ready interactions with matter, limit its usefulness except as a weapon.

Nescog, the—(prop n) NEw Systemwide COllapsiter Grid. Sol system's successor to the Inner System Collapsiter Grid or Iscog; an ultra-high-bandwidth telecommunications network employing numerous supraluminal signal shunts.

Neuble—(n) A diamond-clad neutronium sphere, explosively formed, usually incorporating one or more layers of wellstone for added strength and versatility. A standard industrial neuble masses one billion metric tons, with a radius of 2.67 centimeters.

Neutronium—(n) Matter which has been supercondensed, crushing nuclear protons and orbital electron shells together into a continuous mass of neutrons. Unstable except at very high pressures. Any quantity of neutronium may be considered a single atomic nucleus; however, under most conditions the substance will behave as a superfluid.

Neutronium barge (also **Neutronium dredge**)—(n) A space vessel, typically one billion cubic meters ($1000 \times 1000 \times 1000$ m) or larger, whose primary function is to gather mass, supercompress it into neutronium, and transport it to a depot or work site. Although less numerous, smaller neutronium barges also existed for transport only.

Nubia—(prop n) Subtropical Luner nation of the southern hemisphere, on the former Nearside, with a population of approximately 100 million.

Older—(prop n) Informal title or ethnic slur applied to immorbid Queendom residents by the morbid, mortal peoples of Lune.

Oort cloud—(n) A roughly spherical shell surrounding any solar system, in which gravitational perturbations have amplified the concentration of large, icy bodies or "comets."

Sol's Oort cloud extends from 30,000 AU at its lower boundary to 100,000 AU at its upper, and has approximately 300,000 times the mass and one-billionth the overall density of the much smaller Asteroid Belt. The orbits of Oort bodies can have periods of millions of years, and may be inclined in any direction. The total mass of Sol's Oort cloud exceeds that of Jupiter.

Ophiuchus—(prop n) A large, dim, nonzodiacal constellation, "The Snake Holder," beginning between Scorpius and Sagittarius near the Sol ecliptic plane and extending some 50 degrees northward.

Oxygen candle—(n) A mixture of sodium chlorate and iron, typically enclosed in a metal housing, which smolders at 600°C, producing iron oxide, sodium chloride, and approximately 6.5 man-hours of oxygen gas per kilogram of candle. Widely used in spacecraft, submarines, caves, and mines where breathable atmosphere may be intermittently unavailable.

Palasa—(n) Barnardean term for aristocrats or other privileged individuals, often considered derogatory.

Pantrope—(n) Any organism whose morphology or genome has been altered for the purposes of pantropy. Applied especially to human and human-descended beings.

Pantropy—(n) Literally: complete change. The practice of altering the genome or morphology of an organism to enable its survival in a new environment. From the English "pantropic," or "found everywhere," and/or the Greek "pan" (completely) and "tropos" (turning or changing in response to a stimulus). Attributed to James Blish.

Passfax—(n) Any fax machine including both an input and output plate operating simultaneously. Such devices are employed where presorted buffer mass is unavailable or where mass buffers are smaller than the objects being produced.

Periapsis—(n) The point along an orbit at which gravitational potential is minimized and kinetic energy is maxi-

mized. The point of "minimum altitude" above the orbit's focus or centroid.

Petabyte—(n) A measure of data storage equal to 10^{15} bytes
or 8 quadrillion digital bits.

Pharyngitis—(n) Inflammation of the pharynx. A sore
throat.

Philander—(n) A title granted to formal consorts of the
Queen of Sol. Only four Philanders were ever named.

Photobraking—(n) The gross reduction of velocity by means
of a photosail.

Photosail—(n) Any nearly two-dimensional device whose
primary function is to derive mechanical energy from the
pressure of reflected light, including sunlight, starlight, and
radiation from artificial sources. The term "solar sail" is
sometimes applied colloquially, but in fact solar sails are a
subset of photosails.

Photosphere—(n) The hot, opaque, convectively stable
plasma layer of a star beginning at the photopause, responsible for most thermal and visible emissions. Usually less than
1000 kilometers deep, with temperatures of several thousand kelvins and the approximate pressure of Earth's strato-
sphere. The photosphere floats atop the deep hydrogen
convection zones of the stellar interior.

Photospinnaker—(n) A photosail anchored and/or controlled by guylines, with no direct physical attachment to its
parent vehicle. In practice, most photosails other than mill
sails are photospinnakers.

Photovoltaics—(n) Materials or devices capable of generating an electrical voltage with the input of light energy,
through the liberation of bound electrons in a preferred direction. In many isolated devices, wellstone pseudomaterials
must be photovoltaic in order to maintain their other properties using ambient radiation.

Picometer—(n) A measure of distance equal to 10^{-12} meters
or one-billionth of a millimeter.

Picosecond—(n) A measure of time equal to 10^{-12} seconds or one-billionth of a millisecond.

Pid—(n) Possibly an abbreviation of "period." A measure of time equal to 20 Barnardean hours or 71,875 standard seconds. There are 23 pids in a Barnardean day. Attributed to Bascal Edward de Towaji Lutui.

Piezoelectric—(adj) Decribes a substance, often crystalline, which produces a voltage when pressure is applied to it, or which experiences mechanical deformation in response to a voltage.

Pilinisi Sola—(prop n) Formal title of the Prince of Sol.

Pilinisi Tonga—(prop n) Formal title of the Prince of Tonga.

Pion—(n) An unstable, spin-zero meson possessing one-ninth the mass and +1, 0, or −1 times the charge of a proton, and a half-life of 2.6×10^{-8} seconds.

Planette—(n) Any artificial celestial body consisting of a stony or earthy lithosphere surrounding a core or shell of supercondensed (neutronic) matter. The vast majority of planettes are designed for human habitation and include Earthlike surface gravity and breathable atmospheres.

Plibbles—(n) Fruits of the plibble tree. Colloquially: deranged or misinformed.

Podship—(n) Any vehicle designed to operate both in space and on the tuberail system of a planetary surface. Employed extensively in the Barnard, Wolf, and Lalande colonies.

Positronium—(n) A material consisting of "atoms" made from one electron and one positron orbiting their mutual center of attraction. Unstable in free space, positronium is generally stored in magnetic nanobottles between the fibers of bulk wellstone.

Print plate—(n) The largest single component of a fax machine, responsible for assembling and disassembling finished goods at the atomic level. Print plates are generally flat and most typically rectangular, although with effort they can be fashioned as cylinders or other three-dimensional forms.

Prokaryote—(n) Any member of a domain of single-celled organisms lacking intracellular organelles and an organized nucleus. Some prokaryotic cells are capable of forming systematized colonies, with minor details of cellular morphology and activity varying as a function of position within the colony. However, no true multicellular prokaryotic organisms have been identified in any star system. Prokaryotes are thought to be descended from archaea.

Pseudoatom—(n) The organization of electrons into Schrödinger orbitals and pseudo-orbitals, made possible with great precision in a designer quantum dot. The properties of pseudoatoms do not necessarily mimic those of natural atoms.

Quantum dot—(n) A device for constraining the position of one or more charge carriers (e.g., electrons) in all three spatial dimensions, such that quantum ("wavelike") effects dominate over classical ("particle-like") effects. Charge carriers trapped in a quantum dot will arrange themselves into standing waveforms analogous to the electron orbitals of an atom. Thus, the waveforms inside a quantum dot may be referred to collectively as a pseudoatom.

Reportant—(n) Any person or mechanism gathering information for public distribution.

Rodenbeck, Wenders—(prop n) Playwright and Poet Laureate of the Queendom of Sol.

Sensorium, neural—(n) Any system for channeling synthetic neural inputs into the brain. Sometimes employed as a form of torture, but generally considered a medium for education and entertainment, especially in remote environments.

Shift, Barnardean—(n) A measure of time equal to 10 Barnardean hours or 35,937.5 standard seconds. There are two shifts in a pid, and 23 pids in a Barnardean day. Attributed to Bascal Edward de Towaji Lutui.

Sila'a—(n) A pinpoint fusion generator or "pocket star" consisting of a wellstone-sheathed neutronium core surrounded by gaseous deuterium. From the Tongan *si'i* ("small") and *la'aa* ("sun").

Sketchplate—(n) A thin, rectangular block or sheet of wellstone sized and preprogrammed for the portable display and input of text, drawings, and physical simulations.

Skyhook—(n) Any device or structure spanning the region between a planet's atmosphere and the surrounding vacuum, especially as part of a transportation system.

Smalter—(n) A fax machine specialized for the extraction of useful elements from ore or waste, and/or the dispensing of purified elements as part of an industrial process.

Spall—(v, n) To break up or reduce via the removal of small surface particles, as with a chisel or laser. As a noun, a particle which has been struck from the surface of a larger object.

Squozen Moon, the (see *Lune*)

Stealth—(n) Concealment, especially during movement or action. Colloquially, a synonym for technologically derived invisibility.

Superabsorber—(n) Any material capable of absorbing 100% of incident light in a given wavelength band. The only known universal superabsorber (i.e., functioning at all wavelengths) is the event horizon of a hypermass. (Approximations of 100% absorption are generally referred to as "black.")

Superfluid—(n, adj) Any fluidized material capable of propagating with zero friction and zero viscosity. The vast majority of superfluids are either cryogenic, as with liquid helium, or supercondensed, as with neutronium.

Superinsulator—(n) A material or device which completely forbids the passage of electrons in a given energy band. Universal superinsulators (i.e., functioning at all energies) are unknown and may be physically impossible.

Superreflector—(n) Any material capable of reflecting 100% of incident light in a given wavelength band. No universal superreflectors are known. (Approximations of 100% reflectance are generally referred to as "mirrors.")

Ta'ahine—(n) A maiden or virgin, or a mature woman of high status.

Taha mano ta'u—Traditional Tongan birthday wish. Literally: ten thousand years.

Talematangi—(n) On the Barnardean world of Sorrow, aka Planet Two, a persistent cough brought on by atmospheric halogens and other irritants. From the Tongan *tale* ("cough") and *matangi* ("air" or "atmosphere").

Tazzer—(n) A short-range beam weapon consisting of pulsed, coaxial streams of electrons and metal ions in a guide beam of blue or violet laser light. Tazzers are primarily used to induce temporary incapacity (pain, paralysis, unconsciousness), although lethal versions also exist.

Teleport valve—(n) A device for regulating the flow of atoms or molecules between two discontinuous points in space.

Telomere—(n) The natural end of a eukaryotic chromosome, used in biology as a regulator of cell division. The shortening of telomeres within the cells of an organism is both a marker and a determinant of geriatry. Complete erosion of the telomere results in cellular senescence and is generally considered fatal in the long term.

Terraform—(v) To make Earthlike. In general, to match the gravity, climate, and atmosphere of a planet or planette to that of Earth, possibly including the imposition of a stable biosphere. Enclosed spaces are "climate controlled" rather than terraformed. Attributed to Jack Williamson.

Timoch—(prop n) Capital city of the Luner nation of Imbria, with a population of approximately 2 million.

Titranium—(n) Public domain wellstone substance characterized by moderate flexibility, extreme toughness, and a lustrous gray appearance.

Tonga—(n) Former Earth kingdom consisting of the Tongatapu, Ha'apai, and Vava'u archipelagoes of Polynesia, and scattered islands occasionally including parts of Samoa and Fiji. Tonga was the only Polynesian nation never to be conquered or colonized by a foreign power, and was the last human monarchy prior to the Q1 establishment of the Queendom of Sol.

Tuberail—(n) A monorail system in which the rail, usually circular in cross-section, carries power and other utilities between destinations and for the benefit of tuberail cars and podships traveling along it.

Tui Barnarda—(n) Formal title of the King of Barnard.

Ullage—(n) Waste, inefficiency, or loss. The space in a container which cannot practically be filled, and also the remnant contents of a container or plumbing network which cannot practically be emptied.

Upsystem—(adj or adv) One of the six cardinal directions: away from the sun in any orientation.

Varna—(prop n) A 640-meter-radius planette constructed in orbit around Luna by private investors during the latter years of the Queendom of Sol. Site of the Q1290 Treaty of Varna, granting Right of Return to Barnard refugees.

Vendory—(n) A portable device consisting of a power supply, mass buffer, fax hardware, and small print plate, usually capable of drawing additional buffer mass from the atmosphere. High-quality vendories are technically capable of producing almost any device or substance, but are generally restricted by software and tradition to the production of foodstuffs and eating utensils.

Waldo—(n) Any teleoperation system where movements of the operator's hands are replicated by handlike devices at a remote location. Attributed to Robert Heinlein.

Wellcloth—(n) A fabric woven wholly or partially from well-stone fibers. While sheet wellstone could technically be considered a form of cloth, the term "wellcloth" is generally reserved for fabrics with weave lengths larger than 1 micrometer.

Wellglass—(n) Any wellstone substance which is both optically transparent and electrically insulative, often employed as the default state of wellstone devices. Most typically refers to a wellstone substance closely emulating the properties of transparent silica-soda-lime (SiO_2, NaO, CaO) "window glass" preparations except in terms of mass and toughness. In general, natural substances containing a preponderance of silicon are the easiest to emulate in a well-stone matrix.

Wellstone—(n) A substance consisting of fine, semiconductive fibers studded with quantum dots, capable of emulating a broad range of natural, artificial, and hypothetical materials. Typical wellstone is composed primarily of pure silicon, silicon dioxide, and gold.

Wellwood—(n) An emulation of lignous cellulose ("wood"), often employed as the default state of wellstone devices.

Wideband—(adj) Describes any signal, carrier, or network with a bandwidth greater than 100 MHz or an effective data rate greater than 100 Mbit/sec.

Williamson, Jack—(prop n) American romanticist of the Old Modern period.

Zettahertz—(n) A measure of frequency equal to 10^{21} Hertz, or one thousand billion billion cycles per second.

technical notes

wellstone

For those readers only now joining the series, the programmable "wellstone" material which pervades it may seem a bit startling. However, it's drawn for the most part from established science: other than mass, the observable properties of matter are determined by the electron clouds surrounding the atoms and molecules. By confining electrons in approximately atom-sized spaces, it's possible to replicate these properties, or to produce temporary new "elements" which could never occur in nature. Anyone interested in such programmable materials should check out my nonfiction book on the subject: *Hacking Matter* (Basic Books, March 2003, ISBN 0-465-04429-8).

invisibility

Near-perfect invisibility is a technically feasible (though power-hungry) application for programmable materials. Indeed, if computing power continues its relentless advance, then a form of "stealth fabric" may be achievable even with mid-twenty-first century technology. Anyone interested can look up my *Wired* article on the subject at http://www.wired.com/wired/archive/11.08/pwr_invisible.html

The illusion will work under most circumstances if the material can emit light as bright as the sky, as well as the light reflecting from the ground and other objects. This presents a challenge during daylight, however, since the sun is around 20,000 times brighter than the sky around it. Stealthed warriors will cast shadows if their fabric's light sources are unable to match this brightness, because the light shining "through" them will appear dimmer than the sunlight falling around their edges.

deutrelium

This is my own name for a material consisting of equal numbers of deuterium (hydrogen with one extra neutron) and helium 3 (helium with one missing neutron) atoms. Although ^{3}He is rare on Earth itself, it's quite common throughout the universe, in gas giant planets like Jupiter and Saturn. It's favored by fusion energy enthusiasts (particularly armchair starship designers) because when fused with deuterium, its reaction products are all charged particles, which can be contained with magnetic or electric fields. Other fusion reactions are either less energetic, more difficult to ignite, or produce neutrons or gamma rays which present a radiation hazard. Other than antimatter, deutrelium is the likeliest fuel for practical starships.

Of course, without ertial shielding these could be nowhere near as large as *Newhope*.

the planets of barnard

In the 1960s, astronomer Peter Van de Kamp claimed to have discovered, in the wobbling motion of the stars, a pair of gas giants in circular orbits around Barnard, with periods of twelve and twenty-six years. Since both alleged bodies were slightly smaller than Jupiter, it now seems clear that his instruments and methods were not sensitive enough to make this detection, although his observations continued, and he remained adamant about the discovery until his death in 1995. Meanwhile, George Gatewood published a number of papers—the most recent in the year of Van de Kamp's death—detailing the upper mass limits for Barnard planets based on the *absence* of a conclusive wobble in images taken of the star. However, the planets claimed by Van de Kamp fall within Gatewood's limits, and thus were not disproven per se.

In 2002 and 2003 I corresponded with an astronomer named Chris McCarthy (no relation to me that I know of), who'd been patiently compiling Doppler data on Barnard. He assured me that given everything he knew, a terrestrial planet like Sorrow was entirely plausible, though of course not provable with current technology. He had other measurements which promised to detail the orbits of any large gas giants that existed around the star, but as of this mid-2003 writing his results remained unpublished, and therefore politely secret. However, a related paper, "The low-level radial velocity variability in Barnard's star" by Kurster et al., *Astronomy and Astrophysics*, v.403, p.1077–1087 (2003), tightens Gatewood's maximums with an upper mass limit of 0.87 Jupiter masses between 0.017 and 0.98 AU (8.5 to 488 light-seconds) and 3.1 Neptune masses in the "habitable zone" between 0.034 and 0.082 AU (17 to 41 light-seconds).

Interestingly, this still leaves room for Van de Kamp's planets. For the purposes of this story, I opted for the somewhat romantic notion that Van de Kamp was exactly (if flukishly) correct. ("I know of nothing to rule this out," Chris McCarthy reassured me. "You can certainly let your imagination set the limits.") Thus, one of the planets is named after Van de Kamp and the other after Gatewood, with the small inner planets—discovered much later and with minimal human intervention—being, like the majority of comets and asteroids here in our Old Modern Sol system, nameless. I would have loved to have named a planet after Chris McCarthy as well, but wanted to avoid the appearance that I was naming it after myself or, nepotistically, after someone in my extended family. I did name the system's first and only shipyard after Martin Kurster.

Planet	Distance from Star (AU)	Distance from Star (light-minutes)
P1	0.03	0.25
P2/Sorrow	0.09	0.75
(Mercury)	0.4	3.2
(Venus)	0.7	6.0
(Earth)	1.0	8.3
(Mars)	1.5	12.5
Van de Kamp	2.6	21.5
Gatewood	4.3	36.0
(Jupiter)	5.2	43.0

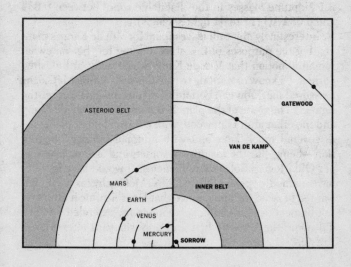

Given the small size of this system I've also abandoned the Earth-centric AU in favor of the light-minute as a planetary measuring stick. Note that P2, with its thick greenhouse atmosphere, falls just outside the habitable zone defined by Kurster for Earthlike planets. A comparison of the Sol and Barnard systems follows.

The radius of Barnard is 0.4 light-seconds. Coincidentally, this makes the star appear 1.00 degree wide in the skies of Sorrow—almost exactly twice the size of Sol in the skies of Earth. Since people tend to overestimate the size of the sun anyway, I suspect this difference would go largely unnoticed.

Planets so close to their parent stars are generally presumed to be "tidally locked," with rotation rates synchronized to their orbital period, so that the planet always presents the same face toward the star (just as Luna does toward Earth). However, this is not always the case. Mercury is an example of a planet in "3:2 resonance," completing two revolutions per three orbits. In a similar way, Sorrow takes 1036.8 hours to revolve around its axis, and 691.2 hours to complete an orbit around Barnard. If the planet didn't rotate at all, Barnard would assume the same position in Sorrow's sky at the same point in every orbit, and the day would be 691.2 hours long. However, the rotation has the effect of shortening this to 460.8 hours.

Barnardeans consistently refer to the day as being 460 hours long, reflecting the fact that a "Barnardean hour" is 3593.75 seconds long—6.25 seconds shorter than a standard hour. Technically speaking, the 0.8 hour day-length difference should be rounded up rather than down, but since 461 is a prime number, no convenient clock could ever be constructed around it!

I'll note that these numbers are no invention of mine; if a truly habitable planet exists around Barnard's Star, it needs to be near or just beyond the outer edge of the star's liquid water band—as far from the star's flares as possible—with a thick greenhouse atmosphere to keep things warm and protect against radiation. And preferably, yes, it should have some sort of day-night cycle rather than a pure tidal lock. Also, given the scarcity of heavy metals, it must be larger than

Earth or its gravity won't hold the atmosphere down. In other words, it needs to look very much like Sorrow, or it couldn't be there at all.

notes on the tongan language

All the Tongan words used in this book are authentic. However, with hundreds of years of history between ourselves and the events of the story, I've taken some slight liberties with the meanings and nuances of certain phrases. Therefore, any use of this book as a language reference may get you some puzzled looks from native Tongans. Next time you're in the Friendly Islands, do please keep this in mind.

mursk in lalande, act two

Lalande was another metal-deprived dwarf, with three gas giants and one tidally locked terrestrial—the half-frozen world of Gammon. Allegedly it was named after a historical person of some sort, but Conrad had always figured it was really because, as in a well-won game of backgammon, all the black was on one side and all the white on the other. It might also have been named "eyeball," for the frosty whites extending just beyond the terminator, the coal-colored iris beyond it in the daylight, and the clear blue "pupil" of tidally raised ocean.

Conrad's image found itself appearing on the front porch of a brick-veneer ranch house, beneath an awning of translucent gray wellstone. A woman stood before him, out on the grass beyond the porch's concrete. She was barefoot and whipped by a strong steady wind, so that her hair and the hem of her long dress flailed out beside her. She didn't appear cold, but from the look of things Conrad would be if he were actually standing here in front of her.

Behind her, in the distance, was an ocean shrouded in fog.

"Hi, Benny," he said. "Nice to see you again. It was windy like this the last time I was here."

"It's always windy here, Conrad Mursk of the Kingdom of Barnard."

"And always three in the afternoon," he said, looking up through the awning at the sun, resting motionless in the sky. It was difficult to say for sure, with no landmarks around it for reference, but it seemed to Conrad that it was both wider and dimmer than the sun of P2's own sky. Certainly it was much redder.

She laughed. "Always, yes, but not forever. The planet is locked, but the snow and ice builds up on the Darkside, bleeding off the Brightside Ocean. The water gets shallower and shallower, and the Darkside gets heavier and heavier, and every eight hundred years the planet flips."

"I'll bet that's a fun ride."

"We'll evacuate the planet," she said, flashing a don't-be-daft look in his direction. "We're actually due for a flip in just two centuries. Which is good, because the melting glaciers will expose all kinds of fresh ore, which we can really use."

"So the shore *is* farther away than it used to be."

"Yup. It retreats about twenty meters every standard year."

Conscious of the time, Conrad looked around the immediate area. The house was large, and it was up on a hill overlooking the city of Moll. And the hill was grassy where most of the landscape beyond it was bare slate or shale. He hadn't noticed this on his previous visit, but it didn't surprise him now. Finding a pen pal here on Gammon had taken decades of back-and-forth prowling on the Instelnet's low-bandwidth message boards, and anyone who could afford to take him up on the offer was, almost by definition, a member of the planet's upper-crust *palasa*. Wealthy, at least by colonial standards.

"Benny N.," Conrad mused, now looking over the woman herself. "You must think I'm an idiot."

"For what?"

"This doesn't look like a palace," he offered, by way of excuse.

"Ah," she said. "No, it doesn't. So you've found me out, have you?"

"Bethany Nichols, the Queen of Lalande."

She smiled sheepishly. "Guilty. We can still flirt, though, can't we?"

"I don't know," Conrad answered seriously. "Your philander might have something to say about it."

"I don't have philanders," she said. "I have old-fashioned *boyfriends*. And right now, I'm in between."

"Oh, I see," Conrad told her, then made a show of eyeing her even more appraisingly. "If only I had a body. And some time."

Her giggle was pleasant, unhurried. "Maybe someday, Architect. But if I'm going telefuff, I'd rather pick someone closer to home. Lalande is less than five light-years from Wolf system and only six and a half from Ross. We have our own little club: we can actually trade fashions quicker than they go out of style. Whereas Sol is a round trip of seventeen years, and all the other colonies—including yours—are twenty or more. Wolf has an ocean, too, and a biosphere, and a mean case of tidal lock. So really we have a lot in common."

"You can't *see* Wolf from here, though. Can't see Ross, either. Right? Not with the naked eye, not even on Darkside."

"We can see Wolf when it flares. God, they have lovely flares. You think *you've* got radiation troubles, try living on Pup!"

"I've visited there in message form," he said. "Stay out of the water, is my advice."

She snorted regally. "And the air. There's a *reason* the capital is under a mile of rock, along with most of the population. King Eddie is many things, but stupid is not one of them."

"Ah," Conrad said, "so it's Edward Bascal you have your eye on, is it? It wouldn't be the first time he and I crossed swords over a woman."

"Well," she admitted, "he is kind of cute. Younger and more charming than his so-called cousin. A girl could do worse."

Running through what little he knew of her bio, Conrad asked, "Aren't you a playwright or something?"

Her smile grew pained. "Used to be. I fear my muse has fled, and anyway the bitch only ever gave me one solid hit. If you're looking for the next Rodenbeck, I'm afraid it's not me."

"Well," he said, "life is long. You never know." And then a

chime sounded through his virtual bones, and he added, "I'm done here."

"Already? I haven't even shown you my tattoo. Ah well, see you in twenty."

"God willing," Conrad agreed, and vanished.

And while it may be true that the digital summary of these experiences was lost in transmission, they *were* thoughtfully archived in the Brick Palace Library, and moved off the planet's surface in the Turnabout Evac, there to find their way into a letters archive which survived intact for nearly twenty thousand years.

In a quantum universe, as they say, almost nothing is ever truly lost.

about the author

Engineer/novelist/journalist Wil McCarthy is a contributing editor for *Wired* magazine and the science columnist for the SciFi Channel, where his popular "Lab Notes" column has been running since 1999. A lifetime member of the Science Fiction and Fantasy Writers of America, he has been nominated for the Nebula, Locus, AnLab and Theodore Sturgeon awards. His short fiction has graced the pages of *Analog, Asimov's, Wired, SF Age,* and other major magazines and anthologies, and his novels include the *New York Times* Notable Book *Bloom,* Amazon.com's "Best of Y2K" *The Collapsium* (a national bestseller) and, most recently, *The Wellstone.*

Previously one of those "guidance is go" people for Lockheed Martin Space Launch Systems, and later an engineering manager for Omnitech Robotics, McCarthy is currently the Chief Technology Officer for Galileo Shipyards, an aerospace research corporation with projects ranging from rockets to high-altitude balloons to quantum nanoelectronics. He can be found online at www.wilmccarthy.com.

Come visit

BANTAM SPECTRA

on the INTERNET

Spectra invites you to join us
at our on-line home.

You'll find:

< Interviews with your favorite authors and
excerpts from their latest books
< Bulletin boards that put you in touch with
other science fiction fans, with Spectra
authors, and with the Bantam editors who
bring them to you
< A guide to the best science fiction resources
on the Internet

Join us as we catch you up with all of Spectra's finest
authors, featuring monthly listings of upcoming titles
and special previews, as well as contests, interviews,
and more! We'll keep you in touch with the field, both
its past and its future—and everything in between.

Look for the Spectra Spotlight
on the World Wide Web at:

http://www.bantamdell.com.

SF 30 3/04